Come Again

Josie Lloyd's first novel, *It Could Be You*, was published in 1998. Emlyn Rees is the author of two other novels, *The Book of Dead Authors* and *Undertow*. They both live in London.

Also by Josie Lloyd & Emlyn Rees

Come Together

JOSIE LLOYD & EMLYN REES

Come Again

WILLIAM HEINEMANN : LONDON

First published in the United Kingdom in 2000 by
William Heinemann

1 3 5 7 9 10 8 6 4 2

Copyright © Josie Lloyd & Emlyn Rees 2000

The right of Josie Lloyd & Emlyn Rees to be identified as the
authors of this work has been asserted by them in accordance with the
Copyright, Designs and Patents Act, 1988

William Heinemann
The Random House Group Limited
20 Vauxhall Bridge Road, London, SW1V 2SA

Random House Australia (Pty) Limited
20 Alfred Street, Milsons Point, Sydney,
New South Wales 2061, Australia

Random House New Zealand Limited
18 Poland Road, Glenfield
Auckland 10, New Zealand

Random House South Africa (Pty) Limited
Endulini, 5A Jubilee Road, Parktown, 2193, South Africa

The Random House Group Limited Reg. No. 954009
www.randomhouse.co.uk

A CIP catalogue record for this book
is available from the British Library

Papers used by Random House are natural,
recyclable products made from wood grown in sustainable forests.
The manufacturing processes conform to the environmental
regulations of the country of origin

Typeset in Palatino by Deltatype Ltd, Birkenhead, Merseyside
Printed and bound in the United Kingdom by
Mackays of Chatham plc, Chatham, Kent

ISBN 0 434 00822 2 (Hardback)
ISBN 0 434 00910 5 (Paperback)

To our Shidduch-maker and the Wunderkind,
(Vivienne Schuster and Jonny Geller) with our love
and thanks.

Acknowledgements

With thanks to Diana, Carol and Kate, Euan and Camilla, Sarah, Gill and Steve, Phil, Nick, Ali and Lorna at Curtis Brown. Lynne (our fantastic editor), Andy (our publisher and all-round guru), Grainne and Mark, Thomas (for being so patient), Ron and his fabulous team, Katie, Glen and Nigel (for another great cover) and everyone at Random House.

Also, many thanks to Gwenda and David for the inspirational hide-away. Finally, to our friends and all the new in-laws for their never-ending support.

Part I

H

Don't have any friends. That's the simple solution. Or, if you do have friends, change them every six months or so. Rip up those Filofax pages, wipe the memory on your electronic organizer, burn your address book and start afresh. Otherwise, things just get complex.

Because if, say, you land up becoming best friends with someone, there will come a day (like today) when you find that you've been up since nine a.m., with a hangover, on a Sunday, in the rain, carting boxes of their stuff, in your car, across town.

And despite the fact that the last time you helped them move, they swore blind it would be their permanent address for ever and ever, you find yourself sweating at the top of yet another flight of stairs going all Talking Heads and thinking, how did I get here? This is not my beautiful home.

But this is my beautiful best friend. Not that I ever tell Amy she's anything but a ropy old tart. She's got Jack to pay her all the compliments she needs these days. It's my job to keep her feet on the ground, which is pretty tough considering she's so happy all the time. Like now.

'This is above and beyond,' I grumble, wedging my chin on top of the pile of papers on the box.

'Quit your whingeing,' she tuts, smiling over her shoulder at me as Jack fiddles with the lock in front of her.

'Hurry up, Jack,' I beg, shifting my knee under the heavy box whilst trying to balance on the stairs.

3

'We're in!' he shouts, finally pushing the front door open to his and Amy's new flat. Amy squeals and claps her hands.

'It's so exciting,' she squeaks, as I feel the bottom of the damp fruit box buckling in my hands.

'Hang on, hang on.' Jack takes Amy's holdall from her and chucks it through the open door, adding to me, 'Tradition', as he picks her up in a fireman's lift and carries her over the threshold.

'Bit premature, aren't you?' I say, staggering up the few remaining stairs into the flat. 'You're supposed to be married when you do that.'

But Jack doesn't hear me, since he's too busy waltzing up their new hall with Amy laughing and protesting, bent double over his shoulder.

'Where shall I put this?' I ask, just as the box collapses and a jumble of papers and books tumble on to the floor.

'Anywhere will do. Feel free to mess the place up,' says Jack, putting Amy down.

'Cheeky,' I mutter, chucking a book at him as Amy comes over to me and crouches down. I start gathering everything together, piling up the magazines and I'm just reaching for the last one when I realize that it's *Bride*.

'Hello, hello?' I say, raising my eyebrows at Amy. She takes it off me and holds it against her chest.

'Someone gave it to me at work,' she blushes, but I know her too well. She's lying.

She puts *Bride* face down on the pile, then hastily stands and brushes her palms on the front of her old jeans. She knows and I know that she's been rumbled.

For the past few months, she's been bitching to me about how overblown the wedding industry is and how she doesn't want to be just another conveyer-belt, commercially ripped-off bride and I've been totally with her. I've admired, colluded with and encouraged her healthy, low-key, no-fuss attitude to her and Jack's wedding. But three weeks to go and here she is reading bridal magazines, signing up for the whole shebang.

'Let's have a look, then,' I say, following her into the living-room.

'It's going to be fantastic,' Jack sighs, looking round the empty space. 'Plenty of light for me to work in ... We'll have shelves over there in the alcove, a window seat there ...'

'You're not actually suggesting that you're going to do some DIY yourself, are you?' I tease.

'You'll see,' he says, giving me a sideways glance. 'Come on, let's get everything else.'

'You're a slave-driver, Jack Rossiter,' I groan, as he puts his arm round me and leads me to the door. I drag my arms like a baboon, already feeling that they've been stretched to knuckle-scraping proportions by all this carrying.

'The sooner we're finished, the sooner we can go to the pub,' he grins matter-of-factly.

But it takes ages to unload all Amy's kitchen stuff from my car and there's a hired van which is jam-packed full of Jack's belongings. Including some very dodgy canvases.

Amy is in the kitchen, unloading, when I bring up the final painting.

'Isn't this one a bit ... yellow?' I ask, looking at it.

'Oddly enough, it's called "Study in yellow", but I wouldn't expect you TV executive types to appreciate the finer qualities of such things,' mocks Jack, taking it.

I cling on to it to have a closer look. I've never been the greatest fan of Jack's work, siding with Amy in her disapproval of his predilection for painting nudes – and beautiful nudes at that. But this is different.

'I don't know. I quite like it,' I muse.

'My Dad didn't think so. He paid for it, but he said it was too bright for his office and gave it back.'

5

'I think it's perfect for an office. I'd love it in mine. Yellow's supposed to be relaxing.'

'Have it, then,' says Jack, suddenly.

'I can't . . . I . . .'

'No, honestly. Take it, H. One of these days I might go stellar and become so famous, it'll be worth a fortune.'

'Are you sure?'

Amy smiles, walks over to Jack and puts her arms around his waist.

'It's the least we can do to say thank you,' she says, cocking her head so that it rests against Jack's chest.

Freeze!

We? She's been living with Jack for, what, four hours and nineteen minutes and she's acting like those shiny couples in a building-society advert. But then Jack puts his arm around her and, as they both smile at me, I realize he's in on it too. And all of a sudden, I feel all unsettled and like I'm a huge impostor in their space.

'Now then . . . Pub?' asks Jack, breaking away.

'Not for me,' I mumble.

'Come on, H,' says Amy. 'We've got to have a drink to celebrate.'

'No, no,' I hold up my hand and duck for the door. 'I'll leave you to mark your territory – pee on all the walls, shag in every room, or whatever it is you want to do . . .'

'Study in yellow' isn't relaxing. As soon as I hang it in my office the next morning, I feel stressed. I'm thinking of putting up 'wanted' posters for my lost sense of humour.

I never thought I'd be one of those people who got stressed. I thought stress happened to people who spent their lives trading millions in the City, or performing life-threatening operations. I.e. important people. Older people. Not people producing possibly the worst (and, yes, that does include *Miami Vice*) TV shows ever seen on our screens. I.e. me.

I never used to be like this. I used to saunter in to the office (usually late), flick through a couple of programme ideas, phone all my mates and bugger off to the pub at six o'clock. Roughly a 70:30 play-to-work ratio. Ideal.

But today is typical of the regime I've become used to. I was in at the crack of dawn, I've spent half the morning firing off grumpy emails and I haven't even had time to go to the loo.

To make matters worse, Brat, my barely pubescent assistant, has been next to useless all morning. I'm trying to be patient, but earlier I had to send him away for the fifth time to correct the running order of tomorrow's *Sibling Rivalry* show (the one in which Alan, a milkman from Sheffield, accuses his sister Jean, a housewife from Grimsby, of helping aliens to abduct his child) and Brat looked as if he was going to cry. Just now I asked Olive, the receptionist, if Brat (his real name is Ben, but Brat seems to have stuck) is OK and she said that he thinks I'm scary.

Me? Scary? I thought I was a pussycat.

It's lunch-time when Amy calls to thank me for my help yesterday, before confiding that after I left last night she did indeed shag Jack in every room.

'Too much information, thank you very much,' I grimace.

'I love it. Living with Jack's going to be brilliant,' she gushes.

'Glad to hear it. You're going to be doing it for a very long time.'

'You make it sound like a prison sentence.'

'Hmm. Well, you wait. You'll be crawling the walls in no time. He might be behaving now, but give it two weeks and I bet he'll be buying green toilet paper and other such male atrocities.'

'H, you're a cynical old bag.'

'Experienced. Not cynical,' I correct.

'Yes, well, you and the others can warn me all about the horrors of men on my hen weekend. There'll be plenty of time for all that. It's all sorted, isn't it?' She laughs to herself. 'What am I saying? Of course it is. I'm talking to the most organized person on the planet.'

'That's me,' I say chirpily, feeling a pang of guilt. 'I'll email you.'

I put down the phone feeling utterly shabby. I know I'm being ungracious, but I had no idea when Amy asked me to be her chief bridesmaid that it'd be this much hassle. I thought all I had to do was hold a bunch of flowers on the day, make sure I didn't tread on her train and then snog someone unsuitable. How wrong I was. Launching Amy into her life of wedded bliss is turning out to be more expensive and time-consuming than putting on the Olympics.

The big problem with the hen weekend (not hen *night*, note, not hen afternoon, or hen lunch, but whole flipping hen weekend) is that Amy is not content to go down the pub like a normal human being, which would be a piece of cake to organize.

No, no, no. Far from it. If Amy had her way, she'd quite happily commandeer all her random mates on an entire week's holiday. She even suggested ten days in Ibiza, 'just for old time's sake'.

What old times she's talking about, I have no idea. We've certainly never been to Ibiza and she's gone with Jack on her recent holidays, so why she's making such a big deal about leaving 'girlie' life is totally beyond me. She's not some winsome nineteenth-century heroine (much as she's making out she is) being dragged off to the World Of Men. She's already there. If she was being dragged off to the World Of Leather, never to return, then I might understand what the fuss was about. But there you go.

I call Brat into my office and once I've given him some letters to type and tried to make amends for the bollocking I gave him this morning, I change the subject as casually as I can. I sit back in my chair and adopt my friendliest tone.

'Now then, how far have you got with booking somewhere for that weekend I asked you about?'

Brat lights a cigarette and slings a trainered foot on to his trendily trousered knee.

'What weekend?' he asks, dumbly.

I hate it when he does this. He knows exactly what I'm talking about.

'You know. *The* weekend? I asked you to book somewhere for seven people. *Ages ago*?'

I watch him blowing out smoke and shifting uncomfortably in his chair. It annoys me that he smokes in here, but since I'm the only one with a smoking office, it'd be fairly hypocritical to put my foot down.

'Oh that. I couldn't find anywhere like you wanted,' he starts.

I put my elbows on the desk and rub my eyes, before looking at him. 'But you have booked somewhere, right?'

He nods and flicks his ash towards the ashtray Amy stole for me from a posh restaurant in Piccadilly. The ash misses and showers over on my desk.

'Well . . . yeah,' he says, flicking his hand to wipe away the ash and missing half of it. 'I got you a nifty deal.'

'Where?'

'Um . . . Leisure Heaven.'

'Leisure Heaven! That dreadful place they advertise on the TV?'

'It's dead good, honest,' says Brat. 'You wanted saunas and all that girlie stuff and they've got that. There's loads of waterslides and they've even got a disco on Saturday night . . .'

I push my hair back with both hands. 'You *are* joking?'

9

He shrugs his shoulders. 'It's the only place I could find.'

I close my eyes, visions of screaming, scabby children all helplessly urinating in the water filling me with horror. And that's just for starters. Think of a holiday camp-style disco full of teenagers on dodgy Ecstasy!

'What about all those country houses I suggested?' I panic. 'Surely we could get in to one of those?'

'All full. It's too late now, anyway. I've got the brochure, if you want.' Brat gestures over his shoulder to his desk outside.

I nod wearily.

Why did I trust him to make the booking? Why didn't I do it myself? This is a total nightmare. So much for being the most organized person on the planet.

A few minutes later, Brat brings the brochure in, along with a few message slips.

'Thanks,' I mutter, turning round in my chair to face the 'Study in yellow'. In the window, I watch Brat's reflection as he turns and leaves. Is it my imagination, or does he have a smug look on his face?

My afternoon doesn't improve. Eddie spends most of it going ballistic about the schedules and, much to my annoyance, I have to rejustify every decision I've cleared with him in the last month. At the end of it all, he shuts the door and tells me in dramatic whispers about the imminent programme reshuffle from above. That's all I need: the powers that be playing Russian roulette with all my hard work. I've spent months getting this far. *Make my day, Eddie*, I feel like saying when he leaves, winking and tapping the side of his nose. *Go ahead, punk. Make my day*.

It's not until everyone has gone home and I'm left alone in my office at last that I have a chance to look at the pile of message slips. There's another one from Gav. I screw it up and have great satisfaction aiming it at the wastepaper bin and scoring in one. Yes! I wasn't wing-attack in my school netball team for nothing.

I check the emails and smile when I see a new one. I open it up and lean forward to read it.

To: Helen Marchmont
From: Laurent Chaptal

Hello, Helen. Are you ready for me? I will need you from a week on Monday. Call me – Laurent.

I touch the screen.

Laurent. Ah. I can hear him saying his name in his scrummy French accent. I know it's ridiculous to have a crush on Laurent, since every single girl who's ever been within two foot of him fancies him too, but I can't help it. But on the plus side, *they* don't get personal emails from him on a daily basis. And they don't have a whole week of filming with him.

I can't wait.

I must admit, it was a stroke of sheer genius on my part to suggest a visit to our sister company in Paris. I justified the expense to Eddie by saying that it was important that we were more Euro-friendly. And since talking to Laurent, who runs the network in Paris, is the only discernible perk of my job, it would seem a pity not to capitalize on the opportunity of getting him to myself for a bit.

Wishful thinking, I know. It's just that that twinkly Gallic charm of his gets to me. Not that I could do anything about it even if I wanted to. Let's face it, it would be a tad unprofessional to fling myself at him. Still, Paris in the autumn . . .

I untangle myself from the tousled sheets of my fantasy and tell myself to get a grip. It's ridiculous. Laurent is probably already married, or something ghastly.

11

I must need a shag. There's nothing more to it than that.

I finally shut down my computer at 9.30 p.m. My head is pounding and I bolt down a few fluffy Anadins I locate in the back of my drawer. I lock up my office, say goodnight to the cleaners and wait by the lift.

I'm vaguely humming 'Cry Me A River' when the lift stops at the third floor and Lianne, one of the presenters, steps in.

Lianne is not my favourite person in the world. She's about fifty, although she only admits to forty, and is one of those affected people who claims to have worked in 'the business' since television was invented.

Yeah, right.

'Ah, Helen. Everything sorted for tomorrow?' she asks, shaking her giant blonde hairdo.

'Yep,' I lie, for the fiftieth time today. As if I've had time! Today I caught up with yesterday. Tonight is for thinking about tomorrow. Everyone knows that.

'I'll read through the script revisions first thing, then,' she says.

First thing? Why am I bothering to go home? I'll be working all night at this rate. I suppose it's just as well I don't have a lover. A fat lot of good I'd be.

'You're sure it'll be OK?' she asks.

'Don't worry, it's going to be fine,' I say, heaving my bag on to my shoulder and easing my mouth into an utterly unconvincing smile. But Lianne smiles back. She believes me! For a moment I wonder what would happen if I ungritted my teeth and let the words behind them tumble out. *Go and pester someone else, you bossy cow. Do your own script revisions. Do you hear me, you miserable shrivelled eighties throwback? I don't care. I've got a life.*

Except that I haven't.

'Have a nice evening,' she says, when the lift pings open on the ground floor.

My flat is a complete mess when I get in and I'm tempted to turn round and book myself into a hotel. I've been thinking about getting a cleaning lady, but I can't bring myself to do it. It seems too extravagant considering that this mess has been totally generated by me and me alone.

I kick off my shoes and open the fridge. Inside there's a Marks & Spencers ready-made lasagne, a chicken-and-ham pasta bake and a family-sized chilli with rice, all of which passed their sell-by date five days ago. In addition, there's a family-sized bag of Italian salad which has gone brown and slimy, a deluxe Vichyssoise soup which has started to ferment and half a tub of houmous.

Great.

This happens every week. I turn over a new leaf and on the way home from work do a huge, expensive shop, promising myself that this week I *will* eat healthily every evening and no, I *won't* survive almost exclusively on Marmite on toast or late-night take-aways from the Indian on the corner. But it never happens, because every time I throw away all the expired food in my fridge.

I've lived on my own now for about six months, but I still haven't learnt the basics of cooking for one. It's really tricky. Instead I buy family-sized everything, harbouring this little fantasy that someone – I don't know who – will turn up of an evening and I'll open my fridge, peruse its contents and rustle up a gourmet dish in a nanosecond. I don't know where it's come from, because no one ever turns up uninvited. In fact, my social life is totally arranged, usually weeks in advance. Nothing is impromptu in my life any more and even if it was, it certainly wouldn't happen in my flat; I'd be too ashamed of the mess.

I chuck some cereal in a bowl and flick through the post. There's nothing interesting, just bank statements and the usual junk mail that someone, somewhere deliberately targets at me. It's a scary thing that I'm now old enough to qualify for all this stuff: credit-card holiday offers, 'you have already won £2,000' subscription cons, photo-developing envelopes, and nasty mail-order clothes catalogues. I fling them on the sofa and hit the answering machine. There's a message from my brother, complaining that he hasn't heard from me for ages, and then there's one from Gav, my ex-boyfriend.

I sit on the sofa and listen to him speaking on the answering machine, annoyed that the sound of his voice still ties my stomach in knots, or that I can still imagine how it was when he lived here.

'Hi, it's me. Listen, I've been trying to get you at work, but you haven't returned any of my calls. I really need to speak to you, H. Will you call me? I'll be up late, or catch me at work tomorrow. OK. Bye for now.'

Bye for now, I mime at the phone.

Excuse me? How arrogant?

I mean, what does he think? That he can call me and I'll immediately take him back? Does he have the nerve to think that I'm as lonely without him as he *obviously* is without me? The cheek of it! *He* was the one who was scared of commitment. *He* was the one who, after a happy two-year relationship, calmly and quite callously engineered things to get so bad that I had to finish it. *He* was the one who walked out without so much as an 'I'm sorry'.

If he wants me back, he can pull his finger out and do some serious chasing.

Secretly I'm pleased, though. Because I knew he was making a mistake and maybe he's realized it, too. Why else would he be calling me all the time?

On the night he left, I watched him pack his bag, pulling books off my shelf, boxer shorts out of my drawers, shampoo and razors from the bathroom cabinet we'd put up together and I watched him in silence, my heart breaking. Because I didn't want it to finish. I didn't want him to leave. All I wanted was a reason. Just one reason why he'd let our precious relationship slip through his fingers.

It was no use, though. A week before, I'd begged him to tell me whether he was having an affair or not. Another woman seemed to be the only logical explanation for his behaviour. But Gav was outraged by the idea and started ranting furiously. It seemed that any problem we had was entirely my fault and this, didn't I know, was the last straw. How could I expect him to love me when I was so suspicious all the time? How could he be his own person with me pulling him down and smothering him? How could there ever be trust in our relationship when all the time I did things like accuse him of infidelity? It went on and on until he ran out of steam. Then he went silent. And stayed silent for a week.

I tried to make him see things from my point of view, begged him to communicate with me, but in the end I knew I'd failed. So the only option left, without sacrificing my last shred of dignity, was to let him go.

So he did.

It was midnight by the time I had calmed down enough to be able to speak. And the only person I wanted to speak to was Amy. She was the one person who I knew wouldn't judge me, who'd lift the burden of the crushing defeat I felt.

I knew she'd been out for dinner with Jack and I knew it was late, but I held my breath as her phone rang, willing her to be in. Eventually, she lifted the receiver and I curled up on my beanbag, ready to pour out all the anger and grief I felt.

'Amy, it's me.'

'I was just about to call you. You'll never guess what?'

'Hang on. Listen, I . . .'

'Jack and I are getting married! Isn't that great?'

Stringer

I get back from playing squash with Martin at 19.02 and check my watch's stopwatch feature. According to the London *A-Z*, it's spot-on three miles across town from Martin's sports club to my mother's Chelsea riverside house and, seeing that I've knocked a minute off the personal record I set for the distance last week, I smile. This time two years ago, running three hundred yards, let alone three miles, would probably have killed me. Although the September air is chill, I'm sweating like a horse, so I stay put for a few minutes, staring down at the familiar cracks in the pavement outside Mum's house, remembering how, as a child, I used to play hopscotch here with my sister.

Mum and Dad bought this place – a Victorian three-storey redbrick – twenty-five years ago. That was 1974, the year I was born. It was because of my arrival that her and Dad and my elder sister, Alexandra, moved here. Their old place in Putney wouldn't have been big enough for all four of us and what with the money they'd come into following my grandfather's death, it made sense. Mum kept the building on after she and Dad divorced in 1993. Xandra and I had left home by then (Xandra in with her boyfriend and me off at university), so Mum moved herself and her belongings upstairs, and converted the lower-ground and ground floors into two separate, self-contained flats for renting out.

I swing my rucksack down from my shoulders and, digging out my flat keys, trot down the basement steps to the front door of the flat I now rent off Mum. Once inside, I check through the mail. There are two bills: phone and electricity. It's hardly what I need on my current salary (or lack of it). There's a letter from my Quit4Good drugs counsellor, David, suggesting we get together for a 'chat' some time next month. Inside a pink envelope is an invitation to a *Kids From Fame* fancy-dress party that Roger's throwing to celebrate his divorce from Camilla. I wonder, will this eighties revivalism never pass? There's also a postcard from Pete, my best friend from university, who's currently coaching tennis for Camp America out in California. Finally, there's a Ken's Gym sponsorship form for next month's Aerobathon Spectacular in aid of Children in Need. I can imagine the aches already.

'Hi, honey,' Karen chimes, as I enter the sitting-room. She's got a soft Cheshire accent that just kills me. She's huddled up on the sofa. Her favourite Reebok baseball cap is pulled low over her brow, concealing her cropped copper hair. Cradled between her hands is a Sony Playstation game paddle, upon which her fingers are orchestrating a series of frenzied movements. Her eyes are glued to the television screen, where Lara Croft is busting her way through the latest Tomb Raider instalment. 'Who won?' she asks.

I walk through to the kitchen and get a carton of juice from the fridge. There's a smell of spicy food and in the sink is a used saucepan and bowl. 'Martin,' I call out, returning to the sitting-room and slumping down next to her. 'He thrashed me. Nine–four. Nine–two. Nine–four.'

Throughout the many years I've known Martin, I've never taken a game off him. He was at boarding-school with me and then we both went on to study Economics at Exeter University. Where I ended up specializing in DJ-ing and slobbing-out, he stuck with mastering the intricacies of macro- and microeconomics. Ergo: he got a first and I got a third. He's now on the fast-track, an investment banker in the City.

'Did you try that serve I showed you on Sunday?' Karen checks.

Aside from being my flatmate, and the secret, unrequited love of my life, Karen is my ally in the clandestine war currently being waged against Martin on the squash courts of London. The rules of engagement run along the lines of Martin being incredibly successful and me childishly wanting to get one over on him by beating him at something. Karen used to play squash at county level at school and has been teaching me a few tricks on the sly.

'Yes,' I reply.

'And?'

'I made a mess of it,' I admit. 'I got too riled. He was running me ragged. You know what I'm like when I get competitive . . .'

'Don't sweat it,' she says, nudging me with her knee reassuringly. 'I'll take you through it again next week.'

I watch Karen kicking virtual arse as I drink from my juice carton and wind down. She's a one-off. There are no two ways about it. She's the biggest tomboy I know. Her current outfit consists of denim dungarees and scuffed-up Reeboks. There's a sticker-ridden skateboard by her feet. Her room says it all: Manchester United and skate punk posters on the walls; assorted football memorabilia on the shelves; clothes scattered across the floor. (My mother told her it looks like my room did when I was nine, which struck me as a particularly Mum-like observation, seeing as it *was* my room when I was nine.) I don't mind about Karen being messy. The reality is that I get a buzz out of her feeling so at home. It's cosily his and hers, although this illusion is shattered every time her boyfriend, Chris, comes over to stay.

I developed a hideous crush on Karen over the first few

months she was here, and it shows no signs of abating. My stomach flips over every time I hear her keys in the front door and sometimes at work I catch myself daydreaming about her, wondering where she is and who she's with. Nothing has ever happened between us, however, and I don't think anything ever will. She's been seeing Chris since I've known her and I've never made a pass at her. As far as I know, she's completely unaware of the way I feel. Aside from the odd whiff of sexual tension between us, I think that in her eyes our status as just good friends has been cemented and set. That's fairly par for the course with me: falling in love with someone, then missing the boat; listening to my heart, then failing to act on what it has to say. That said, I'd be lying if I claimed hope was dead. There are times – particularly when there's only the two of us, or when she's grumbling about Chris – that I catch her looking at me, and I wonder if the connection jolts her heart as hard as it does mine.

Chris is a strange one. It's hard to be certain, but I think I'd still believe this even if he didn't have chronic halitosis and I didn't think his girlfriend was chocolate and envy him every second he's ever spent with her. Their relationship has been ongoing since their first year at college. They've never lived together and Chris has side-stepped the several advances towards this that Karen has made over the years. He takes the view that cohabitation isn't something they should even consider until their careers are irrevocably established. He's been unfaithful to Karen twice with women he said didn't mean anything to him. The first time broke Karen's heart, the second hardened it. He's on his last warning now. I know all this because Karen has told me. I also know that if I were going out with Karen, the establishment of my career and seeing other people would be the last things on my mind.

Karen has been living here for six months now, ever since I decided to boost my income by placing an advert

19

in *Loot* for a flatmate. The copy I submitted was fairly unspecific: 'Twenty-five-year-old male seeks similar-aged flatmate to share spacious Chelsea flat. Male/Female. Professional/Unprofessional.' All the same, I couldn't believe how many people replied. Karen was the last person I saw. She was happy in her job (as a freelance journalist). Chris had just started working in Newcastle for an engineering firm. She saw him every other weekend and generally had a good time. She wasn't symbiotic in any way. She'd neither drag me down, nor get dragged down by me. She was perfect. She moved in the following weekend. Then came my crush, and then our friendship, all of which brings us up to now.

'Doing anything tonight?' she asks.

'I'm meeting up for a drink with Jack.'

'How is he?' she asks. 'Still loved up?'

'Completely. Do you feel like tagging along?'

She shakes her head. 'Early night for me, I think. Shit!' she curses at the screen, tossing the game paddle across the room in frustration as Lara bites the dust again. 'Those wee nasties do for me every bloody time.' She grabs the juice off me and takes a noisy slurp. 'Alice popped in half an hour back . . .'

My mother. There's something in Karen's tone of voice that makes me edgy. 'On the snoop?' I ask.

'Uh-huh.'

'What did she want this time?'

Karen smiles awkwardly. 'The usual.'

'God,' I groan.

It's occurrences like this that make me wish I hadn't moved back here to begin with. I don't mean that badly. I love my mother to bits. Truly I do. It's just that I sometimes wish she'd leave me to my own devices a tad more. It's not as if I don't understand where she's coming from, but even the biggest of life's casualties should be given the benefit of the doubt from time to time. Deep dark secret: I'm very much the 'after' photo from the lifestyle magazine. I was a mess at the beginning of last year – a bloody mess – and had been fairly consistently ever since my father died in 1996.

He died of a heart attack, keeled over on the way out of a board meeting at Sang, the electronics corporation of which he was European Marketing Director. He was fifty-nine and due to retire in six months. I loved him and when his heart broke, so did mine. Instead of looking to the future, as he'd always counselled me, I buried myself in the present. Dad was so young. The week before he died, he'd taken me out for dinner and everything about him had seemed normal. He'd nagged me about getting myself a postgraduate business qualification, and had told me that I had a good brain and should use it for something more challenging than being a DJ. I say nagged, but Dad was never a nagger, not in the traditional sense of the word. He was just ambitious for me, and I was just too young to understand.

I inherited a pile of cash from him and bought myself a second-hand Porsche 911, rented a house in Notting Hill, got myself kitted out with some state-of-the-art decks, and set about ploughing the rest up my nose. Nothing seemed to matter. Getting wasted and forgetting myself was enough, just so long as I didn't have to think too hard.

The money – thankfully, I now believe – ran out at the beginning of last year, and with it went the lifestyle. The first big surrender was the Porsche. I traded it in for the beaten-up Renault 5 that's parked outside now. Next up was the house in Notting Hill. I moved out of there and, at Mum's insistence, in to here. She said it was because I couldn't afford anywhere else (true), but I also think it was because she wanted to be in a position to keep an eye on me. The last, and most painful, aspect of my former life to go was the coke. I went to rehab at Quit4Good and

21

did precisely that on my twenty-fourth birthday, 15th March, 1998. That's well over a year ago. It was the best birthday present I've ever had. In the wake of that, I steered clear of temptation by quitting DJ-ing and keeping away from clubs. Instead, I swapped one addiction for another and started working out down at the gym every day. I even ended up taking on a part-time job there.

Looking back now, the club scene is no great loss to me. Take away the drugs and what are you left with? Not a lot. I look back on that time and it's a blur: a long and meaningless trip with someone else at the wheel.

The 'usual', however, that Karen is referring to, isn't simply Mum's fear that I'll derail again. Mum's 'usual' is more general than that. It's to do with why it is, at the ripe old age of twenty-five, that I've only just managed to get myself a steady job and – more to the point, I suspect – have yet to introduce her to a steady girlfriend? Why is it, she wants to know, when I've got it all on paper – the looks, the brains, the clean bill of health – that I'm struggling at the back of the human race, when, in her eyes, her cherished son should have long since burst through the winning tape?

There are, of course, answers I can give to these questions. Most obvious of all – and an argument I've set before Mum on a number of occasions – is that not having a steady girlfriend is perfectly normal for someone my age and does not, as she assumes, mean that I'm surfing dangerously close to becoming one of those men my Aunt Sarah would describe as, 'peculiar and best left alone'. Then there's the question of regular and meaningful employment and whether such an ideal actually exists – a myth regularly shot down by ninety per cent of the people I know. Finally, there's the coke issue. In that way, at least, I can be said to have been formidably progressive. Instead of waiting, like many people I know, until

22

their mid-twenties to get in to it (admittedly, often a matter of financial restraint rather than choice), I have already, as they say, been there and done that. Much too much, much too young, certainly, but one less stumbling block for the future, I hope.

'What did you tell her?' I ask Karen.

'That she shouldn't worry. I said that different people develop at different speeds, and that just because you were still living in the same building as your mother, without a girlfriend, and existing hand-to-mouth in a low-pay, high-stress job, it didn't necessarily make you a loser.'

Karen's analytical abilities never cease to astound me. 'What did she say?' I ask.

'That when she was your age she was married and had given birth to both you and Xandra, and that she was in a loving relationship, and that what you were doing wasn't normal.'

'Normal?' I ask despairingly. 'What on earth is normal meant to mean? Doesn't she watch *Jerry Springer*? Doesn't she know that normal doesn't exist any more?' A thought occurs to me. 'Or perhaps she does watch *Jerry Springer*. Perhaps it's the very fact that I'm not a transsexual who's sleeping with my best friend's husband's estranged daughter's step-mother that's annoying her. Perhaps that's why she considers me weird.'

Karen calmly ignores this tirade. 'She didn't specify. She just asked me if I could think of an explanation for your current state of affairs.'

'Can you?'

Karen gives back the juice carton, crosses the room and retrieves the game paddle. She glances at me and purses her lips. 'I told her you were thinking about becoming a monk.'

I almost choke on the gulp of juice I've swallowed.

23

Karen comes back to the sofa and slams me on the back. 'Why the hell did you tell her that?' I splutter.

'I thought it would shut her up.'

I hold my head in my hands. 'You thought what?'

'Honestly, Stringer, I get her coming down here like this maybe three, four times a week. It's OK for you, because you're usually at work, or at the health club, or whatever. But seriously, I had to tell her something. She's been driving me nuts. And I thought that telling her that would shut her up. I mean, you can't argue with God and the Church, can you? And it fits the facts: no girlfriend; lack of success in a monetarist society . . .'

It takes me a few seconds to digest all this. Finally, I ask, 'Did it?'

'Did it what?'

'Shut her up?'

'Yeah.'

'Well,' I say, getting up and heading off to get showered, 'that's something, I suppose.'

An hour or so and a couple of beers later and I've come down from the shock that my mother now thinks her only son is about to get tonsured and remove himself to a monastery on a remote Scottish island.

I'm in Zack's, Jack's favourite bar. I'm sitting at our usual table and Jack, in jeans and a grey T-shirt, is over at the bar nattering away with Janet, the owner. She's serving the drinks. She's in her late thirties and as flirty as you like. The beer-bottle pastiche with which Jack paid off his bar tab at the end of last year hangs in pride of place on the wall behind her head. I don't like it much, but then modern art has never really been my cup of tea.

I've got a lot of time for Janet. I always have done. She's almost fifteen years older than me, but we get along fine. As with the three-year age gap between me and Jack, it doesn't make much difference. One night last year, I stayed up with Janet until five in the morning, chatting at the bar. Jack hung around until gone three, when he made his exit with one of those *Don't do anything I wouldn't do* looks he does so well. He needn't have bothered. Sex with Janet wasn't on the cards. We were two people hanging out. It was the sort of night I wish would come along more often.

I remember the phone ringing at home the next morning. I was only working down the gym then and didn't usually leave the flat until after lunch.

'So, did you bang her?' asked a male voice which I couldn't immediately match to a face.

Bang her? Charming. 'Bang who?' I asked.

'Who do you think?' the voice replied. 'Janet.'

'Ah,' I said, a face slotting into place, 'Mr Jack Rossiter, I presume?'

'Who else would be sniffing around your sex life at this time in the morning?' he asked, reasonably enough, since Jack is the only friend of mine who feels he has a God-given right to act as sexual confessor to his social circle.

'I didn't *bang* anyone, Jack,' I tell him. '*Banging* is what shotguns do when you pull their triggers. If you're asking me if I've shot Janet, then the answer is no. As far as I'm aware, she's probably opening up Zack's this very minute, healthy as the day she was born.'

'Not shot her,' Jack interrupted, 'shot your load. Did you plough her furrow, tickle her beaver, raid her nest, show her your one-eyed trouser snake, slip her the hot beef injection?'

Meet Jack Rossiter: Master of the Agricultural Metaphor. 'Did I have sexual intercourse with her, Jack? Is that what you're asking?'

'Yes.'

'That would be telling.'

'So, tell . . .'

'No.'

25

'Well, I reckon you did.'

I didn't correct Jack; I never do. I know him far too well for that. A repeated denial on my behalf would only have confirmed his suspicions. Whilst letting him infer that I did have sex with Janet wasn't particularly fair to Janet, I didn't actually lie. In this respect, the problem was really Jack's, not mine.

It all stems from the way Jack sees me. He's one of those over-analytical types. He likes everything to be logical and to fall in to place. Round pegs, round holes, so to speak. Crudely put, the hole I fit in to, in his opinion, is any one I choose between any woman's legs. Jack thinks this is how I should be and therefore assumes that this is how I am.

Point in case: Jack's nicknames for me. Most of my friends, sensibly enough, call me by either my first or my second name: Greg, or Stringer. To Jack, however, nine times out of ten, I'm Horse – as in *dark*, rather than *hung like a* (although I suspect he thinks that, too). Before he fell head over heels in love with Amy last year, he also used to refer to me as The Bait. Normal people would tend to associate the phrase with maggots, rag worms, or mouldy bread – anything that a predatory fish might consider tasty. Coming from Jack, however, it's something of a compliment. He means I'm good-looking. He means I'm the type of bloke it's good to have with you when you're out fishing for women.

Jack once said to me: 'You know what women think when they see you? They think tall. They think dark. They think handsome. They think hunk. They think, *Please, God, let him be mine tonight.* But do you know what the best thing is?'

'No, Jack,' I answered. 'Enlighten me.'

'The best thing is that you never let them down.'

As with the Janet incident, I didn't correct him on this, either.

I'm not entirely blameless over the issue of Jack's perception of me. I'm someone who's always gone out of his way to cultivate a public image for himself. Nowadays, it's Jack's Horse, but before that it was Party Animal. That's where Jack and I met: a party. It was three years ago: 1996. I say *a* party, although it was actually *my* party. I say *a* party, because then – before the money ran out – I used to throw so many of them that they didn't actually feel like mine at all.

'Anyway,' he says, returning to the table with a couple of fresh Buds and sitting down opposite me, 'enough about me and Amy. What about you?' He runs his fingers absent-mindedly through his brown hair. 'You seeing anyone at the moment?' he asks, settling back in his chair with a faraway look in his eyes. 'Remind me of what it's like to be twenty-five and single. It seems like a lifetime ago.'

'It's fairly quiet at the moment, old-timer,' I reply, keeping an eye on the door to the gents, through which a man in biker's leathers swaggered a moment ago. I twitch uncomfortably in my seat, needing a leak.

Jack is looking at me sceptically. 'What, you're not seeing anyone?'

'No one serious.'

'Ah,' he says, 'that's more like it. Let me guess: that student you picked up at Lupo's?' he asks, a knowing twinkle in his brown eyes.

The student's name is Mandy. I liked her, but unfortunately nothing much came of it. She was last seen by Jack two weeks ago, climbing into the back of a cab with me outside Lupo's wine bar, Soho – hence his interest now.

'History,' I tell him firmly.

'Too young for you, anyway,' he mutters, realizing that I'm not about to be any more forthcoming on the matter.

'No, old-timer,' I correct him, 'too young for *you*.'

Before he can protest, I change the subject: 'The test lunch. Are you and Amy all right for next Wednesday?'

The test lunch. I mention it casually, but it's actually an incredibly big deal for me. Two months ago, I got a call from Freddie DeRoth. Out of the blue. The last I'd seen of him was at a twenty-first birthday party I'd DJ-ed at in 1997, up at this great ancestral pile in Yorkshire. Freddie was there, running the eats side of matters. He owns this hip London party-planning outfit called Chichi, specializing in catering for the whims of society's A-list. Anyway: the phone call. It turned out that his right-hand man had decided to up sticks and emigrate to Australia, and my name had been suggested as a possible replacement by a mutual friend – my mother, as it turned out. Coked off my face as I'd been the first time I'd met him, I'd got on well with him, so I thought, why not?

I quit my job at the gym and I've now been with Chichi for over six weeks. I wasn't certain if I was cut out for it to begin with. The hours are long, the pay poor, the pressure of people's expectations intense, and the company's reputation a hell of a task to sustain. As it's turned out, however, it's been great. Freddie's something of a mentor, working me hard but teaching me well. For the first time since I graduated, I've landed somewhere I really want to be and I feel a sense of progress.

That's why the test lunch is so important. It's in preparation for Jack and Amy's wedding. It's my first solo job and Freddie has been really good about it, letting me boss it from the start. It's something I want to get right, to show Freddie that he hired the right man and to prove to myself that nepotism isn't the only reason I got the position to begin with. Then, naturally, there's Jack. I want his wedding to be the best party he's ever been to – a tall order in anyone's book.

'Yeah, sorted,' Jack says. 'Amy's booked the day off work.'

'How about you?' I ask. 'What's happening with Zira?'

He sighs. Zira is a restaurant over in Notting Hill. It's very in with the in-crowd, according to Freddie, who keeps abreast of that sort of thing. They've had Jack on a retainer for doing a mural for them for the past three weeks.

'Same old story,' he says. 'They still can't decide what date to close down so I can get on with the job.' He shrugs. 'Still, if they want to keep on chucking money at me each week for doing nothing, that's fine by me.'

'Nice work if you can get it,' I comment, waving Jack's smoke away from my face and taking a swig of my beer.

'OK if a couple of other people come along to the test lunch?' he asks.

'No problem,' I say automatically, meanwhile thinking of KC, Chichi's somewhat volatile head chef, who might well disagree. 'Who? Parents?'

'*My* parents?' Jack queries with a laugh. 'No way. I want it to be fun, not a rerun of *Kramer vs Kramer*. I was thinking more Matt and H. Oh, and Susie, another mate of Amy's. And you, of course – you are going to be eating with us, aren't you?'

'Definitely, but we've got a lot on at work at the moment, so I'll probably be in and out quite a bit.'

'Yeah, whatever. But basically it'll be a nice round six, so we can boy–girl/boy–girl it.'

A nice round six. I picture KC's face; it's not a happy one. Oh well, Jack's the customer, and the customer is always right. KC will have to lump it. 'Who's Susie?' I enquire, dismissing KC from my mind.

Jack fills me in on the details: 'Susie's single. Susie's cute. Susie's cool. Susie's the kind of girl you'll enjoy meeting.'

I roll my eyes. 'You always say that about women.'

Jack smiles. 'I always say it, because it's always true.'

'Name one,' I challenge him.

'One what?'

'Name one time since I've known you that you've successfully set me up with anyone.'

'Ooh,' Jack says, looking hurt, 'that's harsh.'

'Rot,' I snort.

He raises his eyebrows and sits back. 'Very harsh indeed.'

'No,' I pursue, 'come on: tell me how precisely that's a harsh judgement?' He purses his lips, says nothing, and I, in turn, scent victory. 'You can't, can you? You can't name one time, not one.'

His eyes suddenly light up. 'What about Julie Wright?' he demands.

'Who?'

'Julie. The girl I fixed you up with at Chloe's barbecue last year. Five-eight, nice smile, great legs—'

'Brain the size of a planet, boyfriend who plays rugby for Bath?' I finish off for him. 'Oh, yes, I remember her, all right. She was a great success, wasn't she? Posh London git. I think that's how she described me. To my face.'

'That wasn't my fault.'

'No,' I agree, 'and neither was it your fault, I suppose, that other highlights of that evening included having to forcibly eject that lunatic in the leather trousers who attempted to kill you for cracking on to his girlfriend . . .'

'Jons,' he says with a wave of his hand. 'A misunderstanding.'

'Neither was it your fault, I suppose, that the rest of my evening was spent down at A&E with an ice-pack on my eye, after the aforementioned lunatic decided to smack me one on my way home . . .'

'So what are you saying here?' Jack asks. 'That you're no good at pulling, or that I'm no good at setting you up? Because, quite frankly, Horse, I can't take either of those theories very seriously. Maybe it was Julie Wright who was at fault,' he suggests. 'Maybe Julie Wright was, in fact, Julie Wrong.'

'No, Jack. Julie Wright was not at fault. Julie Wright simply hated me on sight – as is her right. You were at fault for not realizing that this is what Julie Wright would think and for trying to fix me up with her in the first place.'

'OK, OK,' Jack finally concedes. 'Things didn't work out as planned.'

'No, they didn't, and do you want to know why?'

'No, but I think you're about to tell me anyway . . .'

'Because you're not Cilla-bloody-Black, that's why. You're Jack. Jack Rossiter. If you were a superhero, your special skills would include bad chat-up lines, cigarette breath and unusual masturbation techniques. What they would not include are uncanny matchmaking abilities, red hair and a catchy theme tune.'

Jack slips a fresh piece of spearmint gum into his mouth. His eyes sparkle. 'I don't see what's so unusual about my—'

'Fine,' I interrupt, 'but apart from that, you admit I'm right?'

'Susie's different,' he insists. 'I'm serious. She's right up your street.'

Right up my street, indeed. As far as women go, I doubt Jack even knows what country I'm in. 'Six in all, then,' I say, pressing on, 'for the lunch?'

'Yeah,' he reluctantly replies, 'six in all.'

I notice that the biker is sitting back at the bar, reading a beer mat and drinking a beer. My bladder feels like it's about to burst. 'Good,' I say to Jack, 'I'll fix everything up for one-thirty. Now, if you'll excuse me . . .' I take a swig from my beer and get to my feet and nod in the direction of the loos.

'Off to siphon the python?'

'Precisely,' I reply, heading off across the room.

31

A couple of girls – one blonde, one dark – who are standing by the bar, give me the once over as I walk past them. The blonde smiles and I return the gesture. I half-recognize her but can't remember her name. Oh well, that's London for you, I suppose. I could have seen her on the tube, or a bus, or in one of a thousand bars. It could have been anywhere.

I walk on.

A stainless-steel urinal runs the length of the wall inside the gents. Standing on the tiled step in front of it are two men. I'm surprised. I've been vaguely monitoring the comings and goings through the loo door and thought it would now be empty. I stare at the men's backs. They're both adopting that ubiquitous, cocksure, slumped-shoulder stance of the male in mid and satisfying piss. The noise of their urine thundering down into the steel trough makes them sound like a couple of camels post-oasis refuelling. They're talking football and one of them turns and glances at me, disinterested, before shuffling sideways to make room for me beside him, returning his attention to the matter in hand.

I stare briefly at the space between them, but it's no good. I know exactly what will happen if I take those two small steps and stand there: nothing. I'll unbutton my jeans and dig out my dick and then I'll freeze. The noise of the two camels will fill my ears and I'll stare at my wizened end, praying for so much as a tear of piss to show its sorry face. It won't, however, because it never does. I suffer from nervous bladder disorder and I find it impossible to pee whilst standing within ten feet of another man. Next will come the shame. The men standing either side of me will finish their business and my silence will reign and no amount of 'Don't you just hate it when that happens?' will get me out of it, because it doesn't happen to them, it only happens to me. They'll

32

want to know why, and so they'll look, and then they'll know. Then they'll know the sordid truth.

And the sordid truth is this: I have a tiny cock.

I have a tiny and, moreover, a cowardly cock which would rather humiliate me in public by hiding in my pubics, than by getting on with the simple task of acting as a channel for my piss.

In the cubicle at the back of the gents, I lock the door and, for the benefit of the two men at the urinal, go noisily through the motions of lifting up the lid, dropping my trousers and sitting down. My public statement: *I am here to crap and not because I am ashamed of the size of my cock.* The urge to piss returns with a vengeance and I sit here, physical relief flooding through me, its mental counterpart nowhere to be found. I stare down at my pubic nest and its hairy eggs.

I have a teeny peenie.

There's no point in beating around the bush, so to speak. There it is, inescapable, hanging (if an object of such little weight can be affected by the law of gravity) miserably between my thighs. Where other men have trouser snakes, I have a trouser worm. Where other men are hung like donkeys, I'm hung like a gnat. Where other men boast a third leg, I'm an amputee. I'm not Jack's python, then, and equally not his Horse – unless he's talking Shetland ponies, of course.

To say I have mixed feelings about this part of my anatomy would be a lie. My feelings are clear and, for want of a better expression, completely to the point: I hate my cock. I hate it with the same passion other men my age might reserve for income tax, military dictatorships, or, say, the song-writing abilities of 911.

At my prep school, which I attended until I sat my Common Entrance examinations at the age of thirteen, it wasn't so much of a problem. I hit puberty early on and, in the shared showers every morning, not only did I

33

tower over the other kids in height, but I also had the added kudos of a fully thatched nether region. That my cock had failed to grow in proportion with the rest of my body wasn't something that was remarked upon. That came later, at public school. Here, the other kids' bodies quickly caught up, and so did their cocks, and that's when my shame truly kicked in.

The sad fact, however, remains that what's mine is mine and, short of radical surgery, is going to stay that way. Not that the thought of surgery hasn't crossed my mind before. On the comedown of a particularly vicious coke-fest, I once went as far as cutting out one of those Male Enhancement advertisements from the newspaper and actually dialling the clinic's number. A woman answered, however, and I chickened out. There was also the feature advertisement for the manually operated SwellSize Rodpump™ I read in the back of a porn mag whilst I was at university. £19.99 and two hours' pumping later, however, and all I had to show was a bruised shrew, and a bad case of tennis elbow.

I've tried looking on the bright side. I've considered that God giveth and he taketh away. I've told myself that if, in my case, God gaveth good looks, good health and a good body, and in return tooketh away vital inches of love muscle, then that's simply the way it was meant to be. I've tried telling myself all of this, but it hasn't worked. Given the choice of reversing my physical attributes, I'd be down at the deed poll office to register the name Quasimodo in an instant.

I hear the sounds of zips and footsteps and the main door to the gents opening and closing as the other men leave. All that remains is the sound of my piss.

'You're being checked out,' Jack says when I get back to the table. 'The two women at the bar. They clocked you before, on your way to the bogs. They're looking over here now.'

'I know the blonde from somewhere,' I tell him. The temptation is there to turn around and have a good stare, but I don't. It would look too obvious. 'I can't quite work out from where, though.'

'So, what are you going to do?'

'What do you mean?'

'Well, you can't just sit here, can you?'

I laugh. 'Why on earth not?'

'Because she's walking over here right now . . .'

'Stringer, isn't it?' the blonde girl asks.

I ignore Jack's obvious amusement, and say, 'Yes.'

She smiles at this, before announcing, 'I met you at a party at the start of last year.'

I don't remember her. Hardly surprising, however, considering how wasted I most likely was at the time. I continue to study her face and, more specifically, her mouth. I decide we might have snogged each other. Certainly no more. Simply a case of lips that passed in the night.

'Oh, yes?' I ask noncommittally. 'Where was that?'

'Some posh pad in Notting Hill. You were DJ-ing.'

'That'll be your old place, then, mate,' Jack says helpfully. Then, to the girl: 'Used to throw good parties, didn't he?'

She nods her head and says to me, 'I'm Samantha, yeah? My friend over there's called Lou. All right if we join you?'

I finish my drink. 'We're leaving,' I say, ignoring Jack's look of surprise.

Jack shrugs, before picking up his own drink and backing me up, 'Yeah. We're meeting some people in town.'

Out on the pavement a few minutes later, when Jack asks me why I blew out such a great pulling opportunity, I tell him that Samantha isn't my type. I tell him this because there's no way I can explain to him – to him of all

35

people – that it's not only men I'm terrified of getting my cock out in front of.

Susie

Oh dear. I'm lying in bed, trying to focus on the ceiling and whilst I normally do this when I wake up, the problem is that neither the bed nor the very fuzzy ceiling are mine.

Oh dear, oh dear, oh dear: yet more poor behaviour by Miss Morgan.

I shift quietly, trying to extricate myself from under the itchy, heavy forearm of . . . of . . . um . . . now, let's see . . . Dave. No, not Dave. Dave was the baldy one.

Damn! What's he called?

He grunts and rolls away and the pungent smell of stale sex wafts up from under the duvet. I look at his back and try to piece together the events leading up to the fact that I've failed, yet again, to wake up on a Saturday morning in my own bed. So much for keeping my dream diary up to date.

Now then, let's see. I can remember having a drink with the gang in the pub, larking about, as you do. Then the next thing I remember, I got chatting to a bunch of musicians, went with them to this snobby club in Soho and I must have come home with this one – the singer, I think. I'm always a sucker for struggling arty types.

After he'd sung several of his own, I'd been reduced to a gooey-eyed slave to my hormones, at which point I offered to give him a massage. My way of giving back some positive energy, of showing him my special skills, I assured him, in my best whisper. Actually, I just wanted to cut to the chase and get my hands on that body of his.

What's his name, now? Come on, I know this.

Ed. Ah that's it.

Ed with the voice.

I'm pretty sure it's Ed.

I ease up on to my elbows and adjust my eyes to the unfamiliar shadows. There's a clock on the far wall ticking quietly and I squint at it. It's a bit blurry without my glasses, but I think it's saying ten to seven in the morning.

Come on girl, time to sling your hook.

I ease back the duvet and slip out of bed. I'm well practised at being as quiet as a mouse in these situations. Mind you, I'm a terrible one for getting the giggles when I'm trying to be silent, but this morning, I'd determined to keep my big gob shut for once, and not wake up Ed. I hate all that embarrassing early morning stuff with a virtual stranger, especially since I didn't clean my teeth last night. I have the breath of a stray Alsatian, I'll bet.

I creep across the carpet on all fours, retrieving the items of my clothing in reverse order to the door. It takes me a while to find my bra, since it's tangled up in the duvet cover at the bottom of the futon. Without my big knockers in it, it looks huge. Certainly too complicated to put on. I stuff it in my bag and take out my glasses so that I can see what I'm doing and assess the damage. My velvet skirt smells disgusting after the pub and my fleece top has a hot rock burn on the collar, but all in all, I'm in one piece. Not *too* bad, considering.

After a silent struggle to get my tights on, thrashing around on the rug like an upturned beetle, I'm finally dressed. I stare down at Ed before I leave. He's very cute in a smooth-chested boy-band sort of way, but I shan't be leaving my number. I've got enough on my plate without adding this one as a side dish.

Anyway, there's no point in being sentimental, is there? I already know I've blown it. See, Ed won't be any different from any other one-night stand. (And I can't be accused of stereotyping here, because my personal statistics on this matter would form a healthy base for a government survey.) The thing is, if you put *out* on the first date, you're automatically put *in* the casual sex zone. Fact.

Oh, I know men are supposed to have grown up and out of their old sexist ways, but we all know that old habits are hard to break. That's just life. You're fine if you're a frigid blushing violet who has a low libido and lots of patience. If, on the other hand, like me, you happen to have the sex drive of your average stallion and the self-control of an escaped bumper car, then getting a boyfriend is a bit harder.

Not that I want to be Ed's girlfriend, mind you. I hardly know him. Besides, I can't imagine he's single with *that* sort of body. But it would be nice to be taken seriously once in a while, instead of being what my grandmother would call 'one of those girls'.

The trouble is, you see, I *am* one of those girls. Always have been. Even when I was little, long before I started having sex, I was forever in trouble with the boys. I think I was seven when I first traded a look down my gym knickers for two Bubblicious bubblegums.

I glance at the clock again, before blowing a kiss off my hand in Ed's direction and tiptoeing backwards out of the room. I creep down the stairs, stopping and holding my breath every time a floorboard creaks, but eventually I make it out of the house without being caught. I post Ed's keys back through the letterbox (old trick) and mentally brush myself down.

There was a time when I would have felt daring and wicked and would've already been excited about telling everyone about my nocturnal conquest, but this morning I can't help feeling that I want to keep this to myself. As I walk through the gate on to the pavement and look back at the flaking paint of Ed's front door, I feel a bit seedy.

Still, there's no point in beating myself up. What's done is done. And anyway, I've no reason to feel bad. I was in control the whole time. It was me who decided to stay and me who decided to leave. If it was the other way round and it was Ed creeping out of my flat like a burglar at seven in the morning, I bet he'd have a cocksure swagger in his step. So why shouldn't I?

Anyway, I've got other things to worry about. Like where on earth I am. I stand under a lamppost consulting my mini *A-Z* for a good five minutes, before it dawns on me that the street name is not listed in the index. Buggeration. That can only mean I'm off limits and scarily outside the boundaries of my three-zone Travelcard. I look around me, hoping to spot something familiar, but it's one of those characterless London streets – all squashed-together houses with crumbling steps and cold windows. I could be anywhere. I can hear traffic in the distance, so I eeny, meeny, miny, mo it, decide to go left and start walking.

I find a petrol station on the main road a couple of streets away and get chatting to the man behind the till. He's called Raj and he assures me that his brother has a minicab and will run me back into town. Whilst I'm waiting, I have a coffee from the machine and surreptitiously read the tabloid headlines. When you put my exploits last night into context, I'm not so bad.

Raj is chattering on, as if he's known me for years, but it doesn't bother me. It always happens. I reckon I've got one of those faces, because people often tell me their secrets. Raj is off on one, telling me that it's certainly been something of a Friday night. 'Lots of bad elements. Terrible for my night staff,' he gesticulates.

I fail to tell him that one of the 'bad elements' was probably me, buying Rizlas and Pepsi Max in the small

40

hours. I think that's when Ed and I were competing in a fine rendition of 'The Bare Necessities'. He was playing bongos with my buttocks and making lewd suggestions with a Magnum bar.

'Terrible,' I say. 'Terrible.'

Maude, my flatmate, and Zip, her lover, are still up from last night when I get back to the flat. They're sitting on the sofa, under a sleeping bag, both nursing cans of lager and watching a video. They are one of those couples that look grungily trendy if you like Calvin Klein adverts, but to me, they look like they could both do with a good fry-up.

'What time is it?' yawns Zip.

'Eightish, or so. Aren't you helping me today, then?' I ask Maude.

She puts her hand over her eyes and groans. 'Forgot. Sorry. We went clubbing with Dillon and everyone.'

I ruffle her purply-red hair as she looks at me through her fingers. 'I knew it! Next Saturday, then.'

'We'll come and see you at lunch-time, promise.'

I laugh at her. 'Oh yes? Well I won't be holding my breath.'

Maude has been my flatmate in my last three flats and I've known her for ever. She's going travelling with Zip, who's sort of moved in before they leave. They were supposed to leave for America about two weeks ago, but they've got a visa problem, apparently.

I don't want them to go. We've got this huge flat that I got through the housing association, quite by fluke, and it's fun all being here together. It's not the warmest or most tasteful flat in the world, but it's lovely – all high ceilings and plenty of light – and I really don't want to lose it when Maude goes. She's paid two months' rent in advance to help me out, so that I won't have to find another flatmate immediately, but it's still going to be horrible without her. She's such a poppet.

I feed Torvill and Dean, my goldfish, before packing all my stock into my laundry bag and heaving it downstairs. By the time I've collected the Mini Metro from the other side of the parking permit zone and loaded up, I'm late. I shouldn't have been so naughty last night. I should have learnt by now that it's a killer to do the market with a hangover.

Dexter, predictably, has saved a space for me next to him and has already erected a plastic roof over my stall in Portobello Market. According to Capital Radio, it's going to bucket down, so I'm grateful. Being next to Dexter is marvellous for business, as his stall invariably has a queue full of people itching to spend money on tat. He won't hear of it, though, and insists that he sets up next to me because *I* attract the punters. This type of flirty thing has been going on for months between us, but we both know he's doing me a favour.

He's already on his second bacon butty by the time I unpack the car and set out my hats. This week, I've got some new velvet to cover my plywood stand.

'What do you think, then?' I ask, when I've pinned it all down.

Dexter whistles at it. 'Very classy,' he says, handing me a piping hot coffee in a polystyrene cup before starting to croon, 'She wore blu–u–ue ve-el-vet.'

I laugh and roll my eyes at him. Dexter is the widest, most sexist, arrogant man I've ever met, but despite myself, I've got to admit that he's quite shaggable, especially in those 501s.

'Got any good stuff this week, then, Dex?' I ask, averting my eyes from his bum and sipping my coffee.

Dexter is a car-boot, jumble and bric-à-brac sale connoisseur, devoting most of his spare time to trawling other people's junk for any tapes or records he can lay his hands on. He's got a staggering selection of the naffest music you can imagine. Bert Bacharach and random tribute bands. It's very 'in' with the posh lot round here and he's a bit of a legend in the market since he makes a fortune. Well, I say fortune, but no one is ever going to get rich quick, standing in the freezing cold in a London market. (It took me just one week to discover that, which is a pity since this was originally my get-rich-quick scheme.) It doesn't matter, though. One day, it will be me: I will win the Lottery.

'I've got a surprise for you,' nods Dex. He flips open his seventies disco turntable, whips a record out of a sleeve and plops it on the centre, before winking at me as he pulls the needle arm across. 'You being Welsh . . .'

A terrible recording of Shirley Bassey singing 'Big Spender' crackles into action. Dexter is smiling cheekily at me, raising his eyebrows for a reaction.

'That's marvellous, *boyo*,' I nod, turning away to stab hatpins into my cushion.

This Welsh obsession is getting out of hand. Last week Dexter wouldn't stop singing 'Land of my fathers', after having seen the rugby, and I couldn't stop thinking, 'And they can keep it,' as Dylan Thomas said. I mean, if Swansea is so wonderful, why am I in London? Answer me that.

I can't say this to Dexter, though. I can't be mean to him, because I like him. And anyway, he's a mate. Which is why, when a surprise turns up at lunch-time, he's fine about watching the stall for me.

The surprise is Amy.

'Susie the Floozie!' she says, wrapping me in a huge embrace.

Since I'm wearing my big trainers to match my puffa, I'm taller than her, so I lift her up as I hug her back, before giving her a big kiss.

I'm delighted to see her.

'Hiya, darling! What are you doing here?'

43

She pulls a face and points both hands at her head. 'Wedding experiment.'

Amy's gorgeous brown hair is back-combed, plaited and tousled into an impressive bird's nest. I touch it, tentatively.

'Where did you go for that, then?'

'That place you recommended up in Westbourne Park, you cow. I've never felt such an idiot in all my life.'

'They're usually quite good.' I look around the back of her head. 'Bit unusual, isn't it?'

Amy laughs. 'Unusual? It's dreadful! I can't wait to brush it all out. I'm going to scare Jack first, though.'

'Where's lover-boy, then?' I ask, looking round for him.

'Working to keep me in the manner to which I wish to become accustomed,' says Amy, pretending to be smug.

'Shame,' I say, meaning it. Jack's a stunner.

'Hands off,' teases Amy. 'Are you busy? I thought we could go for lunch.'

'Rushed off my feet, as you can see,' I laugh. 'Let's go for sausages and mash.'

I love Amy. She's been my best mate since we were at art college together. She used to be a fellow slacker, never having a permanent job, but she's sorted herself and gone all careerist on me with a fashion house called Friers, so I'm a bit in awe of her these days. Still, the prospect of a good girlie chat in the warm, in my favourite café, is about as good as it can get for a Saturday.

A mate of mine, Sarah, set this place up last year and it's doing really well. When I introduce her to Amy, she finds us a table at the back and takes our order. I'm feeling a bit wobbly, not having slept much last night, but a big plate of mash should sort me out.

'Three weeks today! How are you feeling?' I ask Amy, leaning over towards her and taking her hand in mine. I still can't get used to seeing her engagement ring on her finger. It's so grown-up. I gaze closely at the diamond in the middle and twist her hand so that it catches in the light.

'Fine,' she shrugs.

'Only fine? If I were you, I'd have spontaneously human combusted with excitement by now.'

I look up and smile at her and when she smiles back, I laugh, because I know she's excited. I can see it in her eyes. She looks healthier than I've ever seen her, her eyes sparkling and her skin clear. Lovely.

Whenever I see Amy these days, I go all gaga in a Walt Disney princess sort of a way. It's just that what's happening in her life at the moment is so *romantic*. She's found Jack and he's wonderful and her wedding is going to be like a fairy-tale. I'm going to be her bridesmaid and I can't wait for it all – the dressing up, the posh cars, the beautiful flowers, the belting hymns, the speeches, the dancing. *All* of it.

Amy twists her ring on her finger and looks at it proudly, before taking a sip of Diet Coke. 'I can't believe it's come round so soon,' she murmurs, dreamily.

'Now listen, you,' I say, 'you will throw your bouquet to me, won't you? I won't forgive you if you don't.'

'You're so soppy, Sooze,' she chuckles.

I crinkle my nose at her and rest my chin in my palm. 'I know.'

We chat for a while before Sarah comes back with two huge plates of food.

''Scuse,' she says, undoing the top button of her trousers.

'All those sausages catching up with you, eh?' I laugh, noticing that she's put on weight.

'I'm pregnant,' she whispers.

'Never?' I gasp, genuinely shocked. I come in here nearly every week and I haven't sussed. Usually, I can pick up baby vibes a mile off.

'Three months today.' She smiles radiantly.

'Wow! That's amazing.' I give her a kiss before patting her tummy affectionately. 'Are you feeling OK?'

'Not too bad,' she says. 'The only problem is giving up the fags.'

We chat to Sarah for a bit and Amy asks lots of questions.

'Spot the broody one,' I say, when Sarah's gone. I raise my eyebrows at Amy and start tucking in.

Amy laughs. 'Stop it, you stirrer.'

I sigh, staring after Sarah. 'Isn't it wonderful? I'd love a baby.'

'You? With a baby?' Amy scoffs.

'What's wrong with that?'

'You'd be hopeless.'

'I wouldn't.'

'Come off it, Sooze! What would you do with a baby? You're the original gypsy. You're always on the move and you're far too scatty to be responsible for another human being. One sniff of a party and you'd forget all about it and leave it somewhere.'

'No I wouldn't,' I say. I'm not that bad, am I?

Amy widens her eyes at me. 'Anyway, aren't you forgetting something?'

'What's that, then?' I pick up the ketchup bottle and shake it.

'A man,' she says pointedly. 'It takes two, apparently.'

'Oh that,' I say, dolloping ketchup on to my plate. 'I thought I'd nip down the sperm bank.'

Amy laughs. 'So you've definitely stopped seeing him, then?'

The 'him' she's referring to is Simon. Simon the Spineless. He was the permanent lover of my life up until about a month ago. Had been for years.

Not that he was ever mine. That pleasure belonged to Ilka, his Swedish wife. Beautiful, thin, pure, naturally white-blonde Ilka, who bred perfect mini Simons and

Ilka-ettes and apparently devoted her existence to making Simon's life hell. Only when it came to the crunch, it turned out that he couldn't live without her, this witch he'd slagged off for years. Funny that. He swore blind he couldn't live without me and guess what? He isn't dead yet.

'Yes. I've finally had to let him go,' I sniff. 'He struggled, mind, but I put my foot down. "Simon," I said. "What part of the phrase 'I never want to see, hear or touch you again' are you having particular trouble with?" '

'Good.' Amy laughs. She always said that Simon was never going to leave his wife, but even though I'm joking about it now, Amy's a good enough mate not to say 'I told you so'.

'He did call again, mind,' I tell her. 'He suggested that I move in with him and Ilka, "as a nanny", can you believe it, to make things easy,' I shrug.

Amy gasps, before pointing her fork at me. 'I can't see that working, somehow.'

'Good riddance,' I say. It still makes me shudder to think of what a mug I've been. I deliberately set myself up as Simon's mistress, so why did I expect him to think of me as anything else? It was fine at the beginning whilst I was shagging other people too. I used to think seeing Simon was a bit of a laugh and I liked all the attention, especially since I was so skint. He used to make me feel so special, whisking me off to posh hotels for afternoon sex and buying me expensive underwear. It was all so illicit and exciting and, sucker that I am, I fell for him. My charming older man, who thought I was the bee's knees. But now, looking back on it, he was just *grateful*.

'So? How are you finding life now you're *officially* single?' Amy asks.

I suck in my cheeks and stab my sausage. I gaze at it for a moment. 'I can't complain.'

Amy grins at me and rolls her eyes. 'What have you been up to?'

For a moment, I'm tempted *not* to tell her about last night. Not to share the intimate details or elaborate on the finer points of Ed's bedroom prowess, as I have done with every other lover.

It's funny these days. Because since Amy moved in with Jack, things have been different. She's not the smutty gossip she used to be. Either it's because things between her and Jack are too boring to mention, or just simply too private. I suspect it's the latter, but whatever it is, she doesn't compare notes with me like she used to.

'Come on! This is me,' she says interpreting my pause.

I clear my throat, pretending to be coy, but eventually she coaxes the whole story out of me and I liberally sprinkle my description of the night's events with lots of salacious details, the finale of which is a reconstruction of Ed's anatomy using the sausages on my plate. I feel a bit bad about exposing Ed, but I doubt if I'll ever see him again and, to be fair, I am being quite generous.

'You can get Jack to recalculate my promiscuity rating, if you like,' I say, scooping up the last of my mash on my fork.

'At this rate, you'll be off the scale,' she laughs.

Jack's got this mad equation for calculating how much of a tart you are when you're not in a long-term relationship. We had a tremendous laugh working it out in the pub the other night. According to Jack, I've got the highest rating he's ever heard of. I'm not sure whether he's impressed or jealous.

Amy pushes her knife and fork together. 'You don't change, do you?' she says, shaking her head and putting her hand on her stomach.

I love making Amy laugh, but I can't help feeling that these days it's at my expense. Not that Amy has done anything wrong, or is taking the mickey in any way. It's just that she's not complicit any more. And whilst I feed Amy instalments, like a soap opera, we're actually talking about my life. This is happening to me. It isn't happening to her. She's safe and she's in love. And I feel I've exposed too much.

'So? Tell me all about the hen do?' I ask, changing the subject and putting my hat back on.

'Hasn't H called you?'

'Nope.'

'That's strange. She said she was going to. Anyway, it's Leisure Heaven for the weekend.'

'You're kidding? That's brilliant!'

'Are you sure? H didn't sound too keen.'

'Don't be daft, you'll love it.' I stab a hat pin through the back of my hat, so that it secures my rebellious ponytail of thick curls.

Trust H to put such a downer on things. I don't know her that well, but each time I've seen her, she's always been a bit off. She needs to lighten up, if you ask me. She's got this swanky job and is all mobile phones and sharp suits, but she's one of those people who's really stressy. When I heard she was organizing the hen do, I imagined we'd go out for a really posh meal or something. I knew whatever she chose for Amy, it'd cost an arm and a leg for the rest of us. She's like that, see: showy. I said to Amy that we didn't need to spend loads of money to have a good time and offered to have a do at my flat, but Amy said H was taking care of it. I didn't make a fuss. It's best not to.

Still, I'll hand it to H. She must have put in a lot of thought to the whole thing, because Leisure Heaven is a marvellous idea.

'Is H OK?' I ask, as we walk back to my stall. I'm only being polite. I don't really care how she is. To be honest, I can't understand why Amy is such good friends with her.

'She's fine. You'll see her next week, I expect. We're

having a lunch on Wednesday, to test out all the food for the reception. Jack's organized it with Stringer. You'll be there, won't you?'

'A free lunch?' I ponder, before glancing at Amy and linking arms with her. 'Course I will be, stupid. Who's this Stringer fella then?

'He works at the catering company we're using and he's a really old mate of Jack's. I'm telling you, Sooze, he's *absolutely* divine.' Amy raises her eyebrows at me, suggestively.

I laugh at her.

'You won't be able to help yourself,' she warns.

'Well, we'll see, shall we?'

When I get back to the stall, Dexter's being smug. He's sold two of my hats, but since neither of them had price labels, he shifted them for fifty pounds.

'You never did!' I gasp. He must be having me on, because they usually go for fifteen each.

'You shouldn't under-sell yourself, girl,' he advises, taking out a wodge of notes and peeling off a fifty. 'You've got quality. Don't forget it.'

I pocket the money, ignoring the fact that he's looking at my tits.

'So? Fancy a drink later, then?' he asks, rubbing his hands together.

Aye-aye? Fifty quid for two hats? My fat arse! He's after a date.

'Dex!' I laugh, turning to face him. 'You're a shocker.' I pull the money out of my pocket and offer it back. 'You don't have to pay me to ask me out.'

'Oh.' He looks crestfallen, but still refuses the money back. 'Does that mean . . . er . . . you will or you won't?'

'It means I'll think about it,' I smile, turning to serve a customer.

The thing is, I could go out with Dexter but, to be honest, I can't after last night. If I hadn't slept with Ed, then I might go out with Dexter tonight, but it's like being offered bread and butter pudding when you've already had ice cream. Tempting, but too much. I like Dexter, mind, but I'm not sure he's going to turn out to be my ideal man any more than Ed. And there's no point in pretending that Dexter honestly wants to have a drink with me because he's thirsty or wants a good chat. No. We've been flirting for weeks and he wants to shag me. It's very simple to fathom out. To be fair, mind, he might want to sit and talk to me first and play the game, but at the end of the day, our relationship boils down to sex, or the prospect of it. And I can't honestly imagine it developing into anything more. I can't imagine Dexter making me a hot-water bottle, for example, going to the supermarket with me, or coming to my Mum's for Christmas. And I certainly can't imagine washing his dirty pants or sitting out a car-boot sale with him.

So anything between us would just be for fun. And I can do fun. I am queen of fun. Except that I'm fed up with all this flotsam and jetsam that floats about my life. I want something real, something solid. Amy's right. I am a gypsy. I do flit from one flat to another, from one job to another, from one man to another, and it's never bothered me before, but come to think of it, what I really need is something permanent. Anything. Not necessarily a man. A bank account in credit would do.

'So, then?' says Dexter, shuffling from one foot to another as we pack up.

'Not tonight, Dex,' I say, stuffing my unsold hats back into my laundry bag.

'Come on,' he pleads.

'Can't. Sorry.'

'Out with your boyfriend?' He sniffs and smiles sheepishly at me.

I look Dexter in the eye and I can tell he's embarrassed by the fact I'm being so direct.

'No. I haven't got a boyfriend, just other arrangements. Perhaps we could make it another time?'

'Yeah. Sure,' he gushes. His cheeks are pink and he sort of clicks his fingers and punches one hand with the other.

'See yah,' I smile over my shoulder.

Dexter winks at me and smiles. 'Next week, then?' he pants, with a bright glint in his eye like a dog that's just discovered a chair leg to hump.

'Maybe.'

Well, there's no point in throwing him off the reserve list just yet, is there?

In the car, I sing along to the compilation tape Zip made for me last week.

Lovely Zip. She's so smart.

I remember feeling a bit weird when Maude told me she was gay a few months ago and introduced me to Zephone, or Zip, as everyone calls her. It seemed to be such a grown-up thing for her to have decided. I spent a while wondering where it had come from, or whether Maude has always fancied women. Or even, whether she'd fancied me all the time we'd been living together, but there's no point in trying to reason it out. These things just happen and as long as she's happy and fulfilling herself, then I'm happy too.

'Where were you at lunch-time?' asks Maude when I get back. 'We came by.'

I slap my hand on my forehead. 'Sorry. Amy turned up and . . .'

'Don't worry,' she laughs. 'I knew you'd forget.'

'Look,' says Zip, modelling one of my hats. 'I bought it, anyway.'

'How much did Dexter charge you?' I ask, ominously.

'A tenner each,' says Maude.

'Cheeky bugger,' I laugh.

'What?' asks Zip, taking her hat off.

'Nothing, love. Just Dexter trying it on. Why are you two looking so chirpy?'

'The visas have come through,' announces Maude. 'We're going to LA on Monday.'

'Monday? You can't go on Monday! That gives us no time at all,' I protest.

'But we've been waiting for ages,' she says, pinching my cheek. 'And think of all the space when we've gone.'

Zip's full of America and she spends the evening getting more and more excited with each new travel web site she finds on her portable computer. Maude and I open the last reserve bottle of wine that has been languishing in the wine rack since Christmas, and ooh and ahh when Zip downloads pictures for us, but I can't share their sense of adventure. I just feel sad.

On Monday, I'm up early, fussing over Maude and getting in the way. I bundle their rucksacks into the back of the Metro and beg it to get us to Heathrow. They're both so excited, they can't wait to leave, but I'm feeling wobbly. As I walk them to the gate of the departure lounge, I can feel my throat constricting.

'You're crying,' laughs Maude, gently wiping my tears away.

'I don't want anything to happen to you,' I blurt, clinging on to her.

'Shh,' she soothes, planting a kiss in my hair. She seems infinitely self-confident, so much more mature than me, despite the fact that I'm nearly a year older. 'We'll be fine.'

'I'll miss you both.' I sniff loudly. My chin is trembling.

'Come here, silly,' says Maude, wrapping me in a big hug. Zip joins in and I'm enveloped in their warmth.

'Why don't you come and join us out in LA?' says Zip, suddenly, pulling away. 'We'll get you a job.'

'Go on with you,' I bluster. 'This is your trip. Three's a crowd and all that.'

'We'd love you to come,' says Zip and Maude nods in agreement. 'Come on, Sooze, it'll be amazing. My Mum is out there. She'll be able to sort you something out.'

'You're just saying that,' I tut, but even if they are just saying it, the thought cheers me up immeasurably, as if a small part of their bravery has rubbed off on me.

I'll call you,' mouths Maude, putting her little finger by her mouth and her thumb by her ear as she hitches her bag up on to her shoulder, links arms with Zip and walks through the departures gate. And in a second they're out of sight and all I'm left with is my fading smile and my hearty wave withering in mid-air.

Back in the short-stay car park, I have a good therapeutic bawl to get it all out of my system. Everyone seems to be deserting me: Maude to an adventure in America, Amy to get married, Sarah into motherhood.

Where am I going?

I turn the key in the ignition and drive down the slippery concrete ramps to the exit. It's only then that I turn on the windscreen wipers and they stick, because someone has left a flyer on the windscreen. I curse and get out of the car and pluck it off. I'm about to screw it up when I notice its banner line. It reads in block capitals:

CHANGE YOUR LIFE

And for some reason, I put it in my pocket.

Matt

I remove a piece of paper from the bound file and pick up my dictaphone from my desk and walk over to the window, where I catch my half-reflection staring back: short black hair, charcoal-grey suit. My face looks every one of its twenty-eight years and my eyes are baggy and tired. It's dark outside. There are no stars, just the glow of the city lights bouncing back off the smog-soaked clouds. From up here, on the eighth floor of the Robards & Lake building off Piccadilly, I can see across Haymarket, clear over Trafalgar Square and on to the Houses of Parliament themselves.

The room smells of industrial polish and I reach out to open the window, then check myself, remembering that you're not allowed to any more because it mucks up the air-conditioning. Instead, I settle for sitting on the windowsill and hitting the play button on the dictaphone. My voice drones, 'Yours sincerely, etcetera, etcetera,' at the end of the last letter I dictated. I press record.

'Letter to William Davey of Mathers, Walter, Peacock, please, Mrs Lewis,' I begin. 'Dear Mr . . .'

Only it's not so much a beginning, as an end, because the next word that comes out of my mouth hasn't got anything to do with either Davey, Mathers, Walter or, indeed, Peacock. Nor, equally, is it any business of Mrs Lewis's, whose typing skills I'm fortunate enough to share with Peter in Property and Joan in Employment. In fact, the only person in the world that the next word has got anything to do with is me, because the next word is:

55

'Pizza.'

Three years at university, one year at law school, two years' articles and four years' employment with one of London's top legal firms, and what have I got to say for myself?

Pizza.

Not what flavour pizza. Not what extra toppings. Not whether to order fries or onion rings or garlic bread. Not whether to choose cheesy-crusted deep pan or thin. Not even what soft drink I should get to wash it all down with.

Just pizza.

Because pizza, it seems, is where my life is at.

I switch off my dictaphone and continue to stare out of the window. I feel the piece of file paper slip from my fingers and watch it flutter to the floor.

This is the *fourth* night in a row – including Saturday and Sunday – that I've ended up stuck in the office, case-building for my Soho-club-owning client, Tia Maria Tel (he who's always out after dark), attempting to discover a way of successfully demonstrating in a court of law that he's not, as a certain columnist recently declared, 'a dishonest, hypocritical, flatulent arse, who's had more prostitutes over the last ten years than all the sailors of the Royal Navy put together'. According to my client expenses, since I took Tel's case on seven weeks ago, I've chewed my way through no less than twenty-six pizzas on his behalf. And this, as I told Amy when I met her for a quick drink at lunch-time today, is a worry.

'Oh, Matt,' she sighed, squeezing my arm sympathetically across the pub table. 'It's only pizza. It's not like it's God, or the meaning of life, or anything scarily profound. 'Pizza obsession is perfectly normal in a man your age.'

Amy's someone whose opinion I value, so this was a generalization I was prepared to run with. 'It is?' I enquired.

She nodded her head enthusiastically. 'Oh, yes. Jack's the same with curries. I've seen him practically immobilized over a take-away menu. To vindaloo or not to vindaloo, isn't that the question? It's a basic male consumerist dilemma ... too much choice, you know?'

'You're thinking about this in marketing terms,' I pointed out. 'It's not that simple for me.'

'It's not?'

'No.'

Amy raised her eyebrows and waited for me to continue. I stared back for a moment. Talking through your psychological demons (even the dough-based kind) with someone is kind of personal. Still, Amy, via Jack, probably knows more about me than anyone on the planet. They have no secrets, in the same way that Jack and I used to have no secrets.

'It comes down to the fact that my life hasn't always revolved around pizza,' I began. 'It comes down to the fact that my life used to be about bigger issues. You remember that time when you and Jack came up to my office?' She nodded. 'You remember the view from my window?' Again, she nodded. 'Well, when I started working in London, that view inspired me. And not just that view either, but the whole city. I saw it as pure *Wall Street*. There I was, fresh in to town, ready to take control, yet to meet my Gordon Gekko and have the wool torn from my eyes. Back then, I'd get a real buzz from the whole thing, just standing up there, looking out, knowing that I was a part of it all. Potential. I suppose that's what it spelt out to me, Amy. London was a wide open space, and I could fit in any place I wanted.' I took a sip from my Coke and leaned back in my chair. 'I even had a fantasy, you know. Not a sick fantasy,' I quickly added. 'Nothing involving farmyard animals, bearded nuns, or long pointy sticks.'

Amy smiled slyly at me. 'That's not what Jack told me . . .'

I rolled my eyes at her. 'Seriously, Amy, I imagined that, by this age, I'd have got where I wanted in my career. I'd have got myself a house, I'd have—'

'But you *have* got all that,' she interrupted.

'I know.' I sighed. 'But I thought it would all mean something. I thought that I'd be –' I shot her a warning look – 'I know this sounds corny – happy . . .'

'And you're not . . . ?'

'No,' I told her, suddenly experiencing a huge surge of relief over fronting up to someone about all this stuff. 'No, I'm not. None of it seems to mean anything. And it was easy before, you know, when Jack was living with me, when we were both in the same boat. Everything seemed fine. He wasn't complaining, so why should I have been? Only now that he's moved out . . . I don't know . . .'

I noticed Amy frowning at me. 'I'm sorry,' she said, 'about stealing your best mate.'

'No,' I said hurriedly, 'it's not that. Christ, that's the last thing I'm thinking. You two being happy and being together means the world to me.' And it does, it really does.

'Good,' she laughed, relieved, 'because I'm not giving him back.'

We stared at each other for a beat and I felt myself smiling too. It's a funny thing, watching your best friend fall in love. So many aspects of your relationship with them alter. I remember Jack last year, when he and Amy first met. It was all confidences between us then. *Did I approve? Was he getting too involved? Was she really the only one for him for the rest of his life?* And it was a buzz for me, too, watching these two people reaching the conclusion that they were one hundred per cent right for one another. Then, though, came the realization that my relationship with Jack had altered, probably for ever. No matter what he might say to the contrary, I was no longer his best friend. Amy was.

I groaned, coming back to our conversation. 'It's just, Christ, Amy, I don't know where Jack leaving my house leaves me.'

'Single?' Amy suggested.

'But I've been single for ages. Jack moving out shouldn't make any diff—'

'Of course it does. I mean, yes, you were single before, sexually . . . but emotionally and everything, you always had Jack, didn't you? Partners in crime. All that stuff. I met you two at the same time, remember,' she said with a glint in her eyes. 'I remember *exactly* what you were like. It was the same with me and my close friends. When you've got mates, who needs partners?'

'So you reckon it's a girlfriend issue, then?' I asked, failing to catch the sarcasm in my voice. 'Easy as that?'

'I don't know about that, Matt, but having someone or something else to think about might stop you obsessing about pizza quite so much.'

I look away from my office window and consult my watch. It's one minute past nine and the moment of decision is upon me. Pizzas are chargeable to clients from nine onwards, my stomach is rumbling. I've yet to follow Amy's advice of getting myself an alternative obsession, and denial will only make matters worse. With this information at my disposal, it's not a tough call. I reach for the phone to dial up some dough. But then the phone does what phones have a habit of doing in offices just when you're quietly minding your own business: it rings. I stare at it, a look of mild offence no doubt settling in for the duration on my face. Then I pick it up.

'Hello, Matthew Davies speaking,' I say, praying it's not Tia Maria Tel, who's already called three times today.

'All right, Matt,' Jack's voice comes on the line. 'How's tricks?'

I smile. Jack's voice is one of those sounds that automatically put a smile on my face. I sit down in my chair and put my feet up on the desk, relaxing, I think, for the first time today. 'Tricky. How about you? What's new?'

'Nothing much. I'm starving. Just got out of a meeting with some posh hairdresser down the road from you. He wouldn't shut up, kept me there for hours. Kept banging on about wanting an *industrial* centrepiece to put in his front window ... Maybe I should drive a car through it and leave it there. Call it *Ramraid*. Do you think that would be *industrial* enough for him?'

'Are you asking me that as a lawyer or a friend?'

'Friend.'

'In that case, I'd say it was a distinct possibility.'

'Any chance of borrowing your Spitfire for the job?'

'No, Jack. No chance at all.'

'Didn't think so.' He sighs. '*Industrial*, indeed. I ask you, mate, what *is* the world coming to?'

'The world,' I calmly inform him, 'is coming to an end. In the new millennium, psychos and zealots will take to the streets, signalling the beginning of a thousand years of darkness, during which there will be a perpetual cacophony of wailing and gnashing of teeth.'

'Mmm ...' Jack considers this response for a moment, before deducing, 'You're not having a good day, are you?'

'I've had better.'

'You want to tell Uncle Jack about—'

'Hawaiian, or Four Seasons?' I interrupt.

'Eh?' Jack queries.

'Hawaiian, or Four Seasons?' I ask again.

'What?'

'It's one minute past nine, Jack,' I say tiredly. 'You're

starving and you're just around the corner. You know I'm working late this week and you know I get to order free pizzas after nine. So what's it to be? Hawaiian, or Four Seasons?'

He finally accepts the fact that he's been rumbled. 'Hawaiian. Heavy on the pineapple, yeah?'

'OK.'

'Half an hour all right?'

'Fine. Get security to buzz me and I'll come down and get you.'

That'll be Jack, then. Jack Rossiter, my best friend in the whole world. Jack Rossiter, the grubby little kid who used to fight with me in the playground during lunch breaks over who got to be Batman and who Robin. The same grubby little kid who repeatedly stole my records, cigarettes and hair gel throughout the eighties. The same Jack Rossiter who hooked back up with me in the nineties in London after university, became my lodger, borrowed my car, my clothes, my money, my food, and, from time to time, my girlfriends. The same Jack Rossiter who's capable of making me laugh until my eyes water. The same Jack Rossiter who I'd march through the gates of hell to rescue. And the very same Jack Rossiter whose new lease of life has inadvertently cast a black shadow across my own.

I think back to my conversation with Amy at lunchtime, all that stuff about needing something bigger than pizza in my life, and suddenly I find myself glaring at the phone I've just put down. And even though I know it's childish and pathetic, there's no use in denying it: I feel jealous of Jack, jealous to my core.

I snatch the dictaphone off the desk and press record.

'Letter to God, please, Mrs Lewis,' I say briskly. 'Dear God. Matt Davies here. You probably won't remember me, but I'm the lucky soul who got beamed down into a

61

human body at 03.13 G.M.T. on 4th April, 1971. Mother, Gina. Father, Mike.

'Anyway, down to business. I've never been much of a churchgoer, but I do know my statutory rights, and although I've never actually seen a specific clause relating to divine warranties, I'm working on the assumption that such things do exist.

'The basic problem is that it's recently come to my attention that my life's not going the way I expected. It's a matter of fairness, I suppose. You see, God, there's this guy. His name's Jack. Jack Rossiter. He's been my friend since I can remember. Now, don't get me wrong here, God, Jack's a great guy and I wouldn't wish anything bad on him. No thunder strikes, locust plagues, or rent asunderings. I'm not complaining about his circumstances, you understand, just my own.

'What I want to know, God, is how come it was OK for him to quit his job last year and slob about for months on end, only to turn into an overnight artistic success story? And to fall in love at the same time? And to suddenly find himself happy beyond his wildest dreams? Are you telling me that's just the way the cookie crumbles?

'And if it is, then how about giving me just one itsy-bitsy bonus, too? It can be anything. I'm not greedy. A win on the horses. A promotion at work. Jennifer Lopez walking into my office right this minute, asking me if I know how to show a girl a good time. Something simple like that. Just one pinch of that good stuff you've seen fit to sprinkle all over Jack. Just to make the balance even and restore my faith.

'I look forward to hearing back on this pressing issue in the near future, present, past, or any other temporal dimension you see fit.

'Yours sincerely, etcetera, etcetera.

'Thank you, Mrs Lewis.'

I put the dictaphone back down on the desk, and then

check the wall: nothing. No denial from God on that one, then. No celestial scrawl, acknowledging that there's been some sort of mistake that will be rectified forthwith. So it's a fact. Jack's life – by heavenly decree – is *better* than mine.

It was to be expected, I suppose. I couldn't go through twenty-eight years of existence side-by-side with some-one and always end up on top, could I? It wouldn't be right. And, to be fair, I've had a pretty good run for my money up till now. Since that temporary aberration of Jack losing his virginity before me, things have gone almost entirely my way. I got better results than him at A level, got a better degree *and* a better job. I ended up with a great house and a great career. And Jack ended up paying me rent.

Only then he met Amy and everything changed.

And I haven't changed. And herein lies the problem. I've stayed the same. And everything I valued before now seems meaningless. I mean, what's the point in having such a great house if I've got no one to have over for dinner? What's the point in working late at the office every night if I've got no one to go home to? And what's the point in earning all this money if I've got no one to blow it with?

Amy's right: I need to find someone.

But where?

Just where the hell do you even start looking for love?

The only answer that hits me is a negative one: not here. Not here in this office and not now. Guiltily, I glance down at the dictaphone. I rewind the tape and erase my rant at God, then cross my heart for good measure. Then I call the pizza place. Pizza's going to have to do for now.

At nine thirty, I'm at the top of the spiral staircase which descends through the hanging plants and indoor trees of Robards & Lake's atrium. I lean over the edge of the balustrade and see Jack, four floors down, sprawled on one of the sofas in the reception, with what looks suspiciously like an open pizza box on his lap.

'It was getting cold,' he mumbles, wiping the back of his hand across his mouth as I reach him. He watches me stare at the single greasy cube of pineapple in the otherwise empty box. 'Don't stress it, mate,' he says, pushing the box to one side, revealing another, closed one beneath. 'Yours is in here.' His forehead wrinkles. As with all Jack's expressions, time has given me the ability to read it like a book. And this page reads guilt. 'Well, most of it is,' he mumbles on. 'You see, I had to try a bit to make sure it wasn't my Hawaiian . . .'

I accept the box from his outstretched hand and open the lid and my good vibe vanishes. A third of my Country Farmer Triple Spice is missing. But that's not the worst of it. There's a large, Jack-sized bite mark in the centre of the remaining crust. I snap the lid shut, then look from Jack to the box and then back to Jack again. I take a deep breath, because it's not every day that a man has to make a decision between his pizza and his best friend. Jack is not the enemy, I remind myself. He may be a completely selfish bastard with an appetite like a half-starved pig, but he's not the enemy. Jealousy is the enemy. Jealousy over the fullness of his life. And now, jealousy over the fullness of his belly. I breathe deeply once more and remind myself that I'm bigger than this, and that I can and I will overcome these negative feelings. Exercising extreme control, I slowly close the lid and drop the box into a bin.

'Forget it,' I tell him. 'Let's go for a drink instead.'

We duck in to a bar just round the block. By the time we've got our drinks and squeezed in to a corner table, I'm feeling calm again.

'You booked anywhere yet?' he asks.

'What?'

'For the stag weekend. You got somewhere sorted?'

'Um, sure,' I lie. What with everything that's been going on at work, I haven't had a chance. I'd better get on the case soon, or we'll end up sitting in some dull pub in London. 'It's all done.'

'And have you let everyone know?'

'Faxed them last month,' I confirm, and this is true: I have given them the dates. 'Everyone's replied except for Carl, and he's an unreliable bastard at the best of times. Gete's off to Ibiza with Tim and Mark, so they're out.' I count off the party on my fingers. 'So that's you, me, Stringer, Damien, Jimmy and Ug, maybe Carl, and your brother. Seven definites, then, maybe eight. Are you sure about Jimmy and Ug?'

He nods his head. 'Yeah. I can't not. They'd be gutted.' I look at him sceptically. Amy's not the only one concerned about the two Neanderthals in question. 'Don't worry,' he reassures me. 'I'll keep an eye on them.' He grins and chinks his glass against mine. 'Assuming I can see straight.'

'How's it going with you in the new place?' I ask.

'It's good.' He looks at me sidelong. 'Not that I don't miss living with you,' he quickly adds, 'but I thought it would be a major issue, you know, a surrender of my independence . . . that kind of thing. But it's not. It's great being with her full time. I suppose it's different because we're getting hitched. It's a natural progression.'

'Growing up and moving on . . .'

'Yeah. You going to get another bloke to move in?'

'Not decided.'

'You're on to a loser,' he states, shaking his head morosely, and whistling through his teeth.

I look at him, confused. 'Huh?'

'Getting someone as awesome as me. It's just not going to happen. I mean, no matter who you find, they're always going to be a huge disappointment. Christ,' he reflects, 'what an act to follow. You've got to pity the poor bastard.'

'Yeah,' I humour him, 'it'll involve a world-wide search. National advertising campaign. *Wanted: Jack Rossiter's successor. Only applicants possessing a degree in Slob Studies from the University of Blag need apply . . .'*

Jack runs his tongue thoughtfully across his lip before saying, 'Yeah, that should just about do it.' He looks at me expectantly. 'Have you put the ad in yet?'

'No, I'll put one in between the stag and the wedding. I've been too busy with work. I'll get Chloe to give me a hand interviewing the applicants. Should be a laugh.'

He nods his head. 'How is she? I haven't spoken to her for a while.'

Chloe's an old schoolfriend of ours from Bristol. The three of us have been as thick as thieves for years.

'She's got some new guy.' I make speech marks with my fingers as I say, 'film producer', because, obviously, like most young so-called film producers in London, he hasn't actually got around to producing anything more substantial than a line in plausible bullshit just yet.

'You met him?'

'Last week. Round at hers.'

'More info.'

So I tell him. I tell him exactly what happened when I went round to Chloe's flat last week. And I tell him why.

Last Thursday afternoon, I got a phone call from Chloe at work.

Chloe: Your secretary sounds drunk.
Me: Mrs Lewis is a teetotaller. A drop hasn't passed her lips since her husband, George, ran away with the landlady of their local pub five years ago. She has a speech impediment owing to a severe laceration she suffered to her tongue as an infant, after her brother, in

a vile enactment of sibling rivalry, pushed her pram to the top of a hill near their home and then released the brake.

Chloe: Fascinating as that may be, darling, I wasn't calling you up for your secretary's life history.

Me: So why have you called?

Chloe: Because I need your help.

Me: What do want me to do?

Chloe: Come round to my flat tonight.

Me: For dinner?

Chloe: Not exactly, though I can rustle up a snack for you, if you like.

Me: For a drink and a catch-up, then?

Chloe: No, but we will have time for a quick chat . . .

Me: What, then?

Chloe: I want you to be my boyfriend.

Me (suspecting there was probably more to it than that): OK. Will eight o'clock do?

Chloe: Better make it seven. I'll need to brief you on exactly what's required.

Me: Fine. Seven it is.

Come seven thirty that evening, I was sitting down in the window seat in the living-room of Chloe's ground floor flat, overlooking the road. She doesn't have a front garden and passers-by get a clear view of exactly what's going on in Chloe's front room. And what was going on in Chloe's front room was this: Chloe was sitting with her back pressed up close to me and her fine, shoulder-length hair falling against my cheek, as I administered a sensuous massage to her shoulders and whispered sweet nothings into her ear.

Or rather, that's how it *looked*. In reality, there was nothing sensuous about the movements of my fingertips and the sweet nothings whispered between us went something like:

67

'Look, can we give this a rest for a minute? My arms are starting to ache.'

She craned her neck and stared at me for a second, allowing her essentially wicked blue eyes to grind my misgivings away. 'Don't be such a weed, Matt,' she finally said, turning back. 'He'll be here in a minute.'

'What if he takes it badly?' I asked. 'He's not violent, is he?'

'No, he's lovely. He just needs a nudge in the right direction.'

'Yours, you mean . . .'

'Exactly. He's older than us, set in his ways. I just want you to get him jealous enough to make him realize that he's not the only fish in the sea, and that he can't go on stringing me along for ever without giving me some sort of commitment. How are the wedding plans going, by the way?' she moved fluidly on, before I could have a chance to object. 'Have you written your best man's speech yet?'

'Working on it.'

'And Jack and Amy? How are they?'

'Great. They're in their new place. We've got the stag and hen nights coming up.'

'Yes, and I haven't been asked on the hen . . .'

'Well, what do you expect? You and Amy hardly see eye to eye.'

'No,' she corrected me with finality, '*Amy* doesn't see eye to eye with *me*. I've got nothing against her. I think she's perfectly sweet. She's just jealous about how close I am to Jack. Or was . . . Still,' she reflected, 'at least I'm getting to go to the wedding . . . not that it would have surprised me if I'd been NFI to that, as well.'

NFI, as Chloe informed me a while back, is an acronym for Not Fucking Invited. 'Yeah, well, maybe that's a good time for you and Amy to make your peace. Who knows, you two might end up good—'

'Shush,' she hissed, tensing up, 'here he comes.'

68

I continued to massage Chloe's shoulders, and began to mutter the alphabet sexily into her ear, whilst surreptitiously looking out of the window. Chloe's new boyfriend, Andy, was getting out of his ruby-red Alfa-Romeo Spyder. He was good-looking, about thirty-five, and was dressed like an extra from Operation Desert Storm: baggy combat slacks, a Portobello Market khaki T-shirt, desert boots and a photographer's multi-pocketed waistcoat. His hair hung in untidy bleached streaks on his shoulders.

'You sure he's not violent?' I asked Chloe. 'Only all that ex-army gear . . .'

'Don't be so mean,' she chastized. 'He's cute.'

At this point, I observed the cute Andy stop in mid-swagger and literally freeze on the pavement as he noticed the two of us. I counted the seconds off by my heartbeat – one, two, three – and then saw movement again, as Andy got down to some seriously aggressive grooming of the male kind: sticking out his chest, dropping his Wayfarer shades down off the top of his head over his eyes, and running his fingers with deliberate slowness through his hair.

'I still can't believe I'm doing this,' I muttered, continuing to massage Chloe as I felt Andy's eyes boring like drills into the side of my face. 'Remind me again,' I continued. 'Why *am* I doing this?'

'Because you're a good friend and you know that I'd bail you out if you were in a similar fix.'

'OK,' I tell her, 'but if he attacks me, I expect you to defend me. To the death, if necessary . . .'

'Don't worry,' she assured me, getting up to answer the door. 'It won't come to that.' She stopped at the doorway to the hall. 'And remember to niggle him,' she reminded me. 'Make him a little insecure. But don't be downright offensive. If things work out between us, you'll be seeing a lot more of him . . .'

I was mates with a guy called Paddy at university. Like me, he was there to study law. But unlike me, he had the uncanny ability of never ending up in situations he didn't want to be in. He put this down to his uncompromisingly honest approach towards life. He always spoke his mind and if he didn't want to do something, he'd just come out and say so. After observing him in action a few times, I narrowed down his manipulation-free existence to a single facet. It wasn't Paddy's uncompromising honesty that saved him from being roped into dreadful situations, it was his deployment of the word *no*. When Paddy said *no*, it was apparent to all and sundry that he most definitely meant it. Whilst remaining within the boundaries of civility, it was an essentially antisocial statement of intent capable of killing debate in an instant. I never once saw it questioned.

As Chloe brought Andy through in to the living-room and he stood there – shades in his hand, eyeing me suspiciously – I decided that selective use of *the Paddy No* would be my weapon of choice for the forthcoming duel. From what Chloe had told me about him, Andy was a man used to living life on his own terms. I suspected he'd never suffered a decent *no* in his life.

Chloe, standing between us, smiling brilliantly, seemed impervious to the testosterone leak that was presently flooding Andy's pants. 'Andy, this is Matt, an *old friend* of mine. Matt, Andy.'

Andy grunted at me and, following his lead, I grunted back.

'Beers, boys?' Chloe asked.

We both nodded, two prize-fighters, not taking our eyes off one another for an instant. Chloe left the room to fetch the beers and, in her absence, the stare-off continued unchecked for a few seconds. Andy, I'm glad to report, though if truth be told it was a close thing, was the first to crack.

He weighed his shades in his hand. 'What line are you in, then, Matt?' he eventually asked.

'Law.'

He considered this for a moment, before realizing that his enquiry wasn't going to be reciprocated. 'I'm a film producer,' he stated, watching me for a reaction.

'Really? And what exactly have you ... *produced*?'

He lit a cigarette. 'I'm working on a short at the moment.'

'A shorts what?'

'Film.'

'And what are your shorts about?'

'Short,' he corrected me.

'Whatever.'

'It's a love story.'

'Cute.'

'Do you like films?' he asked.

'*No.*'

'But you go to the cinema, right?'

'*No.*'

'Watch television?'

'*No.*'

He watched me, waiting for me to elaborate; I didn't.

'So,' he eventually asked, fishing for a reason for my presence, 'do you live round here?'

'*No.*'

Again, he waited for me to go on. Again, I didn't.

'London, though, yeah?' he finally asked.

'Yeah, I've got a nice little *bachelor* pad.'

He took the bait. 'You're single?'

'I wouldn't exactly put it like that,' Chloe interrupted, returning with three open bottles of beer, and distributing them before tactically taking an armchair at the side of the no man's land between Andy and myself. 'Matt's a bit of a shark, aren't you, darling?' she went on, looking up and smiling at me winsomely. 'Exes all over London who he likes to . . . keep in touch with?'

I smiled easily. 'Something like that.'

Andy looked between us. 'How did you two meet?'

'Us?' I reflected dreamily. 'Oh, we've known each other since school. We're – how shall I put it? – very *close* . . .'

'I see.'

I gave him a couple of seconds for the ramifications of this to sink in, before adding, 'How about you?'

He glanced at Chloe and cleared his throat. 'Chloe and I are seeing each other.'

Bingo. If Chloe wanted commitment, here it was. 'Really?' I said, looking over at her. 'You're a sly one, aren't you, keeping that one from me . . .'

'We've only known each other a few weeks,' Andy quickly added.

'But you are seeing each other?' I asked. 'As in boyfriend, girlfriend?'

He looked shiftily at Chloe for a split second, before fixing me with a stare. 'Most definitely,' he said.

'Well, well, well,' I said to Chloe, stifling a grin, before turning back to Andy. 'Well, let me offer you my congratulations, Andy. Chloe's a tough woman to pin down. She's got very high standards in men, you know. *Very* high,' I repeated. 'Not the kind of person who stands for any flakiness. Take it from someone who's tried . . .'

A mixed expression of confusion and relief flooded Andy's face. 'You two are exes, then?' he asked.

I smiled at him for the first time since he'd come in, and then winked at Chloe. 'Only if you count a ten-second snog aged fourteen in the school bus on the way to see *Macbeth*.'

'Yes,' Chloe exclaimed, 'and you told everyone, you little shit.'

'See what I mean about high standards?' I asked Andy, ignoring Chloe. 'Cross her and you're dead meat. She

72

didn't speak to me for a whole year. I suggest you watch your step and take good care of her. If not, you mark my words, she'll be off out of your life like a shot.'

Andy walked over and put his arm round Chloe's shoulder. 'I'll bear that in mind.' He raised his bottle to me. 'Thanks for the advice.'

I checked my watch. 'Shit,' I announced, getting up. 'Is that the time? I'd better get going.' Chloe started to get up, too. 'Don't worry,' I told her, 'I'll let myself out. Feeling like a bit of a gooseberry sitting here, anyway, to tell the truth . . . You love birds . . .' I walked over and shook Andy's hand. 'Good meeting you,' I told him, and then, unable to resist, I glanced down at his lap and added, 'And good luck with your shorts.'

Here in the bar, Jack smiles and shakes his head in amusement. 'Nice one. How's it going between them now?'

'He's been as good as gold since. Chloe's delighted. He's even taking her away to Bruges at the weekend.'

Jack laughs. 'Christ, it'll probably be her next.'

'What will?'

'Marriage, of course.'

I shake my head. 'Uh-uh, mate. It's not like that.'

'What's not?'

'Her being *next*.'

He looks bemused. 'Haven't got a clue what you're talking about,' he says, taking a drag from his cigarette and shooting me a mischievous look.

'Yes,' I correct him. 'Yes, you do. You know precisely what I'm talking about. I'm talking about your assumption that just because you've gone and decided to tie the knot, it's only a matter of time before me, Chloe and everyone else you've ever met goes and does the same thing.' I glare at him. 'Chloe's not a domino, Jack. Just because you've toppled doesn't mean she will as well.'

73

'That isn't what I said.'

'That's what you implied.'

'No, Matt,' he says, shaking his head, 'that's what you inferred.'

'Same bloody thing.' I smile thinly. 'You, my friend,' I tell him, 'should be a bloody lawyer.'

He takes a swig of his wine and another drag on his cigarette. 'Anyway,' he says with a shrug, 'even if I was talking about marriage, what's the big deal? No reason for you to get all bristled up about it. You've got no objection to marriage per se, have you?'

'*Per se*?' I consider. 'No, no, I haven't. I have no objection to marriage *per se*. I am, for example, as you well know, delighted about you and Amy getting married. Per *me*, though – well, that's a different matter altogether.'

'I don't see why. I mean, look at you. You're from a happy background. You get on with your sister. Your Mum and Dad are happy.'

'I fail to see what my background's got to do with—'

'It's got *everything* to do with it,' he interrupts.

'Everything, how?'

'Everything, in that if someone like me, whose parents hate the sight of each other, can fall in love and want to settle down, then someone like you must have a pretty good chance of wanting to do the same thing.'

'Whoa.' I hold up my hand. I know Jack means well, but quite frankly, I can do without his analysis of the long-term social ramifications of the disintegration of the nuclear family unit right now. Feeling insecure about being single is one thing, but feeling guilty about not being married yet is quite another. 'It may have escaped your notice, Jack, but wanting and doing are two separate things. And finding's something separate again.'

Jack narrows his eyes. 'Meaning?'

'Meaning that there's little point in us sitting here

discussing the hypothetical compatibility of Matt Davies and the institute of marriage, if there's absolutely no chance of this hypothesis shifting from the realms of fantasy into the realms of reality in the near future.'

Jack narrows his eyes further. 'The English translation of which is . . .'

'. . . that I don't have a girlfriend, Jack, let alone a girlfriend that I love, let alone a girlfriend that loves me back enough to spend the rest of her life with me.'

Jack considers this for a moment, then sits back in his chair and folds his arms. 'So find one,' he finally ventures.

'Find one what?'

'A girlfriend you can fall in love with.'

I eye him suspiciously. The echo in his voice is too loud to ignore. 'Have you been talking to Amy since I met her for lunch?'

Jack smiles innocently. 'Might have,' he chimes knowingly, 'but that's beside the point. Why not? That's the question. Why not get yourself a girlfriend? Lots of advantages . . . don't you think? Think of all the money you'll save on baby oil and Kleenex . . . and that's just for starters . . .'

I stare at him for a few seconds in disbelief, before replying. 'Do you want to know what I think?' I ask, pressing straight on. 'I think you're stark raving mad, that's what I think. I can't just go out there and find myself someone to fall in love with just because I *feel* like it.'

'Why not?' He looks at me like I'm stupid.

'Because it doesn't happen like that, that's why bloody not,' I splutter. 'The odds against it must be—'

He waves his hand dismissively. 'Nah,' he says, 'you don't want to go believing all that crap.'

'All *what* crap?'

'All that crap about there only being one person out there for you.' He lights another cigarette. 'I mean, look at

75

me and Amy. All that Überbabe shit I used to bang on about last year. All that waiting for my perfect woman to come along, when Amy was there, staring me in the face the whole time. All I had to do was look. Just give things a go . . .' He glances round nervously, before leaning forward and shielding his mouth. 'It's like the *X-Files*,' he whispers, 'they're out there somewhere. It's just a matter of sussing out where.'

'OK, smartarse,' I tell him, figuring I've got nothing to lose. 'Where do you suggest I start?'

'Easy,' he says, not batting an eyelid. 'H.'

I give Jack a complicated problem that's troubled mankind since the birth of time and he, in return, gives me a letter of the alphabet. Great. 'What are you talking about?' I demand.

'Not what,' he corrects, '*who*. I've got it all worked out. Amy's best mate, H.' He waves his hand. 'You know, the girl she was with at Zanzibar that night. Helen. Short, dark hair. Totally Winona. A complete babe. Really easy-going. You two clicked straight off.'

Oh, yeah. I remember H. I have a definite memory of her telling me, in no uncertain terms, to get the hell away when I attempted to get a snog off her at the end of the night in Zanzibar. I feel myself blushing, remembering my excruciatingly embarrassing failed move. I wonder if Jack's clocked the fact that I've bailed out on every social event that H might have been at since.

'*That* H. Oh, yes, Jack. Very smart,' I say with a rueful smile, 'but forget it. She gave me the brush-off, remember? Had some long-term boyfriend, she told me.'

Jack nods his head enthusiastically. 'Sure, but times change. She's single now. What?' he asks, catching my expression. 'Didn't I tell you?'

'No, not that it matters. Times change, but tastes don't,' I point out. 'She gave me the brush-off then, so she'll give me the brush-off now.'

Jack wags his finger at me. 'Some people have morals, Matt. Consider the possibility – no matter how outlandish it might first appear – that the reason she blew you out was because she was in a monogamous relationship at the time, and not because she didn't fancy the pants off you.'

Two pertinent points from Jack Rossiter in one evening. It's not like him to blow his annual allowance just like that. I'm intrigued. Perhaps he's on a roll. Perhaps he will be able to give me some sound advice. 'Has she said something to you?' I ask, and as I do, I can't help feeling that playground rush of excitement and hope.

'Not exactly,' Jack says.

My rush freezes. 'Oh.' I take a couple of seconds to recover. 'So, when you say she *might* fancy the pants off me, you mean just that.'

'No, I have a hunch.'

I consider this for a moment. H *was* fun that night in Zanzibar. *Really* good fun. But what's the use? Boyfriend or no boyfriend, when it came to the crunch, the chemistry just wasn't there.

'Forget it,' I tell Jack. 'Once bitten, twice shy. Let's leave it there. Save both of us the embarrassment.' He stares at me levelly, the kind of stare a schoolteacher gives you when you claim your homework's been eaten by the dog for the fifth day running. 'Come off it, Jack,' I continue. 'Think of the practicalities . . .'

'What practicalities?'

'Well, Zanzibar was a year ago, wasn't it? It would look pretty weird, me calling her up now and asking her out for a date.' I hold my fist to my ear, mimicking a telephone. 'Hi, H. Matt, here. No, no. Matt who you met in Zanzibar last year. No, not the island in the Indian Ocean. The night-club. I was the guy who came on to you like a twelve year old, slap-bang in the middle of the dance floor. Yes, the *arsehole*. Ha, ha. Yes, *that* Matt. Well,

I wanted to know if you fancied coming out for dinner some time. I was going to call you last year, only I've been kind of busy and didn't get round to it till now. Yes. Yes, that *is* pretty warped, isn't it? What? Psychiatric help? Well, it's not something I've ever really considered before. Hello? Hello?' I lower my fist and frown at Jack. 'Can you believe it?' I ask him. 'She hung up.'

Jack raises an eyebrow, unimpressed. 'You don't need to ask her out on a date,' he states.

'How's that?'

'She's coming along to the lunch tomorrow.'

'What lunch?'

'The test lunch for the wedding,' he explains with a grimace. 'The, er, massive test lunch that Stringer's organized so we can all try out the food and decide what we want on the actual day. The massive and terribly tasty test lunch that I was going to tell you about last week, only I sort of forgot, which is why I'm telling you about it now . . .'

I stare at him in disbelief. 'You're not serious, are you?'

He screws up his face. 'Yeah. And it's really important you're there. Best man and all that . . .'

'Forget it. I'm up to my eyeballs in work. You should have told me about it earlier, and—'

Jack looks at me imploringly. 'Please . . .'

I'm about to tell him to go jump, but something stops me. It could be the news that H is now single. It could even be the cute, hang-dog expression that Jack's wearing right now in an attempt to emotionally blackmail me. Most likely of all, though, the swaying factor is that Jack ate my pizza.

'When you say *massive* lunch,' I finally ask, 'just how big are we talking?'

Stringer

'What about you, Stringer?' KC calls out.

I'm trapped in the Epicentre of the Vortex of Chaos, otherwise known as Unit 3, Sark Industrial Estate, Chichi's West London base. It consists of a warren of offices, dining-rooms, kitchens, walk-in fridges and freezers.

From the outside, it looks like any other low-rent, prefabricated two-storey building. A passing innocent might assume that inside regular people are carrying out regulated tasks as part of their regular working existences. A passing innocent, however, would be wrong – utterly wrong – because a passing innocent would never have met Freddie DeRoth, owner of Unit 3 and master of all therein, and a passing innocent would never have met Greg Stringer, owner of very little indeed, and Master of Keeping the Whole Ship Afloat.

Now, I'm not slagging Freddie off. Far from it. He's an industry legend. The party planner's party planner, so to speak. A genius, no less, when it comes to showing other people how to have a good time. He practically introduced the concept of party theming to the UK. Give him the right budget and he'll create anything you desire, from a Romanesque orgy for four hundred, complete with toga-clad slaves bearing whole roast deer, to a simple picnic in the park for ten.

It's just that Freddie is an ideas man, and Freddie's ideas don't stoop so low as to the practicalities of actually running a business. He likes to plan the events and to be there, front of house, to bask in the glory. This is perfectly understandable. It is, after all, his glory. The boring side of the business, however – the logistics of staff, transport, venues and supplies – he leaves to me. Some days, this is a challenge. At other times, it's like being tossed a live hand grenade: all you want to do is throw it back, curl up in a ball, and wait for the explosion to pass.

Today is one of those days.

I've been sitting here at my desk in the tiny admin office by the kitchens since seven thirty this morning with the phone practically glued to my ear. I've got Jack and Amy booked in here for their test lunch at one thirty. Tamara's managing a two-hundred-guest television-awards bash at the National History Museum tonight, and Freddie and Tiff are down in Wiltshire, theming a diamond heiress's fiftieth birthday party. The where-abouts and wellbeing of eighty-six staff, four fridge vans, sixty cases of vintage champagne and a performing goat called Gerald, whose speciality is loudly bleating whilst standing on his hind legs, are merely a sample of the prize-winning turds today has decided to dump on my doorstep.

Thus far, it's SNAFU (Situation Normal: All Fucked Up). I'm a grand total of twelve waiters/resses short for tonight. Freddie, Tiff and their respective convoy of catering and staff vehicles are running two hours late, stuck in a five-mile tailback on the M4. Dave Donovan of *One Man and His Fish* caterers has reliably informed me that if I want fifty lobsters for tonight's NHM bash, then I'd 'better get fucking swimming'. Through tears and anguished sobs, Tamara has confessed that Gerald slipped his tether half an hour ago, and was last seen charging maniacally around Hyde Park, terrorizing pigeons and poodles alike.

'Yo, Stringer,' KC shouts again. 'What about you?'

I've been vaguely aware of intermittent laughter coming from the kitchen for the last twenty minutes or so, and can only assume that KC has once again been chairing a lewd and lascivious debate amongst the kitchen staff. Oh well, any distraction is welcome right now. I walk over to the open door.

'What about me, what?' I ask, leaning cross-armed against the doorframe.

Long-haired, bloodshot and scruffy beyond belief, KC is both a consummate chef and a highly regarded hashish aficionado. He's been working for Freddie for three years now – ever since he moved over from Australia on his thirtieth birthday. He looks up from the vast table of canapés he's been prepping for tonight's television awards. He's wearing baggy trousers, a T-shirt and has a blue-and-white apron tied around his waist. The T-shirt has a picture of the Pope with a superimposed spliff sticking out of his mouth, and bears the legend: *I like the Pope. The Pope smokes dope.*

I like him (KC, that is – I've never met the Pope), but I don't think he's quite made up his mind about me yet. I also don't think that asking him to cook a test lunch today for what he regards as me and five of my mates has helped much either. However, we haven't come to blows yet and – he stands upright, all six foot four of him – I hope we never do.

'Virginity, mate,' he says, his accent coming on strong. He wipes his hand down the side of his apron. 'We've just been discussing when we all lost ours. Jodie here,' he continues, nodding at a pretty graduate who's been working for Chichi for the past few months in an attempt to pay off some debts, 'got her cherry plucked when she was sixteen by her bloody guitar teacher at school.' He waggles a knife between his two other helpers, a teenaged boy and girl sent round by the staffing agency this morning. 'And Mickey and Alison plucked each other's the weekend before last. The weekend before last,' he reflects with a rueful smile, watching the two of them exchange coy glances. 'I ask you, mate, how bloody old does that make you feel?'

'Ancient,' I tell him, turning to go.

'Hang on,' he says. 'What about you?'

'What about me?' I ask.

'Well, fair's fair,' he explains. 'You can't go listening in on other people's intimate stories without trading in one of your own, can you?'

'I haven't been listening in on anything, KC,' I point out. 'You called me out here and spilt the beans on everyone, remember? If it's anyone's turn to dish the dirt, it's probably yours.'

A mistake. Rather than putting KC off the idea of continuing the conversation, all my request actually does is up his interest. No sooner have I issued my challenge to him, than he takes it up with a relish probably not hitherto witnessed in his life since his discovery that tobacco and hashish, when smoked together in sufficient quantities, were capable of inducing a lengthy and beneficial high.

'So, Stringer,' he drawls approximately ten minutes later, following the finale of an enthralling narrative, complete with a choreographed display of which the BBC's dramatic reconstruction department would be proud, 'fill us in on the scrubber who was stupid enough to get filled in by you the first time round.'

At this exact moment, there's a silence. It's a silence of ignorance, and a silence of shame. It's the silence of a schoolboy who's been asked the easiest question in the world, but doesn't know the answer.

I feel sick and this sickness comes as no surprise. This isn't the first time I've felt this way. It's been going on since I was fourteen and Richard Lewis came back to our boarding-school on the first night of the summer term with a pair of white cotton knickers in his blazer pocket. I remember standing with him and about ten other teen-agers in the yard at the back of our boarding-house before lights-out time, smoking cigarettes, passing the knickers from hand to hand, digging each other in the ribs, and giggling when Dave Tagg was caught stealing a sneaky sniff by pressing the gusset up against his face. I also remember studying Richard's face as he told us about the previous Wednesday night when a girl he knew from home, Emma Roberts, had agreed to go down to the caravan at the bottom of his parents' garden at their home in Berkshire. He told us how he'd curled up with her on the fold-down bed and slowly undressed and – and this was what we'd been waiting to hear – shagged her. Then he showed us the knickers again, because they were his proof, and because without them and without Emma Roberts' name tag sewn in to them, we wouldn't have believed a word he'd said.

I'm not Richard Lewis, however. I'm Greg Stringer. I have no proof. All I have are lies.

'The very first time?' I query.

'Yeah,' KC presses.

I walk over to the preparation table, pull up a chair and sit down. 'Her name was Emily,' I begin.

Her name was Mrs Emily Warberg.

'How old were you?' Mickey asks.

'She was twenty-one and I was seventeen. She was a student at Manchester University. I was in my last year at school.'

She was forty-nine, the mother of Alan Warberg, a boy from home I used to hang out with in the school holidays. I'd known both her and him since they'd moved in to the street when I was twelve. Her husband's name was Rob and he worked for an advertising agency.

'An older woman, huh?' KC exclaims. 'You lucky bastard. What was she like?'

83

'Emily was beautiful. Blonde hair, blue eyes. Five ten. A real stunner.'

Mrs Warberg was the Bride of Frankenstein, a diet-junkie, and scrawny to the point of emaciation. Her legs were like broomsticks and her shoulderblades sharp. She smoked forty Rothmans a day and hadn't exercised once in the time I'd known her. Her hair was bottle blonde and her roots cobweb grey. She wore padded bras and drank vodka neat from a bottle she kept on top of the fridge.

KC puts down his knife and perches on the edge of the table, rapt. 'Radical,' he mutters. 'Where d'you nail her?'

'I called round at her house one Saturday night,' I continue. 'Emily lived down the street from me. It was the Easter holidays and I was at home revising for my A-levels. She was home from Manchester for the Easter break. I'd seen her at this party the weekend before and we'd chatted and kissed a little. Nothing more, though. Anyway, this Saturday night . . . Her mother was an economics teacher at the college down the road, and I needed some help on a mock paper I was doing, so round I went . . .'

One Saturday night in the Easter holiday, I went round to Alan's house for a spliff.

KC guffaws and pulls his knee up to his chin. 'Help you with your homework. Jeeze, man, how cheesy can you get?'

Jodie glares at him and he shuts up.

'I knocked on the door,' I carry on. 'It wasn't her mother or father who answered the door; it was Emily. She looked me up and down and smiled and blushed and asked me how I was. She muttered something about having been quite drunk at the party, and then I blushed as well and asked her if her mother was in and she said no. I was about to go, when she said she'd done Economics A-level and could probably remember some

84

of it, so why didn't I come in for a drink and we'd see if we could work it out between us.'

Alan's mother opened the door about five minutes after I'd first rung the bell. She stood there, leaning against the doorframe in her dressing gown and slippers, staring at me unsteadily. I could smell the drink on her breath. She said, 'Oh, it's you,' and pulled on her cigarette and told me to come inside. I followed her through to the sitting-room and she sat down on the sofa, and slopped vodka into a couple of tumblers. She patted the sofa next to her and said, 'Alan's gone to the football with his dad. They won't be back till late.' She offered me a cigarette and I took one and sat down.

'Come on,' KC urges. 'Cut to the chase.'

'It was great. It was everything you could want. We sat in the kitchen and had a couple of beers and laughed about what we'd got up to at the party. Then she rolled a number and we smoked it. Then . . .'

It was awful. It was the most uncomfortable I'd ever felt. I sat next to Mrs Warberg and smoked her cigarettes and drank her vodka. She talked about her life, slating her husband and complaining about her lack of fun and lack of sex. Then she poured herself another vodka and downed it and then gazed at me for what felt like an age. Then . . .

'Then Emily asked me if I wanted to go upstairs with her, and I said yes. She took my hand and we went up to her bedroom. I lay on the bed and she put on a record, lit a candle and switched out the light, and came and joined me. We kissed for what felt like hours and then we made love, and if that sounds cheesy to you, KC, it wasn't. It was perfect. She was the most wonderful person I'd ever met. She was intelligent, gentle, beautiful and kind. It was how I'd always dreamt it would be.'

Mrs Warberg reached over and took my hand and pulled it towards her and slid it beneath her dressing gown and shoved it roughly between her legs. She told me that it felt nice and that I wasn't to worry about what Alan and her husband would say, because there was no reason for them ever to find out. Then she undid her dressing-gown belt and shrugged it off, knelt down on the ground beside me, naked, and unbuckled my belt. I simply sat there, feeling drunk, feeling sick, unable to look at her. That's when it happened. That's when she saw my cock and started to laugh.

'That sounds really special,' sighs Jodie.

'Yeah, lucky you,' KC admits.

It wasn't special. It was gutting. I remember how Mrs Warberg flicked my cock with her forefinger. 'Well, darling,' she slurred, pulling her dressing gown back on and lighting another cigarette, 'I don't know what you expect me to do with that little pinkie.'

'Fair do's,' KC says. 'That's pretty cool.'

'Yes,' I say, 'it was.'

There have been other attempts, drugged-up fumblings in the dark over the years with equally wasted girls. I might even have got it in a few times, but nothing I could face up to in the morning. I shake my head. It never ceases to amaze me how something so small has managed to have so great an impact on my life. It leaves me gutted and alone.

'Will we be all right for serving lunch at one thirty, KC?' I ask.

He walks over to the cooker and picks up a piece of paper. 'American-style crab cakes with creamed spinach for starters. Wild mushroom sauté for the non-carnies. Grilled mustard-butter quail for the main. Veggies get mushroom and spinach lasagne. Then for pudding you said fig, honey and mascarpone tart.' He looks up. 'That right?'

'Perfect.'

He looks me sceptically up and down. 'Yeah, well your mates had better be here on time, because I'm not hanging about if they're not. I promised Freddie I'd be down the museum for two thirty to sort out some kitchen space.'

'Don't worry,' I say, thinking of Jack's poor record on punctuality and suddenly feeling none too confident on this score. 'They'll be here. And they're not mates,' I remind him, 'they're fee-paying customers.'

'Bullshit,' he snorts, 'I've seen the estimate you've done 'em. They're getting it rock bottom, so they'd better appreciate the trouble I'm going to . . .'

'They will, KC,' I reassure him. 'And so do I.'

He grunts at me, unconvinced, and returns to his work.

One o'clock comes and matters are looking up. Through a variety of blackmail, bribery and downright begging, I've lined up the missing waiters and waitresses for tonight's NHM do. The M4 tailback has cleared and Freddie has checked that everything at the fiftieth is to his satisfaction and is now on his way back to London. In a remarkable turnaround, *One Man and His Fish* have discovered a surplus of lobster, and have sent them over in a fridge van, along with a brace of sea trout by way of an apology. Of all this morning's woes, only Gerald the Performing Goat remains at large, and good luck to him. After all, a goat's got to do what a goat's got to do.

Jack and Amy get here early, at one fifteen. It's tipping down outside and I show them upstairs to the dining-room I've spent the last half-hour setting up with Jodie. We've laid on the full monty for them: linen-boxed table; candles; crystal and china. Jodie is on hand to take their coats and offer them a drink. Jack and Amy seem pleased as punch, so I scoot back downstairs and check with KC that everything is running according to schedule.

'One thirty, you said,' he reminds me matter-of-factly. 'So one thirty it'll be.' He glances at me suspiciously. 'All your mates here yet?'

'Two of them,' I mumble, before adding, 'the bride and groom', hoping it will appease him slightly.

It doesn't. 'The crab cakes'll taste more like crab craps if they don't have 'em while they're hot,' is all he says.

As it transpires, only one crab cake suffers this fate, and so I only have to deal with one sixth of KC's wrath. The crab cake in question belongs to H, and it suffers this fate because H arrives late. An hour and a half late, to be precise. The others are well in to their pudding by this time, and KC, thankfully, is well on his way to the museum and out of my hair for the rest of the afternoon.

The first word that H says to me when I open the door to her downstairs is 'Don't.'

She's soaked from top to toe, looking for all intents and purposes like she's stuck her head down a toilet and pulled the flush several times. Black streaks of mascara run from her eyes to her chin and on down her throat, giving her the impression of a badly made-up Pierrette. More worrying, however, is the look on her face. It's not simply a look that could kill. It's a look that would take great pleasure in torturing you for several days first.

I feel my heart beat and, after gently clearing my throat, ask, 'Don't what?'

'Don't say one fucking word,' she snaps, shoving past me and standing shivering in the hall.

Contravening her wishes at this moment would definitely have a detrimental and possibly irreversible effect on my health, so instead I settle for mutely pointing her up the stairs. I follow her and, at the top, watch her stride down the corridor towards the sound of voices. She sticks her head round the dining-room door and, as the voices inside collapse into silence, says in an icily calm voice, 'Amy. Outside. Now.'

Seconds later, Amy comes out and takes one look at H before leading her by the hand into a side storeroom and closing the door behind them. I tiptoe up the corridor and stand outside, ear pressed to the door, quietly listening.

'Problem?' Matt whispers, appearing seconds later.

I grimace. 'If you're the driver . . .'

He stares at me blankly and I press my ear to the door again.

'Of the stationary bus she crashed in to on the way here,' I inform him.

He winces and takes over the eavesdropping duties.

'The stationary bus she *reversed* in to on the way here,' he corrects. 'The stationary bus she reversed in to on the way here, that she doesn't want any of us knowing about, because if anyone so much as sniggers, she's going to cut out their tongue and rip off their head.'

'Cut out their tongue *and* rip off their head?' I check. 'Isn't that a tad excessive?'

Matt purses his lips and nods his head.

'Keep out of her way for the time being, then?' I suggest.

'Yeah,' he agrees, 'probably best.'

It's odd, but neither H's satanic mood nor her late showing for lunch manage to put the complete downer on my day that I might have otherwise expected. It isn't that the meal has been a success, although it has. (Jack and Amy adored the food.) Nor is it that everyone has been in good spirits, although (with the obvious exception of H) they have. Nor is it because KC, as part of some deranged hippy retribution for getting him to cook for us, has laced our food with some of his more unusual herbs. (He hasn't.) It's actually more to do with having had a cracking time chatting to Susie. We clicked the moment she sat down and have hardly paused for breath since the meal began. I haven't laughed this much for months. It's like she's got this limitless energy that you just can't help getting high on.

'What the hell's all that about?' Jack demands, as Matt and I walk back into the dining-room.

'She's trashed her car,' I announce.

'How?'

Before I can speak, Matt interjects: 'Don't know. We didn't hear the details.' He looks to me for confirmation. 'Did we, mate?'

'No,' I agree. He's right. It's probably best not to stir matters up. If H wants what happened kept secret, then that's fine by me.

Susie looks shocked. 'Was anyone hurt?'

'No,' I say, 'nothing to worry about.'

'Probably best not to mention it when she comes back in,' Matt adds, walking round the table. 'She's got a bad case of *tantrum maximum*.'

I sit back down next to Susie and there's silence for a few minutes as the muffled, raised voices continue from next door, and we all stare at our shoes, embarrassed. It's a shame really, because the rest of the meal has gone so well. Everyone's had a giggle and, equally as important for me, it's been a professional success, with the food and wine getting the thumbs up all round. It means a lot. Especially Jack and Matt's reaction. I don't think I can remember them ever looking at me with admiration before. Certainly not in a work scenario. It's almost like a coming of age. I feel Susie gently nudging me in the ribs and look up.

'What's the cheesy stuff?' she asks, nodding at her plate.

'Mascarpone,' I inform her.

'Mascar-bloody-gorgeous, more like,' she says, taking another spoonful. She turns to face the table at large. 'Come on, then, boys,' she says, her blue eyes wandering over myself, Matt and finally Jack. 'Fill us in on the smutty venue you've got booked for your stag weekend.'

Jack shrugs and nods at Matt. 'Nothing to do with me,' he says. 'Matt's keeping us in the dark.'

'Well, Matt?' Susie enquires.

He grins at her. 'You know the rules. The hens aren't allowed to know.'

90

'Ah, go on now,' she says dismissively. 'Don't be so retro. I won't tell.'

'That's not the point. Besides,' Matt continues, 'not even the stags know. Not even Jack. Only me. And it's staying that way till we get there.' He leans forward conspiratorially. 'What I will say, though, is that it's got the Matt Davies Official Seal of Approval on it and is consequently going to be the best weekend of our lives. Guaranteed.'

Susie nods her head in approval. 'Sordid weekend, more like,' she says.

'What about you lot?' I ask her. 'Have you got anywhere booked yet?'

'H has got it all sorted . . .'

'Where?' Matt pounces.

Susie pulls an imaginary zip across her lips. 'Sorry, Matt. Top secret. Same as you. If I told you, I'd have to kill you.'

'How about a clue, then?' he asks.

'Like what?'

'Like which city?' He winks at Jack, then turns back to Susie. 'Just so we know which one to avoid . . .'

'Easy,' she says with a smile, then, 'It might not be a city.'

'What,' Jack scoffs, 'you mean you're off to the countryside? No clubs? No bars? No guys? You'll go nuts.'

'For your information, Jack Rossiter,' she says, smiling, stabbing a finger at him, 'there's more to life than that.'

'Like what?' he challenges.

'Like fresh country air, and beautiful scenery, and stacks of Me Time.'

Jack looks horrified. I'm not surprised. His idea of the Great Outdoors is sitting in Hyde Park with a crate of Stella Artois and a chicken drumstick.

'*What* time?' he asks.

'Me Time,' Susie explains. 'Time for a bit of self-contemplation. Time to relax without worrying about the future – or anything else for that matter . . .'

Jack rolls his eyes and pats his mouth with his hand in a yawning gesture. 'Bor-ring,' he tolls. 'You won't last five minutes.'

'Come on,' I intervene, feeling that it's about time someone took Susie's side, 'it won't be that bad.'

She puts her arm round me and gives me a squeeze. 'See,' she says. 'A real man. Not like you pretty-boy, city-boy wimps.'

I have a snapshot of Susie exactly as she was when I met her at the front door earlier: curly blonde hair poking out from beneath her mad velvet hat; five foot six and curvy; a great big grin. Then there's her accent: to die for, like that Cerys woman, the lead singer of Catatonia. In the few instances we haven't been speaking directly to one another, I've found myself monitoring her out of the corner of my eye, aware that she's doing the same. It's put butterflies in my stomach.

'Sorry I'm late,' H says, interrupting my train of thought. She's standing in the doorway next to Amy. Her face is set like a death mask.

'No problem,' I tell her. 'Grab a seat. The food's cold, though, I'm afraid. The chef's had to go somewhere else.' I force a smile, hoping that her strop is now officially over.

It's not. She nods as if she expected nothing less and slumps into her chair and reaches for the water bottle. She fills a glass and drains it. Then there's silence. I notice Matt staring at me, attempting, I think, to prompt me into doing the host bit by breaking the silence. My mind goes blank, however, and I look away and wait for someone to suggest that the meal is over, as it obviously now is.

Half an hour later and we're all standing downstairs, looking out into the rain.

'Thanks for making it,' I tell H. 'As I say: sorry you missed the food.'

'Forget it,' she mumbles, giving me a perfunctory peck on the cheek, before stomping out into the rain.

Matt watches her for a few seconds, before whispering into my ear, 'Magnificent, isn't she?' Then, out loud to the others: 'I'd better get going, as well.' He kisses Amy and Susie goodbye and shakes hands with Jack and me. 'I'll give you two a call next Monday to let you know where and when we're going to hook up for the stag weekend.'

He catches up with H at the edge of the car park and they stand there talking in the rain.

'Aye, aye,' Jack comments, his voice laced with insinuation, watching the two of them.

'How about you, Sooze?' Amy asks, ignoring him. 'Do you need a lift anywhere?'

'Ah, that'd be fantastic, love. Left the Metro back home, so down the station would be brilliant. You sure it's no problem?'

'Of course not. We don't want you drowning, do we?'

'Thanks,' Susie says, then groans, patting the top of her head. 'Oh, bugger. I've left my hat inside.' She shoves her bag into my hand and hurries off. 'I won't be two ticks. I'm pretty sure it's upstairs.'

'Hang on,' Amy calls after her. 'I'll come with you.'

The moment they've both disappeared up the stairs, Jack nudges me in the ribs. 'Looks like you're well in there, Horse.'

The leather handle of Susie's bag is warm from when she was holding it. I feel my own hand squeeze instinctively round it. 'All right, Jack,' I confess. 'I admit it. For once in your life, you might have a point.'

He stares at me blankly and grunts, 'Huh?'

'About Susie,' I remind him. 'It was nice meeting her . . .'

'Yeah,' he enthuses, 'and just like you, a total scrubber. It's a match made in heaven.'

Jack's attitude never ceases to amaze me. 'Total scrubber,' I mimic. 'Don't you think that what she gets up to in private is her business?'

'Not when she gets up to it with everyone, no,' he says without pause for thought. 'I reckon that makes it public property.'

I roll my eyes at him. 'Yes, well, we'll have to agree to disagree on that one.'

Amy and Susie reappear before Jack can reply. Susie waggles her hat at me. 'Left it in the toilet,' she informs me, pulling it down on her head, and taking back her bag.

'It looks great,' I tell her, but there's a flatness in my voice which takes me by surprise. I think it might have something to do with what Jack said about her. It's not the part about her sex-life. I meant what I told him about that: it's her business. I think it's because of what he said about me being in there. It hadn't really occurred to me, not bluntly like that, at least. Now that Jack's put it into my head, however, I do accept it as a possibility, and because of that, what he said about her being so experienced leaves me depressed. But what did I expect? That she was a virgin? That we could go to bed and have a great time because she wouldn't know any better? I take a deep breath and smile at her. At the end of the day, however, I don't suppose it matters. I like her and that's enough. We'll be friends, exactly the same as it is with Karen. 'Where did you get it?' I ask her, trying to inject some enthusiasm into my voice and feeling better the moment I succeed.

'Oh, best store in town . . .'

'Where's that?'

She grins. 'My stall. Portobello market. Saturday mornings. You should swing by some time. I'll treat you to a coffee.' She cocks her head to one side and peers up at me through sparkling eyes. 'Come to think of it, I might treat you to a coffee anyway. Or something a bit stronger, if you fancy.'

'That's very kind, but—'

She shoots me this big beamer of a smile. 'Fab. How about tonight, then? We could chill out, you know? Have a laugh. What time d'you knock off here?'

'I can't tonight. There's a job on at the Natural History Museum. I've got to be there in an hour and I doubt I'll get away much before 3 a.m. . . .'

She looks at me like I'm being shoddy. That isn't how it is. It's simply the truth. I rack my brain, trying to think of an alternative date to meet up, but fail. Bar the stag weekend, I'm working every night now right up until Jack and Amy's wedding. I shrug apologetically.

'Some other time, then . . .' she suggests.

'Yes,' I say, giving her a goodbye hug and a kiss on the cheek, 'some other time.'

H

Wednesday, 15.30

'Want a lift?' asks Matt, jangling his keys. I'm standing in the car park, rummaging in my bag for my mobile, already soaked. Matt nods towards the green Spitfire next to me.

I might have known he'd have a car like this.

'It's OK, I'm calling a cab,' I say.

It's not that I don't want a lift. I do. I want anything that will get me out of here and where I want to be. Which is at home.

Alone.

Preferably with dry clothes on.

'Come on, get in,' he says. 'It'll take ages for a cab to find this place.'

Reluctantly, I open the door and try clambering into the bucket seat without getting my suit skirt wrapped round my ears. There's a bag of golf clubs in the back seat and Matt rearranges them so that I can push my seat back. I think Matt wants me to be impressed. He looks expectantly at me and smiles as he starts up, but I don't smile back. I hate golf and I hate poxy show-off cars like these. I'm also not sure I can stand any more small talk.

I'm sick of trying to be nice. Of everything being *nice*.

'Nice food,' says Matt.

Aghhhhhhhhhhhhhhhhh!

Nice food is not how I'd describe it. To be honest, all wedding food is pretty disgusting. I challenge anyone to enjoy it, even if it's the type of nosh that Stringer would have us believe is worthy of three Michelin stars. As far as I'm concerned, he's wasting his time. On the day, everyone will be bored shitless from hours of photographs and all they'll really want is a stiff drink, not a tepid, sit-down meal with a bunch of strangers, whilst Jack and Amy preside over everyone from the top table.

I can't bitch to Matt, though. Apart from the fact that he likes Stringer, he and Jack are thick as thieves and it would only get back to Amy. And if it got back to Amy, she'd probably change the whole menu and give me a nervous breakdown in the process.

Matt puts his arm around the back of my seat, looks through the tiny plastic rear screen and reverses. The car makes a whining sound. It's nowhere near as good as mine is.

Was, damn it.

'You look different from the last time I saw you,' observes Matt, putting the car in to gear. I can feel him looking at me, but I wish he'd concentrate on driving. One accident is enough for me today. Besides, I don't want to be looked at. I haven't got any make-up on.

'I was pissed last time you saw me,' I point out.

'And now you're just pissed off?'

'Let's just say I haven't had a very good day,' I say, lighting up a cigarette.

Matt spins the wheel round with one hand. 'What happened?'

'My car got written off, if you must know.'

'Bummer,' he says.

I open the window an inch and blow smoke towards it. It blows back in my face, along with a splash of rain as Matt speeds off towards Vauxhall Bridge. I sulk in the passenger seat. How dare he be so flippant? My life is not a *bummer*, it's much worse than that, not that I'd expect Matt to understand.

Maybe Matt senses my irritation, because when he

pulls up smoothly to the traffic lights, he leans one arm on the steering-wheel and turns to face me.

'How did it happen?' he asks, gently.

To my surprise, he looks genuinely concerned, his eyebrows knitted together. I hadn't noticed before, but he's got very green eyes – dark green with hazel flecks in them.

'How did *what* happen?' I snap. He may be a lawyer but I'm not going to be cross-examined by him, thank you very much. I'm not falling for his phony sympathy.

'The car. I mean, you could have been badly injured.'

I fold my arms and look out of the window. The glass is covered in drops of rain and I watch them slide in to one another, before noticing my pursed-lipped reflection.

'I'm fine.'

'What about the other people?'

'What other people?'

'In the car that hit you,' he says, easing away from the lights.

'They're OK,' I stall, as we career round the feeder lane on to the bridge.

'You've got all their details, I take it?'

Who does he think he is? Chief Inspector Matt Davies? I take a drag of my cigarette and tap my foot.

'It's complicated,' I mutter, hoping that he'll take the hint.

But he doesn't.

'All the more reason to sort out the insurance quickly.'

'I'll deal with it,' I say pointedly, turning to face him, my back teeth gritted together.

'It's best to,' he nods. 'These things can drag on, especially when they're not your fault.'

'*I know.*'

We drive on in silence for a while and I watch the windscreen wipers flick water away. I drop my cigarette butt out of the gap in the window, fold my arms and shiver.

'Only, I can help with the claim if you want,' offers Matt. 'I've got some experience with this sort of thing.'

Will he just *shut up*?

I shift in my seat and turn on him. 'Look, I've got it all under control. There are lots of people and vehicles involved and it's quite complex...'

'A big collision then?' he interrupts, glancing at me.

'Yeah, pretty big.'

'What? Two or three cars?'

'Something like that.'

'Poor you. Coming from all angles?'

'The back, mainly, if you must know,' I spit.

He pauses as he drives on. 'So you didn't reverse in to a bus or anything, then?' I jolt round and face him.

'How did you know?'

Matt's eyes are dancing with amusement. 'Stringer overheard you talking to Amy.'

Stringer. I might have known.

'Great!' I snarl.

'Calm down,' chuckles Matt. 'I didn't tell anyone else.' He glances over at me. 'It's *funny*.'

'It doesn't seem very funny to me,' I sulk, but I know I'm over-reacting. He's caught me lying my arse off, because I'm too proud to admit what I've done. Matt's still laughing, and despite myself I feel myself breaking into a smile. I hit him on the arm.

'Stop it.'

' "Lots of people and vehicles involved... Volvos, juggernauts, the works, officer, all shunting up my back end," ' he mimics, sucking in his cheeks to look ultra-serious.

I laugh, despite myself.

'I felt a bit of a twat, to be honest,' I confess, surprised

99

how relieved I feel to talk about it. 'Especially since I got out and kicked the car. The bus I'd hit was full of people and they saw me shouting like a lunatic.'

Matt shakes his head and laughs. 'Forget it. Everyone does things like that once in a while.'

'Really? I thought it was just me.'

'No way. Think about the last time we met! I made an *total* twat of myself. You can't out-twat *me*.'

I snort, remembering Matt grabbing me and smooching me around on the dance floor. We'd met him and Jack at a new club in town that I'd taken Amy to, to get her mind off Jack. I'd never set eyes on either of them before, so I was completely fooled by their identity. And once Amy had got over the shock of seeing Jack and had swooned off with him in a haze of rekindled romance, I was abandoned with Matt who was being unbearably smug about his set up.

'True,' I nod, remembering. 'You were a huge twat that night.'

'What happened to you, anyway?' he asks.

'After you'd tried to shove your tongue down my throat?' I ask, pleased to see that he's blushing slightly. 'I went home,' I continue. 'To barf.'

'Thanks very much!' His cheeks are even more pink.

'Well, honestly! You'd tricked me and I felt like a complete idiot. Anyway, what did you expect? That you'd get Jack and Amy back together and to make it all neat and tidy, you'd pull me? To make a cosy foursome? Personally, I can't think of anything more nauseous.'

'All right, all right,' he says, holding up his hand. 'I've admitted I was a twat.'

'Good,' I nod. 'Accepted.'

He changes the subject and asks me about my job, but I feel exhausted and find myself switching off and giving him my stock 'I work in TV . . . sounds glamorous . . . it isn't' speech. Eventually, we get to Hammersmith Broadway and I give Matt directions to my street. He stops outside my flat.

'So,' he pauses. 'What are you doing tonight?' He waggles the gear stick in neutral.

'Working. Having lunch today wasn't exactly convenient.'

'I know the feeling,' he says. He looks up the street for a moment and turns back towards me. 'I was going to ask if you wanted to have something to eat. Um, with me?'

I'm about to make a flippant comment, when I catch him out of the corner of my eye. There's no mistaking his expression.

He's making a pass.

Oh God. I don't think I can cope with this.

I shake my head hurriedly, in a panic. I just want to get out of here.

'Some other time then?' he presses.

I don't believe this. I spend five minutes talking to Matt and he thinks he can ask me out on a date. Blokes! They really do my head in. I've made my views very, and I mean *very*, clear about cosy foursomes, and now this.

'No,' I say, fumbling with my seat belt. 'No, I can't, I . . .'

'A drink, then?'

I stop fiddling with my seat belt, take a deep breath and turn to face him. 'Matt, I don't want to go out with anyone. Not you. Not anyone. OK?'

I try to open the car door, but the lock is tricky.

'I'm not *asking you out*, I'm just asking you out,' he says, leaning across me and pulling the catch. 'There's no need to bite my head off.'

He pushes my door open and sits back in his seat and I can see how different he looks with all the kindness gone from his face. He looks really offended, as he puts the car into gear.

'Thanks for the lift,' I mumble, clumsily getting out.

I stomp up my stairs and let myself in to the flat. I don't listen to the answering machine as all I want is to shower today away. I rip off my clothes and head for the bathroom. It's only when I'm naked, the icy water splashing all over me, that I remember that since I'm home earlier than usual, the hot water hasn't come on.

Just great.

A lousy end to a lousy day.

I wrap myself in towels and dive under my duvet, pulling it over my head.

How was I supposed to know about Matt? I thought he was coming on to me. It sounded like he was and he hasn't exactly got a good track record.

But maybe he was just being friendly. And if he was, I've really blown it now.

I groan and roll over. I can try to justify it all I want, but the truth is, I'm being an over-sensitive, over-defensive bitch. And I can't afford to be bolshie with Matt. I am going to see him all the time. Not just at the wedding, but afterwards as well. Let's face it, I won't be able to avoid seeing Amy with Jack most of the time when she's married. And if Jack's around, the chances are that Matt will be too. And that's fine, I suppose. Matt's funny in a slick sort of way and whilst he doesn't exactly make my stomach flip, he's hardly Quasimodo.

But the whole thing makes me sick.

Really sick. Because it's just too couply.

I *hate* couples. Everything about them, even platonic ones. I don't want to see couples and I certainly don't want to be in a couple. I want out.

How has everything changed? One minute, everyone was happy being single, but now it seems that everyone around me has become desperate to find a mate. And more worryingly, those that have (even Amy, who I think

of as pretty independent) have started defining themselves by their 'other halves'.

I don't want another half. I'm perfectly whole as I am. I
don't even want to be put in a pretend pair, just so that I
become more socially acceptable not being on my own.
I don't want it. I don't care. I'm sick of other people's
baggage and bullshit. I just want to be on my own. In the
Outer Hebrides. Where there's no one to team up with
but the seals. And that's fine by me, because teaming up
doesn't work.

Certainly not with men.

I bury my face in the pillow and close my eyes tightly,
but the tears squeeze through. I hold my breath, but it
doesn't work and a strange sobbing noise escapes me. I
don't want to be crying, but I am. Because what
happened today just isn't fair. I wrap my arms over my
stomach, but it doesn't work. There's pain in there. Real
heartbreak pain that I can't tell anyone about and that I
can't avoid any longer. And on top of it all, I'm so angry.
With myself and with Brat.

Actually, it's all Brat's fault.

It was so busy this morning and the docudrama that's
going out tomorrow had to be re-edited before lunch. I'd
told Brat that I was going down to the editing suite alone
and not to disturb me, unless it was important.

About an hour later, I was just finishing up when Eddie
opened the door. 'Any news from the lawyers?' he asked.
We've been waiting for a reply on a libel action for days.
Typically, though, the lawyers are being slow.

'Come in a sec,' I said, gesturing him in. I was pleased
he'd turned up, since I wanted his opinion on the final cut
of the programme. Lianne was with him and she stood by
the door, fiddling with the cuff of yet another new jacket,
as I showed Eddie what I'd done.

Absent-mindedly, I turned on the speaker phone as we
scrolled through the rushes, Eddie leaning over me.

'Has that fax come through?' I asked Brat. I could hear him hastily rustling through papers.

'Um. There's only one here,' he squelched through his chewing gum.

'What does it say?'

'Um . . . Well, I think you should read it, it looks, kinda, well, sort of, important.'

'Brat, I haven't got time. Just read it, OK?'

'But . . .'

Eddie gestured to the screens and I stood up, letting him have my seat. 'I haven't got all day.'

Eddie moved the phone away, so that he could put down his pad of paper to take some notes and I leaned over to turn up the speaker volume.

'Dear H,' began Brat. 'Um. This is what it says, right . . . I've been trying to reach you . . . um . . . but you're obviously busy . . .'

'Come on,' I called, pulling a face at the phone. Eddie smiled.

'Um . . . um . . . I wanted you to hear it from me, but since you're not returning my calls, this is the only way . . .'

Eddie and I both looked at the phone ominously.

'You were right,' continued Brat, through the speaker. 'Um . . . I was . . . I was having an affair with Lindsay . . . um . . . from work and we're . . . we're getting married . . . I thought you should know . . .'

Eddie cleared his throat noisily, but there was silence all around me as Brat trailed off.

'It's from Gav,' he explained, unnecessarily. 'That's all that's come through.'

'Nothing from the lawyer, then?' I said, as calmly as I could.

'Wasn't he your ex?' asked Brat.

I pounced on the phone and pressed the button to cut him off.

'No news,' I said to Eddie, challenging him not to comment as my cheeks burned up.

'This seems fine,' he said, pointing to the screen. 'I'll catch you later.'

Lianne gave me a pitying grimace as she crept after Eddie through the door and closed it quietly after her.

I slumped into the chair, feeling as if I'd been shot.

Minutes later, the phone rang.

'What?' I barked.

'Aren't you going for lunch with your friends?' asked Brat, in a pathetically sympathetic tone. 'You're going to be late.'

I grunted and slammed down the phone.

Outside, I raced around the corner to where the car was parked on a meter, crunching it in to reverse, jamming my foot down on the accelerator. Of course, I hadn't looked. I doubt if it would have made any difference if I had. There was no way I could have missed it.

The number 38.

I get in late the next day. I haven't really slept. At least, I don't think I have. I cried long and hard for a while, but it's hard sustaining serious weeping on your own. I started to feel childish and ridiculous, and so I stopped. Ever since, I've been in a weird twighlight zone of numbness.

I sit for a while chain-smoking in my office, playing out pyschodramas in my head. They're all to do with confronting Gav, but I can't really connect with any of them. Anyway, they all trail off as soon as I see his face.

At ten o'clock, Brat knocks on the door and brings me a cup of coffee.

'I didn't know, right,' he starts, gormlessly, 'that Eddie and that . . .' he trails off, putting the coffee down on my desk, as if he's poking something through the cage of a grouchy lion.

It must be all round the office. I bet Lianne couldn't wait to tell everyone.

Bitch.

'That what, Brat?' I ask, reaching for the coffee and sliding it across towards me. 'That you chose to read out a fax from my ex-boyfriend, in front of half the office, detailing not only his wedding plans, but his on-going infidelity whilst he was with me?'

He flaps his arm about ineffectually. 'I didn't know, did I?' His bottom lip is drooping.

'No, you didn't,' I say, more kindly.

Brat sniffs and seals his lips together in a semi-smile. 'Lousy thing to do, I reckon ... faxing you.' He nods, agreeing with himself.

'Yes, all right,' I say, taking a sip of coffee. 'I know.'

'What are you going to do?' he asks.

I look at him for a long moment and bite my lip as I make up my mind.

'Sit,' I say, nodding to the seat on the other side of my desk. I rip off my list and throw him my pad of paper and a pencil. 'I want you to take this down.'

Brat sits with the pad perched on his knee, looking like a very awkward secretary.

'Fax,' I say. 'To Mr Gavin Wheeler from Helen Marchmont.' I put my feet up on the desk, lean back in my chair and light a cigarette.

'You can fill in all the date and that stuff,' I add, glancing at Brat, who is busy writing, his tongue gripped between his teeth.

'Congratulations on your engagement,' I begin. 'What a delightful way of hearing about it.' I take a drag of my cigarette. 'Good luck to the frumpy Lindsay and my condolences on her cheap and nasty engagement ring.'

Brat looks at me, but I motion him to write it down.

'I'll give you a year, tops, before she's divorced you.' I pause, giving time for Brat to catch up.

'Is divorced with a "c" or an "s"?' he asks, tentatively.
'C.'

'Are you sure about this?'

'I haven't finished yet.'

I take a long drag. 'But please don't think I'm bitter,' I continue, blowing out expansively. 'I'm overjoyed to be free of . . .'

'Slow down!' says Brat, scribbling, but I'm on a roll.

'Your lies and your pathetic . . .' I pause, looking at my cigarette for inspiration, '. . . ineffectual penis,' I say. 'I'm sure that Lindsay doesn't feel a thing either.'

'H!' interrupts Brat, wincing.

'What?'

'Isn't this a bit, you know . . . strong?'

'I think it's very reasonable. And honest,' I add, taking my feet off the desk and stubbing out my cigarette. I flip through the Rolodex on my desk. 'Send it to the general office number, will you?' I ask, scribbling Gav's numbers on a Post-it. 'Oh and a couple of copies to his department, too. If he replies, or phones, I don't want to know about it.'

Brat is sitting motionless in the chair, gawping at me.

'Well, go on,' I say, flapping the note which is stuck to the end of my forefinger.

Brat tuts as he peels it off my finger. 'Ballbreaker,' he mutters, as he starts shuffling out of my office.

'You better believe it, honey,' I grin.

On Friday night, I agree (with good grace for once) to meet Amy and Jack in the Blue Rose after work. I feel a bit bad about being in such a foul mood on Wednesday when I saw them at their test meal, so I should make the effort. I'm feeling demob happy since I'm off to Paris on Sunday to meet up with Laurent, so I might as well start as I mean to go on.

I like the Blue Rose. It's down near the river and Amy

and I have spent many a night sitting outside at the trestle tables or inside on our favorite sofa by the fire, which is exactly where I see her as I walk in. Her eyes are closed and she has a big cat's grin on her face as Jack nibbles her ear and whispers something in it. Amy sighs and turns to kiss him.

I watch for a while, putting my head on one side as I stand by the door. Snogging is such a strange thing to do. I gave up smoking for six months once and I remember looking at people lighting up and thinking how bizarre it looked. Even though I'd been (and continue to be) addicted to the devil's weed, I still couldn't wrap my head around why people would suck on something that's on fire. And now, not having snogged anyone that I care about for ages, I have the same sensation when I look at Jack and Amy. Why are they doing it? Do they find that pleasurable? Does Amy actually enjoy it? Especially since Jack looks a bit sloppy. Nothing worse than a bad kisser. At least Gav was OK in that department.

But I'm not going to think about Gav.

Git.

'OK, OK, time's up,' I say, pulling up a bar stool to the table and sitting down.

Amy breaks away and giggles.

'Going green and furry, are you?' asks Jack.

'No, I'm not a gooseberry, Jack, I'm just nauseated.'

'You're jealous,' chirps Amy, leaning over and giving me a kiss on the cheek in greeting.

I screw my up face and scrunch my eyebrows at Jack, 'Per-lease.'

Jack makes a lustful noise and lunges towards me, giving me a sloppy kiss. I pull a face at him and wipe my cheek.

'You know H doesn't approve of public displays of affection,' Amy scolds Jack.

'Well, honestly. If you want to shag, why don't you just

108

go home and do it, or have a bunk-up in the alley round the back? You don't have to mind me.'

'We can't,' says Jack. He and Amy smile at each other in frustrated sympathy. 'Red day.'

Not the Persona *again*. Amy has had so many red, green and yellow days, that I'm convinced she's a traffic light half the time. I've seen the offending all-seeing, all-knowing pregnancy prediction device quite a few times in her loo and I've a good mind to tamper with it, just for a laugh. I'd love to know what would happen if I dipped one of her test sticks in dog wee.

'I'm doing an egg thing,' explains Amy.

What is she, woman or hen?

'Chucky egg, chucky egg,' teases Jack, getting up. I'm glad he's not taking the fact that Amy's ovulating seriously, either. 'Drink?' he asks me.

'Vodka and tonic, please.'

'Can I borrow your mobile?' he asks, glancing at Amy. I don't know what the look means, but Jack's up to something.

'Sure.' I pull it out of the back pocket of my jeans and hand it over to Jack. He disappears to the bar.

'Are you feeling any better?' asks Amy, leaning forward and touching my knee. 'You weren't in a good way on Wednesday.'

'Sorry,' I mumble. 'Bad day.'

She looks at me. 'So? Was it just the car?'

I take a deep breath. 'Gav's getting married.'

She looks really shocked and her newly plucked eyebrows spring towards each other in concern.

'Why didn't you tell me?' she asks.

'You were busy ... the wedding meal, and I ...'

'H! You're my best friend. I tell you *everything*. I'm always there for you, you dope.'

I nod and look at my hands. 'He faxed me.'

'He *what*?'

'He faxed to tell me.'

Amy grabs me and pulls me on to the sofa, next to her. 'You poor darling,' she says, folding me in a hug. 'I'm so sorry.'

'It doesn't matter,' I say, pulling away. 'I was upset, but I'm OK now.' I tell her about my fax back to Gav and she laughs.

'Don't ever not tell me what's going on,' she says, eventually. 'In here.' She rests her forehead against mine.

'Grrrr,' I say, smiling at her.

'That's my girl.' Amy kisses me.

'Ex-cel-lent. Girl-on-girl action,' interrupts Jack, nodding and putting on a ridiculous accent, as he sets down a large vodka and a small bottle of tonic water on the table.

'Idiot,' says Amy. She sits back in the sofa, holding my hand. Jack pulls a face and puts my mobile on the table.

'Cheers!' I say, leaning forward and pouring the tonic into my glass. 'Let's get shit-faced.'

I'm just finishing my second vodka when Matt comes in. Jack greets him warmly, but he's obviously surprised to see me.

I pull a face at Amy, but she shrugs in surprise.

'I'll get a drink,' Matt mumbles, avoiding eye contact with me.

'I'll help,' I offer, eyeballing Jack and getting up to follow Matt to the bar. He's still wearing a suit from work and he looks tired, a shadow of stubble around his chin. He orders our drinks and leans on the bar.

'Matt,' I begin. 'About the other day . . .'

He glances coldly at me. 'Forget it. If you don't want to be friends, it's fine. Really.'

He pays for the drink and I fiddle with a bar mat as he drops the change in his pocket.

'I do want to be friends,' I say, feeling suddenly nervous. 'I got the wrong end of the stick. I was in a dreadful mood and I'm really sorry.' I look up at him, steeling myself. I'm not used to being this humble. 'I shouldn't have accused you of . . . well, you know. It was out of order and I don't want there to be any awkwardness between us, especially with the wedding coming up.'

I wait for him to say something, feeling small, but he doesn't. I fold my arms across my chest. Matt narrows his eyes at me, but he seems to have something caught in his throat and for a moment I think he's going to sneeze.

He says something incomprehensible and looks away.

'Sorry?' I ask, leaning forward.

'I'm glad we're sorted,' he says eventually.

'Me too,' I say, but I'm taken aback by his tone.

'To tell the truth, it was awkward for me too,' he says. 'Because, as you'll no doubt be relieved to hear, I don't fancy you. I don't mean that nastily, H. It's just that you're not my type.'

Matt snatches at his pint and spills some of it over his hand as he puts it to his lips. 'Sorry,' he shrugs.

I gawp at his wet hand and then watch him make his way back to Jack and Amy.

What?

What does he mean, he doesn't fancy me?

Why not?

What's wrong with *me*?

I follow after him, feeling embarrassed, humiliated and indignant all at once. I genuinely thought he was coming on to me in the car and so I thought apologizing just now for my behaviour would sort of let him off the hook and smooth everything out. I thought I was being brave and fearless, but now that I've found out he really doesn't fancy me . . .

Oh my God. This is serious. Not only am I terminally single, but I've lost the ability to read the signs with men. First I thought Gav was contacting me because he wanted to get back together and now this.

What if I've lost it? I thought I was a good judge of character. But obviously not.

Amy and Jack are back on the sofa together, so I sit down next to Matt. The leg of my stool is caught in the carpet, so I have to sit quite close. Still, who cares? Not Matt. That's for sure.

'You look cosy,' says Jack clinking glasses with Matt. Amy smiles at us and looks as if she's going to break into a royal wave. *My husband and I are so pleased that we're all such jolly good chums and I'd like to bless all couples who are as fortunate as we . . .*

To my surprise, Matt clocks it. 'Cut it out, you two,' he warns.

They do and without them clucking over us, Matt starts to behave as if we've known each other for years, competing to put the worst song on the juke-box and downing drinks in between. And maybe the alcohol makes me more perceptive, but all the time, I start to notice more and more things about Matt: his pink and white fingernails, the way his stubble patterns his chin, the mole on his ear lobe, the tuft of dark hair I can see when he undoes the top button of his shirt and loosens his tie, the way his face lights up when he laughs. But I guess those are just the details you notice when someone is unavailable.

Eventually, the bell for last orders rings.

'Come on, beddy-byes.' Amy tugs Jack's sleeve.

'Yeah, all right already,' says Jack, nursing an inch of beer.

'It's bridesmaids' fittings in the morning. I've got to be up early. And so have you,' she warns me. She's horribly sober. 'Have you got those details for the weekend?' she asks.

'Oh yeah,' I slur, digging two A4 envelopes out of my bag. 'One for you and one for Susie.'

'Give it to her tomorrow,' says Amy, taking one of

them and putting the other one back in my bag. She pulls Jack to his feet.

'See you in the morning, then,' says Amy, kissing Matt and I good night. Jack waves us goodbye and gives Matt a big slap on the back.

When they've gone, Matt turns to me. 'Will the little missy be having one for the road?' he asks in a Scottish accent.

'Aye,' I laugh, getting up and flopping down on to the sofa. 'That'll be grand.' The cushion is still warm from where Amy has been sitting. Actually, another drink is the last thing I need, I'm already completely plastered, but I can't cope with the thought of going outside yet. Matt joins me a few minutes later and we sit side by side, slumped down on the cushions.

'They're like an old married couple already,' he says, nodding to the door through which Amy has just pushed Jack.

'Not really. You should've seen them when I arrived. Teenagers! They were practically eating each other.'

'Ugh. How unpleasant!' Matt pulls a face as he clinks glasses with me.

I laugh. 'It looks really weird, watching other people snog. All tongues and stuff.' I waggle my tongue out of my mouth drunkenly.

Matt laughs. 'They don't do it like they used to in my day.'

'When was that, then?'

'Can't remember. I watch old black and white movies and do it vicariously.'

'Ah, but they don't snog properly in old films. They just touched lips, like this.' And before I know what I'm doing, I lean over and press my lips up against Matt's. I sit back and we both giggle, but I'm blushing.

'See, it's not a kiss at all,' I bluff, glancing at Matt, but my heart has started to race.

Either I'm monumentally pissed, or . . . or . . .

'Na na-na-na-na,' he says. 'They *did* kiss, they just didn't open their mouths.' He leans towards me and gently presses his lips against mine, before gently prizing them apart with his tongue.

It's the gentlest kiss and I feel myself falling in to it, as if I'm landing on the softest pillow.

'There,' he says, pulling away, as if nothing has happened.

'That was rubbish,' I squeak. 'It's much more like this.' I grab Matt's head and pull him towards me and kiss him back harder. This time it goes on longer and I press against him, burning up as my head processes the following thoughts:

I'm kissing. I can still do it.

I'm kissing Matt. He can do it, too.

But hang on, he can do it well . . . really well . . .

Matt pulls away slightly and smiles and I smile back, thinking what a laugh this is. And I don't care. I don't care about any consequences. Because I feel deliciously drunk and all that matters is right here, right now. I don't care about anything else.

I've pulled. I can still do it.

'It wouldn't work, us being in the movies,' Matt says eventually, grabbing my hand and pulling me to my feet.

'I know,' I say, reaching for my jacket.

'There's got to be chemistry for it to work properly,' he says, his eyes locked with mine. And I know what they're saying. I know what they're offering.

We kiss again, more urgently as we bundle through the door. I don't know who's leading who, but it doesn't matter, because I've decided that this might be just what I need.

'It's good that we don't fancy each other,' I gulp, between kisses.

'You don't fancy me, either?' says Matt, his hands urgently grasping the back of my head.

'No. You disgust me,' I say, grabbing his bum.

'The feeling's mutual,' he says, slipping his hand under my shirt.

'Good,' I gasp, as he almost lifts me off my feet. 'Let's go to your place.'

Susie

Saturday, 08.30

Since last week I've made a few life decisions. And number one on my list was:

1. <u>Change Everything</u>.

So. This is the new me. I'm going for it. I'm going to be different. And I'm taking a little break from my random routine to make it work.

I've decided not to do the market today since I'm meeting Amy for the final dress fitting and I yawn decadently in the full knowledge that I have two blissful me-hours all to myself instead of yomping about with loads of silly hats and flirting with Dexter.

Because that was the old me.

This is the new me.

I reach for my glasses and my notebook by my bed and open it up at a clean page. I've managed to keep a dream diary for a whole week now and I'm quite chuffed with myself. I'm not sure whether I can make head or tail of it, mind, but maybe it'll all become clear in time. It's a bit confusing, see. It'd be fine if I dreamed about one thing, or my dreams had a general theme, but they're always fragmented. Sometimes, I feel as if I've spent all night channel-hopping, without ever having had the satisfaction of watching a whole programme all the way through. Maybe being an impatient dreamer is a psychological condition.

I grab my pink felt-tip pen, but my grip hasn't woken up yet, so today's wonky entry reads:

Use Pick 'n' Mix for cover in Woolworths shoot-out. (Save three children and a Jack Russell.) Pacify shocked mother as grandma (87) installs mirrored Jacuzzi in her Mumbles bungalow. Mum invites me to stay with mystery man – ? Green gooey aliens instigate food fight in junior school dining-room (repeat). Mrs Jones, the dinner lady, killed this time. Maude (half woman, half Richard Branson) and me in round-the-world yachting race (very wet). Melts into . . . Counting buttons in factory. Siren for break shrieking, but I'm not allowed to go. (Depressing.)

Roughly speaking then, disregarding the last dream, which is obviously to do with money, since I'm unemployed again, I reckon my issues are about successfully fighting demons and having a socially acceptable lover. I chew the already-chewed plastic end of the pen and survey the list. Not too bad, then. I'll give the night seven out of ten. I flick through the other pages. Seven is good news. My dream scoring, which is pretty arbitrary, is on the up which means that the Change Your Life programme is definitely working.

Nearly one week and already I've changed beyond all recognition.

It all started on Tuesday. I'd been clearing up the flat, missing Maude and Zip as I tidied up their room, when I found an envelope by their bed. 'Don't think the customs men at LAX are lax about this! Enjoy!' said the scribble on the front. Inside was their entire stash. I sniffed the contents of the bank bag. Skunk. Strong skunk at that.

I almost threw it out, and then I thought of Maude and thought, why not? It would be rude not to. So I kicked off the vacuum cleaner, made a pot of tea and flopped down in front of the telly.

I'm not so good at getting drunk, but I love getting stoned on my own. Before long, I was shouting advice at the people on the chat show and admiring myself for being so incisive and witty. That's the thing with getting stoned for me: I always have the most blinding ideas and feel like I can solve the most traumatic of problems. Shame is, I'm always too stoned to remember anything.

Two hours later, when I'd practically melted, I found myself staring inanely at the TV, communing on a rather alarming level with the Teletubbies. They seemed to be speaking to me. Just to me! And I was understanding what they were saying. La-la was explaining that Dipsy was a proto-Fascist with designs to take over the entire town of Tunbridge Wells, brainwash the population and parachute them in to Parliament Square, on 31st December, 1999, in order to blow up Big Ben before the millennium could strike, thus stopping time itself and bringing the relentless march of democracy crashing to its knees once and for all.

Armed with this crucial information, I was just about to roll myself another spliff and was absent-mindedly rooting about for some roach paper when I found the Change Your Life leaflet that had been left on my car windscreen the night before, at Heathrow. I'd ripped a corner off it before I pulled my eyes away from the screen and realized what it was.

Five minutes later, when the Teletubbies had finished, I lurched towards the TV and switched it off. Maude and Zip were almost certainly arriving in Los Angeles right now. And what was I doing? Lying on the living-room floor on a Monday afternoon, behaving like a student.

'Take action now,' urged the leaflet.

I decided to go by bus.

I adore buses. I think they're lovely. They certainly make being in London an absolute treat. I plugged in my Walkman, sat at the front up top and let my eyes float over the scenery, until the conductor tapped me on the shoulder. 'All change, love. South Kensington. You're the last off.'

The office of the Change Your Life programme was on the ground floor of a shabby Georgian mansion house near the Science Museum. When I stumbled in to the room, six people were sitting nervously in an array of tatty armchairs. They all had computer labels stuck to them, with their names written in schoolteacher's handwriting.

'I'm . . . er . . . er . . . here,' I said, grinning inanely, as they all turned towards me.

'Welcome to CYL. You're just in time,' said a woman, jumping off her chair in the bay window and welcoming me in. I squinted at the label stuck to her mohair jumper. 'I'm Claire. Your group leader.'

Claire's mouse-brown hair was scraped back into an elastic band and round metal glasses were hooked over her sticky-out ears. She looked as if she'd be far more comfortable running the poetry section of an obscure library than running a personal motivation course.

'By stepping through that door, you've taken the first, most important step towards getting what you really want,' she recited, in a little-girlie voice, blinking at me like an uncovered vole.

'OK,' I nodded, slumping down in to a dusty armchair and realizing that I was still completely off my head.

Claire produced a label for me and cleared her throat. 'Now before we start,' she said, smiling at each of us in turn, 'let's sort out the money, shall we? Just to get it out of the way, so that we can get on with *Changing Your Life*.'

I was so stoned and so pleased to be sitting in a comfy chair that I had my chequebook out in no time.

'You'll see,' assured Claire, clasping her hands in front of her, like a Sunday school mistress. 'This will be the best money you'll *ever* spend. The CYL programme guarantees that if your life hasn't changed by the end of the course, then we will refund you completely.'

'You won't regret it,' beamed Claire, taking my illegible

cheque from me and handing me a photocopied Change Your Life Guaranteed certificate. The words blurred since I'd forgotten my glasses, but it didn't seem to matter. It was the rent for a month, but if I was guaranteed . . . who cared? I kicked off my shoes and pulled my feet up under me in the chair, ready to learn.

An hour or so later, I was completely engrossed. We'd heard all about Angie, who was desperate to leave her abusive husband and felt that she badly needed a makeover, and Gerald, trying to shake off the shackles of a miserable past, and I was beginning to think that this was better than Jerry Springer, Rikki Lake and Oprah all put together.

'So,' sighed Claire. 'Michaela. Why are you here?' She cocked her head earnestly at the large woman sitting next to me.

'I do so want to change,' whispered Michaela, running a large false fingernail under her thick eyeliner. 'I want to go back to how I was.'

'And how were you?' asked Claire.

Michaela's large features crumpled.

'Take a breath,' counselled Claire, breathing in and blowing out, as if she was trying to blow Michaela's wig-like hair off. '*Breathe* in to the emotion.'

I followed her breathing pattern, until I was nearly hyperventilating.

Michaela looked at her huge hands. 'I used to be a man,' she sniffed. 'I wanted the change, but now, now I'm a woman . . . I'm really . . .'

'Take your time,' soothed Claire and I realized I was staring, open-mouthed at Michaela. Now I'd really heard it all.

'Can you share the emotion with us?'

'I'm just so sad,' choked Michaela. 'And lonely.'

'Why are you lonely?'

'I can't find a relationship. I can't find anyone who'll go

out with me. There was this guy, Matt, once, but he rejected me when I told him and since then I've tried and . . .' Michaela adjusted her shoulder pad.

'You'll find someone,' I blurted, flinging myself at Michaela and giving her a bear hug over the arms of our chairs. 'Honest you will. It's not so bad being a woman . . .'

Michaela recoiled from my unsteady advance.

'Thank you, Susie,' interrupted Claire. 'It's important to show support. But we'll have a chance for that at the end of the session when we've got to know each other a little better.'

'But she's lovely. Look at her. If I was a bloke . . .' I began in earnest.

Claire shot me a warning glance. 'I'd like to talk about the word "relationship" for a moment. This may help you all.'

I listened, trying to concentrate as I watched Claire's mouth carefully, mouthing some of her words as they hit my fuzzy head like Velcro darts. 'Project on to others . . . take responsibility . . . relate . . .'

'Susie. Tell us your thoughts,' said Claire, suddenly. All attention turned to me. 'Tell us what you want to change about your life.'

I was silent for a moment. 'Everything, well, um, I don't know . . . not that much, really. Not *everything*. Some things. Some things definitely. Like er . . . like.' I bit my lip, looking up and trying to grasp my train of thought that had just derailed towards the ceiling. 'Other people . . . and . . . things.' I looked up at the group. They all looked confused.

'I want . . . things. Like you were just saying.'

'You want to relate to people in different ways?' clarified Claire.

I sat in silence nodding slowly, trying to formulate my argument. All I could think about were my school dining-room alien dreams. What did I want to change about my life? Sitting in that room full of these people, everything seemed just dandy with me.

'That'd be . . . ? Yeah.' I shrugged. 'Men. I'd like a boyfriend.'

Afterwards, back at home, when my head straightened out, I was mortified. Claire must have thought I was a complete fruitcake and besides, I don't think I do want a boyfriend.

The next day, when I woke up with noticeably fewer braincells, I felt sick remembering the money. I fished out the guarantee, but I'd have to go for months to complete the course before I got my money back. With a sinking sense of dread, I opened the course manual. Just how much of an idiot had I been?

But when I started reading, surprisingly it all started making a lot of sense. I spent all of Tuesday in bed reading and by the Week Twenty-four guidelines, I was feeling very positive indeed. I hadn't done anything, mind, but at least I'd come up with a purpose, as the manual suggested. I wrote it down on a large piece of paper:

My purpose is: to become friends with an attractive man and to present myself in a non-sexual way.

I said it over and over again, loads of times, to make it have positive energy. I left it overnight with a crystal on it and it worked. Because on Wednesday, I met Stringer.

And I knew, as soon as I saw him, he'd been sent as a challenge. Because normally I would've flirted outrageously because, just as Amy had predicted, he is absolutely divine. But when I sat next to him, at the meal, I made a conscious effort to think with my head for once. So instead of checking Stringer out, to see whether he was either a quick shag or a long-term prospect, I talked to him as a friend. And I think I did quite well.

I close my eyes, preparing for my morning meditation. I've been doing this every day since Wednesday and I'm sure it's going to work.

I wriggle on the bed and breathe deeply. I make sure my eyes and face are relaxed and work through my body, until all tension has gone. It doesn't take long since I've only just woken up.

I remember the advice in Chapter One of the CYL manual and the four steps to changing your life. Step one: define your purpose. Step two: visualize achieving your purpose. Step three: allow yourself to fill out every detail. Step four: think big.

I focus my mind and the image of Stringer comes to me. I picture us outside on a mountain, having a picnic. Everything is in soft focus. The sky is blue, with a few fluffy clouds, the trees are a lush green, the birds are singing and Stringer is lying, propped up on one elbow, sucking on a stem of grass. I'm kneeling beside him, wearing a flowery summer dress and I know that we're friends. And I'm comfortable being friends. And I'm happy sharing my thoughts and secrets with him like this. I look out at the view, feeling totally content, but when I turn back to Stringer to speak again, his eyes are smouldering with sex and, despite myself, I can feel myself becoming hopelessly turned on. He's looking me right in the eye and I'm leaning across to him and reaching into his trousers, and it's big, really, really big . . .

No!

I jolt upright in bed and rub the vision away from my eyes. This *keeps* on happening and I can't stand it. I want to know Stringer without sex being involved. How can I have a lasting friendship with him, when every time I think about him I'm stripping him off in my head and pouncing on him?

Obviously, I've got a very long way to go.

I get out of bed, sling on my kimono, feed Torvill and Dean and cook myself some poached eggs on toast. Over breakfast, I have a rethink and come up with some more purposes. Honestly, it takes up so much time defining what I intend to do, I don't have time to do anything.

Fortunately Maude calls to relieve me from my head. She sounds tanned. You can tell by her voice. She's all white teeth, frayed shorts and shining skin and I can picture her on rollerblades as she talks.

'It's amazing,' she gushes, once she's recounted the journey and described Zip's mother's house. She's awe-struck by the swanky kitchen from where she's calling and makes me listen to the sound of the ice-making machine on the fridge. 'I wish you were here.'

'So do I,' I smile, leaning back against the hall wall and peeling a banana.

'Well, why don't you come out?'

'Don't be silly,' I tut. 'I can't come out there. What would I do?'

'I'm working on it. This is the place for you, Sooze, I'm telling you.'

'Maude!' I laugh, pulling off a piece of banana. 'You're crazy mad. This is my home.'

'But you're wasting precious time. You're festering.'

'I'm not festering,' I protest.

'But there's the whole world out there. You've always said you wanted to travel . . .'

'I know, but I can't give up everything just like that.'

'Why not? You have done before. What have you got to give up? You're not making any money. If you gave up the market and sold your stock, you could get some money together . . .'

'How come you're on the other side of the world and you're still organizing my life for me?' I smile.

'Because you need organizing,' she replies.

'I don't,' I say, before telling her all about the Change Your Life course.

She laughs. 'Then visualize yourself in the sunshine, with your friends around you, chilling out, having fun, going to the beach . . .'

And I do think about the ocean as I'm struggling across London on public transport. When I give up my seat on the bus for a woman, her shopping and her child, I cling on to the overhead rail and look out of the window at the traffic and the drunks on the pavement and the dirty, damp windows of the shops and I do think about clean air and sunshine and mountains and vast expanses of country to explore.

The sight of Amy cheers me up. She's sitting in the coffee shop in Hammersmith Broadway with her hair plaited in two coils over her ears.

'It's supposed to be the trendy look for this season,' she says, pursing her lips in disappointment. 'According to *Your Wedding*.'

'This season! What a load of rubbish,' I laugh. 'Come on, take it out,' I say, attacking her plaits. 'People will start requesting "Edelweiss" any minute.'

'Thanks,' she mutters, as I unravel her. 'What am I going to *do*?'

'It'll be fine,' I soothe. 'Get it cut and wear it down. You're most gorgeous when you go natural.'

'Oh, thanks!' she says, hitting me. 'Why am I bothering at all? According to you, I'd look best in a hessian sack.'

'Correct.'

'Sometimes I think it would be better just to elope and get married on a beach in a bikini.'

'And miss Leisure Heaven?'

'True,' she sighs.

'All set, then, for next weekend?'

Amy nods. 'H has got the details for you.'

'Who's coming?'

'Well, there's you, me, H, Jenny and Sam from work, Lorna, an old mate from home and Jack's sister, Kate. We've got two chalets booked so there's more space.'

'I can't wait. I will be in your chalet, won't I?'

Amy shifts in her seat. 'I don't know, I think H will sort it out.'

That means I'll be relegated, I bet. H is so pathetically possessive about Amy, which annoys me a bit, because *I've* known Amy longer.

'Bags I share a room with you,' I smile and Amy nods. 'Talk of the devil,' I say, turning round as H rushes in.

'Sorry. Overslept,' she mumbles.

'Overslept?' guffaws Amy, nudging me. 'So, what time did you leave the pub?'

H ruffles her short hair. 'Not long after you.'

Amy raises her eyebrows. 'How's Matt?'

H looks at me and then back to Amy. She shrugs and sticks out her bottom lip. 'Matt?' she says. 'Fine, I think.'

'Come on, you two,' says Amy, narrowing her eyes suspiciously at H and sliding off her stool. 'We're already late.'

I link arms with Amy as we go outside to hail a cab and H skulks behind us. I love chatting to Amy about her wedding plans, but H doesn't seem interested.

Her odd mood doesn't improve when we get to the wedding shop, which is heaving. We practically have to rugby-scrum our way into the changing rooms and it's very hot inside. H strips off cautiously, probably because she's wearing slinky black underwear. She pulls and tugs at the dress, wriggling in front of the mirror.

'It looks dreadful,' she whispers to me. 'Look at this.' There's a big gap down the back and she pinches in the material, whilst trying to keep the straps from falling down.

'You've been losing weight, haven't you?' I say, eyeing her skinny body. 'You should eat properly.'

'I don't have time,' she says.

'How are they?' calls Amy. She wants it to be a surprise, so she's waiting outside the curtain with our bags and jackets.

'They're beautiful,' I call.

H scowls at herself in the mirror, but then pink really isn't her colour.

'I'll fix it, if you like,' I offer, going to help her. 'Don't bother Amy with it, she'll only be upset.'

'Amy will want the dress to be right,' says H, haughtily. 'Of course the shop will fix it. That's what we're paying for.'

'Suit yourself,' I reply, wanting to hit her for being so patronizing. 'Ready?' I call, before pulling the curtain back. Amy's hands fly to her mouth, which is the desired effect. To be honest, next to H, I feel like Jessica Rabbit, but it doesn't matter. I do a twirl, feeling great, and I say so. I wonder what Stringer will think.

'What about you?' Amy asks H.

'It's fine,' she grunts, but anyone can see she's not fine. She looks like a little girl in her mother's dress. I'm a bitch, I know, but hooray for boobs.

We potter about the shops for a while, until it's lunch-time.

'Let's go for sushi,' suggests H. I'm all for a sandwich, but H is adamant. She insists it's good for a hangover and she knows this posh Japanese place nearby.

'You want eggs in the morning, if you've drunk too much,' I tell her, but she's not having it.

'Still off the sex, Sooze?' asks Amy, when we're all seated.

'Yes.'

'What? All sex?' asks H.

'I wasn't aware there were different types.'

'You can have sex just for fun,' says H. 'Sometimes it's cool to have a one-night stand. No questions asked, just a good service, if you know what I mean,' she says, tipping soy sauce into a saucer.

'H!' says Amy.

'What?' she says. 'You've had loads of one-night stands. Remember that bloke in Portugal?'

'That was ages ago!'

'So? There's nothing wrong with it,' shrugs H.

'I used to think that, but now I think one-night stands are the pits,' I confess. 'The thing is that casual sex is like smoking. Once you've done it, it's impossible to stop.' I look at Amy and smile. If anyone knows these things, it's me.

'But you've *always* had casual sex, Sooze,' she says.

'Exactly. And I'm fed up with it. If you do it with someone you don't know, you just end up feeling tacky and cheap, but if you do it with someone you know,' I look earnestly at Amy and H, 'it's rubbish. It just gets messy and ruins everything.' I stretch my hands out on the table. 'So I've decided. I want to be friends with the opposite sex from now on. I want to go formal.'

Amy looks at me as if I've just told her that I'm having radical plastic surgery.

'It's possible, I suppose,' she ponders. 'So you're going to have a proper relationship at long last?'

'There's no such thing as a "relationship", Amy,' I say, remembering Claire and the CYL manual. 'Where people go wrong is that they think a relationship is a *thing*. But it's not. You can't contain or define a relationship, which is why people have problems with them. It would all be different if people said, "I'm having a problem relating to so-and-so about such-and-such", instead of "My relationship is crap".

I'm on a roll, convinced by my argument, but H interrupts.

'Bollocks,' she says. 'What about a friendship? That's a relationship.'

'And it's a thing,' chips in Amy. 'It's a thing that would upset me if it went wrong with either of you.'

'Yes, but our friendship isn't going to go wrong,' I say, meaning her and me. I can't speak for H, because I wouldn't be friends with her myself.

'Well, it probably won't go wrong, but it could do,' says Amy. 'I'd go nuts if I found out that either of you had been lying to me, for example.'

'We're *relating* to one another in a friendly way. Being honest is a choice, it's not a condition of friendship,' I say, confusing myself with too much therapy speak.

'Excuse me,' says H, standing up to go to the loo.

'Did I say something wrong?' I ask, watching her go.

'She's just hungover.' Amy screws her nose up at H's bag before giving me a cheeky grin. 'What about you and Stringer, then? Did you like him?'

'We got on, but . . .'

'Just to warn you – he might not do the friends thing, if that's what you're after. Jack calls him Horse. As in dark horse.'

'A stallion, eh?'

Amy sniggers. 'That too, probably. All I'm saying is he might not be what you're looking for.'

'Why not?'

'He's only interested in sex. As far as I know, he's never had a girlfriend. A long-term one, that is.'

When H comes back from the loo, she pays the bill, much to my relief, because it costs an arm and a leg for two mouthfuls in here. It's nice of her to pay, but she's doing it to stop herself from feeling bad about being stroppy. Still, if she wants to flash her money about, that's fine by me.

I mooch around the shops with Amy after H has gone to do her shopping for Paris, but I'm feeling a bit stirred up by what she said about Stringer being a dark horse. He didn't come across to me like that at all. I thought he was sweet. Posh, mind, but a gentleman. He's not the sort for flippant encounters. And why hasn't he had a girlfriend? I think he's just the sort of person you could cooch up to, have a good heart-to-heart with. But then, maybe he's just like me. Maybe he's fed up of casual sex. Maybe he's ready to change too.

'Do you think I should call him?' I ask Amy, as I trail after her in Habitat.

'Susie, you're terrible,' she laughs, picking up a picture frame. 'Don't get obsessed by Stringer.'

'I'm not.'

'Listen. If you're so determined, just call him.'

'I asked him out already, but he was busy. Do you think I should ask him again? Just for a drink or something?'

Amy thinks for a moment. 'I don't see why not.'

I wait until we get back to Jack and Amy's for a cup of tea before I have the courage to ring.

'Go on, I know you're gagging to. You might be able to see him later,' suggests Amy. She takes the phone and punches in the number for me and then hands it over. I flap my hands, changing my mind.

'It's ringing,' Amy smiles and I snatch the phone from her.

'Hello?' I hear Stringer's voice and glance up at Amy.

'Hi, Stringer? It's me. Susie.' I've been thinking about him so much, that I half-expect him to know that it's me already.

'Oh right,' he says, formally. 'Hello there.' I grip the phone tightly. My hands are all sweaty. Why doesn't he sound more pleased? Amy's staring at me.

'I wondered if you were doing anything tonight,' I blurt. 'We could, er, go for a drink or something.'

There's a pause. 'I don't think so,' he says. 'Not tonight.

130

I'm busy. Terribly busy, actually. I'm chock-a-block right up until the wedding . . .'

'No problem,' I interrupt chirpily. 'No problem at all, that's fine. Really,' I smile. 'It was just on the off chance . . .'

'I'm sorry, Susie, but I'm right in the middle of something . . .'

I gasp, feeling embarrassed. 'No, no. Sorry. Right then. Well, I'll see you at the wedding . . .'

'Yes. See you there. Cheerio.'

I put down the phone and give it back to Amy. 'What did he say?' she asks, frowning.

'Cheerio.'

'He must have said more than that?'

'He's busy. It's short notice,' I shrug.

This is not a good sign. It's not a good sign, because if I just want to be friends with Stringer I shouldn't be feeling so desperately disappointed that he doesn't want to see me.

'Oh, Sooze,' laughs Amy. 'Why do you always fall for the bastards?'

'Stringer's not a bastard.'

Amy gives me an 'Oh, really?' sort of look.

This is rubbish. Why do I feel like this when I don't even fancy him? And how am I supposed to progress to week two of being a non-sexual person if Stringer's denying me access?

Matt

My mind's one big question mark.

I finally look up from the mobile phone that I've been clutching in my hand for the last half-hour or so. It's one of those crisp, clear September days. The sky above is blue and cloudless and a cool wind sporadically blows, whipping the freshly fallen leaves into spiralling eddies. I wish I'd worn something warmer, but I spilled coffee on the cuff of my suit this morning and my others are at the dry cleaner's, so I've had to make do with this linen summer number instead.

I'm sitting on one of the benches in St James's Square, just off the Haymarket. Aside from myself and this scatty-looking woman who's sitting beside me, the square's emptied out since lunch-time. And with the thick hedges running the square's perimeter blocking out the noise of passing traffic, it's as quiet as London ever gets. Great, in other words, if you've got someone to snuggle up against. But a total dog if you don't.

And I don't.

And I haven't had for quite some time, not since I used to sit here with Penny Brown, my one and only long-term girlfriend.

Penny and I met doing articles at Robards & Lake in 1994. Like me, she was fresh from law school, a student suddenly wearing a suit and acting like an adult. We clicked right from the start: same sense of humour, similar ambitions. Penny used to joke about other couples we knew who lived their lives hand in hand. She could

132

never see the point, giving up your independence like that, putting your relationship before your career. She once told me that she'd worked out that if you took all the hours that most people invested in their relationships, and diverted them in to their careers instead, they'd get where they wanted to be twice as fast. That was the time and place, Penny reckoned, to open up your life for real to someone else. And not before.

And I ran with it. I didn't give myself time to stop and think about whether I really agreed. I was in love with her and assumed that, deep down, she felt the same – even though she never told me, and even though I was always too afraid of scaring her off to ask. I decided that not saying it didn't matter. All that mattered was how we felt. And I knew how I felt. I was happy. Happy with her, happy with the sporadic nights and weekends we spent together. If she wanted to take things slowly, then I'd wait. The way I saw it, we were on the same career paths, so we'd both reach the place she wanted to be at the same time. It made sense to wait. She – and all the glimpses I'd seen of what she had to offer confirmed this – would be worth the wait.

But she wasn't.

There was no love. Not in her. Not for me. That's what she told me in June 1995 when I asked her. Right here. On this exact bench. Looking at this exact view, minus the falling leaves. It was the day she told me that it was over between us and that she'd met someone else, someone she'd fallen in love with, and someone she wanted to spend her time with. It was the day she left me here and walked back to the office, not because she needed time on her own, but because our time together was over.

I felt like my world had vanished before my eyes.

Jack finishing with Zoë Thompson the month before was probably my salvation. He'd been seeing Zoë for two years – a whole six months longer than I had Penny – and was determined to treat our new circumstances as a positive step forward. Don't look back. Don't dwell. He wouldn't take no for an answer. He filled me in on all the good stuff that was coming my way. Every night was going to be a big night out. He'd move in to my house with me and we'd create the kind of bachelor pad that would make other bachelor pads looks like chapels. And, of course, there were the women. We were going to have fun and act our age. No serious relationships. No compromises. Nothing till the real thing came along.

And up until recently, this attitude has been my own. I've stayed not wanting a serious girlfriend. The same as Jack was before he met Amy, I've been happy being single and safe. I've gone on moving from one close encounter of the bird kind to the next, a consummate drifter. It's only now that I've reached the conclusion that this is no longer enough, that my life has become a hollow place. I've seen Jack and Amy together and I've wanted that unity for myself. I've woken up and smelt the coffee, only to find that I don't have a cup of my own.

And in response, I've finally gone and done it. I've finally gone and asked someone to stay in my life for longer than one night.

I've been sitting here for two hours, sifting through the evidence of the events which occurred in the Blue Rose public house and my own house on Friday night, between the hours of eleven p.m. and two a.m., in the company of one Helen Marchmont, a.k.a. H. And all I've managed to come up with so far is one big question mark.

I blame Jack and Amy. The separate seeds they planted in my head last Tuesday have grown. And now H is in my head, as surely as if she were rooted here. But the question in my mind isn't simply a *why?* I know why she's here in my head. It's because I invited her. It's because I decided that she was going to be the one for me. It's more of a *where/why* combination. *Where* is she now?

And *why* isn't she here with me? Because I don't want this any more. I don't want to be sitting here on my own with no one to cuddle up against. I stare down at the mobile phone in my hand. Not when I could be sitting here with her.

I called Jack as soon as I got back from dropping H off last Wednesday, following the test meal round at Stringer's work. I mean, who else would I have turned to to brainstorm over how to get embroiled in a relationship other than the one person I know who's recently, without even going out there looking for it, achieved just that?

'So?' he asked.

All I could picture was her eyes. Those eyes. How I hadn't been thinking of them every waking second since I met her last year was beyond me. 'I think she's fantastic,' I gibbered. 'Awesome.'

Jack was delighted. 'There. What did I tell you? Mr Matchmaker strikes again. Twice in one day, no less. I should start taking commission.'

'Twice?'

'Yeah. You and H, and Stringer and Susie.'

'Eh?'

'Come on, mate,' he chided. 'You must've picked up the vibes . . . They're sweet on each other, two sugar cubes in a bowl. Great news about you and H, though,' he went on. 'What's happening next? You going on a date?'

I hated to puncture his enthusiasm, but there was no point in lying to him. 'Not exactly.'

'Not exactly how?'

'Not exactly in that when I said I thought *she* was fantastic, I didn't say the same sentiment applied in reverse.'

'Don't be ridiculous,' Jack scoffed. 'Of course she thinks you're fantastic. You're Matt, for God's sake. Matt Davies. Matt Davies, who is best friend of Jack Rossiter,

135

who is fiancé of Amy Crosbie, who is best friend of H. All the compatibility connections are there. You're made for each other. It *has* to work. It's a mathematical certainty.'

Jack's logic was flawless, but still I had doubts. 'Not necessarily.'

There was a silence, which Jack read like a signpost. 'You blew it, didn't you?'

I bit down on my lip. 'Sort of,' I admitted.

He hissed down the phone in disbelief. 'Jesus, I leave you alone for five minutes . . . What happened?'

'I think I got a bit carried away . . . jumped the gun . . .'

'Go on.'

'I asked her out on a date when she'd just made it massively clear that she didn't want to go out with anyone at the moment.'

'And she said no . . .'

'Yes.'

'Well, what's wrong with that?'

'Everything.'

'Why?' he came back.

I wished we were talking face to face. I couldn't tell if he was being sarcastic. He certainly didn't sound it. 'What are you telling me?' I asked. 'That "no" 'is suddenly good?'

'Yeah. Under the circumstances, "no" 'is a pretty good answer. Not as good as yes, of course. "Yes" would have been perfect. But "no" 'is OK. "No" you can work with. "No" just means that she's got the hots for you and hasn't realized it yet. Either that, or it means that she's playing hard to get.'

'Or,' I pointed out, because one of us certainly had to, and I certainly dreaded as much, 'it means that she hasn't got the hots for me and is perfectly aware of the fact.'

'It's a possibility,' Jack conceded, before hurrying on, 'but not one you should dwell on. Too negative,' he chastized. 'You mustn't even consider giving up till you know for sure.'

'OK,' I said, 'so where do you suggest I go from here?'

'The first thing is to decide upon your strategy.'

'Strategy?'

'You've *got* to have a strategy.'

'I have?'

'Of course. How else is the campaign going to be a success?'

'What campaign?'

'Operation Marchmont.'

'Marchmont?'

'H's surname. Her first name's Helen, by the way.'

'Oh,' I said. 'What strategy do you recommend?'

'I don't know. You're the lawyer. You work it out.'

A-ha. So there was a sure-fire strategy and campaign to win the wondrous Helen, but I had to come up with it myself. Great. I knew this had sounded too good to be true. I stayed silent, listening to the sound of the static and Jack's breathing on the line.

'Come on, mate,' he encouraged after a few seconds. 'I can hear those brain gears grinding from here. Think of all those exams you've passed. You can do it.'

And then it dawned on me: maybe Jack was right. Maybe I could work out a strategy. After all, why should love be left to chance? That worked for people like Jack and Amy, sure, but they were the lucky ones. What about the rest of us? Where was the harm in a little analysis of the situation, a little problem-solving? That's how I approached every other area of my life, so why not this, the most important of the lot?

'OK,' I said, determined to give it a go. 'The way I see it is this. H either fancies me or she doesn't. If she doesn't, then all is lost. If she does, however, and either hasn't realized it yet, or is playing hard to get, then my best course of action is to ignore her completely.'

'But surely if you do that—' Jack objected.

But I was on a roll. I was Einstein and I didn't want anyone messing with my equation. 'Romantically, I mean. Ignore her romantically. Even better, in fact, I should work from the assumption that to be desirable, you have to appear unavailable. I'll tell her that I don't fancy her. Straight to her face. That way, if she does fancy me, she'll be furious that I've rejected her.'

Jack grunted in approval. 'And once she's furious with you for rejecting her, she'll want to win back her pride by pulling you?' he deduced.

'Correct. I reckon it's the best shot I've got. What do you think?'

Jack thought. Seconds passed. Then Jack spoke. 'It's perfect, you sly old rat. Treat her mean, keep her keen. Just like—' He halted. 'Still,' he added, 'I do foresee one problem . . .'

'What?' I demanded, mildly annoyed that such a thing could exist, and already doubting its provenance if it did.

'How,' Jack asked, 'without going out on a date with her and thereby inadvertently demonstrating that you fancy her, are you going to find an opportunity to explain to her that you don't fancy her, thereby making her fancy you?'

Damn.

'Good point,' I said, suddenly stumped.

But then Jack chuckled. It was a good chuckle, the kind of chuckle that inspires confidence. 'Strike that,' he announced. 'I've got the perfect solution.'

It sounded dangerous, but maybe, just maybe . . . 'Go on,' I said.

'Keep your mobile phone switched on and wait for my call. I'll fix up a time and a place for you two to meet *accidentally*. That way, she's none the wiser, and you get to say your piece.'

It was brilliant.

'You're on,' I said.

And as it happened, I didn't have long to wait. On Friday evening, Jack called me on my mobile at the office. 'Operation Marchmont is go,' he hissed down the line. 'We're in the Blue Rose, so get your arse down here now.'

By the time I got there, he was sitting with Amy and H over by the fire. I walked over and said hello to Jack and Amy. H, though, I totally blanked, not even so much as looking her in the face. This, though, I admit, had nothing to do with any attempt at disdain on my behalf. More terror. From the moment I'd sighted her on entering the pub, my heart had leapt directly into my mouth, and as I'd watched her on my approach to the table, it had taken to using my tongue as a trampoline. Fearing that if I stayed a second longer it would launch itself on to H's lap, I mumbled something about getting a drink, and swiftly turned and headed for the bar.

'Matt,' she said, catching me up. 'About the other day . . .'

I turned to face her, keeping my mouth firmly shut. Her eyes looked in to mine and my heart did the mouth thing again. Only this time, it did it worse. My throat dried. My tongue turned to Fuzzyfelt. And my stomach flipped. I was going to crack. My lips were twitching, starting to stretch . . . oh, God, no . . . her eyes . . . those eyes . . . I was going to smile. I thought Nelson. I thought Churchill. I thought Eisenhower. *Be a man, my son, be strong*.

I summoned up my coldest look, straight from the bottom drawer of the freezer. 'Forget it,' I said, my voice clipped. 'If you don't want to be friends, it's fine. Really.'

I paid for my drink.

'I do want to be friends,' she said, looking at the floor in embarrassment. 'I got the wrong end of the stick. I was in a dreadful mood and I'm really sorry. I shouldn't have accused you of coming on to me. It was out of order and I

139

don't want there to be any awkwardness between us, especially with the wedding coming up.'

She folded her arms across her chest.

Her chest, for Christ's sake, her chest . . . I felt my eyes begin to drop . . .

Napoleon.

Monty.

Patton.

What's-his-name? That bloke who won the battle of Agincourt.

I cleared my throat. 'I meant . . .' I began, my voice a rasp. 'I meant,' I tried again, overcompensating this time and sounding like I'd just inhaled the contents of a helium balloon, 'what I said about just wanting to be friends.' Then I remembered a seminar I took on public speaking and concentrated on speaking clearly and slowly. 'AndI'mgladwe'resortedonthatfront,' I blurted out.

She looked up at me quizzically. 'Sorry?'

I noticed a trace of a smile on her lips. She thought this was funny. It was the break I'd been looking for. 'I'm glad we're sorted,' I snapped.

'Me, too.'

I avoided her eyes and hesitated and drew breath. Here came the hard bit.

King Arthur.

Henry the Eighth.

You can do this.

'To tell the truth,' I said, 'it was awkward for me, too, because, as you'll no doubt be relieved to hear, I don't fancy you. I don't mean that nastily, H. It's just that you're not my type. Sorry,' I added, hurriedly picking up my drink and squeezing past her.

I headed straight back to Jack and Amy, knowing that only yards behind me, the first bomb of Operation

Marchmont had just gone off, and feeling infinitely relieved that, for now at least, I was out of range.

The effect of the blast was immediate, and astoundingly, considering my miserable efforts, beneficial. On her return to the table, not only did H park her bum right next to mine, but she started talking. To me. And smiling. At me. With *that* smile. And looking at me. With *those* eyes. It was like time had been rewound, back to Club Zanzibar last year, like that first aborted snog had been erased and we were working from a clean sheet once more. We were friends again. We were having a laugh. We were getting drunk together. I was relaxing and enjoying myself. My heart had retreated to its natural place. But most important of all, we were flirting.

The conversation in the cab on the way back to my place after Jack and Amy had left us alone went:

H: I haven't gone home with a bloke since I split up with Gav.
Me: Neither have I.
H: I'm drunk.
Me: Me too.
H: Maybe I should go home.
Me: If you like.
H: Do you think I'm being a slag?
Me: No.
H: Do you wish I was?
Me: No.
H: I think you're a slag.
Me: Why?
H: Because that's what Amy says.
Me: You shouldn't believe everything you hear.
H: Do you have one-night stands?
Me: Sometimes.
H: Do you enjoy them?
Me: Sometimes.

H: Are they easy to walk away from?
Me: Usually.
H: Even with people you know?
Me: Usually.
H: Do you think he can see?
Me: Who?
H: The driver.
Me: See what?
H: This.
Me: What are you doing?
H: You.

And the conversation in my kitchen went:

Me: Do you want a drink?
H: No.
Me: Coffee?
H: No.
Me: Something to eat?
H: No.
Me: Cigarette?
H: No.
Me: Do you want to go to bed?
H: Yes.
Me: Now?
H: Yes.

And the conversation in my bedroom went:

Me: You look edible.
H: So eat me.
Me: Mmm . . .
H: Ah . . .
Me: Should I wear a condom?
H: Is the Pope a Catholic?
Me: I don't think he approves.
H: I don't think he's slept around as much as you.

And the conversation the following morning went:

Me: I brought you breakfast.
H: What time is it?
Me: Nine.
H: Shit.
Me: What?
H: I'm meant to be meeting Amy and Susie in half an hour.
Me: Can't you be late?
H: No, I promised.
Me: It's eggs Benedict.
H: Sorry. No can do.
Me: I'll give you a lift.
H: It'll be quicker by tube.
Me: Suit yourself.
H: Where are my knickers?
Me: Behind the TV.
H: Who put them there?
Me: I did.
H: What on earth for?
Me: A delaying tactic.
H: What?
Me: To stop you doing a runner.
H: I'm not doing a runner.
Me: Yes, you are.
H: No, I'm not. I enjoyed last night.
Me: Enough to do it again?
H: Sure.
Me: When?
H: I'll call you.
Me: When?
H: Are you trying to close me?
Me: Are you ducking out on me?
H: I'm away next week. Working. In Paris.
Me: All week?

H: All week.
Me: See you at the wedding, then . . .
H: Sure. See you at the wedding.
Me: Goodbye.
H: I'll see myself out.

I check my watch: it's nearly three o'clock. No wonder the square's empty. I should probably get back to work soon. One more cigarette, then I'll scoot. I rest the mobile phone on my lap and light one up, inhale. I stare in to the branches of a tree. I might just be being paranoid. That's what Jack said when I spoke to him on Sunday about what had happened.

'She slept with you, didn't she?' was his reaction. 'What more proof do you need that she's into you?'

'She was drunk, Jack. We both were.'

'So what?'

'So, in the morning, when she was sober, she did a runner. Her sober reaction to waking up in bed with me was to flee the scene of the crime.'

'She was meeting Amy. She told you so and it's true. Amy met her yesterday morning. Dress fitting.'

'OK, then, what about her being away *all* next week?' I demanded. 'You're not telling me that's not an avoidance tactic?'

'Her Paris trip? Sorry to disappoint you again, Matt, but it's gospel. She's been banging on about it for weeks.'

'Oh.'

'Just cool it.'

'Listen, Jack. Is it all right if we keep this to ourselves for now?'

'What, you mean, not tell Amy?'

'Yeah.'

'Why?'

'I'd just rather, that's all. You know, in case nothing comes of it.'

'But it will,' he insisted.

'Yeah, but all the same . . .'

'OK, mate. Whatever you say.'

'Swear?'

'Swear,' he solemnly replied.

'Thanks. What about Amy? Has she said anything to you?'

'What, about you two shagging? No. Why?'

'No reason.'

Only it wasn't no reason, it was the biggest reason in the world. All people are different; I acknowledge that. But at the same time, there are some universal traits which apply to just about everyone. And bragging to your mates about a top shag is one of them. H didn't brag, though, did she? She didn't tell Amy, because if she had, then it's a certainty that Amy would have told Jack, and it's an equal certainty that if Amy had told Jack, then Jack would have told me. (Such is the nature of trust in a close social circle.)

I've analysed this over and over again and have come to the conclusion that there are three likely explanations for H's silence on this matter:

One, she could be embarrassed about her drunken behaviour, and doesn't want to tell anyone in case they think worse of her, particularly her closest friend.

Two, she sees nothing wrong with her behaviour, but is totally grossed out that it was me she behaved that way with.

Or three, she might be cool with the way she behaved and simply be keeping quiet until she sees if it's just another notch on the headboard or the start of something more serious.

Now obviously, short of repeating my observation to her that she's not a slag, or having plastic surgery to

145

transmogrify me into her perfect guy, I'm pretty stuffed if it's explanation one or two. Three, however . . . three I can run with. So long as I get to see her, then I can show her that together we can really go places. That's what I wanted to do the morning she left. I wanted to fix her breakfast. I wanted us to lie in bed, talking the day away, getting to know each other. Because I know this can go somewhere if we only give it a chance. I see her. Jack was right about her. She's right for me. Of course she is: she's perfect. And I can prove it to her, as well. But when? The sooner the better, that's for sure. The wedding's a whole two weeks away. Leave it till then and whatever momentum we've got going for us now will have reached stasis.

I stare back down at my mobile phone and toss my cigarette away. Then I take out a piece of paper from my pocket. There's a phone number on it, written in my squiggly handwriting. The paper's well-thumbed, which is hardly surprising since this must be about the thousandth time I've looked at it since I hastily copied it down on Saturday morning. I feel sick just looking at it. I know it's wrong. But what other hope have I got?

I'd copied the number from another piece of paper that I found in H's bag on the floor of my room the night she stayed. I wasn't being nosy. It was just kind of sticking out. With some other pieces of paper. Which I just kind of read as well. Granted, the pieces of paper came from a sealed envelope marked 'Hen Party Details' – the same sealed envelope I'd watched H return to her bag in the Blue Rose after giving Amy a copy. But who was I to fall deaf when opportunity knocked?

I resealed the papers and put them back in H's bag and glanced over at her on the bed. The bedside lamp was still on from the night before. H was lying on her front, facing me, sound asleep. Her head and torso were uncovered by the sheets and I gently traced a finger along the perfect skin of her forearm. Then I folded my scribbled piece of paper up and slid it inside the pillowcase beneath my head.

'He's coming for you,' the scatty-looking woman sitting next to me on the bench suddenly hisses, ripping me from my reverie.

For a moment, I'm too shocked to say anything, and simply stare at her agog. She's in her early twenties and looks like she's just stepped out of a club, all dark shades and jewellery.

'Who is?' I ask, recovering my composure.

'The devil,' she says, grabbing my wrist. 'Beelzebub. Satan.' Her grip tightens. 'Call him what you want.'

'I see,' trying not to sound too freaked out.

'I mean it,' she insists. 'I saw him last night. In Hyde Park.'

'Do you mind?' I ask, prising her fingers free. 'Only it's starting to hurt.'

'He's coming for you,' she snaps. 'To punish you for your sins.'

Accuse a lawyer of anything dodgy and, chances are, they'll have a guilty reaction. Especially if, like me, they have a somewhat seedy past. My mind flies immediately back to 1981 when, dressed as Batman and Robin, Jack and I carried out the – still unsolved – broad-daylight robbery of Calder Road Post Office, Bristol. But there's no way this woman could know about Jack's cunning pocketing of twenty-four mint humbugs and my equally dastardly theft of two liquorice pipes, three strawberry whips and a packet of Spangles, is there? I study her face for a few seconds, just to be sure, but all she does is stare right back.

'You should get some sleep,' I finally tell her, slipping my phone into my greatcoat pocket.

She looks at me slyly. 'You don't believe me, do you?'

'That the devil's currently at large in Hyde Park? No, I don't.'

147

'He's taken the form of a goat and walks on his hind legs.'

'Yes,' I say as comfortingly as I can, getting up to go, 'I'm sure that's true.'

'He's called Gerald,' she shouts after me. 'I saw it on the sign he wears around his neck. I . . .'

But I'm no longer listening. I cross the square to the iron gate, the piece of paper still in my hand. Once there, I stop and take out my phone, my blood fizzing with adrenaline. Hurriedly, I thumb in the first few digits. But then I freeze. I can't. The woman's right. Do this and the devil's going to be on my case for the rest of my life. More terrifying still, so will H. She's never going to believe it's a coincidence. I mean, the odds are preposterous. At the same time, though, she's never going to be able to *prove* that that's exactly what it is. All she'll have is supposition. So be brave. This is your only chance. So what if it's wrong? Doesn't the end justify the means? And if the end is getting H, shouldn't you be prepared to use every means at your disposal? The answers to these questions come snapping back in an instant. Who cares? Yes. And yes again. So without another thought, I do it. I do something so evil that *The Exorcist* would look cute and cuddly in comparison. I finish dialling in the number.

'Hello,' a woman's voice answers. 'You're through to Leisure Heaven. Lisa speaking. How can I help you?'

'I'd like to make a booking, please. For this weekend. Friday and Saturday night.'

'How many in your party, please, sir?'

'Seven definites. Maybe eight.'

'Bear with me, sir. Our computer system's down at the moment.' I listen to the sound of rustling papers and muffled curses for several seconds. Eventually, Lisa comes back: 'You're in luck, sir. I can do you two chalets. They're the last ones and they both sleep four to six guests. How will that do?'

'That, Lisa,' I say, pulling out my wallet and extricating my credit card, 'will do very nicely indeed.'

Part II

Stringer

Friday, 16.00

'You swine!'

I grab Ken by the throat and twist him round to face me. 'It isn't so funny when it's the other way round, is it?' I snarl, before adding, 'You geeky little squit,' for good measure. I take a second to shine my torch at the back of my hand where he scratched me. As I suspected: blood. 'Cut me up, would you?' I demand, turning back to face him and examining his sharp little hands. 'All right. Well, here's where you start paying.' I stare into his eyes, but all he does is stare impassively back. He hasn't got so much as a hair out of place. He's a cool one, all right. I'll give him that. He's exactly how he was when he used to hang out with Barbie and my sister. Well, fuck him. The past means nothing. No one messes with the Stringer Man and lives to tell the tale. I tighten my grip and twist, and then it happens: his head comes clean off in my hand.

'Are you all right in there?' I hear Karen calling out in a muffled voice.

I toss the Ken doll's head over my shoulder and tread his and Xandra's other dolls underfoot.

'Fine,' I call back, shoving a *Judge Dredd* annual and a threadbare gingham shirt to one side. I make another sweep with the torch and continue to edge forward into the built-in storage space at the back of my room, banging my elbow on a Fisher Price garage in the process and making the bell ding. I can't believe the amount of tat that's been squeezed in here. There are toys I haven't seen since Xandra and I were tots. Our school reports and uniforms are here as well, along with lots of other junk. I remember Mum sneaking it all down here about a month after I moved in, saying that if I wasn't using the space then she would. It's cramped in here – only about three feet high – but goes back about six foot. I bang my head on the ceiling for what feels like the hundredth time in as many seconds. Then I curse Matt. I curse Matt and I curse Jack, and I curse the whole stag concept. Then, just for good measure, I curse Jimmy and Ug, because their presence on the stag weekend is what's really getting me down.

Karen's muffled voice asks again: 'What are you doing? Building a den?'

'Oh, ha-ha,' I shout, chucking a cobweb-bound fishing reel out of the way. 'No, I'm bloody well not.'

'What, then?'

'A hat, actually. I'm looking for a funny hat. It's black with rubber moose antlers on the top.'

There's a pause. 'Why do you want to find that?'

'I don't. Matt does.'

There's another pause, then, 'He's not in there, too, is he?'

'No,' I tell Karen, 'he's asked us all to bring one. A funny hat. A ha-ha-ha, hilarious hat. For the stag weekend.' I grab Big Ted by the throat and claw him roughly behind me. I'm going to find this hat if it bloody well kills me. 'It's in the fax he sent me,' I continue to shout. 'On my bedside table. See for yourself.'

I march in to the kitchen about five minutes later with my moose hat gripped firmly in my hand. Karen's sitting at the oak table, a mug of coffee cradled in her hands. The table is covered with magazines, papers and books, all research for the article she's currently working on. Her laptop sits on the only place left: her lap. She doesn't look up from the screen and her hands are motionless. I look over her shoulder and see she's waiting for some research paper from the Guggenheim online archives to finish downloading. Still she doesn't move, utterly tranced-out.

'Are you all right?' I ask.

'Sure,' she replies.

I know her too well to take this at face value. She's dwelling on something, something bad. I lean on the table and stare at her until she stares back. 'Really sure?' I enquire.

'I don't know,' she says, shaking her head, before stumbling on, 'It's just Chris. He's . . .'

'He's what?' I ask.

'Well, you know he was meant to be coming down tonight?'

'Yes.'

'Well, now he's not coming until tomorrow. He says he's got to stay late at the office and that by the time he finishes it will be too late to get a train.'

'Oh.'

'Exactly,' she says. 'Oh.'

This isn't the first time Karen and I have had this conversation, but as with the times that have gone before, I find it difficult. If it's an absolute opinion she wants from me on what she should do about Chris, I have one: ditch him. The trouble is, it isn't something I can tell her, not without risking giving away my own feelings about her. The one time I did let loose about what I thought of him a few months ago, we were drunk and I don't think she remembered the conversation. She certainly never mentioned it to me again. 'What did you say?' I settle for.

She groans, putting her mug down on the table. 'I said fine. Just like I always do.'

'But that's not what you think.'

'No, I . . . I don't know, Greg. It's the usual thing. Him living up there. Me down here.' She sighs. 'And I don't know what he's doing, and since he was unfaithful that last time, I just . . . Oh, God, it just pisses me off. Why

155

should I have to sit here feeling insecure on my own on a Friday night?'

'The simple answer to that is that you shouldn't.'

'I know.' She hesitates for a moment, before continuing. 'And maybe that's what I should tell him.'

'What?' I ask, feeling my heart beat begin to race. 'You're going to break off with him?'

'I don't know.'

I sit on the edge of the table. She looks so sad, it cuts. 'Do you love him?' I ask, inwardly pleading for her to please, please say no.

She stares at the wall. 'I don't even know that any more. I love him for who he used to be, for who I used to think he was,' she corrects, looking back at me. 'But I don't think we're the same people we were when we fell in love.'

'If you don't love him any longer, then perhaps it's already over,' I suggest.

'Yeah,' she says, slowly nodding her head, 'perhaps it is.' She sucks in a deep breath and then exhales, forcing a weak smile. 'You found it, then,' she observes, picking up her mug and peering over the rim at my moose hat as she takes a sip.

'Yes,' I reply, realizing that the Chris conversation is closed. I search for something else to say, finally opting for, 'Have you got Matt's fax?'

She picks it up from the table in front of her and runs her eyes over it. 'Men never really grow up, do they?' she asks, her tone world-weary. ' "A penalty system will be operating for the duration of the weekend," ' she quotes in a sarcastic voice, ' "for what is generally considered as *unstagly* behaviour." ' She shoots me a withering look. Karen's condemnation of the fax only serves to double my anxiety over the weekend. Still, at least she's smiling now. ' "Appropriate fines will be administered where deemed appropriate." Isn't that a bit pathetic?' she asks.

'Tell me about it.'

'It's not very like Matt, is it?'

'No, but Jack said he wanted the full works, so that's what Matt's giving him. By the book.'

She peers into my face. 'Are you all right, baby? Here's me going on about my problems, and there you are, looking like you haven't slept in a month.'

'I'm shattered,' I admit. 'Last night's guests didn't leave until after three, and then I had to be back in there at eight this morning to check it was all cleared up.' My head spins at the thought. I've been averaging about four hours sleep a night over the last week. I blink heavily. It would take me seconds to fall asleep. 'All I want to do is curl up in bed for twenty-four hours.'

She looks back at Matt's fax. 'And instead you've got to do this . . .'

'Precisely . . . and that's just the half of it . . .'

'What's the rest?'

I let out a long overdue growl. 'There are these two blokes going on the stag: Jimmy and Ug,' I tell her. 'Or Jimmy mainly . . .'

'And?'

'They're into their gear. The works, you know. I swear, you give them a week-old dog's turd and they'll try to smoke it or snort it. I *know* they're going to come loaded. They're going to be carrying a stash the size of the Taj Mahal, and do you know who they're going to want to share it all with?' I don't wait for a reply. 'Me. That's who, because as far as they're concerned, that's what I'm into, no matter how many times I tell them I'm not any more . . .'

Karen knows all about my narcotic history. I confessed all a few months ago. 'Have you spoken to David at Quit4Good?' she checks.

'Yes. He thinks I'll be able to cope.'

'And you don't agree?' she surmises.

157

'I don't know. You know what I was like, Karen. One line. I know that's all it will take and I'll be off again, and once that happens, well, shit . . . I don't know . . . I really don't . . .'

Karen looks at me sympathetically. 'These two – Jimmy and Ug – they're close friends of yours, I take it?'

'Friends? Yes.' I think about this for a second, before contradicting myself: 'No.' I think about it again. 'I don't know. I used to hang out with them a hell of a lot. They're into their clubbing. All-nighters . . . dawn raiders, you know? But friends? I don't know. They haven't been since I kicked. I've been avoiding them . . .'

'If that's how you feel, then maybe you shouldn't go . . .' Karen suggests.

I feel myself frowning. 'That wouldn't be fair to Jack. They're his friends, have been since college. He's OK with them because he never went down that path with them. No, this is my problem, not his.'

She nods at me. 'Then face it head on,' she advises. 'Just tell them to piss off about the whole thing. They can't force you in to doing anything you don't want.'

I consider this and accept it as the truth. 'You're right,' I say. 'I can do this.'

'I know you can.' She studies my face. 'Is there anything else that's worrying you?'

I smile wearily. She knows me so well. 'Money.'

She glances at the fax for a second. 'Yeah, I saw. "One hundred quid kitty" ' – she continues to read – ' "each".' She looks up at me. 'Jesus, Greg, how on earth are you going to afford it?'

The blindingly obvious answer to this question is that I'm not. Including the overtime I've been getting from Chichi this week, I'm completely up to my eyeballs in debt with the bank from last year. Then there's the money I owe Mum for rent – I'm two months behind. It's all right for people like Matt and Jack. They've *got* the money. A hundred quid probably doesn't mean that much to them. A few restaurant bills, or a weekend's clubbing. Herein lies my problem: it doesn't occur to them that anyone else might not be able to afford that style of party money. There's no point in whining about it. It's my fault that I'm broke. Nobody else's. Also, it's hardly like I'm out in the cold with nowhere to stay, is it? No. I'll therefore have to lump it and get back in to the overtime next week. I shrug at Karen. 'I'll manage. I'll have to, won't I?'

'Well,' she comments, 'like I said, you could not go.'

'I can't do that.'

'Yeah, you can. You can do whatever you want. Like with the drugs, you can live your life how you choose.' She glances back down at the paper. 'It looks like it will be a load of thigh-slapping, chest-beating crap, anyway.'

'I know, but I can't bail out. It wouldn't be right, and besides, I've already given Matt a cheque to cover transport and accommodation.'

She tuts. 'Do you even know where you're going?'

'All we've been told is what pub we're meeting at.'

'Well, it's your call,' she says with a sigh, then, 'Do you want me to run through the checklist with you? We don't want you getting fined right at the start, do we?'

I look at my watch: it's four twenty. I'm going to have to shift it to get to the pub by five to meet the others. 'Thanks,' I tell Karen, picking up my backpack in to which I've already packed my clothes and washbag.

'Item number one,' she reads. 'A funny hat.'

'Check.' I sling the hat into my bag.

'Item number two: a packet of condoms.'

'Check.' I sling them in on top.

'Item number three: an unusual bottle of spirits (NB. any repeated bottles will result in fines for all parties concerned).'

159

I hold up the bottle of apple schnapps, before placing it into my bag. 'Check.'

'Item number four: a piece of women's underwear.' Her brow settles in a frown. 'You're not planning to wear them, are you?' she enquires. She looks me archly up and down, teasing, 'Now there's a sight I wouldn't mind seeing . . .'

'No,' I say, suddenly awkward. 'At least, I don't think so.'

'Shame,' she reflects. There's a pause and then she looks up at me and raises her eyebrows. 'So, women's underwear . . . Check?'

'Actually,' I say, feeling myself begin to blush, 'I've been meaning to ask . . .'

Susie

Friday, 16.30

'You promise me you'll be OK?' checks Amy, dumping her stuff for the weekend by the door of her flat. She's got a whopping suitcase and she's intending to take her double duvet – because, apparently, it smells of Jack. I would have thought all she'd need for Leisure Heaven was a swimming costume and some liver salts. Still, that's Amy for you – always a creature of comfort. She leaves her pile of clobber and stands beside 'Scented' Lover, her arms akimbo.

'Now don't let them shave your eyebrows or chain you up naked and leave you, or anything,' she nags again. 'Promise me!'

Jack's sister Kate and I roll eyes at each other as Jack laughs and puts one foot up on the kitchen chair. He's about to depart for his stag weekend and is already in King Lad mode, especially as he's got an audience of girls. He winks at me as he does up the lace of his trainer. Since he stopped living with Matt, Jack's appearance has taken a steady turn for the worse. Gone are the designer clothes, but there's something quite sexy about a man who isn't colour-coordinated. He stands up and stretches out his arms, grinning. He looks ready for battle.

'What about the stripper? Can I diddle her?' he asks.

Amy whacks his arm. 'That's not funny,' she pouts, as he pulls a hat out of his pocket and pulls it on. It's got a nasty holiday logo on it.

Kate covers her eyes. 'You're *so* embarrassing, Jack.'

'You're not going to wear that?' I laugh.

'It's nothing to do with me,' he shrugs. 'Matt's orders. I'll get fined if I don't,' he says, dancing round. But Amy doesn't see the funny side as Kate and I laugh. She clutches Jack's rucksack on the wooden kitchen counter, fiddling longingly with its strap as if she's a heartbroken parent on her child's first day at school.

Jack takes it from her and swings the bag on to his shoulder, like a cowboy with a saddle. 'This is all rubbish. I can't see why we can't all be together,' says Amy. 'They're going to do horrid things to you, I know they are.'

Jack puts his hand on her shoulder. 'Listen. Matt'll be there. He'll look after me.'

'It's not Matt that I'm worried about . . .'

'Come here, you,' laughs Jack, pulling her into a hug. 'It's all going to be fine. You've got the girls . . .' He smiles at us over Amy's shoulder.

Kate sucks in her cheeks and shakes her head.

I like Kate, although I've only met her once before at Amy and Jack's engagement party. She's quite shy and definitely a one-to-one person, so we sat together in the corner and pretty much ignored everyone else. I took to her immediately since she reminded me so much of myself when I was that age. She'd just graduated at the time, having done a languages degree, and despite being absolutely skint, she was full of plans and schemes. I couldn't imagine any of them working, mind, but I encouraged her not to sell out to the lure of a proper job until she'd given things a go for herself.

I felt mature and brave at the time, but to be honest I'm the last person to offer any tips on getting ahead. After all, I'm five years further down the line and what have I got to show for myself? *Failed* plans and schemes. Nothing permanent. Nothing that pays any money, or gives me any credibility. I haven't even been anywhere, despite all my grand plans. The only progress I've made is to get to first-name terms with the woman at the DSS.

'Yes. Well, I'll miss you,' Amy says, as she fiddles with Jack's shirt.

'Now come on, don't be daft!' I bustle. 'We're going to have *loads* more fun.'

'See?' agrees Jack, letting Amy go, and she laughs, but she's staring at Jack as if it's the last time she'll ever see him.

I pinch his cheek, affectionately. 'You'd better believe it, sunshine. You should be the one that's worried. The Tarzan-o-gram is a bit of a dish, so I hear!' I stick my tongue in my cheek.

Jack smiles. 'She's got her chastity belt on,' he stage whispers. He looks at the kitchen clock. 'Gotta go, girls. I can't be late for the boys.'

I can tell he's excited, but I have to admit I'm with Amy on this one. It would be good if we were all together. Never mind though.

'Off you hop then, love. Don't do anything I wouldn't do,' I smile, reaching up to kiss his cheek.

'That leaves the way clear, then,' he chuckles.

'Look after her,' he mouths at me and I nod before turning away so that they can have their emotional farewell.

'Jack's the worst of that lot,' Kate laughs, reaching up to the cupboard. Her T-shirt rides up above her trousers and I notice that she's got her belly button pierced, just like mine. 'If I know my brother, he'll be the one leading them all astray.'

'Don't tell her that,' I whisper.

The kettle clicks off and Kate opens the box of tea-bags.

'Tea!' I exclaim. 'I think we all need something stronger than that. I certainly do.'

I delve into my bag and produce the enormous bottle of vodka I've brought. The last donation from duty-free cheapskate Simon. I've been saving it for a special occasion and I think this'll do nicely. Besides, I've taken the last emergency money out of my building-society account for this weekend, so I'm determined that it's going to be a good one. With difficulty, I pour the vodka from the giant bottle into the mugs. I put extra in Amy's.

'I'm glad you brought something to drink. I meant to, but I'm a bit short of cash,' begins Kate.

I touch her arm. 'You save your pennies for your Australia trip. You'll need your money for all that wonderful travelling. I'm so envious.'

Kate smiles and for once, even though I am envious of her, I feel like I'm the grand benefactress. 'I'll bet we'll do the lot, this weekend,' I warn, tapping the bottle. 'Or by tonight. Now where's H got to?'

'She called earlier. She's running late. She wants us to go over to her place in a cab and then she'll drive from there,' says Kate as she undoes the lid of the tonic bottle.

Well, that's typical, isn't it? How can she have the nerve? I've come all the way from South London and Miss High and Mighty can't even be bothered to drive half a mile. I know I haven't got a job, but honestly. She's known about this for ages. I've got better things to spend my emergency dosh on than a cab fare, just because she's being a prima donna.

'Her loss,' I shrug, curbing my desire to bitch, as I push the mugs towards Kate.

Amy appears, blowing her nose on a large wadge of green loo roll. 'We should get going, too.'

'Don't worry about that yet,' I say, handing her a mug. 'There are more important things first. We've got to get you in the mood.' I put my arm around her and we all clink our mugs together.

'To the hen,' toasts Kate.

'Cluck,' says Amy.

I give her a squeeze. 'I've got a feeling in my waters that we're going to have the time of our lives.'

Matt

Friday, 17.00

'Gotcha!'

Relief floods me. This is the fifth drive-by I've executed outside the appropriately named Stag & Hounds boozer in the last twenty minutes and – at last – I've found somewhere to park. I'm angry with myself. Soho on a Friday afternoon: the boozers' Mecca. What did I expect – even if we are meeting up before most Londoners knock off work? Clear and empty streets? I pull over to the side of the road and grind the gears noisily for a couple of seconds as I attempt to locate reverse. Someone behind me blares his horn and I curse. Why the hell did I decide that this was a good place to meet up? *Hell*. The very word sends shivers down my spine. I put the madwoman in the park out of my mind. It's not hell I'm heading for, I remind myself. It's H. It's heaven.

I'm going to have to be careful this weekend if everything's going to go according to plan. Or *plans*, seeing as there are two of them afoot. There's the Jack plan: to give him a stag weekend he'll – one way or another – remember for the rest of his life. And there's the H plan: to get as close to her as I was last Friday night: to win her heart like she's already won mine.

I'm aware that there's a danger that these two plans might be mutually exclusive. I know, for example, that H might freak if she suspects my double-booking of Leisure Heaven is deliberate. I also know that Jack, in spite of his recent conversion to Coupleanity, is looking forward to a weekend of unbridled male solidarity. And I also know

166

that in spite of his advice concerning the paramount importance of strategy in the winning of H, he's going to go apeshit when he discovers that I've unilaterally decided to turn Leisure Heaven into my personal chessboard of love, with him and the other guys and girls making up the pieces.

The last serious acting I did was in 1988 when I auditioned for our school's sixth-form production of *One Flew Over the Cuckoo's Nest*. I'd seen the film and when I went along to the lunch-time auditions, it was with the wicked grin and insane eyeballs of Jack Nicolson, as perfected in the bathroom mirror at home the night before. I didn't get the part of MacMurphy. That honour went to Danny Donaldson. This wasn't, as I rumour-mongered in the pub that evening, because he was porking Mrs McKinnery, the sixtysomething head of drama. It was because I couldn't act. Not outside the bathroom. Not under pressure. The moment I'd set foot on the stage, I'd gone to pieces. Mrs McKinnery's verdict on my thespian pretensions, after my allotted five minutes of strutting and snarling had passed, had summed it up perfectly: 'What's the matter, boy? Are you looking for the toilet?'

And that's my worry now: my inability to act convincingly under pressure. Exactly the same as it was when I told H I wasn't interested in her that night in the Blue Rose. The only way I'm going to avoid a castration from H and a lynching from Jack is to act innocent at the pivotal moment when they discover their joint weekend destination. *Perfectly* innocent. Manage that, and this could turn out to be the best weekend of my life. Fail, and it could well be my last.

This moment aside, though, so far with the Jack plan, so good. No one suspects a thing. Since booking us all in to Leisure Heaven on Monday, everything's run smoothly. I've given Tia Maria Tel the finger workwise and pulled out my finger stagwise. Everybody knows where to meet and when. I've told them what to bring. I've got enough booze in the back of the minibus to launch the *Titanic* into.

Apart from the transport, everything's great. And that's down to Stringer more than me. I toggle the gearstick again, but the only discernible effect is an increase in black smoke coming from the back. I picked it up an hour and a half ago, over in Clapham, from this rental company Stringer put me on to: Easy Riders. More like Sleazy Riders. Stringer said Chichi use them from time to time when they need extra staff transport at short notice, and that they're cheap and reliable. Cheap and fucked, while unlikely to win any gold medals at the National Marketing Awards, would have been more accurate.

The van's thundercloud grey, with mushy-pea green go-faster stripes running round its midriff, kind of a cross between Scooby Doo's Mystery Machine and a hearse. The interior's not much better, with worn-out seats and a peculiar odour of goat's cheese coming from somewhere near the back. Then there's the *pièce de résistance*: thanks to a jammed cassette, all the sound system's capable of playing is, according to the empty case, *80s Chart Classics: A Panpipes Compilation*. Radical chic, indeed. And fine if you could turn it off. Or down. But you can't do either. Because it's stuck on volume eight and won't be budged. It's like being trapped in elevator hell and God only knows what H is going to think if she sees me driving this wreck. Mind you, what she'll think of the *minibus* being there will probably be the least of my worries . . . I grind the gears again and this time something clicks. I check behind me, worried that it's the noise of the bus breaking in half, then slowly reverse in to the parking space.

Where the Jack plan's running according to schedule, the H plan is still stuck in its starting blocks. This, it has to be said, is largely down to H herself. Or the complete absence of her, at any rate. There's been no word from her. Not so much as a syllable. Not since her oh-so-casually executed *I'll see myself out* in my bedroom last Saturday morning. Hopefully, this is down to opportunity. Hopefully, she's been rushed off her feet what with being in Paris and finalizing stuff for the hen weekend, far too busy, no doubt, to call me up to shoot the breeze. This, at least, is what my heart says. And if that is the case, then this weekend will be exactly as I've dreamt. She'll be delighted to see me and we'll have twenty-four hours of non-stop fun together.

My head thinks differently. My head thinks motive. Perhaps it's nothing to do with lack of opportunity at all. Perhaps she simply doesn't *want* to talk to me again. And perhaps she just wants to forget the whole incident altogether. I'm not defeatist by nature and this isn't a possibility I want to dwell on too long, because it would depress me beyond belief.

'Oi!' someone shouts over the finishing bars of a particularly masterful piped rendition of 'Like a Virgin'.

I look out of the window and see Damien's chubby face wedged firmly against the glass. I hit the window button and watch his lower lip stretch obscenely down. Damien's a mate from Bristol. He was at school with me and Jack and now programmes computer-games title sequences for a company in Brixton. He pulls his face back and his features spring in to place. Blond receding hair. Blue-grey eyes shielded by John Lennon glasses. Cheeky grin. And looking paler than ever, probably because he's going to become a dad in about eight weeks' time.

'Nice wheels,' he says, stepping back and casting an appreciative eye over the Passion Wagon's bodywork. 'And tunes, as well,' he adds, grinning even wider, bunching his hands round his mouth in a panpipe mime. 'Could that be the dulcet tones of panpiped Dire Straits?'

I notice that the track's changed and bow my head to his eighties wisdom. 'It could indeed.'

'Nice. Good to see your taste hasn't improved since we last met.'

'Up yours.' I shake hands with him and smile. This is the first time I've seen him since the news about his impending fatherhood broke. 'Congratulations,' I tell him. 'On the incoming child. You found out who the father is yet?'

'Very funny.'

'How's Jackie?'

'Good. Pretty much taking it in her stride. We've been lucky. No complications.' He kicks the front wheel, changing the subject. 'How far's this hunk of junk got to get us?' He looks at me sidelong. 'That's if you're prepared to tell me where you're taking us yet . . .'

'All in good time.' I turn off the engine. 'Are you the first one here?' I ask.

'Nah.' He nods over at the pub. 'I spotted you from the window. Jack and his brother . . .' He frowns. 'Billy, is it?' he checks. I nod. 'Well, they're up at the bar. And Jimmy and Ug rang about ten minutes back. They're in a cab. Should be here in the next five minutes.'

Jimmy and Ug are old mates of Jack's from college. They run a fifties seconds clothes shop on the New King's Road. They even look alike: both of them about five ten, stocky with short-cropped dark hair. Jack and I refer to them privately as the Suicide Twins, on account of their propensity to party till they drop. I like Ug well enough. He's not the sharpest suit on the rack, but he's harmless enough. Jimmy, though, can be a real pain, especially when he's wired, which these days he generally is. I remind myself about my promise to Amy that I won't let anything happen to Jack.

Damien checks me out from top to toe as I climb out. 'You're looking a bit smart, aren't you?'

I feel myself flush. 'Yeah.'

My shop-fresh Hugo Boss slacks and Romeo Gigli shirt can hardly be described as suitable stag attire. The last stag I went on was Alex's, last year. I wore my oldest shirt and jeans, fully aware of the direct correlation between beers consumed and beers spilt. Today, though, dressing down is not an option. H will be there tonight, so there's a chance I'll bump in to her. And where H is concerned, I'm a peacock: all strut and display. The last thing I need is my feathers looking ruffled and tired.

'Who else is coming?' Damien asks.

'Stringer,' I say, locking the door. 'Carl called last night. He can't make it. Flu. So it's just the seven of us.'

'The magnificent seven,' Damien intones with grim resolve, pulling a Bay City Rollers Fan Club hat that must have been his Dad's from his pocket and ceremoniously donning it.

We turn round to face the pub.

'Right,' I say, starting to cross, 'let's get this show on the road.'

H

Friday, 17.30

'Come on, come on,' I mutter, looking out on to the street for the fifth time. I've been waiting for Susie, Amy and Kate for half an hour and if we don't leave soon, we're going to be stuck all night in rush-hour traffic.

I pull my mobile out of the recharger and make sure it's working. I scroll through the numbers in the memory and my thumb hovers above the green call button. If I press it now, I'll be straight through. It's no use though, I've already called once and he wasn't answering and I'm too nervous to leave a message. Anyway, he's probably left already.

I fall backwards on my cast-iron bed and feel my body bounce on the soft mattress. I look up at my Japanese paper lampshade and sigh. I could stay here all night, just dreaming. I'm so tired and dazed after Paris and today at the office I hardly had a chance to catch my breath, so lying here, the silence broken only by the noise of the traffic, I revel in the precious solitude. I feel like I've been catapulted back in to my life in London and all I want is the chance to reflect. To remember. To enjoy it all over again in my head.

I rub my eyes, missing this moment, even though it's not over yet. Knowing that any second the door buzzer is going to go and once again, I'm going to have no time to myself. I wish this wasn't happening. I wish it was next weekend, so that I had a chance to get my head straight and work out how I feel.

I take a deep breath, smile to myself and spread my

arms out on the bed. I can't believe I haven't told Amy yet. She'll die when she finds out. How can so much have changed in my life and yet she doesn't know?

I wish it was just her and me this weekend and the others weren't coming. I need to be alone with her to analyse every bit of it. I need to talk her through the sex, to work out all the pros and cons, to decide whether it's worth having a relationship with him.

All I actually want to do is *tell* someone. I'll burst if I don't. And if I tell Amy, it'll make it all real. Not just a memory.

Even though I've been expecting it, the buzzer rudely interrupts my thoughts. I groan as I peel myself off the bed.

'Coming,' I yell through the intercom and grab my shoulder bag. I rake my hair in the hall mirror. I look a total state. Thank God it's only the girls.

Susie and Amy are on the pavement, giggling and trying to find change for the cab driver. I look at Amy and, to my horror, notice she's wearing a cheap and nasty wedding veil, is covered in lurid make-up and has four coloured condoms safety-pinned to her jacket.

Hmmm ... classy. Susie's influence, I bet.

'Where've you been?' I ask, handing over a tenner to the embarrassed cabby. I wave his change away and stare at Amy. So much for my hopes of a heart to heart. She looks absolutely wasted.

'We had a few to warm up,' she hiccups, holding up a half-empty bottle of vodka. 'But we're ready now,' she slurs.

Kate stumbles out of the cab with all the bags, including what I assume to be Amy's bulging suitcase and a massive duvet. She stands flimsily on the pavement, smiling lamely. As usual, I have the overwhelming urge to say 'Boo' to her very loudly.

Amy kisses me before linking arms with Susie and

skipping over to my car. Since I wrote off the Golf, I've had a 3 series BMW on loan from work. As I click the alarm button on my keys and the doors snap open, they both jump, before cracking up into peals of laughter and bundling in to the back seat.

I wish it wasn't me driving.

'You'll have to give me a hand,' I say to Kate, before marching off towards my flat.

'How are the others getting there?' Kate asks, as I overload her with shopping from my dash around Tescos earlier. There's no way I'm venturing out of walking distance of the twenty-four-hour garage without coffee, cigarettes and painkillers.

'Jenny's bringing Lorna because they live near each other and Sam's coming separately, later on,' I reply, dumping a large bag in her arms and throwing a kitchen roll on top. 'OK there?'

The whole concept of this weekend makes me want to hand over the keys of the car, barricade myself inside my flat and let them all get on with it. I know it's my fault we're going there, but I have to say, Leisure Heaven *is* my ultimate idea of hell.

I catch my reflection in the glass as I lock the front door and realize that I look like thunder. I take a deep breath. Come on, I tell myself. This is Amy's weekend and it's a one-off. Next week she'll be getting married and after that I'll have all the time in the world to talk to her. Surely I'm big enough and ugly enough to cope with this. Just go with the flow. I close my eyes briefly.

I will be strong.

I will not crack.

'All set, then?' I ask, getting in to the driver's seat and making a big effort to be jovial. Susie leans between the two front seats.

'Marvellous car, H,' she says, feeling the leather seats. She stinks of booze.

'Well, I thought we'd do it in style,' I smile. No wonder she's so gushy. I doubt if she's ever been in anything more plush than a public bus. Mee-ow! I check myself.

'Let's go!' says Amy, slapping her knees, drunkenly. 'Let's go.'

'You betcha!' I reply.

But my plan to do just that fails. Instead of bombing down the M4 at 100mph as I'd planned, we crawl along in stop-start traffic, which isn't exactly soothing. Remembering my resolution, I ignore my irritation as Kate leans back and puts her feet up on my dashboard whilst she rolls her own cigarettes. In the back, Amy plays with the stereo controls and I watch her and Susie in the rear-view mirror as they swig vodka and plan the weekend. They both want to go on the waterslides when we get there.

The only place I want to slide is in to bed.

By 8.30 p.m., I'm completely knackered and we've run out of cigarettes and petrol. At last we find our exit from the motorway and cruise in to the first station. It's a relief to have some peace and quiet. I stand holding the petrol pump, feeling the car bounce as Amy and the girls muck about inside.

I get my phone out of my pocket and check for messages, but with a sinking heart notice that he hasn't left one. I did give him my number, didn't I? I left in such a rush that maybe I wrote it down wrong. But surely he should have called by now? All I want is a few words. A moment of solidarity. After all, I'm sure he's just as stressed as me.

I tap the last drips of petrol into the fuel hole. If I'm going to call, I've got to do it now, because if he calls me there's no way I can talk to him in the car. I'm about to press the green button when I look up and see a revolting gypsy van swerving on the road. As it screeches past me, someone from inside leans out of the window. Out of the corner of my eye, I can see that he's got an odd-shaped hat on and he bellows something at me, before the van careers away.

I give him the finger as I replace the petrol nozzle. 'Wanker!' I shout.

Why have I got such a bad feeling about this weekend?

Matt

Friday, 20.30

'Get your tits out!'

Checking the wing mirror, I see Ug's hairy bare torso sticking out of the window, his head adorned with the cheap plastic breast he, Jimmy and Jack fought over in the fast lane of the M4, following a drunken foot chase through the gridlocked motorway traffic outside Slough. Any hope that his bellowed comment has been swallowed up by the minibus's sliptrickle (slipstream being too ambitious a word for this vehicle) immediately vanishes. The girl standing by the side of the garage, now some forty yards behind us, raises her middle digit in salute. There's something familiar about her stance, something I can't quite place . . . But then I'm distracted by a cheer from the back.

Checking the rear-view mirror, I see Ug stumbling back to join Jack, Jimmy and Damien, who are sitting on the back seat. Jack's brother, Billy, is comatose in the row behind me, sleeping off the beers he drank in London. There's a pair of his wife's knickers around his neck and an empty bottle of Tia Maria by his side. I glance across at my co-pilot, Stringer, who's sprawled against the passenger door with his eyes closed and tissue paper sticking out of his ear. The poor sod's shattered, not due to booze, just work. I told him to catch some zeds and that I'd wake him up when we reach our journey's end. On current progress, that could be some time in the next millennium.

Turning my attention back to the road ahead, I see that for the first time since we left the motorway the traffic's starting to thin out. Not that this will make any difference to *our* journey (this rust bucket's top speed is 55 mph). Panpiped 'Save a Prayer' by Duran Duran bleeds from the sound system and the exhaust rattles disconcertingly. There's a roar of laughter from the back.

'Hey, Matt,' Jimmy shouts. 'What's all this about you shagging H?'

H

Friday, 21.15

'I don't believe it!' I slap the reception counter with my booking form.

'As I said, we've got your booking,' trembles Shirley, the Leisure Heaven receptionist behind the desk. 'Only there must have been some mistake. There was a double booking. There's only one chalet available for your party. I'm sorry.'

'Sorry?' I choke. 'Sorry? There are seven of us! I've had this booked for weeks . . . Months! You'll just have to find us another one. *Now*!'

Shirley is fiddling with her desk as if she's looking for a panic button. 'There isn't one. We're fully booked, madam.'

I grit my teeth, clamp my hand to my forehead and turn away before I hit her, or someone, or something. I'm too tired to deal with this.

'What's the matter?'

It's Susie. I might have known she'd interfere.

'There's been an administration cock-up,' I say, glaring at Shirley. 'Apparently we've only got one chalet. I specifically booked two. Where are we all going to sleep? That's what I want to know? Look, why don't you just get me the manager?'

Susie shoves me out of the way and smiles sycophantically at Shirley.

'I'm sure it's not your fault. We've had a very long journey,' she slurs, glancing at me and pulling a face. 'One chalet'll be fine. We'll all cooch up.'

How dare she!

'I'll sort this out!' I snap, barging my way back towards the counter, but Susie bars my way.

'There are other people waiting,' she points out. I look behind me at the long queue of punters, lining up like lemmings for this . . . this . . . *hell*. They're all staring at me as if I'm stark raving mad. As if I'm the odd one out.

'If you'll just give us the keys, I'm sure we'll manage,' Susie says, crinkling up her eyes annoyingly. Shirley smiles at her gratefully and hands over the keys.

'You're in the French Riviera section. Apart-i-ment 328,' she mumbles.

'Thank you,' says Susie, taking the key.

'Please remember that your car has to be moved to the car park by 8 a.m.'

'*What?*'

'It's a car-free zone. Didn't you know? It's bikes only,' says Susie. 'We'll hire them in the morning.'

I scowl at Shirley and storm towards the exit sign.

Right. Brat's going to pay for this! I tear out my mobile phone and angrily punch in his – for use in emergencies only – home number. A home firing. Could this be a first, I wonder? But surprise surprise – there's no reception.

I stamp outside and bite my lip hard as I stare at the dark sky above the regulation pine trees. I thought Brat would've checked the booking, but then again, I didn't ask him to. I should have done it myself in the first place. What was I thinking of, leaving all this to someone else? Now I'm going to have to explain to Amy that it's all my fault.

I check my phone again, feeling an increasing sense of panic. But there's still no reception and if there's no reception that means I'm cut off from civilization all weekend . . .

Which means *he* won't be able to call me.

This is a disaster.

I try my phone again, but it's useless.

'What's your problem?' demands Susie, catching up with me.

'My phone doesn't work!'

'Well, you don't need it here,' she says, looking puzzled and then scowling as I growl in frustration.

'This is Amy's weekend,' she points out. 'Will you just calm down?'

'I am calm!' I shout. She raises her eyebrows and I know I'm over-reacting. I hate this place, already. It's worse than a prison camp.

'Don't spoil this? OK? Just don't,' she threatens, grabbing my arm. I'm too cross to shake her off as she marches towards Kate who is standing by the queue of cars, talking to Jenny who has just arrived with Lorna. Amy's asleep in the back of the Beamer.

'. . . Horrible van. We played tag with them for ages,' laughs Jenny in her ridiculous Northern accent. 'There were this right group of lads. But we saw them a few miles back and they'd broken down. Flat tyre, by the looks of things.'

That must have been the van I gave the finger. Maybe there is a God after all.

'Found her!' announces Susie, pushing me forward, so that I trip in to the hen party.

Stringer

Friday, 21.30

It's amazing. I feel like I've been here for ever, like this is my home. I stare across the lushly vegetated valley to where the foothills of the Andes start their climb towards the clouds. It's so beautiful, I never want to be anywhere else. I never want to set foot in London again. I simply wish to remain here. For here there are no stag parties or crappy old minibuses. Here there is only the simple communal existence of the tribe. I watch an eagle soar high on the crest of a thermal. The woman at my side – her name is Karoonamigh (meaning she whose hair shines golden as the sun) – squeezes my hand tightly and I know that we shall never be apart. I turn back to the village shaman and he smiles his ancient, toothless smile.

'Have you any further requests, child?' he asks.

'Your words will be my truth,' I answer, sitting cross-legged before him and making the sign of peace. 'I am happy. My soul is at one with the earth.'

He nods in understanding and raises his panpipes to his lips. ' "Footloose" by Kenny Loggins,' he says. 'A particular favourite of mine.'

Matt

'Whu . . . ?'

'I said, wake up.'

'Whu . . . ?' Stringer repeats, beginning to stir. He opens his eyes slightly and squints at me through their sleep-clogged slits. Then he reaches over the gearstick and grips my hand. 'Karoonamigh?' he asks in a quavering voice.

I stare uncomfortably at my hand for a second, before turning the engine off. The absence of panpipes drops the minibus into silence. 'Karoona-what?' I ask.

'Karoona—' His eyes open properly this time and he sits up, startled. His hand recoils as if it's just been stung. 'Oh, hi, Matt, it's you.' He glances at his hand reproach-fully, muttering something about a weird dream, then looks around, confused. 'Are we there, then?' he eventu-ally asks.

'That depends on where you mean. If you're referring to our final destination for the stag weekend, then I'm afraid you're going to be very much disappointed. But if' – I indicate the dimly lit building to our left – 'you mean the Black Bull Inn, middle-of-bloody-nowhere, Wiltshire, then you're spot on. We've broken down,' I conclude. 'Flat tyre. No spare. Easy Riders strike again.'

Stringer shifts uncomfortably in his seat. 'Have we got cover?'

I pick my RAC road-cover card off the dashboard. 'They should be here in about another half-hour.'

He removes his seatbelt and swivels round. 'Who's that?' he queries, turning back to face me.

'The corpse?' I ask, not bothering to look, assuming that his enquiry concerns the prostrate and motionless Billy.

'With the puddle of drool under his chin . . .'

'That'll be Billy. He hasn't moved since we turned off the motorway.'

'Oh.' He takes another look. 'Do you think he's all right?'

'Ug took his pulse,' I inform him. 'Says he's fine.'

'I didn't know Ug could count high enough for that,' he comments, peering out into the dark. 'Where's the rest of the squad?'

I nod towards the pub. 'In there. You want to join them? You might as well. There's no point both of us being stuck out here. Sober' – I turn the engine back on and Living in a Box's eponymous single starts up – 'and freezing.'

'Look, mate,' Stringer says. 'About the minibus. I'm sorry. I screwed up.'

I shake my head at him. Stringer's one of those people it's almost impossible to get angry with – particularly when he's got tissue paper sticking out of his ear.

'Forget it,' I tell him. 'It's my fault for not fixing us up with something else.'

He opens the door and gets out. 'Do you want me to get you a soft drink or anything?' he asks.

I shake my head. 'No, I'm fine.'

I watch him walk over to the pub, then pull out the Leisure Heaven brochure they sent me from the glove compartment. I scan through it again. It's great. Great for parents with young kids who want to muck about all day in the extensive adventure playground and waterslides complex. And it's great for people who love the country-side. And it's great for healthniks like Stringer who want to take advantage of the wide variety of indoor and outdoor sports on offer.

But apart from that, it's shit. It's shit for Jack, who probably wants this weekend to involve memories that will stay with him for the rest of his life. And it's shit for Jimmy and Ug, who are probably hoping we're heading for some hush-hush rave that's so leftfield that even they haven't heard of it. And it's shit for Damien, who probably wants to go on a record-breaking pub crawl. And it's shit for Billy, who, judging from the state he's in, probably wants to report to a doctor at the first available opportunity and have a total mind, body and soul transplant.

I just hope I manage to track H down, because without that, I'll have gone and sold my friends down the river for nothing.

Susie

'It'll be fine,' I whisper.

Amy looks anxiously towards the bathroom door. 'But she's been in there for ten minutes.'

'She's just wound up and stressed, that's all. I know H. A few moments alone and she'll get over it. But she's right,' I add, looking round as we put the bags down. 'How are we all going to fit in? Look at this place. It's hardly big enough for four.'

Amy follows my glance around the tiny chalet. We're in the wood-effect kitchenette, unpacking H's shopping, whilst H herself sulks in the bathroom. Jenny, Kate and Lorna are in one of the bedrooms, sorting out the bedding. Fortunately, Lorna, being a bit of an outdoors type, has brought a sleeping mat with her. She's also brought a stereo and she's put on a Best of Funk CD.

'Forget H. How are *you* feeling?' I ask, boogying along.

Amy looks at me. Her eye make-up is smudged and she's got bloodshot eyes. She crinkles up her nose. 'My head hurts.'

'You fell asleep, you daft moo. You're hungover before you've even started. You need some more,' I say, waggling the bottle.

Amy groans. 'Do I have to?'

I smile and re-pin the veil I've made her. 'Yes. You're the hen, remember.'

'But I thought tonight was supposed to be the quiet night,' she whines. 'I thought we were all just going to chill and then we'd celebrate tomorrow night.'

'I like tequila! It makes me happy,' sings Jenny, in reply, conga-ing out of the bedroom with a huge carrier bag. She's changed in to leggings and trainers.

'So much for that idea,' tuts Amy, shaking her head at me, as I laugh.

Jenny is Amy's mate from work and she seems like a real laugh. Sam, her other work friend, is coming along later.

Jenny pulls salt, lemon and a bottle of tequila out of the bag.

'Slammers, girls?' I call, and Lorna and Kate come through.

H opens the bathroom door. Nice of her to join the party, at last.

'Are you OK?' asks Amy.

'Yes, fine,' she says, quietly. 'I could do with a drink.'

I pull the glasses out of the cupboard and fill them up, but there aren't enough to go round. 'We'll have to go in relay.'

'It's OK. I'll have a beer,' says H. 'Sorry about all this.' For once she sounds genuine.

If it comes down to it, I don't mind sleeping out here, but I'd rather be with Amy.

'I'll toss you for the other bed, if you like?' I smile at H. 'Heads – you're in the bedroom with Amy. Tails – I am.'

'I'll sleep on the sofa,' pipes up Amy, looking anxiously between us.

'No!' I say, flicking a coin. I clap my hand over it. 'It's tails,' I say, showing H. 'Tails for Wales, never fails.'

I learnt that one off my old Dad.

'Settled then,' I smile, but H looks like she's got something stuck in her throat. 'You lot are all right in the other bedroom, aren't you?' I ask, handing out the tequilas to the girls and they nod. Jenny passes round the slices of lemon and the salt pot.

I think this weekend's going to be a complete laugh.

'Right then,' I say, when we're all ready. 'One, two, three . . .' We all slam our glasses down, lick the salt off our hands, down the tequilas and shove the lemons in our mouths, except H, who fiddles with her beer can and looks like she's biting her tongue.

'Shall we go and get something to eat?' she asks.

'Let's go to the Global Village Dining Complex,' I suggest, looking it up in the guide. 'We can take the tequila with us.'

'It's miles away,' says Amy, looking over my shoulder at the map.

'Shall we risk it in the car?' asks Jenny.

'Good idea. I'm sure we'll all fit in to H's.'

H hesitates, then looks at Amy.

'That's OK, isn't it?' asks Amy.

'Fine. Come on then, let's go.'

On the way out, Amy grabs my arm. 'Do you think Jack's all right?'

'Are you missing him?'

She nods and I smile at her. She looks so sweet. 'He's probably missing you too. Come on. I'll look after you, darling, don't you worry.'

Stringer

Jimmy's the first to break the silence that's suddenly descended in the minibus.

'You have *got* to be joking,' he says, staring in disbelief, along with everyone else in the back of the bus, at the Leisure Heaven sign in front of us, eerily lit like the Frankenstein place in Rocky Horror. He looks at Ug imploringly. 'Tell me you've spiked my drinks and none of this is actually real.'

All Ug does is shrug wordlessly and continue to stare at the sign, transfixed.

I think we're all fairly shocked, to tell the truth. When Matt told us he'd used our hard-earned money to book an awesome weekend destination, I doubt that any of us envisaged Leisure Heaven. Personally, I've got nothing against the place. There's tennis, squash, swimming and a host of other activities. Personally, however, doesn't come into it. I can understand why the others are a tad miffed. Exercise and fresh air are hardly intrinsic elements of their lifestyles. Ug removes the plastic breast from his head for the first time this evening. The situation, it seems, is that grave.

'Well, Matt,' he asks, '*is* this for real?'

Matt parks the minibus by the reception lodge and switches off the engine. Delicious silence reigns in the place of panpipes for a few moments. Then Matt turns round and stares straight into Ug's eyes.

'I want you to know, Ug,' he says, his eyes moving on to traverse the other onlooking faces. 'I want you *all* to

189

know: Leisure Heaven is a wonderful place. We have no transport worries. We have no licensing hours to contend with. Out here in the wilderness, there is *nothing* that can interfere with the pure and unadulterated fun that I have planned for us.' He looks back at Ug. 'Do you understand?'

Ug frowns for a moment. 'Sort of,' he says.

'Good,' Matt replies.

Jimmy, however, isn't as simply convinced. 'But it's a dump,' he snaps. 'An anti-fun zone. Everyone knows that. They treat you like sheep the moment you drive through the gate. You spend your whole weekend queuing and the nearest club's about two hours away and there's nowhere to score . . .' Jimmy glances at me. 'You got any gear on you?' he asks.

I tell him, 'No.'

'Why not?'

I reply automatically: 'You know why not.'

He smiles slyly. 'Come *on*,' he says with a sneer. 'Once a player, always a player. You telling me you haven't got so much as one itsybitsy pill on you? Not one spare line? Not one cheeky plug?'

I make a circle with my forefinger and thumb. I can feel myself flushing, angry with him for putting me in this situation and not backing off, but I'm determined not to lose it or let him know that he's succeeded in winding me up. All it will do is make matters worse. 'Zero,' I tell him.

'Will you two just chill out?' Ug says, rearing up at the back. 'I've got a fat bag of grass back here. There's plenty to go round.'

Jimmy turns on him. 'Why didn't you say something before?'

'Because you didn't ask.'

'What else you got?' Jimmy asks.

'That's it,' Ug replies.

Jimmy mutters something and turns back to me. 'Just

dope, then.' His top lip curls. 'And I suppose you're not interested in that either . . .'

I don't even bother to reply.

'Don't kid yourself,' he says. 'Because you're not kidding me. Not for a second. Hey, Ug,' he calls, keeping his eyes on me. 'What d'you reckon? You think Stringer here's going to make it through the weekend without getting back into the good old ways?'

'Leave it out,' Matt interrupts.

Jimmy looks at me, disgusted, for a second, before turning his attention back to Matt and staring him full in the face. This is a stupid move. It's almost as stupid as badgering me about drugs. Matt, apart from myself, is the only sober person here, so when it comes to staring, he's at a distinct advantage. Compared to the rest of them, he *is* Clint Eastwood. Jimmy gives it his best shot, but he only lasts seconds before his eyes are flickering over the others, searching unsuccessfully for support. I blank him big time. The dipshit. Where does he get off hassling me like that? I can't believe Jack's got him tagging along. A case of too much history, I suppose. We've all got people from our pasts we don't let go when we probably should. The trouble is, Jimmy's one of mine and I just can't seem to shake him.

'Come on, guys,' Matt says. 'We'll have fun. Trust me on this one, OK? I've never let you down before, have I?'

'Yeah, sod it,' Jack says, chucking Jimmy a beer and cracking one open himself. He pulls his 'I Went Potty In Lanzarote' hat down low over his brow. 'He's right. Let's just get on with it.'

'Good,' Matt says, getting out. 'I'll go and check us in.'

I turn back to face the front and notice that my fist is clenched. I picture the letters of Jimmy's name tattooed across my knuckles. But then my fingers relax and I don't feel angry any more. Why get angry over something so far back in my past? Why waste my time on someone like him? I glance back at Jimmy and this time all I feel is amazement that I was ever friends with him to begin with.

Matt

Friday, 22.32

Cometh the hour, cometh the man . . .

H

Friday, 23.00

Amy burps loudly and sways in her chair as she points at me. 'You're twelve. I know you are.'

I say nothing. I knew she was coming round to me and I've been dreading it. I'm too sober and I don't want to play her girlie bonding games. Especially with this lot.

'H has slept with twelve blokes!' she announces. 'Same as me and thingy,' she waves in a random direction down the table.

I hate this. And I hate feeling estranged from Amy. I smile vaguely at her at the other end of the table, but inside I feel like she's a million miles away. I know it's her hen weekend, but I thought the whole point about sharing all the secrets of my sexual and emotional history with her was that she's my best friend and that's what best friends do. Because they keep each other's secrets. They don't make them public knowledge. These are her friends, not mine. It's horrible listening to her blurting out all the stories that I thought were ours – and just ours – across the checked plastic tablecloths of Mexican Mecca. But I suppose my rules of information privacy and Amy's don't apply on a hen weekend.

Which is why I don't want to correct her and admit that I've slept with more than twelve people. To be honest, I'm not sure I even want to tell her about it any more: ever.

Susie squeals with hysterical laughter and the others join in as Amy swaps her worst shag story: losing her virginity; and her most filthy: Nathan. I don't join in. I've heard those stories a thousand times. They were better when they were fresh.

'Jack's the best, though,' she slurs. 'He's gor-or-geous.'

I rub my eyes. Jesus I'm tired.

'Oh, oh!' gasps Amy, suddenly, opening her mouth and pointing at me. 'H! H! What about that bloke ... what's his name ... your one, who had a willy like a banana?' She screams and puts her hands to her mouth. 'He was dreadful!' She hiccups loudly. 'H couldn't walk for a week!'

She gets up and does an impression of me walking like Raw Hide and the girls seem to find this hilarious.

I beckon the waitress over. She's dressed in what looks like stained chamois leathers and has corks dangling from her hat. They keep hitting her on the chin.

'Can we have the bill please?' I ask.

Ten seconds later, she dumps it on the table, rudely. It has '*Thanx*' scrawled on it.

Oh dear. It looks like the literate and, I must say, highly educated staff have run out of patience. I wonder why? Could it be that Mexican Mecca's third Michelin star is in danger of being knocked off? Or maybe they just feel we didn't appreciate their house speciality – tortilla à la salmonella. Or maybe Amy and her gang have embarrassed them once too often.

Susie jeers at me. 'No, H. No. More drinks, more drinks,' she yells. 'Take the bill away.' I ignore her and attempt to smile at the waitress in sympathy.

'We've got to get back for Sam,' I explain to a pouting Amy, putting down my Visa card. We'll be here all night if this lot start trying to co-ordinate money. Besides, I'd pay anything to get out of here. All I want to do is go to bed.

Except that, thanks to Susie, I don't have a bed.

Stringer

'So what's the story behind these splendidly lurid red cacks?' Damien asks, walking over to me and taking the knickers which Karen kindly donated from my pocket.

Anything – even this rather dubious exercise – is a welcome distraction from Jimmy's bitching about Leisure Heaven.

'Well?' Damien prompts me.

For the past fifteen minutes, Damien has been engaged in an in-depth analysis of the choice of women's underwear brought along by the members of the stag party. He's sozzled and there seems no end to the amusement he's been able to derive from uncovering the provenance of each garment. For a man who lists the word *moist* amongst his favourite words, this somewhat unreconstructed approach to the dressing habits of the opposite sex comes as no surprise.

I look at Damien's fingers fondling Karen's knickers and for a moment am transported back to the yard at my boarding-house at school, listening in awe as Richard Lewis tells me all about his teenage conquest of Emma Roberts. Panic seizes me for a second as I consider the possibility that Karen's knickers might have a nametag sewn into them also. But Damien's voice dismisses this thought, because all Damien's voice asks me is, 'Whose are they?'

'Marilyn,' I respond, coming out with the first name that springs to mind.

'Description.'

'Blonde, buxom and babe-ish. An actress,' I hurriedly improvise. 'Glam roles.'

'Like Monroe,' Jack comments absent-mindedly.

Hmmm. Strange, that . . .

'So what happened?' Damien asks.

I spin them a yarn with all the necessary ingredients to make them believe I'm telling them the truth. Key words include: foxy, filthy, famous and, of course, multiple orgasm.

'Smart,' Damien comments when I've finished. He looks at the knickers wistfully for a second, before handing them back to me, saying, 'I've always wondered what it would be like to sleep with an actress.'

With Karen's knickers back in the palm of my hand, I can't help feeling a pang of regret. I think back to Karen snorting over my request to borrow them for the weekend. After failing to persuade me that I didn't have to add my name to the ranks of stag-night saddos, she relented and we went through to her bedroom. She opened her knickers drawer and told me that, if I was going to be a sexist jerk, I might as well be a sexist jerk with taste.

It's the next few minutes – as she laid out the pick of the pack on her bed – that stick in my mind the most. I should have been able to approach the situation with an air of normality, an air of amusement – like she did. But it wasn't normal for me. It was extraordinary. It was only afterwards, on my way to meet Jack and the others, that I came to terms with the true significance of the event. A sense of unease gripped me, not over my – admittedly suspect – reaction to witnessing Karen cataloguing her smalls, but deeper than that. I made a wish to make myself feel better. I wished on the never-never that a day would come when being in that situation with Karen would be as normal to me as seeing the sun in the sky. I wished that those knickers in that drawer would be nothing more remarkable than some of my girlfriend's clothes.

Here, now, I wonder how she is, and I hope she's not feeling too blue. I think about Chris perhaps being out at some club in Newcastle with another woman. I wonder what tomorrow will bring and whether Karen will make the decision to change her life for the better.

'Hey, Stringer,' Ug calls out from the window at the front of the apartment. 'Come here and check out the talent.'

I roll my eyes at Matt and then walk over to join our local Neighbourhood Watch officer, Ug.

'Go to it, Horse,' Jack calls over from where he's squatting on the floor drinking beer.

Two minutes later, I'm walking out of Apartment 327 in the French Riviera and along the twenty yards of concrete pathway that leads to Apartment 328.

It's a relief to get some fresh air. Jimmy's bitching aside, matters have been getting fairly out of hand. Jack and Damien have gone all rival on the booze front and Jimmy and Ug instigated a spliffathon the moment they entered the apartment. I admit it: there's a bit of me that wants in. It's all down to Jimmy, getting my brain ticking on the minibus. What if he's right? What if I am only kidding myself? What if there's a part of me that will always want to revert to who I was? And after all, it's only a bit of spliff. It's not like it's anything hard.

I breathe deep and try to shake the itch. I'm exhausted, that's all. My defences are low, the couple of beers I had just now are making me woozy. All this jealousy and anger, looking at Jimmy and Ug and half-wishing I was with them, half-wishing they weren't here at all, it's nonsense. That's what I've got to remember. I'll regret it if I get involved. It would be a waste of the effort of all these months. I know the rules. *No* to *all* drugs. Spliff included. I know myself. If I broke that one cardinal rule, the whole house of cards would collapse. I'd be back in that dark zone, dependent, incapable of concentrating, or relaxing, or enjoying myself without the expensive on board. I'd be locked back into that never-ending chain of night-time trips across London in search of a score off some fuck-up I either don't know or don't care about. I shake my head. I don't *need* it. It's nothing to do with Jimmy and Ug. I can cope with them being here, can't I? I'm strong enough for that?

I reach the woman as she's opening the boot of her red Peugeot 205, bathed in the glow of the night lamp above her apartment door. 'Hi,' I say, cheering myself up with a smile. 'Welcome to Leisure Heaven.'

She looks me up and down and I do the same to her. She's about thirty-five, attractive. Her expression when she speaks is half-suspicious, half-amused. 'You don't work here, do you?' she guesses.

'No,' I admit. 'I am, however, along with a number of my associates' – I turn sideways and indicate our apartment – 'staying over there. I'm here to extend an invitation to yourself and anyone you're with to join us for a drink either now or tomorrow . . .' I give her my best smile. 'Or whenever . . .'

'That's very kind,' she says, pulling her bag out of the boot.

'Do you want a hand with that?'

'No, I'm fine. But thanks anyway.' She hesitates. 'What's your name?'

I consider this for a moment. 'You can call me Welcoming Committee.'

'Well, Welcoming Committee, you can call me Sam. I'm planning on going to the Aqua Spa tomorrow morning. Maybe I'll see you and your friends there.'

'You can count on it.'

She grins and glances over at the twitching curtain in

our apartment. 'I will,' she says, heading off towards her
apartment.

Susie

'Sam!' says Amy, as we crash in to our apartment. Sam's wrapped in blankets and is lying on the sofa, reading a magazine. She breaks out of her cocoon and gives us all a hug, as Amy introduces her to Lorna and Kate.

H is not here. She got nicked driving us back from the food plaza and the nasty Leisure Heaven official made us get out of the car. H was banished to the car park near reception, so she'll be gone for ages. I'm glad. She's being such a spoilsport.

'Sorry, we weren't here. We've been in the . . .' Amy waves her hand at the door and looks through one eye.

'Restaurant,' I finish for her.

'When did you get here, mate?' Jenny asks, grabbing a bottle of wine and opening it.

Sam collapses back down on the sofa. 'About half an hour ago. I was too tired to move, so I helped myself,' she smiles. She's eaten most of H's food and is on her third can of lager. 'I guessed I was probably on the sofa.'

'Whoops,' says Amy, losing her balance and collapsing on the floor.

'You will *never* guess what?' says Sam as Jenny hands out glasses of wine.

'What's that, then?' I ask, propping Amy upright.

'There's a group of boys next door and one of them came over to say hello. I'm telling you, girls, he's an Adonis.'

'Oh goodie!' says Jenny.

'No word of a lie. We have landed on our feet, ladies.

He's just . . . uh . . .' Sam rolls her eyes. 'Amazing. He was totally charming. I told him we'd meet him at the Aqua Spa tomorrow.'

'Tomorrow? Why wait? The night is young,' Amy slurs. 'Go on, Sooze. Go get that man.'

'You want me to check him out for you, do you?'

She nods vigorously. 'Yeah. Go get him. I want to see. He might do a strip for me. I deserve a strip, don't I, girls? I'm getting married, aren't I, and everything?' She hiccups loudly.

'You want him? I'll get him,' I say, brazenly flinging open the door.

I can hear loud music from the next chalet, but the curtains are all drawn. I go to the door and look back. Amy's giggling and peeking round the doorframe. Jenny is above her and Lorna's on the other side with Sam and Kate. They look like a Scooby Doo cartoon and I can't help giggling.

'Go on,' hisses Amy, waving me on.

I hitch up my boobs and turn back. An Adonis, eh? I might be a changed woman, but for Amy I'm back to my old ways tonight.

I knock loudly at the door.

Matt

'Leave it,' I shout.

There's another bang on the door. Jimmy glares at me, still angry from before. 'Why?' he demands, his hand on the doorhandle.

'It's probably the park security. Open the door and we'll have to deal with them. Ignore them and they'll have to go away. We've turned the music down, so they've got no reason to be here now, have they?'

''S'right,' Ug slurs, placing a restraining hand on Jimmy's shoulder. 'Just simmer. They'll get bored.'

Jimmy glowers at me, but releases the handle. Damien gets up from the sofa and walks unsteadily over to the ghetto blaster he brought down with him. He turns the music down a notch further and the knocking at the door stops. In its place, the sound of Billy vomiting reaches us from the bathroom.

'Jesus,' Stringer says with a grimace. 'He's like a drain. When's he going to stop?'

'Don't look at me,' Jack says, taking a slug of Smirnoff Black. 'I'm only his brother.'

'Runs in the family,' Damien teases, sitting down on the floor and breaking out a pack of cards. 'Genetic lightweights, the lot of you . . .' He shuffles the cards. 'Five-card stud,' he announces. 'Who's in?'

Stringer shakes his head. He looks like a kid, all weary and determined, not wanting to embarrass himself by going to bed before the adults. I catch my reflection in the mirror and realize he's not the only one. My face is

203

drained. I'm going to be looking like the Grim Reaper by the time I track H down tomorrow. I glance at Jack, who's joined Damien. I wish he hadn't told the others about what happened between me and H and I hope to God no one goes gobbing off about it in front of her. That'll be me finished.

Stringer

'Right, boys,' Damien, now practically cross-eyed with drink but showing no signs of relenting, slurs, 'time to up the stakes.'

How high? I wonder. Liver failure? The way he and Jack have been going for it, that seems the likeliest result from here on in.

'Twot?' Jack enquires.

Meaning, I think, *to what*.

'Naked,' Damien declares. 'Loser strips. Outside streak. Past the apartment next door. And the one after that. And that. Then back. Assuming we don't lock the door, eh?'

'You're on,' Ug grunts.

I say, 'Forget it.' Apart from having absolutely no intention of dropping my trousers in front of anyone, I'm too exhausted to keep my eyes open. 'I'm going to bed.'

'Come on, Stringer,' Damien implores. 'The night's still young . . .'

I look round at the empty cans and bottles and snack packets and pasty faces. Then I look back at Damien. 'No, it's not. It's old and wrinkled and in need of some beauty sleep.'

And with that, I walk next door and collapse on to the bed next to Matt's in the bedroom we bagged earlier. A few minutes later, I hear Matt come in and crash as well. We're both too shattered even to say goodnight.

H

I get up from my patch of scratchy carpet and walk to the window. I have no idea how Sam is able to sleep. Let alone snore as loudly as she's doing with next door making such a racket.

I pull the curtain back, wishing I had a gun. The door of the next chalet is open and some bloke runs stark naked into the night. He's got what look like knickers on his head.

I recoil from the window and shuffle in to the bathroom to stare at myself in the mirror.

I can't even escape to the car.

The bastards have confiscated my car.

I finger the bags under my eyes in despair. I should take solace really. I've had the worst night of my life, more or less. It can't get any worse.

The door behind me is flung open and I turn round. Amy stands in it in her bra and knickers, her face deathly pale.

'Are you all right?' I ask.

She nods, but she looks rough as hell. 'Sorry about the car thing.'

I smile at her. She looks so vulnerable. 'It doesn't matter.'

She stumbles towards me. 'No, I know you're cross,' she slurs, 'but this is all great and you're my best mate and I love you . . .'

But she can't finish. Because what comes out of her

mouth next lands all down the front of my (new) Calvin Klein pajamas.

I suppose it's the thought that counts.

Susie

Saturday, 11.30

Ohhhhhhh . . . my . . . head.

Susie

Saturday, 11.45

'Uuuuuuuuuuuuuuungh?' I can't open my eyes. I extend
an arm and pat the hard single mattress next to me.

'. . . .Amy . . . ?'

There's no response and my arm falls like a dead
weight as I groan into the pillow.

I slowly turn my head through one hundred and eighty
painful degrees and crank open one eyelid. I'm alone. I
open my other eye and gaze sightlessly at the space
where Amy should be, whilst I attempt to prise my
tongue away from the roof of my mouth.

The curtains are slightly open and a shaft of dusty
sunlight fills the tiny bedroom. The double radiator has
been blasting out hot air all night and the window above
is a wobbling mirage.

Hot. That's what's wrong.

I'm too hot.

I'm a chicken on gas mark ten.

I sit up and swing my legs off the bed and cradle my
fragile head in my hands. I'm wearing a T-shirt (back to
front) and a bra (also back to front with the cups half-way
up my back) and one leg of a pair of tights. The other
unfilled leg dangles withered by my knee, but I don't
care.

Dizzily, I get to my feet and grope along the wall to the
door.

I lunge into the kitchenette, fill up a glass from the tap,
down it, then fill it again.

Sam grunts and raises her head from the sofa. 'Whatcha,' she says.

H is sitting at the table. She's got one arm around Amy's shoulder and is holding a glass of water to her lips.

'Drink it slowly,' she coaxes.

Amy stares up at me, her eyes ringed purple. She's wrapped in a yellow blanket and her face is green. The overall impression is that of a bruise. A shivering bruise.

'Blimey. Looks like we've got a casualty,' I wince. 'Anyone want a cuppa?'

'Please,' grunts Sam and collapses. Amy screws up her face as if she's about to cry.

'Don't worry,' soothes H. 'You'll be OK now.' She strokes Amy's back.

'Come on, Amy. Chin up. Round two, ding-a-ling,' I say, taking the coffee out of the cupboard. 'We've got another twenty-four hours to survive.'

'I don't know how you can be so chirpy,' says H. 'After all that tequila ... I'm surprised you haven't pickled yourself.'

I raise my eyebrows at her. Pinch-lipped fuddy-duddy that she is. If she gets any more anally retentive, I swear, she'll launch herself off her chair.

'If you're referring to last night,' I begin, which she obviously is – the last night she so studiously tried to put a dampener on – '*I* was enjoying myself. This is a hen weekend. We're here to have fun,' I point out, filling up the kettle and noticing my giant bottle of vodka which is now empty. 'Amy had a brilliant time, didn't you, love?'

Amy nods, but H looks at me sternly. 'She was *very* sick last night.'

So it's my fault, is it? Wasn't it Amy herself who started off the drinking games after we'd got no response from Adonis and his mates next door? But I can't be bothered to defend myself. It's far too early in the morning.

'I'm sorry, love. Pukey, were you?'

'All over H,' Amy croaks.

I know it's mean, but I can't help laughing.

Sam raises her head from the sofa. 'I bet you were delighted,' she says to H, glancing at me in mirth.

H looks at Amy. 'It doesn't matter. That's what friends are for,' she says.

I put Amy's coffee in front of her and she smiles at me. 'Get your laughing gear round that, darling. You'll be right as rain in no time and ready for a hair of the dog.'

Amy groans.

'A hair of the dog is the last thing she needs. We're going to the Aqua Spa,' announces H, looking scornfully at the coffee. 'I've booked us in for a couple of massages at twelve o'clock. I think that's the best way to help Amy recover.'

'Oooh. Very posh. Shall we book something, too?' I ask Sam.

'You won't be able to. We've got the last two treatments. You can join the others at the swimming-pool,' says H. 'They've gone to get us some bikes.'

Sam sits up and takes her tea. 'I told that bloke next door we'd all meet up at the Aqua Spa. I think we should go and line up the talent for tonight.'

'I don't want to see anyone,' moans Amy. 'Don't make me.'

'I'll come with you, Sam,' I nod, opening the bread packet and dropping a couple of slices into the toaster.

If H is determined to monopolize Amy this morning, then I might as well hang out with Sam and have a laugh. 'We can all go together.' I smile at H. 'Won't that be nice?'

Matt

Saturday, 12.30

It's well known that a wise general always chooses the ground upon which he'll fight, thereby placing his enemy's forces at an immediate disadvantage and increasing his own chances of victory. He might, for example, were he fighting in a desert, choose the ground around the oasis, thus ensuring water for his own troops, whilst his enemy went without. Then again, were he fighting in the countryside, he might choose the high ground, thereby allowing him to cut down his enemies during their struggle to reach the summit. There are no circumstances, however, under which I can imagine any general, no matter how incompetent, choosing to start his campaign from table thirty-seven of the packed Chick-O-Lix franchise in Leisure Heaven's Global Village.

Now, whilst going some way to explaining why I never chose a military career, my presence here in that exact location is also indicative of my current state of mind. I feel insecure. The ground upon which I must fight for H's heart is not of my own choosing, but rather hers. And it's therefore myself who's at an immediate disadvantage, not her. For the first time since I initiated my strategy to win H, I feel demoralized and engulfed by an air of hopelessness. Today is the day I'll see her again. It could be any second now. I look round, feeling ridiculously on edge.

'You look like shit,' Damien tells me, dejectedly prodding his Spicy South Seas Chick-O-Lix wings around his plate.

'No,' I counter, 'you do.'

'You look so shit that if another piece of shit saw you it would go out of its way not to tread on you,' he counters.

'Yeah? Well, you look so shit that if I trod on you, I wouldn't just wipe you off on the kerb, I'd cut my entire leg off for fear of infection.'

'You *both* look like shit,' Stringer points out, thereby bringing our intellectual exchange to a premature close.

And he's right; we do. Not even my CK jeans and Diesel shirt can hide that. I stare at Damien and remember my own face staring back at me from the mirror this morning. Excluding Stringer, we're the finest specimens of manhood our apartment has managed to produce this morning (the rest of the guys still being out for the count). Rough isn't the word. Try dog. Because that's what we are: dog-tired; dog-eared; hangdog; and dog-breathed. I move my eyes to Stringer, mentally preparing a tailored insult for him. But I'm stumped. Because he doesn't look like shit. Not a bit of it. He just looks healthy. Horribly healthy. And it's not even as if I drank any more than he did last night. The sad truth is that I probably drank less. And the even sadder truth is that I went to bed at the same time as him, so I can't use that as an excuse either. Which leaves me with the saddest truth of all: I can no longer afford to take my body and my health for granted.

It's something I've been aware of for a while now. I mean, there was a time, not so long ago, when the alcohol I consumed last night would have had next to no effect on me, either at the time or the morning after. In my prime – the halcyon days of my early twenties – I doubt last night would even have registered as an event. Back then, I could have coped with far more. Ten pints of premium-strength lager and a double portion of Chicken Madras? No problem. A slight headache, perhaps. And maybe a dodgy gut, as well. But nothing as mortal as this.

And then there's the amount of zeds I used to get by on. Crash at four a.m. and up and in to work by nine? Piece of piss. Three nights running? Bring 'em on. And what about the sex? I was better at that, too, wasn't I? Perhaps not in my technique, but in my morning-after service, moist definitely. I still possessed that miraculous youthful trait: the desire for more action outweighed the desire for more sleep. A morning muff-dive, Mrs? The pleasure was all mine. And there was no embarrassment. I knew I was young. I knew that my night and morning faces were barely distinguishable, and that if someone had found me attractive enough to shag me the night before, then they weren't going to go reaching for a bucket to hurl into at the sight of me the following day.

But that was then, and this, sadly (my head continues to throb and my stomach to churn), is now. A thought occurs to me. Was that why H did a runner? Because I looked so rough the morning after? Is that the way it's going to be from here on in? Maybe that's what Jack foresaw. Maybe that's why he's marrying Amy; because soon he'll be too old to find anyone else. And maybe that means it's all the more important that I sort things out with H. I rest my head in my hands and gaze down at my stomach. That'll be next, slumping out over my belt like dough from a baking tin. Then illness. Then . . .

'Jesus,' I say aloud, 'it's come to that.'

'What?' Stringer asks.

'Hypochondria, obesity and death. That's all I've got left to look forward to.'

A waiter in a rooster outfit comes over to our table and gives us a big, fake smile. 'Was that a' – he flaps his wings in time – 'cluck, cluck, clucking good meal, then, guys?' he asks.

'No it fuck, fuck, fucking wasn't,' I snap back.

'I was only—' the waiter starts.

'Yeah, yeah, yeah,' I say, 'doing your job.' I hold up my

hands. 'And you're doing it fine. I'm sorry. Hangover, yeah? You understand?'

He nods his beaky brow and clears our plates.

'Are you all right, mate?' Stringer asks me once the waiter's gone.

'Yeah. It's just . . .' I look at Stringer and open my mouth to speak, but what's the point in discussing the negative effects of the ageing process with someone who – because he takes good care of himself – looks ten years younger than me, rather than the three he actually is? 'Forget it,' I say. 'Like I told the waiter, I'm hungover.'

I scan the room again, searching for H . . .

Stringer

I feel like one of those characters in a fifties sci-fi flick, who's cottoned on that their hitherto stalwart companion has altered in a subtle yet significant way, thereby raising the question of whether they are indeed themselves at all. Standing against a black-and-white studio backdrop, I hear my thoughts coming out in a cheesy voiceover, saying: *Matt doesn't normally snap at the Chick-O-Lix waiter like that . . .*

This Matt – the one sitting opposite me, looking beaten and drawn – isn't the Matt I've grown to know and love. *That* Matt – the pre-Roswell Incident Matt – doesn't snap at anyone, let alone someone unfortunate enough to be making their living from dressing up as a life-size pullet. Laugh at them, certainly, but not snap, never that. I watch him look nervously about for what must be the fiftieth time since we sat down. It occurs to me that if I were a customs official I'd check his bag.

I ask him again, 'Are you all right?' But this time he doesn't get as far as formulating a reply. He simply takes a swig of his strawberry-flavoured Chick-O-Thick-O-Lick-O-Shake, and stares into his cup.

I turn to Damien instead.

'Tell me,' I say. 'How does it feel?' What's happening to him and Jackie all seems so alien. It's the whole confirmation of sex and what it can lead to. It's everything I can only imagine, multiplied by a million. He looks at me blankly, smoothing down his hair. 'Eight

216

weeks to go,' I prompt, 'before we'll have to start calling you Dad.'

'Oh, that.' He looks between us. 'Freaky, you know . . .' I shake my head, because I don't know. I don't even come close. 'It's like . . . I don't know . . . you know when you leave home for the first time and you move in to wherever it is you're moving in to?'

Matt continues to stare into his shake cup and I say, 'Yes.'

'And you're scared, because you know it's going to involve change,' Damien continues, 'but at the same time you're really excited, because you know that whatever happens now happens because you've made it happen . . .'

'Like you're taking responsibility,' I say.

'Yeah. Well, it's a bit like that. I mean, when he's born – I say it's a he, but we don't know, because of the way *it* was positioned when we had the ultrasound done – when he's born, he's going to change everything, isn't he? Me and Jackie will be the same people all right, only at the same time we won't, because it won't be us we're looking out for, but him as well.' He takes a mouthful of his Coke. 'I mean, we won't be able to go out on the lash or anything like that, because we're going to have to be at home all the time. Like this weekend. If this was going on two months down the line, then I doubt I'd be able to come.' He sighs and then smiles. 'I don't know. Some of it's good and some of it's scary. We'll see. It'll work itself out.'

'I think you're lucky,' Matt says, speaking for the first time since the pullet-bashing episode.

'Really?' Damien asks.

'Really.' Matt smiles. 'I think the good stuff way outweighs the scary.' He looks up and there's something longing about his expression. 'You're having a child with the woman you love. I don't think there's anything that can compare with that. And certainly not' – he lights a cigarette and waves expansively – 'any of this. Anyone can have this. Anyone can get wasted with a bunch of mates. It's the easiest thing in the world. What you've got, though . . . that's different. That's what most people would kill for. You've moved on and that's what we all want to do in the end: move on and see what comes next.'

'Even you?' Damien quizzes.

'Yeah,' Matt confirms, 'even me.'

Damien gazes across the room for a few seconds, before asking, 'What about you, then? Anything new going on?'

'Not really,' Matt says.

'H?'

'What's this?' I ask, catching the discomfort in Matt's face.

Matt turns to me. 'You don't know?' he queries. 'I thought everyone knew. I thought the Jack Rossiter In-flight Information Service had seen to that in the minibus last night.' He nods to himself in understanding. 'Oh, yeah . . . you were asleep.'

Damien supplies me with the finer details. 'They did it.'

My mind goes back to the test lunch. I see them driving off in Matt's Spitfire into the rain again. 'No surprise there, then,' I say.

'What?' Matt asks.

'Well, you two were getting on pretty well, weren't you?'

He shrugs. 'No more than you and Susie . . .'

'Who's Susie?' Damien asks, scanning my face.

'Another of Amy's mates,' I tell him, 'but before you go getting any ideas about Jack and Amy running a match-making service, forget it. Susie's a friend.'

'So says you,' Matt snipes with a grin.

I smile back; it's good to see him getting back on form. 'It's the truth.'

'Looks like it's back to you, then, Matt,' Damien says. 'So, leaving the issue of you and H shagging aside, *is* there anything serious going on?'

I'm expecting a standard Matt Davies answer at this point, something like: *No, nothing serious. It just happened and now we've both moved on.* It doesn't come. What comes in its place is: 'I want to make something of it. This time.' He looks between us. 'Seriously,' he says. 'I really do.'

And he does. You can tell from simply looking at him.

Saying that I need the loo, I tell them I'll meet them over at the Aqua Spa once they've finished their drinks. I offer Matt some cash for my food, but he waves it aside.

'Forget it,' he says. 'It's on me.'

Outside, I collect my bike from the railing. The rest of Leisure Heaven's inhabitants – our apartment, naturally, excluded – are up and in force, walking, running and cycling past in tracksuits and trainers. My reservations about Jimmy's judgement, humanity, etc., apart, I do admit that he has a point about this place: it is a bit of a dump. From the moment I got up this morning to ditch the minibus in the car park and hire a bicycle, it's been one queue after another. That's not why I'm in a hurry to get to the Aqua Spa, though. It's simply that I don't want to have to go through my usual rigmarole of changing behind a strictly wrapped towel in front of the other blokes, because they'd only think it – and, by definition, I – was weird.

After I've cycled there and got changed, I'm more than ready for some serious R&R. I go for a quick dip in the cold plunge pool simply to get my circulation going. Then, yearning for a bit of what Susie called 'Me Time', and not wanting to bump into the girl from outside the apartment last night without the others being here, I sneak off to the sanctuary of the steam room.

Once there, I sit myself down on the lowest shelf with a towel on my head to reduce some of the effect of the all-enveloping menthol vapours. I hold my hand in front of my face and then move it away. There's such a fog of steam in here that with my arm fully stretched, I can't see my hand at all. I'm the only person in here and I sit still, concentrating on keeping my breathing loud and regular, something I learned at a yoga class down at the gym. Listening to the *tsss-tsss* of the steam machine, I feel myself drifting into deep relaxation.

H

Saturday, 13.05

'Feel better?'

Amy nods and adjusts the strap of her swimming costume. 'Thanks for that. It was wonderful. I feel vaguely human again.'

Wonderful is not how I would describe our joint pummelling on the ex-hospital beds in the Health Haven. Nor human. Tracy's non-stop banter, extolling the virtues of her workplace, was as relaxing as giving birth.

I follow Amy through the plastic abattoir doors in to the Aqua Spa, past the sauna and steam rooms. The whole place smells of sweat and eucalyptus and I can almost feel the verruca scabs crunching beneath my feet. A piped recording of Richard Clayderman's greatest hits seeps through the soggy atmosphere and beyond the gaudy fake-plaster fountain there are steps leading down to a pool fizzing with chlorine. Everywhere, there are sweaty fat women and tattooed men oozing body odour, along with an assortment of skidding, screeching children. Through the foggy, dripping windows, I can see Sam and Susie running out of the outside sauna and tipping buckets of icy water over each other, but Amy has her hand on my shoulder and she's lifting up one foot to remove a soggy bit of tissue paper, so she doesn't see them.

'Shall we find the others?' she asks, standing again.

'Not just yet,' I say, diverting her attention before she sees them and quickly opening the door to the steam room. 'Let's have a gossip, just you and me. I haven't seen you all week.'

Inside, to my relief, I can only make out one bloke, sitting hunched forward with a towel on his head. He's snorting loudly and sounds as if he's about to have a coronary. But just the one weirdo is a bonus, I suppose. This is about as private as Leisure Heaven's going to get.

Amy slides on to the plastic shelf and breathes in.

'This is nice,' she sighs, flopping backwards and stretching out.

If this is the only chance I'm going to get to have Amy on her own, I've got to speak now, before the others find us.

'Amy?' I begin.

'Hmmm?'

'There's something I want to tell you.'

She knows me well enough to be alerted by my tone. 'What?' she asks. Despite the steam, I know her eyes have sprung open.

'It's about last week.' I bite my lip. I don't know why I'm feeling so nervous, telling her, but I am finally about to confess. 'I've been trying to tell you . . .'

Amy sits up. 'What?'

I nod. 'I've met someone.'

'Is it Matt?' she gasps, grabbing my arm. 'I had a feeling about that night . . .'

'No!' I snap, exasperated, shaking her off and pulling up my legs to hug my knees. 'Just forget Matt, will you? No, this is someone real. Someone really special.'

'Who? Where?'

I grin at her. 'Last week. In Paris. You know that guy I told you about . . . Laurent?'

'The old one?'

'He's not old. He's only thirty-nine. We sort of, got it together . . . Big time.'

Stringer

Saturday, 13.07

What the hell is going on?

What the hell are Amy and H doing here?

And who the hell is *Laurent*?

I've got to find Matt.

Now!

H

Saturday, 13.07

We're interrupted by the weirdo with the towel on his head. He makes a strangled grunting sound and lurches past us as if he's about to spew up all over the mock-Grecian tiles.

'Good riddance,' I mutter as he flings open the door and hurries away.

'Nice bod, though,' says Amy, thoughtfully.

'Not a patch on Laurent's,' I counter. I'm glad we're alone at last. It means I can give her all the juicy details. 'Oh, Amy. I'm telling you, he was the sexiest man I've ever met. I mean, the best . . .'

'Well, come off it,' Amy interrupts. 'No offence, H, but you must have been gagging for it. It's been ages since you had a good seeing to. Any old sex was bound to feel amazing.'

'Amy,' I plead, wishing that she'd take me seriously. 'This is different.'

I sigh, wiping the sweat on my leg. 'From the moment I arrived in Paris and I saw him, I knew something was going to happen. I've spent so long thinking about him and I'd convinced myself it was stupid, since we have to work together. But on the first night he took me out to supper to talk through his ideas and our eyes kept meeting. It was so romantic.'

I gaze into the steam remembering the small, smoky restaurant with the jazz pianist, the endless carafes of red wine in the candlelight, whilst the rain softly pattered against the window of our private alcove . . .

'So he wined you and dined you? What's so special about that?' Amy doesn't sound convinced.

'He's . . . I don't know . . . a real man. He's established and successful and likes wonderful things. And he's interesting too. He travels all over the place and he's really passionate,' I ponder, remembering how we stayed up in my hotel room, eating room-service picnics and talking until dawn. 'It was just as if everything . . . I don't know . . . we gelled.'

'Well, he certainly sounds like a charmer.'

I'm silent for a moment, then I look at Amy through the steam. 'I think I'm in love.'

Amy takes a deep breath and holds it as she stares at me.

'Only I don't know what to do,' I babble on. 'I can't stop thinking about him and I thought he'd call, but there's no reception in this . . .' I'm about to slag off Leisure Heaven, but I stop myself just in time, '. . . place. I just want to hear his voice. To know that everything's OK.'

Amy breathes out suddenly. 'Oh, H. Are you sure you know what you're doing? I mean . . . how would it work? You've got a life here.'

'But surely we can get round that? Surely if it's meant to be, it's meant to be? You're always saying that.'

'I know, but a long-distance relationship? Is that really what you want?'

'Nothing's perfect.'

'But how do you know he's going to commit? I mean if he's thirty-nine and is tripping off round the world every two seconds . . .' She reaches out and touches my arm. 'I know you. It'll drive you nuts.'

'It's not like that,' I sulk, wishing she'd stop asking questions and say something positive.

But I don't know what it *is* like. That's the problem.

'I'll know what to do when I talk to him,' I say.

Amy sighs again. 'Just be careful. That's all.' She's silent for a moment. 'Still, I'm glad you've got Gav out of your system.'

'Yes. Sod him.'

'It's such a shame about Matt, though,' she muses.

'Why do you keep banging on about Matt?' I mutter. 'I told you. Nothing happened. Nothing will ever happen between us. I don't even fancy him.'

'OK, OK,' she says. 'It just would have been so nice.'

I thought I'd feel relieved having told Amy, but now I feel more jangled than ever, especially since I've carried on lying about what happened with Matt. It's just that if she knew about me and Matt, she wouldn't understand about me and Laurent.

But she doesn't understand about me and Laurent anyway.

Why does everything have to be so safe with her? Just because Laurent's not like Jack, she can't see the potential. But I can. I could have stayed in Paris for ever. I hug my legs tighter and shrug up my shoulders. I think Amy senses my disappointment because she slaps me on the back.

'But hey. Good on you, girl! At least you've got your quota of sex in. Judging from all the talent I've seen so far here, it'd be a disaster if you'd been holding out for this weekend,' she laughs.

Stringer

Saturday, 13.12

Where *are* they?

The male changing-rooms are empty apart from a couple of middle-aged, tattooed men getting dressed. There's no Matt and there's no Damien to be seen. I check my watch. They must be here by now . . . but where?

'Who d'you think you are then, mate?' the larger of the two tattooed men asks me in a gruff voice. 'Lawrence of bleedin' Arabia?'

I stare at him vacantly for a couple of seconds, then click: the towel is still wrapped round my head. I rip it off. 'Two men,' I gasp.

'What?' the man asks.

'Two men. About your height. I'm looking for two men. I need them. Now.'

The man takes a step forward. 'Now, look here, you bloody pervert,' he warns.

But I don't hear what he says next, because I'm running through to the showers. They're empty as well. I stop and try to catch my breath. I attempt to calm myself down. Don't panic. Panicking will only make matters worse. Think matters through and everything will become apparent. A logical and sensible solution to this predicament will present itself.

I try following my advice. Amy and H cannot be here, because Amy and H are meant to be somewhere else on Amy's hen weekend. Clear. However, Amy and H *are* here, which means that Amy's hen weekend is taking place here. This can only mean there's been a cock-up.

There's been a gargantuan and appalling cock-up. Then I remember what the girls were talking about in the steam room, and realize that the cock-up doesn't stop there. Oh, no, that's merely the start. In addition to Matt and H somehow turning the law of probability on its head by booking us all in to the same location, H has fallen for a Frenchman, and couldn't care less about Matt, and Matt does care about her, and if they see each other, then they'll both think they're hallucinating, and since H is seeing this French bloke then, once she realizes that this isn't an hallucination but is stark reality, then the last person she'll want to see is Matt, but because Matt's thinks she's so great, he'll be really excited that she's here, and if that happens, then . . .

Forget it. Panicking was less confusing.

I run back through the changing rooms and past the two men who shout something obscene after me. Then I dash out into the spa.

At this juncture, I can only be certain of two matters. I must find Matt, and I must then seek psychiatric help.

Matt

'Do you want the sports section?' Damien asks.

We're at the complimentary newspaper and magazine stand in the Aqua Spa's conservatory. As far as improving our personal fitness goes, not a lot's happened so far. Since getting here about five minutes ago, all we've managed to achieve is bagging ourselves a couple of loungers for crashing out on whilst we read the papers – and one for Stringer as well, assuming he's not going to spend his morning here doing press-ups or whatever it is he's in to. Looking around, I have to admit that, if you turn a blind eye to the sweaty bellies and pasty thighs of the majority of the clientele, this isn't a bad place to spend the morning chilling out. It's warm and relatively peaceful. And leagues better, no doubt, than the bombsite formerly known as Apartment 327. I wonder if the other guys have surfaced yet. It seems unlikely – unless, of course, a passing team of paramedics equipped with full-on resuscitation gear happened to chance by since we left the scene.

Chilling out, though, it has to be said, isn't a state of mind I'm necessarily capable of getting in to right now. Freaking out, yeah, the same as I've been doing more or less consistently since I awoke this morning. Freaking out I can do with the best of them. On the bike ride over here, I tried thinking myself straight on this one, but it didn't work. Short of bribing one of the entrance-gate staff into telling me where H and the girls are staying, I'm just going to have to keep my ears and eyes open and wait for opportunity to knock. They're here somewhere, that's for sure. And it's only a matter of time till I find out where.

'I said, do you—' Damien repeats, waving the sports section in front of my face.

'Yeah, yeah,' I tell him, 'I heard you the first time.' I prod my stomach with my finger and, picking up the food and living section, mumble, 'The way I'm feeling right now, I think this one's more up my street.' I tuck my drawstring into my swim shorts and turn to walk back to the loungers, when:

'Thaghullsaargheer.'

I stare into Stringer's face. He's flushed and sweating like he's just pulled his head out of an oven. 'Excuse me?' I say.

He grips me by the shoulders and shoves his face up close to mine. 'Thaghullsaargheer,' he repeats, sending a fine spray of spittle on to my cheek.

I push him back and glance at Damien. He looks as bemused as I feel. 'That's charming,' I say to Stringer, 'but do you mind telling me what it's meant to mean?'

He rolls his eyes and nods at me and takes a series of deep breaths. 'They're here,' he finally pants. 'Girls.'

'Christ, Stringer,' Damien says, 'get a grip, mate.' He shrugs apologetically at a sixtysomething woman leafing through a magazine next to us. 'You'll have to forgive him,' he tells her. 'He doesn't get to see naked flesh very often.'

The woman frowns in disapproval before walking swiftly away. I turn back to Stringer and ask, 'Come on, mate, what is it?' But even as I ask, I become aware of a tiny alarm bell ringing at the back of my mind. '*What* girls?' I ask.

But he doesn't need to say any more, because at that exact moment, someone behind us squeals.

Susie

'Oi! That's him. That's the Adonis. Hello! Cooey!' Sam waves her hand furiously and I follow her gaze to a group of boys, who all turn round at once.

My mouth drops open.

Because that's not her Adonis – the one she's been harping on about in the sauna. That's *my* Adonis.

Stringer.

I push Sam out of the way and clamber out of the jacuzzi and clutch at my towel as I race in to the conservatory. Stringer's face is bright red. He's standing next to Matt and some other guy, looking absolutely gobsmacked, but I'm so shocked and happy to see him, that before I know it, I've flung my arms around him in a big embrace. His body feels strong and muscly and I grab on so tight that my towel drops to the floor.

'This is Stringer!' I gush, as Sam arrives. She looks really confused. I pick up my towel in a fluster. 'I can't believe it!' I laugh, kissing Matt. 'What are *you* doing here?'

I hear H's strangled gasp before I turn to see her and Amy. They're both at the door of the steam room.

'Look who's here!' I shout. 'Isn't it an amazing coincidence?'

H

Saturday, 13.17

I can't move. I feel like I'm under water. I look at Amy, but she rushes away from me. I stare, aghast, because right there in front of me are Matt, Stringer and Damien, along with Sam and Susie, who is gushing for the Commonwealth.

'We just saw them!' she prattles to Amy. 'They must all be here. All the boys. And all us girls together at the same place. Isn't that amazing? That's just what you wanted all along . . .'

Stringer looks like a scared guppy fish, his mouth opening and closing. Matt shakes his head at Damien who roars with laughter, looking at Amy.

'This can't be serious!' he chuckles.

I put my hands on my hips and stare at Matt, but his eyes scoot away from mine.

And that's when it clicks. That's when I know that there's something very, very wrong here.

This isn't a coincidence. There's no way.

'Amy?' says Matt, looking aghast. 'Do you mind telling me what's going on?'

'I could ask the same of you!' I say, marching over and glaring at Matt. 'How *dare* you!' I storm.

'How dare I *what*?' he counters, immediately defensive.

'Don't play the innocent. You know exactly what.'

Matt holds up his palm and looks around the group. 'Well, obviously I don't. And since I haven't got a clue what you're talking about, why don't you spell it out for me?'

'Fine,' I snap, starting to count on my fingers. 'One: there is no way that this is a coincidence. Two: which means that you've deliberately set out to sabotage our weekend. Three—'

'Hang on a second,' interrupts Matt. 'We've had this booked for ages.'

'Bollocks you have!'

'Calm down,' says Amy. 'It doesn't matter.'

'Doesn't matter! Doesn't matter! This is a girls' weekend. I'm not having it ruined by this lot.'

'You're the ones in the wrong place,' says Matt. 'We were here first.'

'I don't believe this!' I rant. 'And I don't believe you!' I narrow my eyes at Matt, but this time he holds my gaze.

'There's no need to get so upset,' says Susie. 'I think it's funny. We can all have a laugh together.'

'Is Jack all right?' asks Amy.

I turn on her. 'It was you, wasn't it? You told Jack where we were going?'

Amy looks mortified. 'I didn't,' she blunders. 'I didn't, H. Honestly.'

Matt comes forward and touches my arm, but I shake him off.

'Listen,' he says, totally calmly. 'There's obviously been some kind of mistake.'

'Mistake? You bet your arse there's been a mistake.'

'Let's just all calm down and work this out,' he continues, glancing at my swimming costume.

'There is nothing to work out,' I hiss through clenched teeth, backing away from him. 'You're a liar.'

Matt puts his hands up defensively. 'That's really out of order, H. This isn't fair.'

'Where's Jack?' bleats Amy.

'Oh, for fuck's sake,' I blaze, before turning on my heel and storming out.

Matt

Saturday, 13.20

As I watch H marching towards the changing rooms, the same thought occurs to me as when I saw her walking out into the rain after the test lunch round at Stringer's work: she's magnificent. *Everything* about her is magnificent, from the way she tosses her hair to the way her bum cheeks flex inside her swimsuit to the shape of her bare legs beneath. And I want her. I want her even more now (if it's possible) than I did in the minutes of silence I sweated through after she left my house. It's the sheer perfection of her. Even her anger. It's so *out there*. Nothing weak. Nothing half-hearted. Pure spirit. *Magnificent . . . the stuff of dreams . . .*

But then it hits me. Hard. Like a punch in the gut.

This *isn't* a dream. It's not even a nightmare, because if this *were* a nightmare, then this would be the precise moment when my brain would trigger whatever defence mechanism it is that's responsible for snapping me back in to consciousness and the safety of my bed. I'd sit up – sweating and panicked – but otherwise unharmed. And, gradually, I'd relax, realizing that I wasn't actually in peril at all, but had merely been the victim of my own imagination, and perhaps a wedge too much cheese before bedtime. But there's no easy escape clause here. Because this is infinitely worse than a nightmare. Because this is reality.

And Amy drags me firmly back into it. 'H!' she shouts. 'Don't—'

I watch Susie placing a restraining hand on Amy's

wrist, preventing her from giving chase. 'Leave her,' Susie says softly. 'Give her a few minutes on her own.'

Amy looks horrified. 'But—'

'Just a few minutes,' Susie stresses. 'She'll calm down. You mark my words.'

I feel nauseated. Head-spinningly sick. This isn't how it was meant to be. What's gone wrong? Sure, I expected surprise. I was counting on it. I wanted H to have that thump in her heart, the same as I did when I saw her just now when Susie called to her over by the steam room. I wanted her to feel that rush of blood on first sight. And anger. Yes, even a little anger. But only temporarily. Only until she realized that it was *me* she was angry with. Only until she realized that because it was me, it didn't matter, because I'd never have meant her any harm. And then . . . then I thought she'd laugh and throw herself in to it, just like I would have done if our roles had been reversed. Because that's what this is about, isn't it? Her being my missing half? Her being the one person I'll always be able to laugh with?

I feel the eyes of the assembled group slowly focusing in on me – like a jury turning to deliver a guilty verdict. Susie's still prattling on, chilling Amy out. Think, Davies! Think! Think strategy. It's still not too late. So H is angry with you. She's angry with you because she thinks your motivation for doing this is part of some lads' stunt to trash the hen weekend she's so carefully organized. This leaves you with two courses of action. Firstly, you can own up to the whole thing and tell her why you really did it. If you do that, then, yeah, she might forgive you, but on the other hand, she might be so pissed off that she'll never want to speak to you again. Add to that the possibility that she might tell the boys that they've been taken for a ride as well, and it's a pretty dud proposition. So take the second course of action: stick to the lie about it being a coincidence. Glue tight. Then maybe there's a chance that she'll believe you and let this weekend go back to what I planned it as – a reunion and not a divorce. But believe in it. Believe in it to your core, or no one's going to believe in you. Now's your chance. Method acting. Enter Matt 'Brando' Davies, the finest actor of his generation. I concentrate on this metamorphosis and look around the group once more. And this time, the looks on their faces are no longer ones of condemnation. They're looking to me to sort this one out. And that's exactly what I'm going to do.

'Matt,' Amy's saying. 'Matt. Tell me. What the hell's going on?'

'Christ knows,' I lie, 'I'm as confused as you.'

A rapid group Q&A ensues:

Amy: Where's Jack?

Me: Back at the apartment. Still in bed.

Amy: Why's he in bed? Is he all right?

Me: He's fine. Just hungover.

Sam: I told you, Susie. Didn't I tell you?

Susie: You sure did.

Amy: You sure did what?

Sam: The geezer from last night who said he'd meet us here. The Adon . . . the Welcoming Committee. This is him.

Amy: Eh?

Susie: Stringer. It was Stringer who Sam met last night.

Amy: You mean you're . . . What number apartment are you in?

Stringer: Three two seven. The one next to yours, it appears . . .

Susie: What time did you all get here?

Stringer: Late last night. We broke down.

Damien: Who are you?

Stringer: This is Susie.

Damien: The one Matt mentioned in Chick-O-Lix?

Stringer: I don't know what you're talking about.

Sam: Who are you?

Amy: I want to see Jack.

Me: Do you want me to come with you?

Amy: Yes.

Me: Now?

Amy: Yes. But . . .

Stringer: Matt?

Me: Hold on a minute, mate.

Amy: . . . I need to check on H. Can you give me a few minutes?

Me: Sure. I'll meet you outside in five.

Amy: Will you two be OK?

Susie: Of course we will. We've got Stringer and Damien to keep us entertained.

Me: Did you want something, Stringer?

Stringer: Yes, I need a word.

Me: What about?

Stringer: In private. I need a word in private.

Me: Can't it wait?

Stringer: No. There's something I've got to tell you, something about H . . .

Amy: Come on, Matt. Are you going to go and get changed?

Me: Yeah, I'm on my way.

And then I'm out of there, running for the changing rooms. Whatever it is that Stringer's got to tell me about H is going to have to wait, because right now my own concerns about her far outweigh his.

Susie

Saturday, 13.30

Why didn't I get a new bikini? That's what I want to
know. I feel so revolting all of a sudden. My hair is
plastered to my skull in rats' tails, perfectly showing off
my roots. And worse, I'm sitting on my oldest, nastiest,
bedroom mop-up towel, but it's still not stopping my
thighs bulging between the slatted bench in the sauna.
Damien pours more water on the rocks, but I'm boiling
up already. Stringer is opposite and I'm trying not to
notice the beads of sweat trickling down between the
muscles of his chest. I'm going to faint if I don't stop
holding my tummy in.

Sam rakes her fingers through her hair and continues
laughing. She's been a complete pain since we got in here.

'So tell me, Stringer, are all your muscles that big?' she
flirts.

How obvious can she be? Why can't she shut up and
leave him alone?

Tart.

'Come on,' she says, reaching out to grab his biceps.
'Flex them.'

Stringer removes her hand and shakes his head. 'No,
I'd rather not,' he says politely, but very firmly.

Sam recoils from him, obviously annoyed that he's not
flirting.

'Suit yourself, touchy,' she shrugs.

Stringer glances up at me and I smile. It's supposed to
be sympathetic, but inside I just feel triumphant. I sit on
my hands and swing my feet.

'Haven't you got a sunbed booked, Sam?' I ask.

'Oh shit, yes,' she says and gets up to leave. She straightens out her bikini and gives both me and Stringer an exasperated look, before saying, 'I'll see you later.'

'Was I rude?' asks Stringer after she's closed the door behind her.

'She deserved it,' I laugh. 'Take no notice of her.'

'Isn't she your type?' asks Damien.

'No. I don't really have a type, so to speak.'

'So, what about you?' I say, turning to Damien and keeping the conversation friendly. I'm not brave enough to ask Stringer about his choice of women. Especially in this bikini.

'She's pregnant.'

'Ahhh,' I smile.

'Two months to go,' he says wearily.

'So are you all set?'

'No. Of course I'm not. I'll have to give up my life of hanging round saunas with beautiful women of a Saturday afternoon. It's a complete disaster.'

Stringer and I laugh.

Bless him.

'I should go and call her, actually,' he says, getting up. 'I can't wait to tell her about you lot being here. Make her really jealous.'

'Jealous of us? She should feel sorry for us!' I tease.

Damien rubs his hairy thighs and gets up and Stringer and I are alone. There's a pause.

'So,' I say. Stupidly. Pointlessly.

'So?'

'How have you been?' I ask.

'Oh you know . . . busy.'

'Hmm. Me too.'

'Sorry about the meeting up for a drink thing,' he says. I wave my hand. 'Oh forget it. It doesn't matter.'

The door opens and three rowdy blokes come in.

Stringer pulls a face at me. 'Shall we?' he asks, pointing to the door.

When we get outside, the pool is heaving with bodies. Stringer shivers.

'I've got to get out of here,' he says.

'Good idea. Shall we go somewhere? I mean, I don't want to go back to the apartment.'

'Me neither.'

'Well, what should we do?' I blather. 'I mean, are we supposed to be all separated now, or what? Only we could go and explore,' I suggest. 'Lie low until everything has calmed down. I don't know what there is to do here, but it doesn't have to be too crazy. We could go for a ride on the bikes and explore or something . . . ?'

Stringer laughs to shut me up. 'That's seems like a safe plan,' he says.

Safe for whom, I wonder?

H

Saturday, 13.40

Be in. Please be in, I pray, holding the receiver for the third time. I punch in Laurent's number, my pound coins at the ready, but there's still no reply.

I fall out of the phone box and slump on to the concrete wall. I can't believe he's not there. All I want is to hear his voice. It's the only thing that's going to make all this better. I feel so sordid having told Amy about him. It's made Paris seem so far away. I don't want those memories soiled by bringing them in to this ghastly nightmare.

I curl up in a ball and rest my head on my arms. I want everything to go away. This weekend. Everyone here. This place. I can't handle it any more. I want my reality back. I want Laurent back. I want to be back in Paris. I want it to be last week again.

Except that I don't want to have slept with Matt.

Why? Why did I sleep with him?

What was I thinking of?

I take a cigarette out of the packet and my hands are shaking. Everything is ruined. Amy is going to be with Jack and I'm going to have to spend the rest of the weekend with Matt.

What does he think? That I'll jump into bed with him again? If I hadn't met Laurent, then I suppose it might not be so bad, just vaguely embarrassing. But as it is, I can't even face looking at him.

'Sorry, you can't smoke here.' I look up and see a green-uniformed Park attendant.

Another one.

'What?' I spit.

'This is the health spa area.'

I take a deep breath and grit my teeth.

'You'll have to go over there,' he says, pointing towards the lake.

That's *it*.

Matt

'Oh, my God . . .'

Amy cups her hands over her face. I pat her on the back and she looks up at me. I take her hand and squeeze it and, together, we look through the doorway into Apartment 327.

On the grounds of self-preservation, *looking* wasn't something I considered a wise move this morning. Consequently, I restricted my vision to the bare necessities needed to navigate my way around the apartment. It was a case of eyes straight ahead. Straight to the bathroom. Straight over Billy. Straight back to the bedroom. Then straight out of the front door.

And looking into the living-room now, I can understand why. It *looks* like a bomb's gone off in there. A random sample of some of the visual information immediately available includes: half-eaten pizza slices, upset ashtrays, Jimmy, spilt beer cans, empty spirit bottles, gnawed Chick-O-Lix bones, and Ug. But worse than any of this is what hits my nostrils. If a bomb *has* gone off in there, then I can only assume that, rather than being packed with TNT, its payload consisted of a combination of offal and dung. I hurriedly add *smell* to my list of non-recommended sensory data and, taking a tip from Amy, hold my nose accordingly.

'Are you sure you still want to go through with this?' I whine. 'Only,' – I briefly scan the room again – 'it's not going to be pretty in there, and I'd fully understand if—'

But John Wayne had nothing on the true grit Amy's currently displaying. 'Just take me to him,' is all she says.

I do as requested.

On our route to the bedroom Jack was meant to be crashing in, we encounter a barely human creature slumped against the corridor wall. It gibbers. It goggles. It grips a coffee mug in its hand. A closer inspection reveals it to be none other than Billy, Jack's previously deceased brother. On seeing us, his hand tremors, and coffee patters down on to the carpet. More remarkable than this Lazarus-like resuscitation, however, is Billy's recovery of the power of speech, a faculty I know for certain that he hasn't utilized since early yesterday evening.

'Amy,' he grunts, 'whu—'

But Amy's now beyond even this sophisticated level of interrogation. Instead, she steps over him and in to Jack's room.

'Baby!' she gasps.

And, as she rushes forward to Jack's bed, this simple description proves a highly accurate assessment of his state of wellbeing. He's unable to support himself and his efforts at sitting fail miserably. His hand–eye co-ordination is similarly impaired, witnessed by his attempt to stroke Amy's face resulting in poking her in the eye. Unlike his sibling, Jack's speech is limited to mumbling. This he does into Amy's ear, as she cuddles his huddled form. I catch a couple of words – 'death' and 'enema' – but these aside, I content myself with slipping out to fix us some coffee.

'How could you?' Amy hisses at me when I return. 'You promised.'

Somewhat harsh, considering. I mean, I hardly force-fed the liquor down Jack's throat last night. Still, I can't avoid the truth that I *am* responsible. For *everything*. After all, it was me and me alone who instigated the train of events that brought us here. And it's therefore – yeah, she's right – me and me alone who must accept responsibility for the passengers.

'It's not as bad as it appears,' I say. I kneel down next to Amy. 'Trust me on this one,' I ask her, putting my hand on her shoulder. 'I've seen him a lot worse. He's got incredible powers of recovery. He *will* be OK.'

'Stop doing that,' she warns me.

'What?'

'Looking so pathetic. It's not fair. How am I meant to be angry with you when you look like that?'

I wasn't even aware I was looking pathetic, but now that I think about it, it's hardly surprising: that *is* how I feel. I'm becoming uncomfortably aware that with every passing minute my chances of patching things up with H are getting slimmer. I notice Amy still looking down at me and, even though the last thing I'm in the mood for is joking around, I pull one of my worst faces for Amy in an attempt to cheer her up. 'Is that better?' I ask.

'Much,' she says, a smile breaking through at long last.

Jack's first coherent sentence is: 'Dumb question, but will one of you tell me how come' – he looks at Amy – 'you're here?' He frowns and kisses her gently on the cheek. 'Not that I'm not glad to see you, you understand . . .'

They talk. I listen. The morning's events are covered. There's a big question mark left on Jack's face at the end of her account of the remarkable coincidence that's led both parties to be here at the same time. In adjacent apartments. Jack makes his opinion on the matter pretty clear.

'I've never heard such a bunch of toilet in my life,' he says, leaning forward and pointing his finger at me. 'This devious little sod . . . or H – or, more likely, the pair of them, considering what they got up to – have cooked this up between them. If this is a coincidence,' he concludes, 'then I'm a Dutchman's uncle, whatever the hell that's meant to be.'

'No, really,' Amy starts to react. Only then something strikes her. Hard. And squarely between the eyes. 'What do you mean, *considering what they got up to*?'

Jack doesn't reply, looks down.

Amy eyeballs me. 'Well?'

I take a deep breath. 'Well . . . we . . . I don't know . . .' I fumble. 'It's not really my place to . . . I mean, if H hasn't already—'

'No, she bloody well hasn't,' Amy fumes.

'It's like this,' I continue. 'We got a cab back from the Blue Rose and we went to my place and . . .'

'They slept together,' Jack states. 'They went back to Matt's and they slept together. It was really good apparently.'

Amy stares at her feet. She blinks. She blinks again. 'I can't believe H hasn't told me. She always . . .'

I clear my throat. 'She probably didn't tell you because . . . Forget it. You saw how she reacted when she saw me. She's not exactly—'

Amy ignores me. 'What about you, Jack?' she asks. 'What's your excuse? Honesty. Remember that? No secrets.'

'Now, hang on a minute,' Jack says, suddenly undergoing exactly the type of miraculous recovery I'd told Amy he was capable of. 'This is nothing to do with me.'

'I asked him not to,' I intervene. 'I didn't know if it was going to go anywhere. Don't blame him. If anyone's at fault, it's me. I should have kept my mouth shut.'

'So where *is* H?' Jack asks.

'I don't know,' Amy says. Her voice is small, shocked. 'She stormed off. I couldn't find her.'

'And what about you?' he asks me. 'You still expect me to believe this is down to chance?'

'It is,' I tell him.

He searches my eyes for a couple of seconds, but I don't flinch. Eventually, he nods his head, not fooled for a second, doing this for Amy's benefit, or mine. I'm not certain which; just grateful.

'Well, stranger things have happened,' he concludes. He gives Amy a hug and tells her, 'Guess you'd better go and find her, then . . . Sort this all out . . .'

Amy nods and walks past without looking at me.

I hear the front door slam.

'Sorry,' I tell Jack. 'I messed up. I messed up bad.'

There's a mischievous twinkle in his eyes. 'Bad', he says, blowing the steam from his coffee and taking a sip, 'doesn't even come close.'

Susie

At the top of the hill, Stringer finally stops. I'm puffed as I catch him up.

'Will this do?' he asks.

To be honest, I don't give a monkeys. All I want to do is sit down.

I nod breathlessly and cock my leg over my bike and follow Stringer as he makes his way into the middle of the grass. Maybe he does the Tour de France every year, because he doesn't even seem to be sweating.

I flop down and catch my breath, lying back on the grass with my arms out. Stringer laughs when I sit up.

'It's nice to be alone at long last. A bit of peace,' I sigh, stretching my legs and looking up to the sky. I can hear the birds above me. There's a view down in to the valley and over the trees, the steam rises from the Aqua Spa, but otherwise you wouldn't be able to tell that we're in Leisure Heaven from up here, not that anyone ever gets up here. It's miles away, but it's perfect. I close one eye against the September sun and squint at Stringer.

He's lying on his side and he picks up a blade of grass and sucks it, his forehead crumpled as he squints against the sun.

And then something happens. Like a penny dropping into a juke box, a memory drops from my head into my tummy and starts to replay.

This is the place in my vision.

This was the place, every time I visualized me and Stringer after the CYL course . . .

248

It's here. I'm living out my vision.

I gulp and sit up. This was the problem place . . . the place where I thought of him and his big . . .

I take a breath and try and calm down.

I can do this. I can relate to Stringer as a non-sexual person, I remind myself. We're friends. And I'm fine with just being friends. We're on a friendly picnic. I chuck him one of the packs of sandwiches we bought from the shop at vast expense.

'Odd, don't you think . . . ?' I begin, conversationally. Stringer looks up at me and although I'm looking at him directly, I can feel his gaze in my knickers.

'Hmm?'

'I've been thinking on the way here. Don't you think H was really out of order back then?'

Stringer shrugs. 'I don't know.'

I fold my arms across me protectively. I *will* make conversation.

'She was so nasty to Matt and he didn't deserve it. I mean, I don't know how all this started, but it's not such a problem. We're all here together and it's nice.'

'Maybe it's a sex thing,' he says.

I shake my head, alarmed at Stringer just mentioning the word 'sex'.

'What do you mean?' I ask, looping a curl behind my ear and trying not to look embarrassed.

But Stringer isn't fazed. He sighs and rubs his hand on the grass. 'I'm not supposed to know this, but they've slept together. I guess *that's* the real problem.'

'H and Matt?'

Stringer nods and scratches his head. 'Jack let slip. It was last week apparently.'

'Never! So . . . what? Matt set this all up, you think?'

'I doubt it. He seemed just as stunned as H.'

'Well I never.'

I'm truly shocked. I can't believe she kept that one

quiet. I think back to the bridesmaids' fitting and it all slots in to place. Stringer snorts and laughs at me.

'What?' I ask, smiling back.

'You look so funny. Like an old gossip, sitting there with your arms folded. I never thought I'd see you speechless. You never usually shut up,' he teases.

I can feel myself blushing. I uncross my arms and keep the subject on neutral territory.

'I bet she had a bit of a shocker seeing Matt, then,' I ponder.

Stringer picks at the grass and doesn't say anything. I sneak a look at him, but he's watching his hand and I find myself watching it too. He's got such long fingers.

'Sex always mucks everything up, I suppose,' he says.

'What?'

'Between friends, I mean.'

'Oh, oh,' I blurt, holding up my hand. 'I quite agree,' I say, trying to ignore the stab in my gut.

'Do you?' he asks, looking at me.

I stare back at him.

Of course I agree. I want Stringer to be my friend, right? Which means being honest. This has to be the first step in changing my relationships with men.

Except . . . why couldn't I have picked an ugly one?

'Yes,' I nod decisively. 'Sex between friends is a disaster, it ruins everything. I've made that mistake,' I admit, sounding like a Victorian matron.

I fiddle with my sandwich packet, but Stringer doesn't say anything.

'I always used to think that I might as well have sex whenever I got the chance. But it's too easy. Life isn't just about having fun.'

'Isn't it?' he asks, looking up at me.

'No. Well, yes. But sleeping around isn't that much fun. I want more for myself. Does that sound odd?'

It does to me . . .

I take a deep breath. 'The thing is, I've been on this course and half of it is a load of old claptrap, but some of it really makes sense.'

Stringer reaches into his bag and opens a can of lemonade. He hands it to me. I feel odd talking about the course, but he doesn't bat an eyelid. So I tell him more. I tell him about being stoned and about creating visions. And he just listens and sips lemonade.

So eventually I pluck up the courage to tell him about my real vision. About having a platonic relationship with a man and to stop flirting.

'It's not that I don't like sex. I do. I love it,' I say, blushing. 'I don't know anyone who doesn't. The thing is, I've been reading up a lot and I've decided that I don't just want to jump into bed with people . . . men. I want to be able to relate to them in a non-sexual way.'

I wonder what Stringer thinks of all this, because saying it to him makes it sound ridiculous to me. What can be more odd than telling the most gorgeous man in the world that you're off sex?

But Stringer just smiles.

And it's not a leery smile, or a knowing smile, or a 'yeah, right,' smile. It's just . . . lovely.

I smile back and pat the grass. 'So I'm leaving my past behind,' I say. 'My grotty, *sordid*, past,' I tease, half-testing him. 'Well, you would know. You've got one too, haven't you? That's what I've heard anyway . . .'

Stringer

Saturday, 15.05

'There's a lot less to my past than you'd think. All those stories are . . . well . . .' I falter, '. . . they're not strictly true.'

Susie doesn't answer. I think this is because she's waiting for me to say more. I try holding her eyes on this one, but fail abysmally. The old shame shutters snap down, and I look at my hand instead.

It's difficult. It isn't because it's Susie I'm talking to. That part is easy. She's been open with me, comfortably open. She's simply told me how it is. It came as a surprise when she started. We don't know each other that well, but that could well be what makes it easy, me being a relative stranger. The circumstances remind me of how matters were between myself and David at Quit4Good. Susie didn't need to tell me any of this information. I didn't accuse her of having a messed-up life, or needing to make a fresh start. The thought hadn't occurred to me (and as it is, I think she's being unnecessarily analytical).

My difficulty comes from nothing she's said, but from everything I haven't – everything I *can't*. I'm not a David. It's not as if I'm sitting here listening to her in a professional capacity. A sage nod of my head and a 'How does that make you *feel*?' won't suffice here. It would be unfair, because there has to be an exchange of sorts, doesn't there? It's like swapping football cards when you're a child. You can't simply take Gary Lineker and give nothing back in return. You'd only be construed as being tight.

Rather as with KC in the kitchen, however, I have nothing to swap. There are no grubby little sexual secrets inside this head of mine. In their place is a pristine white scoresheet unsullied by a single mark, and guarding it is a lying habit as all-encompassing as my coke habit once was. I'd like to admit to being Susie's opposite. It would be wonderful for that to form the basis of an unlikely attraction, making this time I've spent with her something greater than an interval in my wider life. Fear, however, remains my king. I can see her now, if I choose to spit out the truth: her mouth agape; her assumption that I'm winding her up; her horror and pity on hearing how messed up I am. I can't go there. I can't allow myself to be set up and knocked back down in that fashion, particularly by someone I'm now convinced – especially in the light of her new outlook on life – I'll become firm friends with.

'It's all role-playing really, isn't it?' I say. 'That's what it's like with Matt and Jack and everyone. We've all got parts to play. That's how it works. Jack's the lad, Matt's the brains and I'm the . . . stud. That's how it is and it's hard, you know? It's really bloody hard for them to accept you as anything else, and equally as hard to be anyone else when you're around them.'

'But you are who you are, Stringer. It doesn't really matter what other people think. It's your own opinion that counts.'

'It's not that simple.'

'Why not?'

'People judge you on what other people say. You're no different. You've judged me on what you've heard about me.'

'I haven't judged you at all.'

'The sordid past thing. You asked, didn't you? You brought it up.'

'OK,' she concedes, 'but now you've told me different.

You've told me you're not a one-man sex machine, and I believe you. So that cancels out what I've heard before. Same as me.'

'Same as you how?'

She snorts. 'What? You're telling me that Jack hasn't gobbed off that I'm a complete slapper?'

'Yes, well, he's hardly one to talk . . .'

'No, but I bet my bottom bloody dollar he's said something to you along those lines.'

'Yes,' I admit, 'he has.'

'And did you believe him?'

'I didn't care.'

'Oh.'

Her eyes flicker. 'I didn't mean it like that,' I tell her.

'Like what?' she asks.

'Care. Saying I didn't care. I didn't mean it to come out like that. I simply meant . . . What I mean is that it wasn't something that interested me.' I sigh. 'God, this is making it sound worse.' I notice a trace of a smile on her face and I try again: 'I meant I wasn't interested in whether you were a slapper or not because it wasn't any of my business. It's the same as it wasn't any of Jack's business to be telling me in the first place.'

Susie looks at me slyly. 'So what made him tell you in the first place? Did you ask him?'

'No.' I'm blustering and sounding like an arse. 'No,' I repeat. 'All right, yes, I was asking him about you, but . . .'

'But what?' she enquires innocently.

'But not because of that. I didn't exactly come out and say, "Hey, Jack. What about Susie? Is she a bit of a scrubber, or what?" . . .'

'I'm glad to hear it.' She pushes her hair away from her face, then asks, 'So what did you say?'

'I don't remember.'

'Try.'

I make a show of scrunching up my face. 'No, I still don't remember. It came up, that's all. All right,' I continue in the face of her raised eyebrows, '*you* came up. In conversation. And Jack told me about you.'

'Same as *you* came up when I was talking to Amy . . .'

'Precisely.'

She dips her head down and looks up at me. 'So where does that leave us?'

I glance around, at a loss for anything to say. 'Sitting on a hill, surrounded by trees,' I suggest.

She considers this for a moment, then says, 'Maybe we should find the others . . . Hopefully, they'll have patched everything up by now . . .'

I remember what I overheard in the steam room. Poor Matt. 'Let's do it,' I say, suddenly feeling guilty for not having filled him in on what's going on in H's head. I stand up. 'Are you still on for getting everyone down to the swimming-pool later on?'

'Yeah. Let's go.'

She holds out her hand and I lean down and take it. It's cold. I pull her to her feet. When she lets go, part of me wishes that she hadn't.

H

Saturday, 15.10

I'm just finishing another cigarette and I'm staring blankly at the overfed, over-tame ducks, when I'm aware of a presence behind me. Biting my lips together, I look over my shoulder. Amy stands behind me, her arms folded. She stares down with a haughty expression.

'All right,' I say, turning back to the lake.

Great. Just what I need.

Amy crouches down beside me and then sits on the patchy grass. I'm about to stub out my cigarette, when she takes it off me and takes the last drag herself. She offers the burning end back to me, but I shake my head. I hug my knees in to my chest as she looks up and blows smoke out slowly towards the ducks. Then she grinds the butt under the toe of her new trainer.

Here we go.

'Why didn't you tell me?' she asks, looking out over the lake.

I don't say anything. So she thinks this is all my fault, does she? I watch a large bird plunge down into the water and pick up a dirty clump of rubbish in its beak. The fish, like everything else in this place, are long dead.

I don't want to talk to Amy. I want her to leave me alone.

'H?' she presses.

'What?' I groan impatiently.

Amy takes a deep breath. 'About Matt? Why didn't you tell me you'd slept with Matt?' She turns to face me, but I don't look at her.

Typical. I might have known. I might have known that Matt would have been mouthing off.

'So he told you, then?' I demand.

'No, Jack did. He told me, just now.'

'Do you think anyone else knows?'

'I don't know. It's possible.'

I suck in my cheeks. 'Great.'

I look at her. She's hugging her knees too and her brows are drawn together. For the first time, in all the years I've known her, I notice that she's getting wrinkles. I know she's annoyed that I haven't told her about Matt and I brace myself ready for the inevitable showdown, but to my surprise, she changes tack.

'I know this isn't easy for you,' she begins. 'I'm really sorry.'

I have to say I'm surprised at this. 'What have *you* got to be sorry about? If anyone's to blame, it's Matt,' I snap. 'He shouldn't have told Jack and he certainly shouldn't be here.'

She ignores me. 'No, *I'm* sorry.' She puts her hand on her chest. She hasn't got her engagement ring on. 'I'm sorry you couldn't tell me,' she says before pausing and looking out to the trees. 'What I'm really saying is that I'm sorry that we're not as close any more.'

She says it as a simple fact and I feel the sadness in her voice. But the shock of her saying it registers as a tight feeling in my chest.

'We are close,' I say, ignoring it.

'Don't patronize me, ' she flares. 'I'm being honest.' She sighs.

I look away, but Amy carries on. 'I know that Jack plays a big part in my life now. And that's my choice,' she says.

'That's life,' I say.

'Yes it is. Life moves on, H. And I'm sorry that I'm not there for you all the time, but you being so angry puts me in such an awkward position. I'm with Jack, but I want you too. Your thoughts and your feelings . . . Because we *are* friends. And that's why I'm sorry that you've shut me out. If you'd stop being so cross with me, then I might be able to help,' she says, softly. 'You're in a scrape, but you don't have to deal with it all by yourself. You don't need to feel lonely.'

I want to tell her that she can't presume what my feelings are. I want to tell her to back off, that it's none of her business. That I don't need *her* to tell *me* that I'm lonely. But the truth is that I *am* lonely and I can feel my throat constricting. Amy cups her hand over mine.

'So what happened with Matt?' she asks.

I tell her about the pub. 'It was just a shag,' I sigh. 'Quite a good shag, actually. But I wasn't really thinking about the consequences. It just seemed like a good idea at the time.'

'And then you went to Paris and met Laurent . . .' she adds for me and nods in understanding. 'Shitty, eh?'

I nod. 'Shitty. And now Matt's gone all stalker on me. I can't believe he's here, Amy. I really can't. I had such a shock back there.'

'I think you made your feelings quite clear.'

'I can't believe he planned Jack's stag do here. He's done this deliberately. He's set all this up . . . because of me.'

Amy strokes my back as if to soothe away my panic. 'Listen. You don't know that for sure. Do you?'

'It's pretty obvious.'

She shakes her head. 'Matt seemed just as gobsmacked as you and I know him and Jack, he wouldn't lie. And if Jack knew about it, he would have said something. You know what rent-a-gob's like. He's rubbish at keeping secrets. I really think it's just a coincidence.'

'It's not,' I wail.

'It could be?' She eyeballs me. 'Couldn't it?'

I shake my head.

'Couldn't it?' she repeats. 'Couldn't it just be possible that Matt had the same idea as you for this weekend? I mean, I didn't tell Jack that we were coming here and you didn't tell Matt, did you?'

I sigh and roll this around my head for a while. I don't see how Matt could have found out.

'OK, OK,' I finally surrender when Amy doesn't let up. 'It *could* be a possibility.'

'And if it is?'

'Well if it is, I've just been horrible to Matt for no reason.'

'Exactly.'

We stay in silent contemplation for a while. I feel all jangled. I'm not sure if she's on my side or not.

'What shall I do, then?' I ask.

Amy wiggles her lips in thought. 'There's only one thing you can do. Be honest. Tell him you're not interested and that you're not looking for a relationship with him. Matt's a big boy. He can cope.'

I bury my head in my hands. The last thing I want to do is see Matt, let alone talk to him.

'Thank God he doesn't know about Laurent. That would really make things complicated.'

'Don't wimp out,' says Amy sternly. 'It's the only thing that will salvage the situation. Otherwise this weekend will be appalling.'

'It already is,' I say. 'The whole point was for us to have a girlie weekend and now that lot's shown up, it's all ruined.'

'It's not all ruined. Stop being such a killjoy.'

'Oh, like you're not going to want to be with Jack all night and Sam isn't going to eat Stringer alive?'

Amy rolls her eyes at me. 'You can't project what's going to happen.'

'I've got a fair idea,' I sulk.

Amy holds up her hands. 'I've had enough of this.' She takes a deep breath. 'Look. If you talk to Matt and sort things out, I promise we'll go out on our own tonight. Without the boys. Once you've talked to Matt, you won't have to see him for the rest of the weekend. Deal?'

And it is a deal, because she's right. And I don't have to say yes, because she knows me too well.

Matt

Saturday, 15.35

'It sounds nice,' is all I can manage in response to Stringer's account of his picnic with Suzie. It's all very Enid Blyton and lashings of ginger beer and I should be more enthusiastic – really, I should. At least he and Susie are doing the adult thing and just getting on with the fact that we're all here. I should be happy for them. I should be relieved. But I'm not. I'm bloody miserable. I've been sitting here, wracking my brains over what I'm going to say to H when I see her next, about how I'm going to make things right between us. And short of repeating what I've already told her, I've come up with a blank. Worse than that, though, is the paralysis. Until she's located, and we come face to face, there's nothing I can do but wait.

'Are you all right?' Stringer asks, continuing to pack his swimming gear, so that he can follow the others down to the swimming pool.

'No, Stringer,' I tell him, 'I'm not. I've spent the last week dividing my time between organizing this weekend and thinking about H. And now the weekend's turned to shit and H thinks I *am* a shit. Happiness and me can't exactly be described as great bedfellows right now.'

'The guys will get over it,' he comforts, sitting down next to me on the sofa and staring out of the living-room window. 'The waterslides will cool them down. And they can't go on blaming you for ever about the girls being here. It's not your fault. Jack knows that and he'll make sure they do, as well.'

'And what about H?' I ask. 'It's going to take more than a quick swim to chill her out. Try a tonne of ice.'

'Yes,' he admits, 'I think you could be right there.' He shifts uncomfortably in his seat. 'Listen, Matt. You know I was trying to tell you something at the Aqua Spa earlier on . . .'

'Yeah,' I apologize, 'sorry about that. Too much shouting going on . . . So what was it?'

Stringer shifts again. This time I look at him. He can't hold my gaze. Instead, his eyes drop. 'I don't know how to tell you. I don't know if it's my place to . . .' he begins, then falters.

'What?' I ask him. Whatever it is, it can't be worse than what's already gone down today. 'Come on,' I coax, trying to sound chipper. 'Out with it.'

'It's H,' he says, looking up. 'I overheard her and Amy talking in the steam room. They didn't know I was there. They were talking about a bloke. H,' he specifies, 'was talking about a bloke.'

I don't like the way this is starting to sound, but still I ask, 'And?'

He stares at me.

I ask again, 'And?'

'And it wasn't you, Matt,' he tells me. 'The bloke. The bloke they were talking about wasn't you.'

There's a fine line between depression and pain. It's a tightrope and you can fall either way, depending on the way the wind blows. I'm walking it now. And I'm starting to teeter. 'Tell me,' I tell him. Because I have to know, even though I already know the answer isn't one I'm going to want to hear.

'He's a Frenchman. Laurent, or something like that. She spent all last week with him in Paris. She's into him. *Really* into him. I'm sorry, mate. After what you said about her in Chick-O-Lix this morning. About wanting this. I'm really bloody sorry.'

I slip. There's no point in even attempting to grab the tightrope as I fall. There's no point, because I'm welcoming the darkness that's waiting for me below. Because it's nothing more than I deserve for being so stupid as to leave myself open to this kind of pain in the first place.

I bite down on my tongue, feeling like I've been stabbed. So here it is: the flip side of the one-night stand. I suppose it had to happen one day. Because – and this is the advice I gave Jack when he was temporarily rejected by Amy last year – it happens to us all from time to time. But, shit, it sure has picked its moment. I feel tears welling up in my eyes. My throat contracts. I picture H in my mind and all I want to do is reach out and take her hand. But it's useless. She's turned her back on me. It's like she's rubbed the word 'hope' out of existence and all that's left is despair. I clear my throat, and rub at my eyes. I'm not going to cry. I'm not going to be the one left sitting here waiting for her to come back. Because I now know that if I did, I'd be waiting here for ever.

'Do me a favour, Stringer . . .' My voice comes out in a monotone.

'Name it.'

'Don't tell the others about this. Especially not Jack. I don't want his weekend getting ruined any more than it already is.'

He looks at me with sorrow in his eyes. 'OK.'

'Strange, isn't it,' I say, reaching for the bottle of vodka on the table and taking a swig.

'What?' Stringer asks.

'How sometimes when the worst thing in the world happens, you don't freak out, you just switch off.'

H

Saturday, 15.50

'They've all gone down the pool,' says Amy, reading Susie's note in the chalet. I open the window to let some air in.

'You go,' I say. 'I'll sort things out here with Matt. Now get your gear and *go*. Enjoy yourself. You've wasted enough time on me.'

'Are you sure you'll be OK? I can stay and wait if you want.'

'Yes,' I sigh. 'I need to do this on my own.'

'Come down in a bit then.'

'I will,' I lie. 'If I find him. He might not even be there.'

Once Amy has gone, I flip through Sam's magazine, but I know I'm only putting things off.

I'm not expecting to find Matt next door, but I give the door a go anyway. I knock half-heartedly and wait, staring up at the clouds, my nerve deserting me. I'm just about to leave when Matt answers the door.

He looks hungover and cross. He stands in the doorway, his hand on the handle and I look up at him from the step. He's wearing shorts and the hairs on his tanned legs are blonde.

There's a long pause. I clear my throat.

'Can I come in?' I ask.

'What do you want?' He shifts his weight on to one leg and looks at me impatiently. He smells like he's been drinking. His eyes are bloodshot and cold and the hairs on the back of my neck stand up.

This isn't going to be easy.

'I came to apologize. Um . . . I think I was probably a bit out of order,' I say sheepishly, rubbing my shoe on the step, before looking up at Matt. 'I mean, you're right. This is probably a coincidence . . .' I try to laugh amicably.

But Matt only looks down at me, his face inscrutable.

'Only, if you'd planned all this because of what happened last weekend . . . I mean, it was great and everything, but I didn't want you to get the wrong . . .'

Matt interrupts me and shakes his head, giving me a derisory snort. 'You really think that I'd arrange this so that . . . what, H? We could be together. To have sex? Is that what you thought?'

'It had crossed my mind,' I say, feeling riled, but wanting him to see my point of view. 'Well, it seems that way to me.'

'Listen. About what happened between us . . . we were both drunk, you came on to me and I took the opportunity for a no-strings-attached shag. There's no more to it than that.'

'*I* came on to *you*!' I gasp.

'Let's just forget it ever happened.'

I'm so shocked, I can feel my voice choking in my throat. 'If that's the way you want it.'

'I *want* to be alone with the boys and enjoy the stag party that I planned *ages* ago. We *were* having a good time. So I'd appreciate it if you'd run along and keep yourselves to yourselves.' He waves his fingers at me condescendingly before slamming the door in my face.

'Fine!' I yell, turning on my heels and marching back into the villa. I slam our front door harder in retaliation, then slump back against the inside of it. I feel like I've been punched. I shake my head as if to rattle away what's just happened, but it doesn't go.

'How dare he?' I mutter as I march in to the kitchen and angrily light a cigarette. I pace on the grey carpet tiles, feeling furious. Somehow I can feel his presence next door and my skin feels itchy.

I chainsmoke five cigarettes before I can think straight.

But eventually, I've had it.

I grab my swimming costume and a towel. I'm not staying here. I'm going to the pool and I'm going to have a great time with the girls. And if Matt Davies dares to come too, I swear I'll drown him.

Susie

I rub my back up against the jet of bubbles in the hot pool at the top of the waterslide. Amy flops over the entrance ledge and sits next to me. Her cheeks are flushed and she's breathless as she grins at me.

'Susie the floozie in the jacuzzi,' she whoops. 'What a laugh. You coming down again?'

I must admit that since coming in to the pool, we've all regressed to childhood. We've been running about all afternoon, squealing like demented kids.

I reach down and massage my feet. 'In a minute.'

'Well, I'm off!' she grins, falling off the ledge and nearly drowning and I pull her up. She comes up spluttering and we laugh. 'I'll leave you to it, it's too hot for me,' she says after squirting water through her teeth. 'If I were you, I'd have a go on these jets. Jacuzzi orgasms: always the best!' She gets up to leave and hops backwards into Stringer. He looks embarrassed and smiles at her.

'Oh, looks like there's no need,' she says cheekily, screwing up her face and silently mouthing 'Phworrh' behind Stringer's back. She wriggles over the side with a big kiddie whoop and is gone.

'She seems in high spirits,' Stringer says, sitting down opposite me.

'Everyone does,' I smile, wondering if he's heard Amy's orgasm comment and blushing anyway. 'Even H, which is a first. She's cheered up at long last. She's been awful until now.'

'She's been the most jolly I've ever seen her,' he says. He sounds so gentlemanly and posh. He looks out of place in here, as if he's uncomfortable being half-naked.

He's not the only one.

Stringer smiles and looks down into the water. I can see his shorts have bubbled up with air. There's a pause. I can feel powerful jets of water pumelling against my thighs.

'So, you all set for tonight?' he asks, eventually.

'It's the disco for us. What are you doing?'

Stringer shrugs. 'Matt's in charge. I think we're staying in. More lads' stuff,' he says scarcastically.

'Why don't you come to the disco with us?' I ask. 'It'll be fun.'

Stringer laughs. 'With Matt and H? I don't think so. I think we'll all be separated.'

'Shame, isn't it? We could try and hook up later?' I suggest.

'We could do, I suppose. Why don't I try and find you, around eleven, say?'

'You're on.'

'Susie, come on!' I can hear Amy yelling and I poke my head over the stone-effect boulders to see her waving at me from the top of the waterslide.

'I'd better go,' I say, waving back, but just as I get up, I realize that my bikini top is skewiff and half my nipple is hanging out.

And Stringer has seen!

I adjust myself hastily without looking at him and try to leap past him, but I slip and land up falling on top of him in the bubbles. And for an electifying moment we're a mass of slithering limbs.

'Sorry,' I smile, foolishly trying to fix my hair. 'I'll see you later, then,' I say, but I'm all choked up. It must be the heat.

Matt

I do realize that alcohol isn't going to solve the problem, but right now, it's doing a pretty good job of numbing the pain. It's over three hours now since H came round to see me and I threw her peace-offering back in her face, and I've been drinking consistently pretty much ever since. Despite this, though, there's a sour taste in my mouth and, as much as I'd like H to be the cause of it, she's not, it's me. Fortunately, I can't even remember what I said to her, but I do know it was pretty unpleasant. A case of injured pride. Not that she knows that. I didn't tell her that I knew about Laurent, that I knew I'd been passed over. I didn't tell her anything apart from the fact that I wanted nothing to do with her.

I look up and focus on a light switch until the rest of the room steadies. The apartment smells of chlorine. Wet footprints pattern the carpet outside the bathroom, in which Jack's currently scrubbing himself down. A Tribe Called Quest are rapping away on the sound system. The others are either getting dressed, or grabbing mini-kips in preparation for tonight's festivities. Ug aside, that is, who's sitting on the floor like some mad scientist, busy constructing a bong out of a variety of plastic implements he found in a bin round the back of the Global Village. ('Hunter-gathering, mate,' he muttered on entering the apartment. 'It's what I do best.')

'Chuck us that bit of hose, will ya?' Ug asks.

I pick up a piece of green piping from the floor and hand it to him.

269

'Cheers,' he mutters, taking time out for a quick beer guzzle before refocusing his attention on his creation.

'Want some?' he asks after a few more minutes.

'Why not?' I say, squatting down next to him.

And why not, indeed? The less I'm capable of thought tonight, the better. I don't want to think. I don't want to be reminded of the stupidity and basic selfishness of my behaviour up to and including this weekend. All I've concentrated on is myself and what I wanted and how I was going to get it. And now that I've failed, I see it for what it was, an exercise in vanity, a waste of time. I take a toke and hold it deep down in my lungs.

H

I pull out the cork, wrap my lips round the neck of the bottle and tip my head back.

Then I do it again.

Then I grab a glass and fill it to the brim, before barging in to the bathroom.

It's full of steam and the floor is filthy. Amy is leaning forward, trying to see her reflection in a porthole she's rubbed in the mirror. Susie is in the shower and Lorna is rubbing the back of her head with a towel.

'Come on. Get your kit on, everyone. We're leaving in just under an hour.'

Amy looks at me aghast. 'But I want to dry my hair properly.'

'This is Leisure Heaven, for Christ's sake. No one is going to see your hair,' I reply. 'Anyway, it's not negotiable. I'm in charge and I say we're hitting the bars and then the disco.'

I take another slug. 'Anyone want some, before I finish it off?'

'I will,' says Amy, holding out her glass.

'Whose is this shampoo?' asks Susie from the shower.

'Mine,' I reply.

'It's good, isn't it?'

'Aren't we going to see what the boys are doing?' asks Lorna.

'Amy?' I say, swinging my hand out so that she can lay down the terms of our deal for all to hear.

'I think it should just be girls tonight,' she says, nervously looking at me.

I smile expansively and take another swig of wine and feel it burn down.

'Absolutely correct,' I say. 'Tonight is the hen night and we're going to make it a good one.'

I clinks glasses with Amy. 'Come on, hurry up. You're wasting valuable drinking time.'

'Are you all right?' she asks, but I ignore her and barge out.

Susie

Saturday, 22.00

'Can't you put on a bit of Abba?' I yell at the DJ.
'"Dancing Queen", or *something*?'

He ignores me, holding his earphone whilst head-banging to the music. Well, I call it music in the loosest sense of the word. It was fine when we got here, but for the last hour he's been playing this techno rubbish, which has never been my cup of tea. I'm all for some good clubbing anthems, but this is just noise. I glance over the dance floor, which is full of sweaty, grubby teenagers. We must be at least ten years older than everyone else in here.

'Oi!' I bellow.

'What?' he shouts, putting up his finger to make me wait as he puts on another musical travesty. Eventually he comes over.

'What?' he repeats, through chewing gums.

'Can't you put on something we can dance to? Only we're on a hen night and we want to boogie?' I waggle my hips to demonstrate. 'You know? Songs? Remember them?' He looks for a moment as if he's going to gob on me.

'Go somewhere else then!' he protests. I turn away feeling unbearably old. Doesn't he know who he's talking to? I've been to more parties than he's had hot dinners. Cheeky blighter.

'No luck?' shouts Lorna, when I shove my way through the kiddies back to the table.

'If you can't beat 'em, join 'em!' I shrug, waving to

273

Amy on the dance floor. Despite the dreadful music, she's in full swing, waving her veil above her head and waving at us to come over. Behind her a group of lads are eyeing up her legs. One of them, with a barely formed bum-fluff moustache, comes forward and pushes in to her. He makes lewd gestures before undoing his trousers behind her.

I march over and give him a good shove.

'She's asking for it,' he bluffs, agitated at being humiliated in front of his mates. He ruffles up as if he wants to fight me.

'Not from you, she isn't. Now hop it!' I shout.

Jenny laughs. 'I'm old enough to be his mother!'

Amy turns round and notices what's going on. 'Cradle-snatching again, Sooze?' she laughs.

'It's my job,' I smile, feeling like a bouncer.

'Come on, let's get a drink,' shouts Amy above the din.

H has already been queuing for ten minutes when we join her at the bar.

I take over and we push our way to the front and elbow our way up against the bar. H is clearly on a mission. She orders flaming Drambuies for starters and then two tequila chasers.

'Stop!' giggles Amy, slapping her chest. 'I can't do any more.'

'Lightweight,' teases H. 'Get some more in, Susie,' she orders, before flouncing off with Amy.

The barmaid is obviously off her tits. (Not that she has any.)

'You paying for those, or what?' she says.

I look back to the table, after H.

But she paid. Didn't she?

'Can't you put it on a tab?' I panic.

'No. Not in here.'

I'm so dizzy with the tequila, that I don't argue and hand over the last of my cash, despite the fact that I've bought most of the rounds so far. I manage to scrape together enough for a few more beers and tuck them under my arms.

'Show us yer tits!' says one of the youths as I squeeze past him.

'Get lost,' I reply.

'Oooooooo! Keep your wig on, grandma.'

'Where have these children come from?' I ask, handing the beers out. Our table has been nicked, so we lurk by the wall and watch the teeny-boppers.

'This music is terrible,' says Amy. 'I've tried, but I can't dance any more.'

'Then let's drink, instead,' shouts H.

Kate comes and stands next to me. 'This is awful,' she whispers. 'Come on, let's get some air.'

We wander outside, leaving the techno music behind us.

'Well, that's it,' I say, sitting on a bench. 'I'm officially old.'

'No you're not,' says Kate, joining me.

'I am. I used to be able to make a party out of anything, but this time I'm stumped.'

'Amy seems to be enjoying herself.'

'She isn't. She's just putting on a show.'

'We can't admit defeat just yet,' says Kate.

'I know,' I sigh. 'I hate all this pretending that we're all having a great time, just for tradition's sake, when all I really want to do is go and join the boys.'

I look at the flickering neon sign of the club, thinking of Stringer.

'Do you?'

'Yes,' I wail, letting my exasperation out. 'Oh shit, Kate,' I groan.

'What is it?'

'The thing is . . . I've been trying so hard to change. I've been trying so hard not to be a slapper and to have a platonic relationship with this guy. But the truth is, I've just realized that I really fancy him. Like, *really* fancy him.'

'Who?'

'Stringer,' I confess.

She shakes her head and looks confused, so I explain.

'I had a bike ride and a picnic with him today and it was so great. But he doesn't fancy me.'

'I'm sure he does.'

'I just don't know what to do. I'm digging myself a deeper and deeper hole. And all I keep thinking is that Amy wants to be with Jack and I'm single and I want to be with Stringer and all this hen and stag stuff is, well, bollocks, quite frankly.'

She laughs.

'And the worst thing is that I'm blowing my only opportunity to see Stringer and do something about my feelings, just for Amy's sake. And I'm happy to do it, but it seems so stupid. She wouldn't want this.'

'Well, you're the one who's always saying if you want something, make it happen. Why don't you talk to the girls?' suggests Kate.

But half an hour later, when I confront H with the idea of bailing out, she's not having any of it.

'No way. This is Amy's night and I don't think it's appropriate that we leave. Ask Amy, she'll tell you the same thing,' she slurs.

'But . . .'

'No,' she says, looking nasty. 'It's final. None of us are leaving.'

'Why do you have to be so controlling all the time?' I ask.

'Me? Controlling?' says H. 'That's rich.'

This is it. I've had enough of her.

'Oh shut up! You've been bossing us around all weekend.'

'Bossing you around!' she guffaws. *'Bossing you around?* One of us has to be responsible for Amy.'

'So you're responsible for Amy, now, are you? You've done nothing but put a dampener on things and behave like a spoilt brat since we got here.'

'Uh-ho,' coughs H, pretending to be outraged. 'I'm not the one going outside for little sulks. I'm not the one who's refusing to have a good time.'

'I'm the one who's been making sure Amy's having a good time,' I retort, my voice steely.

Amy steps in between us. 'What's going on?'

H glares at me drunkenly, as she takes out some money and hands it to Amy. 'Nothing. Go and get some drinks.'

'You see,' I accuse her. 'You're just a control freak.'

'Susie?' gasps Amy, looking alarmed, the money shaking in her hand.

'I'm sorry, but I don't need you to flash your cash at me, Marchmont,' I say, ripping it out of Amy's hand and shoving it back at her.

'Stop it,' yells Amy. 'Both of you.'

'You're so pathetic,' sneers H at me. 'You're such a slapper that you can't bear to be away from the boys for two seconds.'

'At least I haven't slept with any of them, like you have,' I jibe back, but before H has the chance to retort, I try to calm things down a bit.

'All I'm saying is that this place is shit. No one is enjoying themselves and we might as well go,' I say, in a measured tone. 'You want to go, don't you, Amy?'

She looks between me and H. She looks utterly torn, but this time I'm not going to relent.

'Amy?' asks H, eyeballing her.

'Well, I . . . This *is* a girls' night out.'

'Exactly,' says H, poisonously. 'But if you want to go, Susie, please don't let us stop you.'

'Sooze,' begs Amy, gripping onto my arm. 'Don't go.

Let's stay and have a drink. There's no point in arguing. Especially over me. I'm having a good time. Really I am.'

But H is glaring at me and for a moment I hate her. Really hate her. Amy might be too weak to stand up to her, but I'm not.

'I'm sorry, Amy. I'll see you later,' I choke.

But as I shove my way past the cloakroom and the puking teenagers, I know I've lost. H has manipulated this in to a contest over who is the better friend. It's pathetic and stupid, but I haven't felt like this since I was at primary school.

The same as with Stringer.

Matt

I'm having a pretty tough time focusing. Skunk. Ug's home-grown hydroponic treats. Strong as an elephant tranq. It's knocked me sideways.

One thing at least: the stag weekend's running smoothly. Jack succeeded in placating the others about the girls being here and even Jimmy's relaxed. Just a shame I'm too far gone now to play any part in it. I look across the room at the others, all of whom seem impossibly animated. Jack's holding court over at the table, presiding over a point of technicality in their drinking game. I see him laughing over something Damien's whispered in his ear and, momentarily, I remember what it's like to feel happy. But the feeling's transitory. H fills my mind and the overwhelming pain of losing her sinks back in. And that is what's happened, isn't it? She's gone. Out of my life and back in to her own. Or rather, I haven't even lost her, I never even held her in the first place. Not apart from that one night which already seems dreamed, unreal. I see now, that like all my strategic planning that followed in its wake, it was an illusion. I was on to a loser right from the start because, as with Penny Brown, I was never the man H wanted.

I stare at the carpet and search the floor for any sign of a trapdoor. Straight to hell. I don't care. The way I'm feeling right now, it couldn't be any worse than here.

Susie

I fling my bike at the bottom of the path. The fresh air has sobered me up and now I just feel sorry for myself. This is all such a mess. I glance up at the boys' apartment and can hear the party. All I want to do is see Stringer, but there's no way I can go in there. Not now. Maybe I should just get my things and go home.

I'm fishing the key out of my pocket when I hear his voice.

'Susie?'

I look up and see Stringer sitting on the doorstep to our chalet with his hands in his pockets. I'm so relieved to see him that I run towards him and fling my arms around him.

He holds me for a moment before pushing me away gently.

'Hey, hey,' he says. 'What's the matter?'

I shake my head. I hand him the key and he opens the door and turns the light on.

'I'm so glad you're here,' I say, walking with him in to the sitting-room.

'What's happened?'

'It was a disaster. I had a big row with H,' I start. I want to go on, but now I've found him, there doesn't seem much point.

'Sit down. Calm down,' he says.

I slump on to the sofa, wanting him to join me, but he sits on the chair, the table between us. 'What happened?'

'It doesn't matter. She's just drunk and being a bitch.'

'Do you want a drink?' he asks, looking round.

I nod and point at the kitchen counter. 'There's some tequila.'

He gets up, rinses out a glass and pours me some.

'You have some, too,' I say.

Stringer hesitates, then pours himself a splash. In the silence, I can hear the boys next door.

'What's going on?' I ask.

He shakes his head and sighs. 'Nothing much. It's more or less a repeat of last night.'

'Is that why you're here?'

'Fresh air and fresh company . . .'

'I haven't got any friends left. I want to go home.'

'I'm here now,' he says, soothingly.

And he is. But he's not. He's over there and I really want to hold him.

'If it's any consolation, I'm your friend,' he smiles.

I smile back and pick up the bottle. 'Another one?'

Stringer

'Go on, then,' I say, pushing my glass across the table towards Susie. 'If you can't beat 'em . . .'

Susie obliges, filling my glass meniscus-high with tequila. We chink glasses and drink. She drains hers and slams it down on the table.

'Come on, shandy boy,' she taunts, noticing that I've only drunk half mine.

I do as she says and fight the urge to retch. 'Sorry,' I apologize, my face contorting in to a wince. 'I haven't drunk this stuff in a while.'

'What, you not a big drinker?' She looks surprised. 'I'd have thought that was compulsory, hanging out with that bunch. Don't want to mess up your body, is that it?'

'There's a bit more to it than that,' I mumble.

She slops more drink in to our glasses regardless. 'Tell us about it, then,' she suggests, then retracts, reading my face, 'Only if you want, like . . .'

'The Big A,' I say.

'Eh?'

I feel my skin flushing. I'm not sure I want to get into this. But why not? I trust her. She's not going to judge me. I'm sure of that. 'Addiction,' I say. 'Coke. I used to have a problem. A habit. I used to have a habit. I had to have counselling.'

'I'm sorry,' she says, her lips pursing. 'I didn't know. I mean, you hear about it – people getting messed up – but—'

'But you've tried it and some of your mates have tried

282

it, and some of your mates try it every day, and they seem fine . . .' She laughs at my guessing what she was about to say. 'But I didn't cope,' I explain. 'I got bust up by it. Well and truly. It happens . . .'

'I'm sorry,' she repeats. 'I—'

'No,' I interrupt, not wanting her to feel embarrassed, 'it's all right. I'm sorted out now. I sorted myself out. But the booze. Back at the beginning, when I was getting straight . . . I stayed off booze bingeing. It was too close. There was too much of a link. I still like to have a drink, but not to the point of losing it.' I pick up my glass and look at it. I want to get pissed. I want to get pissed with *her*. I continue to stare at the glass. I've moved on. I don't feel scared of this. There is no link any more. I'm already free. I clear my throat. 'But it's over a year ago now and' – I nod in the direction of our apartment – 'if I've survived Jimmy and Ug . . .' I raise the glass and drink. 'To you,' I say. 'To us. To getting pissed and having fun.'

Our eyes link and my gut plunges like an elevator. God, I want to sigh. Suddenly, there's this deep breath inside me that I want to let loose. Everything is right about this moment, in the same way that everything has been right about this day. Susie's eyes crinkle as she smiles. I wish I could kiss her. I want to kiss her. I want it to be like it is in the movies, where we smile and we kiss and we end up in bed. And then I want it to fade to black, safe in the knowledge that everything is going to be all right. All I want is to be normal and unafraid.

'Smile,' she says.

I do what she suggests, because being here with her I feel that everything is going to be all right. We're going to smile and we're going to laugh and we're going to be friends.

And that's going to have to be enough.

At this point, we both look to the window. Outside, there's the distinct noise of a group of girls thundering out a drunken rendition of Oasis's 'Wonderwall'. There are no prizes for guessing who the choir members are.

Susie glances at me. 'I can't face that lot right now.' She gets to her feet and picks up the tequila bottle. 'Especially not H. I'm sharing a room with Amy. Let's go there. They might leave us in peace.'

Susie

I wriggle backwards on the bed, flattening out the duvet between us, before taking my boots off. I fling them against the wall and cross my legs under me.

'Sorry, my feet smell a bit.'

Stringer's sitting on the edge of the bed and he glances towards me.

'I doubt if they do as much as mine,' he smiles.

'Bet they do. Take your shoes off.'

He kicks them off. I pat the bed beside me and he comes and sits next to me on the duvet, his legs stretched out.

'Look,' I say, pointing at his toes. 'Your second toe is longer than your big toe.'

'So?'

'You know what they say about men with long second toes?' I laugh.

'Whatever it is, it's not true.' Stringer looks down at his feet. 'I've got my Dad's feet.'

'Doesn't your Dad find that a bit inconvenient?' I laugh.

'He doesn't mind. He's dead.'

'Sorry,' I say, putting my hand over my mouth.

'Forget it.'

'What happened?'

As we talk, and Stringer tells me about his Dad, I find myself homing in to him, tuning in to every word, until I'm seeing his life in my head.

Eventually he stops. 'Am I boring you?' he asks.

285

I stretch out my legs. 'No, no, it's fascinating,' I say.

Stringer laughs. 'I've just remembered. He used to do this thing with my feet.'

He reaches down and holds my foot. Immediately I start to giggle.

'He used to tickle me, like this,' he says, running his fingernail down the arch of my foot. I squeal with laughter.

'Get off!' I shriek, falling on to him, but Stringer is giggling too and he won't let go. We're falling all over each other when the door bursts open.

'Susie, I need . . .'

Stringer springs away from me and I see Amy in the door. She's looking between me and Stringer and we're both blushing.

'Sorry,' she says abruptly and shuts the door.

I cough. Stringer straightens his trousers.

'Whoops,' I say.

'Well, that's us rumbled.'

I reach out for the bottle of tequila. Stringer doesn't say anything and we can hear the girls whispering through the wall.

'Down the hatch,' I say, passing it to him.

He runs his hand through his hair before taking it.

'Dutch courage. We'll need it now with that lot.'

'Chill out. Don't worry about it,' I laugh, playfully slapping his arm.

He glances at me, looking bashful. 'I wonder what they're saying.'

'Does it really matter? Is it such a sin to be alone with me in here?'

Stringer takes a swig and wipes his mouth with the back of his hand.

'They think we're having sex, don't they?'

'Well, would it be so bad if they did think that?'

286

And as I watch him wrapped up in his own thoughts, I make up my mind.

'Do you want to know a secret?' I whisper.

'Go on, then.'

I breathe in, looking at his profile and the way his hair is flopping over his forehead and I want him. I want him so much, it hurts.

'I want to,' I blurt.

'Want to what?' he asks, turning to face me.

'I want to . . . with you . . . now.'

He shakes his head and looks away. 'You don't mean that.'

'I do mean that, Stringer,' I whisper, pushing myself closer to him. 'Don't you?'

Stringer

'We're smashed,' I say. Not, I suspect, that this information is going to make any material difference to my predicament. My heart is beating like it's about to take off. I feel the tequila rising in my throat. Her lips are centimetres away from mine.

'So?' she finally asks. 'Do you like smashed sex?'

'That's not the point, Susie,' I fumble. Only I'm too smashed to think of what the point actually might be. At a loss, I settle for silence instead.

'I get it,' she sighs, rolling on to her back and staring at the ceiling. 'You just don't want to sleep with me. I might've guessed. It's always the same. You go and get really into someone and they don't want to know. *C'est la fucking vie.*'

'That isn't how it is.'

I feel her hand squeeze my arm reassuringly. 'Don't worry,' she says. 'I'm a tough old boot. I'll get over it.'

She half-smiles at me and suddenly it's no longer enough. I want everything to be how it was a few minutes ago. I want that closeness back. I don't want to let this go. Not this time.

'Like you said in the woods,' she continues, her eyes now closed, a world-weary expression on her face, 'sex between friends messes everything up. Still,' she concludes, rubbing at her brow, 'you can't blame a girl for trying.'

'No.' The word comes out of its own accord, from my body, not my mind. 'It's not like that,' I say. 'It's nothing

288

to do with not fancying you. I do. I want you . . . I . . . Oh, Christ, I can't do this . . . I . . . I want to . . .' I swallow hard, but it isn't any use. The tears are welling up now. The alcohol is conspiring against me. Or simply what's always been inside. 'I want to so much . . .' I say and my voice is choked and I know that I've gone too far now to turn back.

'What is it?' she asks, reaching out and gently touching my cheek. There's something in her face. Fear? Fear for me?

I heave in my breath and shake my head. 'No, it's . . .'

'Tell me,' she urges, clasping the back of my neck with her hand. She looks directly into my eyes. 'Get it out of your head, Stringer. Whatever it is, just get it out. If you leave it there, it's only going to grow.'

In spite of myself, in spite of the pent-up shame and desperation, I can't help smiling.

'What?' Confusion spreads across her face.

'What you said,' I tell her. 'Just now.' This time, I don't just smile, I giggle, my nerves getting the better of me. 'Bloody tequila,' I moan, wiping my nose on the back of my sleeve. But my grin won't be got rid of so easily. 'What you said just now,' I manage. 'About getting it out. About . . .' It isn't any good, though: the grins are here to stay.

She shakes her head, catching my smile, but she remains confused, scanning my face for a solution to this mystery. 'I don't understand.'

I take another deep breath and try again. 'About getting it out,' I say in one long sigh. 'That's just it. I can't. I never do.' She opens her mouth to speak, but I plough on with my explanation regardless, unstoppable now. 'It's my dick. It's my fucking dick. Not that it's doing any fucking,' I reflect, before adding, 'Not that it's ever done any fucking.'

She looks down at my lap and then back at my face. 'What are you talking about?'

I grind my teeth together in yet another attempt to control the grins, but hysteria has me by the balls, and again, I fail. 'I've never *known* womankind,' I say, doing my utmost to keep a straight face. 'I'm a virgin, Susie. I'm a virgin with a tiny prick.' I shrug. 'I'm a virgin, *because* I've got a tiny prick.'

She backs off suddenly, and leans back on her hands. Her mouth hangs open. All she does for a few seconds is stare at me, reading and rereading my face. Eventually, she exhales heavily. 'You're for real, aren't you?'

As quickly as they came, the grins now vanish. I feel empty, exposed. 'Completely,' I mutter.

She frowns. Then her expression relaxes. 'Go on, then,' she says.

'Go on, then, what?'

'Go on, then, and get it out.' Her eyes are shining. 'Let's see just how tiny this tiny prick of yours really is.'

'Are you serious?' I ask.

'If you are,' she challenges back.

'I am.'

'So do it,' she says, hurriedly taking her glasses from their case on the bedside table, putting them on and focusing expectantly on my waist.

So I do. I don't think about it. I simply let my smashed mind rule my smashed body and I get to my feet, and standing centre-stage in the middle of the bed, I unbuckle my belt and drop my trousers to my knees.

Susie

Sunday, 00.30

And there it is.

He does have a point.

And it is a small one.

'Small and thick, does the trick, long and thin, too far in,' I joke, without thinking.

Stringer is looking down at it as if he can't believe it. Suddenly I regret being glib. I grab his hand and pull him down so that he kneels in front of me. I lift his chin and look him in the eye.

'You've been worrying all this time?' I say, gently.

He nods and my heart swells.

'You daft thing. It's perfectly normal.'

He looks so vulnerable. 'It's not,' he implores.

'It is,' I smile. 'And I should know. I've seen enough.'

I put my hand on his cheek.

'I don't believe you. You're just being nice.'

This feels so intimate. So natural. But I wish Stringer could feel it as well.

'If it makes you feel any better,' I say, having an idea, 'I've got one nipple bigger than the other. Look.'

I strip off my top, lifting my bra over my head.

'There,' I say, exposing myself. 'You've seen one of them. Look, this other one's much smaller.'

'It's not,' he protests, glancing down at me.

'Look!' I lift up one boob. 'Ta da.'

I can see Stringer growing and we both look down. A second later, he catches my eye and we both giggle.

Slowly I slide my hand towards him and curl my

fingers around his erection. We're still looking into each other's eyes and smiling.

'You're gorgeous,' I whisper. 'Because this is part of you.'

I can feel his hand tentatively moving over my breast and I can't help shuddering.

He leans forward and I close my eyes as his lips meet mine. I feel him stiffen in my hand.

'I'm sorry . . . I can't . . . I don't know . . .' he whispers, pulling back.

'Shhh. Don't be scared. I'll show you.'

And I will. Because nothing would make me happier. And after all, I may be trying to change my life and all that, but this *is* my area of expertise.

Part III

Stringer

I park the minibus outside my flat and turn off the engine and glance down at the – now irreparably trashed – sound system. There's a yellow-handled screwdriver sticking out of it, wedged in at an angle of forty-five degrees, from when Ug finally cracked half-way up the M4 and brought the demonic reign of the panpipes to an end. (Such was the violence and single-mindedness of his attack that no one had the guts to ask him why precisely he happened to have a screwdriver about his person.) No doubt I'll be held responsible for the damage by Easy Riders Van Hire when I drop the minibus off for Matt tomorrow morning, but looking across at him slumped in the passenger seat, I don't have the heart to make an issue of this right now.

Matt is not a pretty sight. His black hair is greasy and unkempt, reminding me of the feathers on one of those beached seabirds you see on the television after there's been an oil spill. His face doesn't look much better. Were I to attempt to pin an age on him without knowing him, I'd place him nearer sixty than twenty-eight. The corners of his mouth seem intent on falling below the limits imposed by his chin and the droop of his eyes would put Deputy Dawg to shame.

Mentally, I can only guess at what he's going through. Matt himself has hardly spoken on the journey back to London, apart from to grunt goodbyes at the other members of the stag party, all of whom I've now dropped off. If back-of-the-bus rumours are to be believed, however, his liver is currently in the throes of processing the best part of a bottle of vodka, several shots of whisky, a *Phantom Menace* mug-full of Bailey's Irish Cream, and an unspecified quantity of beers. In other words, or in the words of Ug, to be exact, 'A legend has been born.' Or it's attempted suicide, depending on your point of view.

Matt turns and looks out of the window, noticing, I think for the first time, that the bus is stationary.

'Are you sure you want to walk home?' I ask him.

'It'll do me good,' he mutters, unbuckling his seatbelt and retrieving his bag from behind the seat. 'Maybe clear my head.' He looks at me sheepishly. 'How about you? You gonna be OK about dropping off the minibus for me tomorrow?'

'It's no problem,' I reassure him, noticing a bead of sweat trickling down his cheek. 'Early night for you, mate . . .' I suggest.

'Yeah,' he sighs, shaking my hand, 'like that'll solve everything.' He manages a weak smile, adding, 'I'll see you at the wedding,' climbing out of the minibus and walking slowly down the street.

I get my own bag and lock up the minibus, before walking down the stairs to my front door. I can sympathize with the way Matt must be feeling. I'd almost forgotten quite how bad a big night on the booze could make you feel. My day has been experienced in slow motion. Even now, my reactions and movements are sluggish, and a tide of bile keeps threatening to burst from my throat. I feel like I've got a dose of the flu. Then there's the guilt, the familiar guilt from days gone by, of willingly poisoning my system. All right, so it's probably not as bad as it seems. I got smashed out of my mind. It's not as if it's the end of the world. I do feel compromised, however, as if I've backed down on one principle and it's only a matter of time before I back down on something worse. That's how boundaries work, isn't it? Once you've crossed one and survived, you're tempted to go back for more.

The smell of stale cigarette smoke engulfs me the moment I get inside, and worsens as I walk through to the sitting-room. I don't know which hits me harder, the fact that something is wrong, or the realization that, with everything else that has happened over the weekend, I've hardly given Karen a second thought. My mind travels back to the conversation I had with her about Chris before I left, and starts to work over the possibility that she might indeed have broken up with him during my absence.

This possibility is increased by the state of the sitting-room. It's a disgrace. Sunday newspapers are strewn across the carpet. The small wicker bin by the television is stacked with empty Stella cans and Chinese take-away tins, one of which has been employed as a makeshift ashtray. On the television screen, a neglected Lara Croft is impatiently waiting for her next instruction. I pull back the curtains and open the window. Cool air floods in and I stand here and simply breathe a while. On further investigation, I discover that the kitchen is in a similar state of disarray. On the table is a dried Pot Noodle with an encrusted spoon sticking out of it, and at the foot of the cooker is a half-eaten piece of charred toast.

I knock gently on the door to Karen's bedroom, but there's no reply. I push the door ajar and peer inside. The curtains are drawn and the lights are out. Karen, however, is very much in. I stand here in silence for a second or two, simply staring. She's naked, lying flat on her stomach. The thin rectangle of light cast by the open door illuminates her skin from her ankle to her neck, casting her in a golden glow. She stirs slightly in her sleep and I turn my back and quietly close the door.

Light rain starts to fall as I cover the last hundred

metres before Battersea Bridge. I'm beginning to feel better about myself. It's as if every footfall I make is driving more poison from my system. I run on, raising my arm and checking my watch. I'm nearly five minutes behind my normal timing for this part of my circuit, which doesn't surprise me in the least. My lungs feel like they're nursing a puncture and the stitch in my side is threatening to split my torso in two. Half-way across the bridge, I stop to rest. Wiping the sweat out of my eyes with the back of my hand, I stare down at the murky waters of the Thames. They aren't half as murky as my mind.

For most of today, I've successfully managed to avoid thinking about what happened with Susie last night. I say most, because when I woke up this morning and felt the warmth of her body next to mine, she was fairly hard to avoid. I lay there for a few moments, motionless, uncertain what to do. Jump up and down in unbridled celebration? Or lie there and try and act as cool as possible? I ended up doing neither. I simply concentrated on the regular stroke of her breath on my chest and bathed myself in the sense of deep relaxation it transferred to me. This wasn't a time for thinking. It was a time for being.

Some time later, perhaps sensing that I was awake, she stirred.

'Stringer?' she queried, her voice hoarse, a look of confusion on her face.

I squeaked and then, clearing my voice, tried again. 'Yes?'

'Did we . . . ?' she began, before pausing and lifting up the duvet and peering beneath. The urge was there to twist over and hide myself, but I knew there wasn't any point. What little there was to see, Susie had already seen the night before. I felt my buttocks clench in apprehension all the same as I waited for her sober verdict. When her face reappeared, she winked at me. 'Apparently so . . .' – she fired off a teasing wink – 'big boy . . .'

I narrowed my eyes, but failed to hide my smirk. 'You promised—' I started to remind her.

'I know,' she said through a yawn, 'but now that we've established that your bits are fully functional, I think maybe you should start working on burying your complex. Which should start with developing a sense of humour about it.' Her hand reached down and gave me a gentle tug. 'Which should start now.'

'All right,' I said, pulling her on top of me. 'And what next?'

She dipped her neck down and sniffed her armpit. 'Probably best we should get showered.' She looked up grinning. 'I could certainly do with a wash.'

'And after that?'

'Get back to our respective parties, to stop them gossiping about us, if nothing else.'

'You're probably right,' I said, although we both knew that wasn't what I'd been asking about.

She stared at me, serious for a moment. 'After that, though . . .'

'Yes?'

'Well, it would be nice to see you before the wedding . . . if you want . . .'

'I do.'

'How about Tuesday night?' she suggested. 'We might have recovered by then.'

'Good. Tuesday it is.'

I did mean it when I said I wanted to see her. Then, looking into her eyes, I meant it completely. I remembered how I'd felt in the minutes after she'd fallen asleep the night before, lying there with her in my arms, unable to close my eyes, afraid that if I slept I'd wake to find that none of this had been real. I hadn't wanted to lose the sense of elation that was coursing through me. I'd wanted to hold it close, just like I was holding her. It had been my moment, my coming of age, the integration of the part of me that up until then had always been missing.

I continue to watch the water glide by. The elation hasn't lasted. I always thought that losing my virginity would alter me in some monumental way, affect my whole sense of being and outlook on life, but it hasn't been like that at all. Like an orgasm, it's faded away, so that all I have left is the memory of the events that led up to it. I'm the same person I was before. Nothing has changed. The things I craved then are still missing from my life: sensuality, romance and love. Sex doesn't come with these things attached. I realize that now. All sex does is give you a means of getting close enough to someone to hope for them. Perhaps it's the same for everyone. All of this might be easier to bear if I had someone to tell, like Richard Lewis back in the old schoolyard. Perhaps he'd tell me that he felt disappointed, as well, and not to let it stress me out. I don't have anyone to tell, though, and it does stress me out.

The harsh truth of the matter is that the sex last night was awkward, or at best comical. There's no hiding from that. I have Susie to thank for at least introducing an element of the latter to cover my bowel-melting embarrassment over the former. It was nothing like the false story I told KC in the kitchen, the way I'd dreamt it would be. There was no soft music playing on the stereo, no candlelight and no passionate kisses. In their place was the muffled sound of Amy and the others drunkenly dancing the night away in the living-room, the bright light of a bare bulb, and Susie's giggled instructions. We were drunk. It wasn't romantic and it wasn't sensual. It was a process, like therapy. She was the psychiatrist and I was the patient. She knew what she was about – had probably been there a thousand times before – and I didn't have a clue. I was crap, and I knew it, even if she was being too kind to point it out.

I don't blame Susie for any of this. It couldn't have been any other way. I only blame myself. Excluding the obvious reason that I didn't think I did, why couldn't I have had the balls like everyone else to get it out of the way when I was a teenager? Courage then, I'm certain, would have saved me the embarrassment I'm suffering now.

I would be different, I think, if I were in love with Susie. If that were the case, I'd be standing here now, looking forward to calling her and arranging a date. I'm not in love with her, though, and in spite of what I previously assumed, having sex with her hasn't changed that. We were friends last night and, as we dressed this morning, the only alteration I felt between us was that we'd formed a bond of trust. Emotionally, nothing had changed.

I look up from the water and stare across the river at Battersea Park. I picture Karen lying naked on the bed at home. This picture is clear, unlike the one I retain of Susie last night. I think about the stink of the cigarette smoke in the flat coupled with the fact Karen doesn't smoke, and I consider the absence of Chris. Then I start running back towards the flat.

'Hello,' Karen says. She's drunk and her voice is slurred. 'How was the stag?' Her head is bobbing like she's at sea. 'Anything interesting happen?'

I'm standing in the bathroom doorway, a towel around my waist. The cloud of steam which engulfs me only serves to add another surreal element to an already surreal situation. Karen is sprawled on the sitting-room sofa, wrapped in her tatty, off-white dressing-gown. She's smoking a cigarette with one hand and clutching a tumbler full of whisky in the other. Her face is a wreck, her eyes bloodshot and her skin puckered and raw.

'It was fine,' I say. 'All very predictable.' *Oh, yes*, I don't add, *and I lost my virginity to a girl called Susie and now I don't even know whether this was a good thing or not.* 'The usual male nonsense,' I quietly add.

Karen's head continues to bob. 'Chris finished with me,' she says.

'*He* finished with *you*?' I check, because this isn't what I was expecting at all.

'Yeah,' she says, smoke drifting from her nostrils towards the open window. She notices my eyes following its progress. 'Sorry about the smoke and the mess,' she says with a grimace, 'I've been on a bit of a bender since it happened.'

I stand dripping on the tiles. 'When was that?'

'Lunch-time. Today. Just before he left.' She clicks her tongue and looks resigned. 'That's the sick bit. He shagged me this morning when I was half-asleep, then got up to make coffee, and then came back and broke the news as he was getting dressed. A farewell fuck. After all that time. I ask you: how crass is that?'

I push my wet hair back out of my eyes. 'But I thought you were going to break it off with him. I thought that's what you'd decided . . .'

'I hadn't decided it,' she corrects me, 'I was just thinking about it. I wasn't certain. I still thought we might be able to make a go of it. Stupid, huh?'

'No,' I tell her lamely, 'not really. It was a big decision to make. You had to be certain.'

'Doing it is different,' she continues. 'To do something like that you've got to divorce yourself from the whole event. You've got to be callous and not give a damn.'

'Like Chris,' I deduce.

'Exactly,' she agrees, sipping at her whisky and crushing her cigarette out on the saucer on her lap, 'like Chris.'

I walk over to the sofa and she pulls up her knees to her chin to make room for me next to her. The saucer slips from her lap to the floor, sprinkling ash and cigarette butts across the grey sofa cushion and the carpet. I spot a can of Pepsi Max at the foot of the sofa, reach down and, dusting the ash from it, crack it open and drink. Sitting down and turning to face Karen, I ask, 'How did he break it?'

She laughs wryly. 'That's the best bit. Like a business-man. He just gave me the facts, like I'd just lost a contract, or something. He told me that we both knew that things between us hadn't been good for a while, and he couldn't see any way we could rectify the impasse. *Impasse,*' she scoffs. 'What the hell is that supposed to mean? Who did he think we were, a couple of generals in a stand-off?'

'How did you react?'

She smiles bitterly. 'How do you think? I flew off the handle – obviously. And I made a complete spectacle of myself – obviously.' She looks me straight in the face. 'I accused him of seeing someone else. I accused him of doing exactly what we all know he's been doing.'

'And is he?' I query. 'I mean, did he admit it?'

'Eventually. After about ten minutes of histrionics on my behalf, yeah, he did. Her name's Emma.' She shivers and tugs her dressing-gown tighter across her chest. 'God, I can hardly bring myself to say her name.' I get up and walk over to the window and close it. 'He works with her and – get this – he didn't mean it to happen, it just did,' I hear her saying. 'How can that be, Greg? You're a bloke. Tell me: how does something like that just happen?'

'I don't think it does,' I tell her truthfully, sitting back down before adding, 'It's never happened to me.' I examine her face. Misery and confusion chase one another like clouds across her eyes. She reminds me of

Xandra at our father's funeral. There's reality and there's acceptance, and neither of them have yet sunk in.

'Well, with Chris, it just did,' she continues. 'He just happened to start hanging out with her. He just happened to start hanging out with Emma a lot, and he just happened to start feeling emotions for her, and he just happened to end up in bed with her.' She takes the whisky bottle from the table next to her and replenishes her glass. 'I mean, what an arsehole. It makes me wonder, it really does . . .'

'Wonder what?'

'What I ever saw in him. I don't mean to begin with. I understand my feelings back then, when we were both students. He was a giggle. *We* were a giggle. But these last few years . . .' She sighs and drinks. 'What a waste of time. I'm spineless, that's my problem. I shouldn't have had to wait for him to make the decision . . . I should have had the guts to do it myself a long time ago, instead of clinging on. I should have got on with my life.'

'You mustn't blame yourself.'

Her cheeks flash red. 'Why not? Look at where I've got myself,' she mumbles, her voice suddenly small. 'Nowhere. If I'd got this out of the way before, then I wouldn't be sitting here now, drunk and depressed, worrying about where my life's heading, wasting my energy hating Chris, heaping this misery on myself.'

'I'm glad,' I say. I don't intend to say this, but I do. And there, once it's said, it's out.

She examines my face quizzically. 'You're glad that I've been dumped?' she queries.

'No, I'm glad that it's over between you.'

She nods her head in understanding. 'I knew you would be.'

Caution descends. 'What do you mean?' I enquire.

She looks at me over the rim of her glass. 'Well, you've never exactly been his biggest fan, have you? You told me you thought I could do better. And you were right. And you were right about something else, too' – a trace of a smile appears on her mouth – 'he does have a bad case of halitosis . . .'

I bite my cheek, recollecting our conversation of a few months ago. 'You remember me saying that?'

'I wasn't that drunk.' She raises her glass and briefly examines it. 'Certainly not as drunk as I am now.' She rubs at her brow. 'I remember that and a whole lot more . . .' She looks up and waits for me to react.

'I thought he was a waste of space,' I admit, because there doesn't seem to be much point in holding back my opinion any longer.

'He couldn't stand you either, for what it's worth . . .'

'Why?' I ask, surprised. 'What did I ever do to him?'

'It wasn't anything you ever did to him,' she explains with a shrug, 'it's what he thought you might be doing to me.'

My heart begins to race. 'But that's ridiculous . . .'

'I don't know,' she says, cocking her head to one side and looking me up and down. 'You're a good-looking guy. And you're single. And we're friends and we live together. It wouldn't take a great leap of imagination to wonder if anything was going on between us.'

If my heart was racing before, it's now heading supersonic. 'He didn't ever accuse you of anything, did he? Anything concrete?'

'Not in so many words, no,' she confesses. 'But then, he was hardly speaking from a position of strength, was he?'

'No,' I say, 'I don't suppose he was.'

'I used to watch him watching you when he was down to stay. He used to look between the two of us and try to spot a connection.'

'But there wasn't one,' I point out.

'What?' she asks, leering at me now. 'Not ever? Not even when I first started living here?'

'I don't know,' I stumble.

She smiles sadly. 'I didn't know for certain, either,' she says. 'I just thought ... at the beginning ... I used to catch you looking at me sometimes ...'

'I was curious,' I say.

'About what?'

'About you ... about what kind of person you were ...'

She leans forward and hooks my eyes with her own. 'So you never fancied me? Not even a little?'

My mouth opens. I don't know what I'm going to say. I'm feeling torn. I want to speak my mind, but after all this time, I feel paralysed by the reality of it all. I'm scared. She's drunk and this might not mean anything. It might just be words, nothing more. She might simply want an ego massage from a friend she considers safe. Before I have a chance to reply, however, she wipes any doubts I might have away.

'I'm only asking,' she continues, 'because I fancied you. Because I *still* fancy you,' she qualifies. She rolls her eyes and sits back. 'There,' she says, 'it's out.' She knocks back the remains of her whisky, and gasps at the recoil.

I don't move. I feel like I've just suffered an electric shock.

'I'm having a bit of a day of it today, aren't I?' she reflects. 'Getting all my emotions out in the open ... how very nineties of me ...' She scrunches up her face and focuses on mine. Then she stabs her finger at me in an exaggerated, drunken gesture. 'You can say something, you know. And don't worry if you don't feel the same. I'm up to my neck in rejection at the moment. I doubt another dose is going to kill me.'

Slowly, I reach out and take her hand. I hold it tight, staring down at it, feeling her respond to the pressure I'm applying, wringing my own hand in return. 'That isn't how it is,' I say, my voice almost a whisper.

Her grips tightens and she cups my chin in her hand. I feel her finger stroking my cheek. 'Say it,' she says.

'That I fancy you?'

She nods.

'I do,' I say.

I feel her breath against my face and then it happens: our mouths touch.

'You came in to my bedroom earlier, didn't you?' I hear her whisper, her lips brushing against mine as she speaks. 'You saw me lying there.'

I close my eyes. 'Yes.'

'I wasn't asleep. I knew you were there.'

She kisses me again and, this time, our lips part. Her hand moves across my thigh. I know where this is going and I want it. I want it desperately. As we continue to kiss, however, I remember Susie, and how it felt to be kissing her last night, and I find myself locked in confusion. It was nothing like this. There was none of this intensity, none of this heady mixture of sheer terror and delight, but still, it was something, and something it would be wrong to ignore. I don't even know where Susie and I stand. We're seeing one another on Tuesday, but does that mean we're going out? Does that mean that at this very instant I'm being unfaithful to her, and that I'm no better than Chris? I don't know. I've got no frame of reference for this, no pages of history to flick back over to see what I should do next. All I have is my conscience, and it's that which makes me stop.

'What is it?' Karen asks as I pull away.

'I can't do this.'

She grimaces, confused. 'Why not?'

I take a deep breath, then speak. 'I met someone this weekend,' I say slowly, avoiding looking directly at her. 'Susie. On the stag weekend. She's not impor—' I begin, before stopping myself. 'No,' I say, 'that's not true. She *is* important. She's a friend.'

Karen is moving back away from me. 'It's OK,' she says, her voice flat. 'You don't need to tell me any more. If you're involved with someone . . .' She shudders. 'I'm drunk . . .' She shakes her head and closes her eyes. 'It was stupid of me to lay this on you.'

Quickly, I take her hand. 'No,' I say firmly, 'it's not like that. It's you I want to be with, Karen. Believe me on that, because it's true.'

Karen hears the words, but not their meaning. 'What about her?' She chews her lip. 'Susie. What about her?'

'We had sex,' I say. 'I'm not sure where we stand now. I can't do this – with you – not until I've cleared things up with her. I'm meant to be seeing her on Tuesday. I'll—'

Whatever I've said, it hasn't come out right. I haven't made myself clear. This much is apparent when Karen lurches to her feet and stands there swaying, looking down at me. Her expression is devoid of emotion. I can't read it. 'I'm going away tomorrow,' she says. 'To my parents. It's already arranged. For a week. I'm going away for a week.'

'Please, Karen,' I implore, trying to take her hand again, 'stay and listen.'

She puts her hands demonstratively behind her back and slowly shakes her head, looking down at her bare feet. 'Not now,' she mutters. 'This is too much. Too much has already happened today. I should go now. To bed.' She stumbles past me to the end of the sofa. 'I'm sorry,' she tells me. 'I should have kept my mouth shut.'

Then, with my reply still lodged in my throat, she walks away. I hear her bedroom door shut and I find myself completely alone.

Susie

Monday, 20.00

I can tell I've gone too far: my kidneys feel like Jackie Chan's punch bag.

Where has my stamina gone, that's what I want to know? I'm usually the up and at 'em party girl, burning the candle at both ends and in the middle – with a flipping blowtorch. But just look at me. One bender of a weekend and I'm wiped out. Maybe I can't stand the pace any more. Maybe I'm 'on the turn' as they say back at home. That's it then, is it? Spiky facial hair and tubigrip stockings for me.

I dump my carrier bags on to the kitchen chair and ease up, putting my hands to my back like a heavily pregnant woman.

Today has been terrible. I had terrifying dreams all last night: textbook money worries, if you ask me. I was too spooked to go back to sleep, so I ran a hot bath with the last of my Matey. But my subconscious must have been working overtime, because just as I was about to step in to the bubbles, I suddenly remembered my old post office savings account. I'm pretty sure Gran opened it for me when she had a surprise win on the premium bonds years ago. I was so excited about the prospect of my forgotten stash, not to mention twenty odd years of untouched interest, that I pulled the plug immediately, threw on some clothes and drove to the post office. I suppose it was wishful thinking that they'd hand over the booty with no post office book and only my Blockbuster video card as personal ID, but after an hour of queuing and several minutes of pleading, the man behind the counter told me I was bonkers and I left empty-handed.

Of course, when I got back to the car, the meter had run out and a traffic warden was already filling out a ticket.

'Don't do this to me,' I pleaded. 'You don't understand, *I'm really poor.*'

'So am I,' he replied, ripping off the ticket with a flourish and slapping it on my windscreen.

Cheeky beggar.

'But I can't pay this. I haven't got a job,' I wailed, panic gripping me as I read the fine.

'You should get down the parking services. They've got plenty. Become a warden,' he commented, strolling on like an old-fashioned bobby. 'Or a clamper. Opportunities are unlimited,' he added as he passed me.

'I may be desperate, *but I'm not that desperate,*' I yelled after him, yanking the car door open and growling with frustration.

Things didn't improve. With a sense of bad karma hanging round me, like cheap body spray, I bit the bullet and went to the bank. I cast a little good-luck spell on my cashpoint card, but deep down I knew, even before I inserted it into the evil jaws of the machine, it was going to be devoured. It still hurt when it did it, though. It's the final indignity, having your card reclaimed by the bank. It's so humiliating being this age and this skint. To be honest, I think I was better off as a student and I thought I was on the breadline then.

I sat in the car like a stake-out cop, smouldering with indignation and sipping a take-away cup of tea which tasted suspiciously like cat pee, munching a Burgerama burger – definitely akin to dog poo – and flicking through the free papers I'd picked up from the tube station. Two minutes later, I felt vaguely poisoned and horribly depressed. The only jobs in the paper were for media sales and I'm hopeless on the phone.

Miserably, I fished in the bottom of my bag for some chewing gum, finding a broken bag of tobacco, some furry tampons and my old Simpsons diary. I pulled it out and looked at the scrawled addresses in the back, wondering whether any of the people on my faded list would give me a job, or at the very least consider a loan. But I doubted it, since I'd slept with most of them. I was about to throw the diary back in the bag and continue my gum search, when I spotted the address of Top Temps, an agency Amy recommended ages ago. And I don't know why, but it seemed worth a go.

The Top Temps office near Oxford Street was jam-packed with girls, all younger and smarter (and no doubt more qualified) than me. I waited for ages before I was shown in to this pokey office, furnished by a desk and a rubber plant with lipstick-stained cigarette butts poking out of the soil. I scanned through the form I'd been given. Amy said that reception work would be a doddle, but I had to fib on most of the questions. When I finally got to see a consultant, she looked me up and down and, barely scanning my form, told me it was highly unlikely that she would be able to place me. She suggested that I'd be better off trying my local job shop. There's attitude for you.

Then there was Quikshop to finish me off. All day my body has been saying gimme fruit, gimme vegetables, gimme vitamin pills, gimme Evian, gimme *anything* to make me feel healthy again, but the only place dodgy enough to accept my even dodgier credit card, is Quikshop on the corner. I hate it in there. Most of the locals assume it's a front for a drugs cartel and I think there's some truth in the rumour. The man in there certainly looks like he's capable of slitting your throat. The smell is vile – a cross between spilt beer and a rotten pork pie and the fresh produce section has wrinkled, decomposing objects in it, including the lemons, which have certainly been there since I moved in. Perusing the barely stocked shelves, feeling eyes on the back of my neck, the best I could come up with was tinned tomato soup, stale sliced bread, Semtex cheese (plastic and potentially lethal), and a giant bottle of Coke. Why is it that you can't eat healthily in this city unless you've got loads of money? If it's not enough that I'm going to be begging on the streets soon, I'll be poisoned too.

I wedge up the window and tip the soup into a saucepan. My antique gas cooker has a will of its own, so I stand guard, yawning. The last thing I need to finish off today is to turn this place into a towering inferno.

My flat opens on to a closed-off fire escape stairwell at the back, with snaking rubbish shoots from all the flats spilling down to the pungent bins below. From across the way, the *Eastenders* theme music is accompanied by a bawling child, whilst two floors down, Evander and Tyson, the scary bull mastiff puppies, are chewing each other's ears as usual. The old woman on the ground floor has her back door open and is coughing again, the debris of fifty years of non-stop Rothmans rattling around her lungs. Poor thing. She makes me want to give her a good thump on the back.

The sound of other human lives is comforting, I suppose, but I can't help thinking that it's so isolating, everyone living alone in these huge blocks on top of each other like this. I don't even know the names of the people who are probably cooking their tea on the other side of this wall, not two foot away. Somebody might be dead in there for all I know and judging from the smell, it's a distinct possibility.

There's no point in getting a bowl, since it's just me on my own. Less washing up. I slump down at the table with the saucepan and pull my old portable radio towards me, but there's nothing on. It's all patronizing adverts or discussion programmes about third-world agricultural systems. I twiddle with the dials until I find some dance music and nod my head in time to the beat, but I can't get into it.

Dipping my bread in the soup, I stare at it soaking up the orange liquid and realize that I want to cry. It's partly the alcohol comedown, which I guess is inevitable. I must have singed all my happy receptors, overdosing on such a good time. But then there's the other, childish part of me that always wonders at times like these whether it's better in life *not* to experience something and therefore not feel the loss of it? For example, would my tinned tomato soup taste better to me if I'd never had a lovely bowl of Mum's vegetable cawl before? It's a pointless question really, because I love tinned tomato soup. It's just that I'm missing home comforts. Just like I'm missing the weekend.

I don't want it to have ended. It went so fast and having spent all that time with Amy and finally pulling Stringer, being here alone in my flat, catapulted back in to my dismal life, it feels more lonely and depressing than it did before. I know I'm being daft, because Amy's hen weekend can't be counted as 'normal', but I like having a big group of people to hang out with. It makes me feel like I'm a character in a *Friends* episode. Except with soft drugs and scruffier hair.

Even with H being such a bitch, it was still good fun. And it won't ever happen again. Everyone will be together at the wedding, but after that, Amy will be off with Jack and where will I be?

I wipe out the pan with another slice of bread and dunk it in the sink. Usually when I'm in this sort of mood, I go out. But I'm too tired and I'm also too skint. Just breathing in this parasitic city makes you haemorrhage cash. There's nothing for it but to go to bed. It's the only place I can afford.

I put on my oldest nightie and lie on the duvet, feeling

like a ten year old. The curtains are drawn, but there's no doubt that it's still daylight outside and I can hear the pigeons scratching on the roof. I roll on to my front and grab my book from the table. Maybe I'll make some headway with it, since I've been reading it for weeks and keep falling asleep on the same page. I sigh, wriggling the pillow underneath me, wishing it was Stringer's warm body. Not that I feel sexual in any way, I just want a cuddle. Maybe I'll get one when I see him tomorrow. At least I've got that to look forward to.

I obviously pass out completely because it's after midnight when I'm woken by the phone. I stumble out of bed and pick up the receiver in the hall.

It's Maude.

'You sound half-asleep!' she chirps.

'I was fully asleep,' I yawn, taking off my glasses. I fell asleep with them on and I've got big dents in my nose which I rub.

'Well, wake up, silly.'

'OK, OK, I'm awake.'

'Now listen. I've been doing some serious scouting around for you and I think you'd be crazy not to come over here.'

She goes on to explain the reasons why. How I can get a temporary job quite quickly. How if we all get a car together, we could road-ride across the whole of the States and it'd be the adventure of a lifetime. And all the time I listen to her, I can feel her speaking straight to my heart. Because I have always wanted this kind of adventure and because I'm not ready to settle down here.

'Do you remember that list we made of things we'd do before we were thirty?' asks Maude.

'Yes.'

'Well, what was number one on your list?'

'To see the world,' I admit, remembering my youthful exuberance.

314

'Now's your chance. Whatever it takes, get yourself over here. Come on, Sooze, you're always an opportunity grabber. You've even taken some bad ones, but I promise you – this one's the best one you're going to get.'

Once she hangs up, I rest my hand on the receiver. I can hear the buzz of the fridge and the corridor is illuminated briefly by the orange light of a passing car. Everything is normal, except that everything has changed, because I know Maude has said the magic words to make up my mind.

I scuttle to the bathroom and sit on the loo, feeling overwhelmingly perplexed and excited at the same time. The phone starts almost immediately. Cursing, I run back to answer, thinking it must be Maude again, but it's Stringer.

I'm so shocked by Maude's call, and so close to wetting myself, that I probably sound odd, because Stringer goes all stilted and formal.

'Is it a bad time?' he asks. 'I'll call back. It's late . . .'

'No, no. Sorry, it's fine.' I rub my forehead. I've been looking forward to speaking to him so much, but now I feel caught off-guard. I want to blurt it all out, to tell him all about California, but something stops me.

'How are you?' I enquire instead, sounding like a curt secretary and not like me at all.

'Oh, you know . . .' The way he says it makes me see his face again. The way his eyebrows crumple together and he gets a crease between them. 'Work has been mad. I guess I'm just knackered.'

'Knackered in the literal sense of the word, eh?' I guffaw clumsily. I grit my teeth as soon as I've said it, feeling like an idiot. There's a pause as Stringer clears his throat.

'Susie, about tomorrow . . .'

'Tomorrow?' I say, trying to sound breezy, as if I

haven't remembered we have a date. 'Tomorrow? Oh yes. Is there a problem?'

'It's . . . um . . . a bit tricky. I'm run off my feet with this job and I don't think I'll be able to make it.'

'Oh.'

'But I'll sort something out for the weekend, I promise,' he rushes on.

'Not to worry,' I say, sounding magnanimous, but thinking how far away the weekend sounds.

'Sorry,' he apologizes again. 'I do want to see you.'

'I want to see you, too,' I blurt, but I know I sound odd.

Stringer ignores it. 'So we'll speak later in the week, then,' he says.

And then he's gone. Just like that. As if we'd exchanged business cards rather than bodily fluids the last time we met.

'Shit,' I curse. 'Shit, shit, shit.'

H

Tuesday, 09.30

Flipping open my compact mirror, I check my face and
dab more powder on my nose. I've done this twice
already this morning, but one final touch-up won't hurt. I
dig in my make-up bag and pull out my best Lancôme
lipliner, take off the lid and start re-outlining my lips.

'He's here,' says Brat, suddenly opening the door of my
office and leaning in on the door handle.

'Don't do that!' I snap, as the lipliner shoots towards
my nostril.

'Touchy,' he chides, before slamming the door and I
jump again.

I scowl after him, plucking a tissue from the box on my
desk and looking back in the mirror to correct my
mistake. I don't look so bad, considering I've hardly slept
and I've got a monster spot underneath a ton of concealer
between my eyebrows. I touch the spot with my little
finger and wince.

Come on. Stop putting it off.

I squirt some perfume on my neck, then dab my wrists
in the moisture and rub them together, before taking
some deep breaths as I smooth my clammy palms on my
skirt, but it doesn't help.

Laurent is here.

Here in London.

In this office.

Right now.

I pick up the pile of papers on my desk and put them in
order. Outside, Brat is whispering into the phone, his

hand cupped around the mouthpiece of his receiver. I stand impatiently waiting for him to finish and he glares at me when he finally puts down the phone.

'I need these copied,' I tell him, ignoring his pinched look as I place the papers on his desk. 'And the script revisions?' I ask.

'Well, if you'd give me a minute, I'd do them,' he grumbles.

I exhale impatiently. Since I came back in yesterday morning, Brat's had a real attitude problem. He's probably moody because he was dossing about all week when I was in Paris.

'Perhaps if you made *fewer* personal phone calls, you'd *have* time,' I say pointedly. 'I want them on my desk this afternoon. No excuses.'

I turn and, clutching my folder against my chest, make my way to the lift, wondering if anyone can tell that my knees are shaking.

This is so unfair. I wanted to see Laurent on my own when I saw him again. I imagined us meeting at the train station in Paris, or running into each other's arms at an airport. I didn't imagine he'd be here, in London. I hadn't pictured him in my world. In my office. *With Eddie*, for Christ's sake.

This is just going to be so humiliating. I haven't spoken to Laurent since I left Paris and by now he must think I'm a complete bunny-boiler. I left an excruciating, tearful message from Leisure Heaven, three messages on his mobile on Sunday night, then all of yesterday I tried calling his office, but he was 'in a meeting'.

By five o'clock yesterday, I was in the doldrums of despair and rang Amy.

'He hates me,' I announced.

'He doesn't *hate* you,' she said, obviously not taking me seriously. 'Maybe he really *is* in a meeting.'

'He's not. He's ignoring me. It's all over.'

'Calm down. It'll be fine,' she said, but she didn't sound convincing. She was more concerned about whether she should take Jack to Accident and Emergency, since he hadn't moved for twenty-four hours.

I'd just decided to call it a day and was shutting down my computer when Eddie came in.

'Everything OK?' he asked, breezily.

I nodded, knowing that he wanted something. 'I had a heavy weekend, so I think I'd better be off,' I said in a warning tone, opening my bag.

'Can you be in early tomorrow?' he asked.

'I always am,' I pointed out, shoving a manuscript in my bag, annoyed that he had the audacity to think I was a slacker.

'Only we've got a visitor coming,' he said.

'Who?'

'Laurent. He's over from Paris and apparently he'd like to have a look at our strategy.'

I couldn't have been more shocked if he'd told me the President of the United States was coming to visit, but I managed to hold Eddie's gaze, pretending to be nonplussed as my stomach did a somersault.

'I've got a meeting with Laurent and the other powers that be at nine-thirty, but I thought you might like to pop in and say hello beforehand, since you met him last week,' he said.

'Sure,' I said. 'Thanks.' I packed the rest of my stuff in my bag, my head whirring so much that I didn't notice Eddie standing there, looking expectant.

'Oh ... and ... er ... would you print out those schedules you did for me again, on headed paper? And bring them with you?' he added, before waltzing out without giving me a chance to protest.

I stood, stunned, for a moment, before gathering my jacket and practically running out of the office and back to my flat for an evening of frenzied grooming.

Of course the vain part of me is secretly thrilled, because there is a chance that maybe, just maybe, Laurent has planned this sudden trip because he wants to see me. Maybe he's been unable to return any of my calls, but was so desperate to talk to me that he decided to come in person to make up for not being around. Maybe he's got grand plans afoot to come and stay with me in London. Maybe he wants me to go and work with him in Paris.

Or maybe I should get a grip.

I've got my best Joseph suit on and a little top which I had to handwash and is still slightly damp, despite my desperate attempts at ironing it dry this morning. It feels uncomfortable on my back as I step out of the lift. I check the papers are in order again.

Eddie is in the meeting room with Laurent, showing him a clip of the daytime soap on the VCR in the corner. Laurent is standing, one arm across his chest, the other fist on his chin as he frowns at the screen. He looks tanned and slightly uneasy in his dark suit, but then I've never seen him dressed up before. I'm used to seeing him in jeans and a T-shirt and with his salt-and-pepper hair touching his collar. Seeing him in a suit makes him look like a football star on show and despite my vows to be professional, I can feel a dull ache starting in the join of my specially purchased sheer tights.

'There you are!' says Eddie, noticing me and pressing a button on the zapper. 'Laurent, you know Helen?'

'Hello again,' I say, smiling and lurching forward to shake his hand. The same hand I last saw reflected in my hotel mirror as it cupped my buttock.

'Hi,' says Laurent, simply, his dark blue eyes connecting with mine

'Well, then. I'll just go and get some stuff from my office and collect Will,' says Eddie, making for the door, but I hardly hear him. 'You don't mind looking after Laurent for a moment, do you?'

'Oh, um, not at all,' I smile.

We both watch as Eddie closes the door. Then there's a pause.

'So . . . ?' I say, half-clasping my hands in front of me.

As little questions go, it's loaded, but it's got to be, because we don't have much time and I've no choice.

Laurent looks at me and I'm aware of my lipstick and that I may have just been far too forward, but when he smiles slowly, relief rushes through me.

He *is* pleased to see me.

'So?' he repeats, teasing me.

I study the contours of his face – the way his eyebrow is arched and the cheekiness of the boyish dimples in his cheeks and, without thinking, I step awkwardly across the gap of patterned carpet between us and into his personal space.

'I missed you,' I whisper, reaching out to finger the cloth of his suit, remembering how snugly I fit under his arm.

'Oh Helen,' sighs Laurent. His accent is like a caress and I close my eyes, leaning towards him for a hug. But instead of catching me and holding me tight as I'm expecting him to, he grips me by my upper arms.

'I don't think you understand,' he says, his eyes gentle as he looks down into my face.

'Understand what?'

Laurent straightens up and lets go of me.

'About your visit,' he begins. 'It was . . . how shall I say . . . ?' He looks like he's trying to describe a tricky wine, but in the end plumps for, 'very special'.

I stand very still. Even with his heavy French accent, I can still hear the 'but' in his voice.

'What do you mean?'

'Oh dear.' He looks amused as he clocks my expression. 'I hope you have not got the wrong idea.'

'Wrong idea?'

'We cannot continue this . . .' he waves his hand between us as if dispersing a nasty smell, 'thing.'

'Thing?' I repeat.

Laurent comes towards me again, but I back away, nodding my head as the extent of my foolishness catches up with me.

'You are a beautiful woman,' he says, but I can't bear to hear any more.

'You used me,' I interrupt, shakily.

'I think we used each other,' he smiles, 'for a lot of pleasure.'

I stare at the carpet. I can feel my eyes smarting with anger and the bitter sting of foolishness.

'Can't we be friends?' he asks, putting his finger under my chin and lifting my face to his, but I rip my head away and he lets his hand drop just as Will, our chief executive, bursts through the door, followed by Eddie.

'Laurent, old chap!' he says, his arms stacked with files and video. His cheeks are red as he dumps everything on the table and bounds over to us.

'You've met Helen. Great, great,' he gushes.

Eddie runs his hand through his hair and looks nervously at me as Will embraces Laurent. He always gets nervous in front of Will and I shouldn't really be here. I pick up my file and shuffle the papers inside, feeling my eyes smarting.

'Right. Smashing,' says Will, putting his hands on his hips and nodding eagerly. 'How are things back home?' he gushes to Laurent. 'Your wife?'

Wife?

'And kids?'

I close my eyes. My knees are locked and every muscle in my body is tense.

'They're all fine, thank you,' says Laurent, graciously.

'Great. Smashing,' says Will again, rubbing his hands together. 'Shall we get on, then?'

I stare at Laurent, but my legs feel rooted to the carpet.

'Helen?' says Eddie, pointedly. 'It's nice that you've caught up with Laurent. Now perhaps we could have those schedules, please?'

'Oh . . . right,' I mumble, straightening up and flinging the file in front of Eddie as I stumble to the door.

Susie

'Come on, Sooze. Dirt, please,' says Amy, looking over her shoulder at me. She's by her kitchen sink, repotting a plant, and she's the one that's dirty, with soil up to her elbows and sprinkled around her feet.

'You know everything, already. There's nothing more to tell.' I shrug, laying the table for us, admiring the trendy lilac placemats. I've invited myself round for dinner, since Jack's out and Stringer has stood me up. Besides, if I spend one more minute pacing round my flat with only Pot Noodles for nourishment, I'll go mad.

Amy presses down the soil around the plant and her newly cut hair swings above her shoulders.

'That looks better,' she says, as she puts the fern back in its saucer on the windowsill.

'What's going on?' I ask, sitting down and looking round me. 'It's spotless.'

'Jack,' she laughs. 'When he finally got over his hangover, he had a flip about the state of the place. He hates me being such a slob, so he went berserk with the Mr Muscle.'

I laugh at the thought of Jack with a pair of Marigolds on.

'Guilt, probably,' chuckles Amy. 'I left him to it. Anyway, this domestic splurge won't last. He's getting the final load of his stuff from Matt's, so no doubt we'll be overrun with his bachelor bygones,' she says, screwing up the newspaper from the draining board.

'Eeeeuk! Porn mags, other girls' knickers, cheesy love

letters, bad compilation tapes, I know the stuff,' I nod. 'How rank.'

Amy looks me up and down. 'Jack? No no no. It'll only be old teddies and childhood photographs,' she says sweetly, as she stuffs the newspaper in the swing bin.

'You wish,' I laugh.

She gives me one of her best prison-warden looks. 'We shall exterminate all traces of the past,' she warns.

'Ouch! Quite the tough wife you are, aren't you?' I tease.

'As if!' she laughs, as she comes over to me, wiping her hands on a tea-towel, before throwing it at me.

'Now you,' she cautions, 'stop changing the subject. I want to hear all about Stringer.'

'What?' I ask cagily.

Amy puts her feet up on the chair, picks up a fork and starts picking out the dirt from under her fingernails.

'Well, for starters, does he justify being called "Horse"?' She looks up at me with her wicked grin.

And for the first time ever, I lie to her. 'Absolutely,' I say. 'Mind you, I'd call him more of a donkey.'

Amy squeals with delight. 'I knew it! You can just tell with blokes like Stringer. I knew he had a big nob.'

I smile uneasily, taking a sip of wine.

'So?' she continues. 'What was the sex like?'

And instead of telling her that I felt like the madam of a wild-west whorehouse, taking the cherry of the best-looking cowboy in town; and instead of admitting that it was drunken and clumsy and not the abandoned sex marathon I'd been expecting, without pausing for an instant, I lean on the table and fold my arms.

'Lovely,' I say, simply. 'It was lovely.'

'Lovely?' says Amy, screwing up her nose in disappointment. She puts down the fork and her feet. 'Is that it?'

She gets up and goes and checks the pan on the stove,

325

lifting up the lid. She's installed one of those trendy racks full of shiny metal cooking implements above her cooker and she pulls down a spiky spoon to stir the spaghetti. What's happened to her? The only thing she used to be able to cook was toast, and now she looks like she lives in a Sunday colour supplement.

'There's nothing wrong with lovely,' I say, defensively, but probably with too much emphasis, because Amy turns and looks at me.

'No. Of course there isn't,' she says and I know that she's accepted me into her club. The club of people who don't have to talk about their partners because it's private and special and lovely. Because they're in love. And there's nothing more to say.

And I've longed to be in Amy's club, for ages. Ever since she moved in with Jack and built her domestic heaven. But I'm not ready to join yet. And whilst, by the look on her face, I can tell that she's thrilled about the prospect of me and Stringer, I'm not.

Amy lifts down two plates from the rack and serves out the pasta.

'What is it?' she asks as she sits down, pushing my plate towards me.

'It's not like that. Me and Stringer, I mean.' I look at the steaming plate, breathing in the aroma of Amy's carbonara, but my appetite for once has deserted me.

'Sooze?' she asks.

I blow out a slow breath. 'I'm going away,' I say, bluntly.

'What?'

'To California. I'm going to travel with Maude and Zip.'

Amy sits back in her chair. 'Blimey! When did all this happen?'

'Maude rang me when she got there and again last night. It's a huge opportunity.'

'Oh,' she says, dumbfounded. 'So how do you feel about it?' she asks.

This is the six-million-dollar question and the reason that I'm here. Because although I'm excited, I'm also scared and Amy will know what's right. She's the one person I know who's qualified to take me through the pros and cons of such a huge decision, and to tell me that I'm making the right one. But I'm just about to ask for her advice, when the phone rings. She reaches over to the side and picks up the cordless phone.

'Hello?' she says, putting up her finger to tell me she'll only be a moment. But it's H on the other end and Amy pulls a grimace to me.

'What happened?' she asks, sympathetically, picking up her fork and urging me to start on my pasta.

Typical. This is the most important decision of my life and H has to go and interrupt it.

I stab my fork into my spaghetti, feeling absurdly cross. This is *my* moment and H has no right to intrude, but then I hear Amy taking a deep breath and sighing and I carry on chewing my pasta in silence.

A drama queen, that's what H is. If she had one ounce of self-awareness, she could sort out her own problems without leaning on Amy every two seconds. I mean, it's not as if Amy hasn't got her own worries.

But as I sit radiating bad vibes towards H, it hits me that I'm no better. I'm just jealous because I want Amy all to myself and for her to soothe all my worries away. The difference is, I don't need her to tell me what to do, because I already know. I've known it ever since Maude rang.

All day I've been wrapped in fear, worrying about Stringer, but now as I hear Amy telling H to be honest to whoever she's having a flap about, I apply a little honesty myself.

The truth is that even if Stringer thinks he really likes

me and I really like him, it's just that: like. I'm not in love with him. I may fancy the pants off him, but so will loads of other girls and now he's got his sexual confidence, who am I to stand in his way?

And if I'm really, really honest, his innocence puts me off. I've got a juggernaut of baggage and he's got a completely clean slate and I know that, even if I tried really hard to be a loyal girlfriend, I'd find a way to sabotage it. Because that's what I always do and Stringer won't be any different. I don't want another man I feel I have to look after. I want to be loved and protected, like Jack loves Amy.

But that's a mistake too. Jack doesn't protect Amy. We're not living in the 1940s. I look round their kitchen in the warm glow of the new lights they've installed and it's so cosy. And it dawns on me that that is what love is. When you find the person you'll compromise for and build a life with. When you meet the person whose junk you'll put up with and bad habits you'll live with, because they're your equal.

And I'm not even close to it. Not with Stringer, not with anyone. So in the meantime, I guess I'll just have to stand on my own two feet.

'Sorry,' says Amy, coming off the phone.

'Everything all right?' I say, sucking up a mouthful of spaghetti, but I'm not really interested in H and Amy knows it.

'Having a bit of a double-whammy work and bloke crisis,' she explains.

I don't say anything. There's a pause as we both eat.

'Sorry,' says Amy again, reaching over to touch my arm. 'I didn't mean for you to get interrupted. It's just that she was upset and I couldn't tell her to put it on hold.'

'It's OK,' I smile. 'Bad timing. You can't help it if

everyone wants your advice. I wonder what we'll all do when you get married.'

'Don't say that! I'm not dying. I'll still be here.'

'I know, I know,' I say. 'It's just that everything seems to be changing all of a sudden.'

'But change is a good thing.'

I nod. 'Scary sometimes.'

'Tell me about it!' she laughs. 'I'm going down the aisle next week. How scary is that!'

'It'll be a doddle,' I say. 'It's meant to be.'

'And how about this trip of yours? Is that meant to be, too?'

'I think so. I feel all nervous and excited, but at least I'm not feeling bored. It's going to take quite a bit to get the money together.'

'Have you told Stringer yet?' she asks.

I shake my head.

'You're worried about how he'll take it?' she says and as usual she's hit the nail right on the head. Because that is what's worrying me. I don't want to damage Stringer's confidence, or for him to think I'm running away from him. I know how deep his paranoia has been and the last thing I want to do is rekindle it. I don't want him to think I'm rejecting him. But I can't tell Amy this.

'I'm worried he thinks there's a boyfriend–girlfriend thing going on,' I explain.

'And there isn't?'

'Not really. I suppose there might be, in time. But I don't want it. I want to travel and see the world. I want this just for me. Does that sound horribly selfish?'

Amy smiles. 'Yes, but I'm delighted to hear you say it at last. You always put other people first.'

'So what shall I do about Stringer?'

'You've just got to be brave and tell him straight away, before he gets the wrong idea. And no offence, but

Stringer's had loads of women. I'm sure he'll get over it in time.'

'True,' I laugh, even though it isn't.

'I think it'll do him good to have his ego knocked into shape for once.'

'Maybe,' I say.

Amy fills up my wine glass.

'Well here's to you, my lovely Sooze,' she says. 'I won't half miss you.'

And I smile, sad and happy all at once, because she has no idea how much I miss her already.

H

Wednesday, 11.00

Craning my' neck to see the street name through the windscreen, I fling my *A-Z* on the dashboard as the car cigarette lighter pops out. As I cruise slowly along the row of parked cars, I negotiate the speed bumps whilst lighting my cigarette and squint through the window, trying to find the house numbers on the broken gates and shabby front doors of Barlby Road. It's a typical London street, including the bin men, whom I fail to notice, until one of them thumps my bonnet and I nearly jump out of my skin.

'Oi! Posh,' he yells, the huge rubbish lorry looming behind him as he waves a gloved hand at me.

Blushing, I push the button in on the side of the gearstick and hastily back up, until I find a space behind a battered white transit van and reverse in to it. I suppose the car is posh for round here, but I still feel like telling him the BMW isn't mine and that I'm not really a posh person at all: I'm a small person.

At least, I feel very small today.

I turn off the ignition and the electric aerial whirrs down into the boot and then all I'm left with is the bleeping sound of the bin lorry, a police siren in the distance and the overlapping shouts of the children in the school playground up the road. The sound of a Wednesday morning in the real world.

Real to me, at least.

Feeling shaky, I reach over and pick up Brat's letter from the passenger seat and read the address again. I found it on my desk this morning, just after I'd walked past his empty desk and a stony-faced Olive, who refused to talk to me.

The letter was perfunctory and polite, considering what had happened. In unusually flawless grammar, Brat explained that he was writing to inform me of his resignation, due to the irreconcilable breakdown of our working relationship.

Breakdown of our working relationship. I suppose that's one way of putting it.

It's the irreconcilable I've got a problem with. That's why I'm here. But I can't think about it too much, or I'll change my mind.

Tucking the letter in my pocket, I get out of the car, flick on the alarm and look around me and down the street. Through the gap between the gas cylinders and the council towerblocks, I can see the city skyline rising hazily in the London smog and it occurs to me that it must have been a nightmare for Brat to get from here to the office every day. No wonder he was late half the time.

Brat's house is at the end of the street next to a boarded-up dry cleaners. I push open the squeaky gate, a long shoot from the overgrown privet hedge tickling my face as I walk the few steps to the front door and scan the three doorbells by the pane of ribbed glass. I push the second bell, assuming that it must be for Flat 2, and wait, watching hot, soapy water trickle from a cracked pipe into the drain by my feet.

I tap my foot, feeling butterflies in my stomach as I look through the glass and try to make out the shadowy hallway on the other side.

I was in such a state after seeing Laurent yesterday that I didn't know where to put myself. I went to the ladies' loo on the second floor and paced like a caged loony hyperventilating with anguish. I couldn't cry, because I felt so foolish, couldn't scream because I was in the office, and couldn't berate Laurent, because he was in a meeting with my boss.

I don't know whether I was more cross with Laurent or me. He should have told me he was married, but then, I should have asked. All I wished was that I could open myself up and remove the Laurent experience altogether. But most of all I just wanted to hit something or someone because I felt so stupid. Unfortunately, my silent rant was interrupted by someone coming in to the toilet so I had no choice but to go back to my office with so much pent-up emotion in me that I was a walking bomb waiting to explode.

And eventually I did.

In Brat's face.

It had taken him ages to do the script revisions I'd asked for and as I sat, festering in my office, composing a vitriolic, aggrieved email to Laurent, I watched Brat through the glass, seething a little bit more each time he went off for a cigarette or made a phone call. By four o'clock I'd seethed myself into a full-scale fury.

'Get in here,' I said, through gritted teeth, flinging open my door and glaring at him.

'*Please*,' he muttered.

'Now!' I snapped, twirling round and storming back in to my office.

A minute later Brat came sloping in and I turned on him.

'These are a disgrace,' I said, flinging the script revisions at him and feeling myself losing it, as the papers cascaded to the floor.

Brat looked down at them, but didn't move.

'Jesus. Take it easy,' he said.

'Take it easy! Take it easy!' I spat. 'No, I won't take it easy. You've done nothing since I came back. *Nothing*. And I'm sick to death of your excuses. I asked you this morning for these and you've only just done them and they're so bad that I'll have to start all over again. Which means I'll be here until midnight. Again. Thanks to you.'

'Don't shout.'

I pointed my quivering finger at him, but he was looking at the papers on the floor, his body rigid.

'Yes, I will shout at you. Because you deserve it. You're hopeless. Do you hear me?' I yelled, flinging my arms up as I ranted round the office. 'All you do is smoke and chat to your mates . . .'

'Well, have you ever wondered why?' Brat snapped, cutting me off.

'Go ahead. Enlighten me,' I said, sarcastically, putting my hands on my hips.

'Because you're a bitch to work for, that's why I don't make any effort. Because I've given up. Because you want me to do all your dirty work, yet everything I do, you criticize, which is rich, considering you can't take any criticism yourself.'

'How dare you!' I yelled.

'Shut up!' he shouted back. 'I haven't finished.'

'I don't care,' I said, pointing to the door, my whole body shaking with fury.

'You don't get it, do you?' he said menacingly, tapping the side of his head. 'You're not getting rid of me. Because I'm going. I'm not going to put up with your histrionics any more. I've had enough. I won't put up with it. Just like Gav or any other bloke in their right mind won't put up with you.'

'You can't speak to me like that!' I choked.

'Yes I can. You're just a miserable, single cliché and the saddest thing is that you can't even see what you've become.'

'Brat!'

'And another thing. My name is Ben. Not Brat. The

only brat round here is you,' he said, before walking out and slamming the door.

Ten out of ten for staff management.

There's a silhouette behind the glass as the hall light is snapped on and a moment later, the door opens a crack and I catch a glimpse of Ben. His hair is wet and he's got a threadbare towel wrapped round his waist. He groans and disappears, so I push the door open a little. He's standing with his back against the hall wall, his eyes closed.

'Ben?' I say, trying to sound friendly.

'What do you want?' he says, with forced patience. His eyes are open now and they look bloodshot.

I pull his letter out of my pocket. 'I came about this,' I say.

'It's not up for discussion,' he says, wrapping one arm protectively around his chest and reaching for the door latch with the other.

I put my hand on my side of the door to stop him closing it.

'Please,' I implore. 'Can I just talk to you for a minute?'

'What's your problem?' he says, flicking his head at me. 'Can't face telling Eddie that I walked out on you?'

I press my lips together, feeling the sting in his words.

'No, it's not that. He knows already,' I say, but my voice is husky.

Ben looks at me, silenced for a moment.

'Can I come in?' I ask, looking up at him, but he folds his arms like a bouncer and the answer is obviously no.

'Look. I know you're very angry,' I begin.

'You don't even know the half of it,' he snaps.

I'm obviously not doing very well, so I might as well get straight to the point.

'I came to apologize,' I say emphatically, watching the toe of my shoe on the doorstep, the gesture reminding me of Matt at Leisure Heaven.

I look up at Ben, biting my lip and he stands for a moment before opening the door.

'In that case, you'd better come in,' he says, 'I'd like to hear this.'

Ben's flat is small and extremely untidy. The curtains are drawn and the air is thick with the smell of old socks and cigarettes. I perch on the arm of a brown corduroy sofa in the living-room, whilst he disappears into the bedroom to get dressed.

I'm tempted to do a runner, but I force myself to stay. Instead, I look around the room. On the wall opposite, there are two white rectangles surrounded by a smudged tan line and next to the window, a case of bookshelves with half a dozen books haphazardly thrown on the shelves. On the floor underneath them, there's a round stain on the carpet, surrounded by soil. Either Ben's just moved in, or he's in the process of moving out.

It dawns on me that over the past few months I've spent more time with Ben than I've spent with almost anyone else. And in all that time, I've hardly learnt anything about his life. Until now, seeing his home, which is distinctly Ben-like, I couldn't have imagined him existing in a world other than the office. I hadn't thought about him moving house, or travelling by tube, or sleeping, reading, watching movies or any of the stuff that makes him a normal human – just like me. I guess that's why I've landed up here.

'So?' he says, reappearing in jeans and an old jumper and I spring up guiltily.

He pulls open the long brown curtains to reveal another long line of plant-pot marks, scattered leaves and soil. Then he turns to face me and I know it's now or never.

'I'm sorry to intrude like this,' I say, playing uselessly with my hands. 'But I had to talk to you.'

Ben puts his hands on his hips and stares at me. His

face is set and stern and I look down at his bare feet, feeling nervous.

'I've been feeling terrible about what happened yesterday,' I start. 'And I don't blame you for handing in your notice. I'd have done exactly the same thing if it was me. But the thing is . . . I was completely out of order and I didn't mean half the things I said.'

There's a long pause as I look imploringly across the room at him.

'Well, I wasn't entirely complimentary either,' says Ben, quietly.

'The thing is . . . you're great at your job, which is why I came. I don't want you to quit over me. You've got a good career ahead of you and I talked to Eddie this morning and he'll give you a pay rise . . .'

Ben picks up a cigarette from a packet on the seventies coffee table and lights it.

'So you're trying to bribe me to come back?' he asks, cynically.

I run my hands through my hair and look up at the ceiling. 'Oh shit, Ben, I'm making a real mess of this, aren't I?'

He doesn't say anything, but rubs his toe on the carpet.

'Look. If you came back, you'd be working in a different capacity, more as an assistant and not just a secretary. I'd want you to be involved with everything so that you got to know my job. I did that when I was doing your job and I'm not going to stay there for ever and they'll need someone to take over from me . . .'

But Ben smokes, looking down at the carpet and I don't know if he's taking it in. He's certainly not responding. I look at him, feeling my throat constricting, wishing that I wasn't in this situation. Wishing I could take everything back.

'All I'm saying is that you don't have to have your life messed up just because I'm an emotional wreck.' I cough to clear my throat. 'That's all I came to say. I'm really sorry. I just wanted you to know.'

But I can't say any more, because I've failed him and I can't bear how sad that makes me feel. I turn to leave, but I'm nearly at the door, when he stops me.

'H?'

I turn round, hastily wiping my nose.

'Thanks for apologizing.'

I nod, trying to stop my chin quivering. 'Will you come back?' I beg. My voice sounds husky. 'Please?'

Ben breathes in and puts his hand on his hip. 'I don't think I can. It's . . . it's not the money.'

'What, then?'

'I can't do the job.' He looks up at me.

'You can,' I take a step back towards him.

He shakes his head. 'It's never going to work . . . between you and me. I can't work for someone like you, H.'

'What do you mean?'

'Your job is the most important thing to you. It's your life and that's the way you want it and that's fine. But it's not my life, too. Sure, it's important, but it's not the be all and end all. You take it all so . . . so seriously. As far as you're concerned, if other people don't feel the same way as you, then they're rubbish.'

I feel breath rush out of my lungs. 'I don't . . . I . . .'

'You do, H. You criticize everything I do. I meant what I said yesterday. I didn't mean to sound quite so rude, but I lost my temper. The thing is, you haven't once given me the chance or the time to succeed in anything. It's like you want me to fail.'

'I don't . . . I . . .'

'You expect me to go at your speed all the time, but I'm not you. I can't carry on knowing that every day you think I'm not good enough. I'm sorry, but that's the way it is.'

'Am I really that bad?' I groan, realizing that all the time he's been talking, I've been holding my breath.

Ben nods. 'I know you don't mean to be, but . . .'

'Oh God. I'm so sorry.'

I bite my lip and stare at Ben, seeing him clearly for the first time.

I don't know where we go from here.

'All that stuff about Gav . . .' he says eventually.

I wave my hand and try to smile. 'Don't worry about it. I probably deserved it.'

'No. It was out of order.' He gestures to the room. 'My girlfriend left me, as you can see. That's what all the phone calls were about. I'm not so far off an emotional wreck myself.'

I feel terrible. I hadn't realized he had a girlfriend. Let alone one he lived with.

'You poor thing.'

Ben blows his cheeks out as he shrugs, but his eyes are smiling.

'Shit happens, I guess,' he says.

'It must be something in the air,' I say. 'If it's any consolation, I got ditched too, yesterday.'

'Ditched? Who by?' he asks, looking confused.

'Laurent. You know . . . Laurent from Paris.'

Ben's eyes widen. 'You didn't!'

I nod, smiling at his mirth.

'But he's married! With kids,' he exclaims.

'Yes,' I nod. 'As I found out yesterday, *from Will.*'

'I knew all along,' he says, smugly.

'Well, you could have told me,' I scold, jokingly.

'And you could have told me what to do about Liz,' he scolds back, but we're both smiling.

'Shall we start again?' I ask.

He blows out his cheeks and looks down at his hands. 'I don't know. I'll have to think about it.'

I nod. 'I understand.'

'But you could buy me lunch?' he suggests, and there it
is – his old cheeky grin.

'You're on,' I smile.

Matt

'I'm just popping over the road,' Philip says, getting to his feet. 'Anything you need?'

'Yeah,' I reply, folding up the advert I've just drafted for a new lodger. I seal the envelope and hand it over to him. 'Can you bung this in the post for me on your way out?'

'Of course,' Philip says, taking the envelope and slipping it in to his pocket, before turning and walking across the room.

There's nothing quite like an adjournment for concentrating the mind. The other side's barrister was granted one two hours ago and there's still an hour of it left to run. I'm sitting at one of the tables in the Bear Garden, which unsurprisingly, for somewhere as riddled with quirks as the Royal Courts of Justice, isn't a garden at all. It's a red-carpeted, high-vaulted room with a gallery running round its top. An assortment of other solicitors, barristers and clients are scattered around the tables, shuffling through various briefs and folders, reading newspapers, or simply smoking and gazing idly about. I glance down at Tia Maria Tel's case folder on the table before me. It's as thick as my thigh. Then I sit back in my chair and, guiltily avoiding the stares of the oil-painted judges on the walls, yawn.

I suppose I should get a buzz from just being here. After all, in my line of work, it doesn't get much better than having a case in the High Court. It's the kind of thing I dreamed about when I was a student, the reason I

341

bookwormed my way through all those exams. And I do appreciate it, I really do. This morning, watching the war being waged in Court Room 22 has given me a thrill. I've done my stuff and Philip, our side's barrister, has been well-fuelled with information from the start. A job well done, I think, and I'm pretty confident that Tia Maria Tel's going to get his damages and apology. I should be feeling ecstatic. I should be feeling wired. But sitting here, waiting for it all to kick off again, I don't feel remotely connected to what's going on.

I can't blame my hangover any more for the intense sensation of alienation that's dogging me. Monday, Tuesday, sure. My skin still reeked of alcohol then, so it wasn't too hard to put my state of mind down to a bad case of session-induced paranoia. Yesterday and today, though, with my bloodstream cleared of booze, all I've been left with is the facts of how I behaved at the weekend and the problem of how the hell I'm going to face up to the consequences. And consequences there'll be. Soon. Nine days, to be precise. In nine days' time, I'll be standing beside Jack before the altar of Barking Parish Church. Next to him will be Amy, and next to Amy, her father. Somewhere just behind will be H.

Of course, I tried hating her. I tried telling myself on the walk back from Stringer's flat on Sunday afternoon that she was a bitch. She'd shagged me, bagged me and tagged me, and then jumped into bed with the next bloke who'd come along, without giving so much as one thought to the way I might have actually *felt* about her and what had happened between us. And as an excuse, this line of reasoning sufficed for a while. It worked until at least four in the morning, when I woke in a cold sweat and clawed the sheets from my skin and stared up at my bedroom ceiling, a shivering groan issuing from my throat. Shutting my eyes didn't work. When I opened them, nothing had gone away.

In hindsight, I wish I'd handled it differently. I wish I'd taken Stringer's news about Laurent on the chin and put my one-night stand with H down to experience. I wish I'd acted with civility and dignity when she came round to visit me and not tried to pip her to the post by lying about the way I felt about her. But that wasn't how it was. I acted like a ten year old, and an extremely immature ten year old at that. If I wasn't going to see H again, then maybe this wouldn't be so bad. And again, maybe this wouldn't be so bad if I didn't still care about her. But I am, and I do.

So what am I left with? There's the nagging doubt that if I'd told H the truth – that what had happened between us meant more to me than just drunken sex – then perhaps she might have looked on me with different eyes (an unlikely scenario, I admit). And then there's the imminent bout of excruciating embarrassment I'm going to suffer in her presence at the wedding.

Any solutions to the above? Short of failing to turn up for the wedding, I don't think there are. I can only hope. I can only hope that H will put my behaviour down to being drunk. And I can only hope that some time soon I'll get over her in the same way she's already got over me.

What I shouldn't hope, but what I still do, is that she'll get over getting over me and want me back.

Stringer

Saturday, 15.25

'Thank you so much for your help, Gregory,' Amy's mother, Sandy, says, kissing me goodbye.

'No problem,' I say with a dismissive shrug, trying to hide the fact that I'm pleased as punch inside. 'They were simply trying it on. All venues do.' I can't help smiling. I know what I've just done is only a small thing, but it's *my* thing and I managed it like a pro. I've proved something to myself today – that I can do it – and I feel chuffed to bits.

'All the same,' Amy's father, Hugh, interrupts, 'you were very good in there, and you've saved us a lot of money and we're extremely grateful to you.' He's a quiet, suited man and, as far as I can remember, this is the first definite opinion he's cast today. He must mean what he's just said.

'Yeah, nice one, Horse,' adds Jack, patting my shoulder, before slipping his hand back into Amy's. 'You knocked the wind right out of their sails.'

We're standing outside The Manor, near Barking. It's a mock-Tudor building, designed specifically for wedding receptions and business conferences. We've just concluded a meeting with Christine Wilcox, the Event Planner who's handling Jack and Amy's wedding reception. I'm here in response to a panicked phone call from Sandy yesterday. She and Hugh took a van over to Calais last weekend to pick up a load of cheap champagne and wine for the reception, only to discover on their return that The Manor intended to charge them extortionate corkage fees for every bottle opened on the premises.

In the car on the way back to London, with Jack and Amy in the front, and me wedged in the back, I gaze out of the window and run the conversation with Christine Wilcox back through my mind.

We were sitting at a table in one of the small meeting rooms on the first floor and, with the finer details of the wedding reception (the length of the tenancy, set-up and break-down times for my staff) out of the way, Jack broached the subject of corkage, the real reason we were here.

'The thing is,' he began, 'the corkage you're planning to charge basically defeats the object of Amy's dad going over to France to get cheap booze in the first place.'

Christine Wilcox, middle-aged and sharp-nosed, smiled thinly. 'I'm aware of that, Mr Rossiter, but you must also understand our position. Since you've decided to bring in' – she nodded towards me, checking her list – 'Chichi, your outside caterers, we've automatically lost part of our profit margin. It's therefore up to us to make that up in some other way . . .'

'Oh, come on,' said Amy, tapping her fingernail demonstratively on the table. 'What about the money we've paid for the hire of this place? It was hardly cheap. You can't possibly be telling me that you're not making a whopping profit from that.'

Christine stonewalled her. 'I'm sorry, Miss Crosbie, but The Manor's corkage policy is made perfectly clear in the Booking Terms and Conditions form you signed. As I explained to you at the time, you have the option of buying your wine directly from The Manor and thereby not paying corkage. I don't think you can hold me responsible for your decision to bring your own wine.'

'But the prices on your wine list are astronomical,' Amy protested.

Sandy placed a restraining hand on Amy's arm. 'I think she's saying her decision is final, dear,' she muttered, smiling awkwardly at Christine.

'That's it, then?' Jack asked, sitting back in his chair and linking his hands behind his head. 'You're not prepared to budge?'

'As I said,' Christine stated, folding her arms, 'the Booking Terms and Conditions form makes it perfectly clear . . .'

Jack looked over at me in frustration. 'Stringer?' he asked.

I cleared my throat and gave Christine my best smile, and then, when this had absolutely no effect on her, I cleared my throat again and made a show of flicking through The Manor's wine and corkage list and clicking my tongue in disbelief. I smiled openly at Jack and said to him, 'Astounding. These charges are the same as those at the Park Lane Hotel.' Obviously, this was a total fabrication, but never mind. I turned my attention back to Christine. 'Were you aware of that?' I asked her.

'No,' she replied, a degree of uncertainty evident in her voice for the first time since the meeting had commenced, 'I wasn't. No.'

'Quite astounding,' I repeated, smiling wearily and putting the list on the table in front of me. 'Well,' I began, looking slowly round the assembled people as I spoke, before finally settling on Christine, 'if you're not prepared to lower the corkage charges, I suppose you leave us with no other choice.'

Christine relaxed visibly. 'So which is it to be?' she asked Jack. 'Will you be paying the corkage or using our in-house wine list?'

'No, no,' I interrupted, gaining her attention again, 'I mean, we'll have to do without wine altogether.'

There was silence for a couple of seconds as Christine and I stared at one another. Out of the corner of my eye, I noticed Amy digging her mother sharply in the ribs, signalling her to keep quiet.

'I don't think I'm quite following you,' Christine finally said.

'It's the only way I can see ourselves getting round this corkage issue,' I went on to explain. 'If we don't have wine, you won't be charging us corkage, correct?'

'Yes,' she said slowly, 'but—'

'Well, that's simple, then. We won't. There are plenty of other drinks I can arrange. Cocktails, for example. Chichi does a great line in cocktails. And you can't charge corkage on spirits, can you?'

'Er, no.'

'Splendid.' I turned to Jack and Amy. 'What I suggest is that we forget the wine altogether. I'm sure Hugh won't mind holding on to what he's already bought. It's not exactly going to go off, is it?' One cautionary look from Amy, and Hugh nodded in agreement. 'We'll limit the champagne to the toasts, and we'll use magnums, so the corkage won't add up to much there.'

'Sounds perfect,' said Jack.

'Of course,' I added to Christine, 'you'll lose your profit margin on the wine almost entirely, but' – I flicked the Terms and Conditions with my finger – 'that doesn't appear to be a contractual problem . . .'

I watched the penny drop in her eyes: no wine meant no profit. Go on, think about it, I silently urged.

Christine scratched at her nose, then said, 'Um, in certain circumstances, I am in a position to offer some sort of leeway.'

'A one-off corkage fee, for example,' I swiftly suggested, 'whereby Mr and Mrs Crosbie could pay you an agreed fee and then be able to open as many bottles of wine and champagne as they like.'

'Erm, yes,' Christine reluctantly agreed. 'A one-off fee might make sense in this particular case.' I raised my eyebrows, inviting her to continue. 'Shall we say one thousand pounds?' she offered.

I whistled low. 'That's rather steep and I don't know if it makes it worth our while reversing our decision over the cocktails. Five hundred would seem more reasonable, wouldn't you say, Jack?'

'Spot on,' he concurred, trying not to smile.

Christine considered this in silence for what felt like a long time. 'I'm still concerned about our profit margin. Could you see yourself stretching to seven-fifty?'

'Six,' I said.

'Very well,' she finally agreed. 'Six hundred pounds it is.'

Here in the car, I continue to watch the countryside drift past the window and I'm still buzzing. This is probably the first time I've done something of any real significance in the work arena, and it's great that the recipients are my friends. But then I sigh, wishing that the rest of my life could be so simple . . .

Aside from the note I found from Karen on Monday evening, there's been no word from her. I've left two messages with her parents and she's responded to neither. I can't say I'm surprised at this. The note Karen left was unequivocal. It was short and to the point:

Dear Greg,

Sorry. Sorry. A million times sorry. Can we forget about what happened last night? I hope so. I was upset and confused about how you felt. I hope that when I come back everything can be normal between us again. Please forgive me for making such a fool of myself.

Your friend,
Karen

The living-room was spotless as I sat there reading her note, all evidence of her bender wiped away. I went through to my bedroom and lay on my bed, reading and rereading what she'd written. It was no good, however. There was no secret message hidden between the lines. She'd been *confused*. That was all there was to it. She regretted her outburst and wanted our relationship to return to the way it had been before. What she hadn't accepted was that my *normal* feelings towards her had never been, and would never be, normal. I wanted to remind her of this. I wanted to repeat it to her until she accepted it as the truth. Why couldn't she have stayed and let me finish off what I was saying about Susie? Why couldn't she have let me explain that I was prepared to break things off with Susie so that I could be with her? Why did she have to leave with so much unsaid?

'I saw Matt last night,' Jack calls back.

'How is he?' I ask. 'Recovered from the stag weekend?'

'H is still angry with him,' Amy says. 'Apparently he was a bit ratty with her when she called in on your apartment to sort things out with him.'

'Not surprising, really,' I comment, then noticing Amy's look, explain, 'He was terribly upset. He really fancied her, you know.'

'Yes,' Amy said. 'Well, that's her choice and, if you ask me, it's a pity. I think they'd be great together. All the same, he should have been a little more grown-up about it.'

'There's a little more to it than that . . .'

'Such as?'

'He knows about Laurent, Amy.' I shrug apologetically. 'I told him.'

Amy's face is a mask of confusion. 'But how?'

'I was there in the steam room,' I confess. 'With a towel on my head. You two started talking and it was too late to stop you, and I didn't know what you were doing there, and I was confused . . .'

'Oh, Stringer,' Amy groans.

'Who's Laurent?' Jack asks.

349

'A French businessman H slept with while she was away.'

'What?' Jack exclaims. 'Just after Matt?'

'Yes.'

'Oh, God, Stringer,' Amy cries. 'He must be gutted.'

At this juncture, my mobile rings. I hold up a hand to Amy as I pull it from my pocket. 'Hang on a second. It's probably work. I'm bossing a job at the London Aquarium tonight.' I put the phone to my face. 'Hello?'

'Stringer?'

'Yes?' Then I recognize the voice. 'Oh, Susie,' I say, turning to face the window. 'Hi.'

'Go get 'em, Horse,' Jack calls out.

I ignore him. 'How are you?' I ask Susie, feeling guilty just at the sound of her voice. I've been too busy with work to see her, and haven't had a chance to tell her about Karen. I haven't even spoken to her since Thursday, when I . . . oh, tits . . . when I arranged to see her tonight.

'Fine,' she says cheerily. 'Are you still on for—'

'No. Shit, I'm sorry. Tiff's sick and I've got to cover a job for her tonight.'

'Oh.'

'Listen,' I say, 'can we rearrange?'

There's a pause, then: 'I'd rather it was tonight. What time do you finish?'

'Not until midnight.'

'I'll come along then. Is that OK?'

'Yes,' I agree, thinking that I must get this out of the way before Karen comes back next week, or I'll be back at square one again. 'I'll have a word with security at the main door.'

'See you then,' she says and cuts the line.

I put the phone down and look back at Amy. I notice that I'm sweating. 'Now,' I say, 'where were we?'

Susie

Saturday, 23.30

I feel ridiculous.

Absolutely ridiculous.

I probably look like a lady of the night, standing here, waiting for the last tube to take me to my midnight liaison with Stringer. I certainly feel like one.

I'm not sure why I'm so nervous about how I look, or why I've bothered to put on my floral print dress. It's not as if Stringer hasn't seen me at my absolute worst: in my oldest bikini at Leisure Heaven, for a start. And what about last Sunday morning? I'd hardly have won first prize in a Monroe lookalike contest when we woke up together in bed, hungover and smelly. So why have I trussed myself up like a Christmas turkey, now I'm going to tell him I'm doing a runner? I doubt if it's going to make a blind bit of difference. Perhaps there's a bit of me that thinks if I look feminine and pretty, it'll soften the blow. But actually, now I think about it, if I looked my usual dog-eared self, it would probably make things easier for Stringer. You never know, he might even be grateful that I've let him off the hook.

The tube pulls in and I duck out of the way of a swaying mass of blokes who pass me and career to the other end of the carriage, singing football songs. I smile wryly, feeling nostalgic about the quirks of the city I'm leaving.

I hug my bag on my lap and read the adverts above the windows, since I'm too jumpy to read my book. Anyway, I've decided to give up on it, since it does nothing but send me to sleep. There's an advert for hayfever nasal spray, one for the Tower of London and a first-hand account of finding true love through a dating agency, which is compelling reading, but I doubt it's true.

I put a lonely hearts advert in the back of *Time Out* for a laugh once. I received an astonishing amount of crude replies and went out with this one bloke, Jimmy I think his name was, who told me half-way through his Pizza Hut pizza that he'd brought along the studded dog collar and leash his ex-wife had given him. I did a bunk from the ladies' loos.

See, that's one way to dump someone. Just disappear and never see them again. Or, if they're very persistent, be brutally honest, which is just as effective. *I don't fancy you any more* is my preferred line and on the whole, blokes respond quite well to it.

Thinking about it, in all the relationships I've had, nine times out of ten, I've finished them. I would even go so far as to say that dumping people is one of my special skills, along with joint-rolling, bong-making and blow jobs. It's a pity I can't put any of them on my CV.

But Stringer's different. Because I don't want to run away, or be blunt, because I care about him and I don't want to hurt his feelings. It's not the fact that we had sex that makes me feel worried about seeing him and saying what I've got to say, it's that we've shared our feelings with each other and our secrets. I don't want him to think I'm betraying his trust, as if what he said meant nothing.

You don't know, I tell myself. You don't know until you see him.

Except that I feel even more nervous when I do see him. He's standing in the middle of a reception area in the London Aquarium, issuing orders to ten or so staff as they roll table tops round to the side of the room and stack up gilt and red-velvet chairs against the wall.

Stringer looks tired and preoccupied and I watch him

for a moment, wishing I hadn't forced this meeting. I'm tempted to leave before he sees me.

But he does see me.

I clutch my bag with one hand and wave stupidly with the other.

'I'll be ten minutes,' announces Stringer to his staff, not taking his eyes off me, but I can't read his expression.

'Hi,' I say shyly, walking towards him.

'You came,' he says, leaning forward to kiss me on the cheek. Hardly the rapturous reception I'd feared, but then this is Stringer at work and he's not exactly the world's greatest flirt.

'Yep.' I smile.

'Well, um?' he says, sounding flustered. 'Would you like a coffee or something? I think there's still some in the outmess.'

'OK,' I say.

The tanks are lit up and everywhere brightly coloured fish are darting about. I go over to have a look.

'Here you go,' says Stringer, coming up behind me and offering me a cup.

'Thanks,' I say. 'This is an amazing place, isn't it?'

He nods and stares at me for a moment.

'You're looking very pretty,' he says.

'Yeah,' I say. 'Pretty awkward.'

Stringer laughs nervously and looks away. He rubs his cheek.

'Shall we?' he says, pointing along the way to a private space.

We walk in silence and I look at the fish, sipping my coffee, but when we're out of sight of his staff Stringer stops.

'Susie?' he says, pulling my arm, so that I turn to face him.

I think he wants to snog me.

Uh-oh.

I put my coffee cup down on a ledge and put my hand on his chest.

'Stringer,' I say, gently. 'There's something I've got to tell you.'

'There's something I want to say, too,' he says, pulling away.

This is not the reaction I've been expecting and it throws me for a second.

'OK,' I nod. 'You go first.'

'No, no. You go,' he says, starting to pace.

'We'll be here all night, at this rate. Come on, tell me what it is?'

Stringer fiddles with his hands, looking as if he's tying himself up in knots and I brace myself for some sort of declaration. This could be very messy, but at least if I know how he's feeling, then I'll know how to break my news.

'I don't know how to say this,' he says, eventually and looks up at me.

I reach out and touch his waiter's tunic. I can feel how firm his arm is beneath the cloth.

'Stringer?' I say, searching out his eyes and looking at him. 'How about a bit of advice?'

'OK,' he nods.

'Don't make this difficult. Do what I do and be blunt. It works every time.'

I stand back, away from him and fold my arms sedately in front of me.

'Right,' I say. 'I'm ready. Sock it to me.'

Stringer takes a deep breath.

'Just the facts, mind,' I say and Stringer smiles.

'OK,' he says, wiping a lock of hair away from his eyes, but looking straight back down at the carpet. 'These are the facts: I'm in love with my flatmate, Karen. I have been for as long as I can remember. And I never thought anything would happen, because I was . . . well . . . you know, and she had a boyfriend.'

'And . . . ?'

He blows air up over his face. 'But her boyfriend finished with her last weekend and she made a pass at me on Sunday when I got back from Leisure Heaven. But I told her about you and . . .'

I nod seriously as he peeks up at me and I turn my hand, urging him to go on. My heart is beating fast with a curious emotion, despite my tough-girl act. I can't tell if it's jealousy or relief, but I can feel a bubble of laughter creeping up my chest and tugging at my mouth.

'I'm scared shitless,' continues Stringer to the carpet. 'And I don't know what to do, but I had to tell you before anything else happens with Karen. If it does, that is. She was drunk and I didn't explain things very well and after I told her about you, she walked out.'

I pull a face at him, but he hardly notices.

'The thing is, I don't think I can have a relationship with you, when this is how I feel.'

He exhales. 'There, that's it,' he says, looking up at me.

But I'm giggling, my hand over my mouth.

'What?' he exclaims. 'What's so funny?'

'Nothing,' I laugh.

Stringer puts his hands on his hips. He looks slightly flushed. 'OK. Now your turn,' he says, his forehead crinkling. And he looks so deliciously cute, that I don't know whether to kiss him or wrap him up in a big duvet and hide him away, so that he's protected from us women for ever.

I go over to him, biting my lips together, smothering my laughs.

'Oh Stringer,' I say, wanting to touch his hair as I look up at him. 'I've been in a pickle all week about seeing you,' I admit. 'One of my best friends has gone to California and I've decided to go out and join her, but

I've been so worried about telling you. I thought you'd be offended, and all this time, you've been thinking about *another woman*,' I tease.

'So you're not cross?' he asks, smiling bashfully. 'Only we did . . .'

'Yes, we did,' I agree. 'And it was lovely. But it was just sex. And sex can be all sorts of things, but you mustn't ever take it too seriously. It's supposed to be fun. Remember that.'

Stringer puts his hands in his pockets and we're silent for a while.

'You're going away?' he says. 'When?'

'Soon. After the wedding.'

'How do you feel about it?'

'Scared shitless,' I mimic, 'since you ask. But never mind about me. You'd better talk me through Karen and how we're going to get you out of this mess,' I say, linking arms with him.

And as we walk and he talks away, I feel fine. I don't feel jealous or relieved or any of the things I thought I would. I just feel close to him like I did last weekend and pleased he can still tell me.

'I wouldn't worry,' I say, when he tells me about Karen's note. 'She probably feels like shooting herself. There's nothing worse than waking up and realizing you've made a drunken pass at your best mate. Believe me, I've done it hundreds of times.'

'But what if she really means it? I mean, what if she just wants to be friends when she gets back?' he asks. 'What if that's it?'

I look around us. 'Well, you know what they say,' I joke. 'There are plenty more fish in the sea.' I nudge Stringer in the ribs, but he's having none of it.

'Stringer,' I say, seriously. '*Of course she fancies you. You're a god.*'

'You're not helping,' he tuts at me, but I can tell he feels better.

'Have a bit of faith, man.'

'Do you honestly think she'll listen to me?'

'I'd bet money on it. Which is a lot, considering I haven't got any.'

'Greg?' It's one of Stringer's staff calling him.

'I'd better get back,' he says, apologetically.

'Don't worry. I'll be off now.'

'Are you sure you'll be OK?' he asks. 'I'd take you home, but I've got all this . . .'

'Don't worry about me. I'm a big girl.'

Stringer grabs my arm. 'Susie. About what happened last week,' he says.

I smile and look down at his flies. 'What, that, you mean? I haven't told anyone. I may have a big gob, but I'm not that indiscreet.'

'No, I don't mean that.'

'What then?' I ask.

'I just wanted to say thank you, that's all,' he says softly, cupping my cheek in his hand.

'Go on with you,' I say, but I can feel myself choked up with sentimentality.

'No. Thank you,' says Stringer, pulling me towards him and squeezing me tightly. 'Friends?' he asks, kissing my hair.

'You bet,' I say, pulling away. 'Now, go get that girl.' I prod him in the chest. 'When's she back?'

'Beginning of next week,' he says.

'Well, I'll look forward to hearing all about it.'

'I don't know how to thank you,' he says, as we part.

But as I sit on the top of the night bus, looking out over the city, it's me that should be thanking Stringer. Because he was the one who made me think of my vision. And although, for ages, I thought the vision was about him and having a platonic relationship with him, it was

357

actually about me and giving more of myself than just sex. And I've achieved it.

Stringer

Tuesday, 22.40

'Susie?' I ask.

'Stringer?' Her voice comes down the line, lost against the sound of music.

'Yes. Hi. How's it going?'

'Hang on a tick,' she shouts. 'I can't hear you. The radio's . . .'

I hear the sound of her putting the receiver down and footsteps crossing the floor at her end. It occurs to me that I've never been to her flat, and now that she's going away, never will. I sigh, looking around my own sitting-room. It's as spotless as when Karen left it. I force myself to sit down in the armchair. I've been pacing the room for the last hour, reciting lines like some out-of-work actor waiting in the wings for the big audition. In all this time, I haven't managed to get them right once.

'God, I'm knackered,' Susie says, coming back on to the line.

'Busy day?'

'Busy bloody life,' she says. 'I tell you, mate, this jumping ship to the States malarkey isn't all it's cracked up to be.'

'You're not thinking about changing your mind, are you?'

'Definitely not. Just my possessions. It's staggering, the amount of tat I've managed to collect since I've been in this place. I've filled up enough bags to keep Oxfam busy for a decade, and I'm not even half-way there yet. And that's only my clothes. I can't even bear the thought of

359

chucking away any of my other stuff. And then there's Torvill and Dean . . . Don't suppose you're interested in looking after them, are you? It's just that I can't bear the idea of shoving them down the toilet like Mum suggested . . .'

'I take it we're not talking about the eighties ice-skating icons here?'

She sniggers. 'Don't be silly, you daft pillock. They wouldn't flush. Their skates would get caught in the U-bend. No,' she hurries on to explain, 'Torvill and Dean are my goldfish. They're ever so nice and well-behaved. Fully house-trained. They wouldn't give you any trouble, I promise.'

'Fabulous as they sound, I'm afraid I'm going to have to decline your kind offer. The last goldfish I had died before I got it back from the funfair.'

'Shame.'

'How about Jack and Amy?' I suggest. 'Might make an interesting wedding present.'

'Now, there's an idea.' She pauses for a moment and I don't fill the space. 'Is everything OK, Stringer?' she checks. 'You sound a little bluesy.'

I sigh, looking round the flat. 'Yes, I suppose I am a little.'

'Karen's not back, then?' she asks, guessing the real reason for my call.

'No. Not a word. I tried her parents a few minutes ago, but got the answering machine.'

'You're going to have to sit tight and wait then, aren't you? She's got to come back some time. I mean, there's all her stuff for a start and, as I now know from personal experience, a girl's not easily parted from her tat.'

'You're probably right.'

''Course I am. Now, more importantly, have you decided how you're going to play it with her yet?'

'I'm not sure. I tried working it through in my head,

but it never quite rings true.' I consider my failure and conclude, 'I'll probably end up simply telling her the truth.'

Susie tut-tuts at me. 'Christ, no. Don't go doing that. Not the whole truth and nothing but. That's crazy talk. You go telling her you're head over bloody heels in love with her and she'll probably run a mile.'

'But why?'

'No fun in it, is there? Nothing to chase if you've already got it on a plate. Truth comes later. Trust me on this one, Stringer. You're new to this, so take the word of an old hand.'

I laugh, despite myself. 'If I can't tell her the whole truth, then what *do* I tell her?'

'Don't tell her anything. You already know you fancy each other, so stop arsing about and cut to the chase. Give the girl a snog. That's all she needs to know. She can't be all embarrassed about what she said, or worried about you and me, if she's got her tongue stuck down your throat, can she?'

I hear the noise of a key in the lock of the front door. 'I've got to go,' I say.

'That her?' Susie asks.

'Yes.'

'Well, good luck to you. And as you boys say,' she adds with an evil cackle, 'give her one for me.'

I can almost hear Susie grinning as I put down the phone.

I'm standing when Karen comes in to the sitting-room, a gym bag over her shoulder and a clutch of mail from the hall table in her hand. Her hair has been cut: short, above her ears. It shines like silk. She's wearing black trousers and a grey cashmere top.

'Hello, stranger,' she says, dumping her bag on the floor, looking me apprehensively up and down.

'It's Stringer, actually,' I tell her. 'But you can call me Greg.'

She allows me a watery smile, but her eyes remain timid. She walks over to the sideboard and puts the letters down, staying hunched there for a moment, before turning round to face me. 'I think I owe you an apology,' she says. 'Did you get the letter I left for you?'

I'm about to speak, to tell her that she doesn't need to say sorry and to tell her why, when I stop myself. Instead, I remember Susie's advice and simply say, 'Close your eyes.'

Karen looks doubtful, the corners of her mouth trembling slightly, as if torn between joy and pain. 'Why?'

'Please,' I ask her, 'just do it.'

She does. She closes her eyes and straightens up, folding her arms across her chest. I stay where I am, looking at her. She's so close, but suddenly she seems an impossible distance away. 'Well?' she asks, tapping her foot impatiently.

Then I do it. I cross the gap between us in what feels like a single stride. Gently, I lower her arms and take her hands in mine. She opens her eyes and I allow us a nanosecond's eye contact before closing mine and leaning down and kissing her. I don't know how long the kiss lasts, but when I come up for air, we're still pressed tight together and there's an insane light dancing in her eyes. From her grin, I can only assume the same light is dancing in my own. I don't know who starts it, but the next thing is we're moving towards her bedroom. At her doorway, I stop, letting her go first. I watch as she walks to the bed and turns on the bedside lamp. She sits down and, not taking her eyes off me for a second, starts to unbuckle her belt.

'Karen,' I say, suddenly nervous, the dread of a hundred similar situations coming back to haunt me, 'there's something I've got to tell you.'

Her fingers hesitate in their task. 'What?'

I shake my head and, with it, the demons from my mind. 'Nothing,' I say, walking over to join her. 'It doesn't matter. Not any more.'

Matt

Sky is sitting in the armchair opposite. She's twenty-three years old and stunningly attractive: long, raven-black beaded hair, five ten with captivating grey eyes. We're in the living-room of my house. I'm on the sofa and next to me is Chloe, who's been helping me interview prospective lodgers to take Jack's old room. I've just finished explaining to Sky about the house's more idiosyncratic features: the pool table, and original bar fittings from when this place was still a functioning pub.

'It's just so much fun,' Sky exclaims.

'I think that's probably just about everything covered,' Chloe says stiffly, checking her watch. 'Any other questions, Matt?'

'You mentioned that you'd be doing yoga in the garden, if the weather was good,' I say.

Sky beams at us. 'Oh, yes. I love the feel of the sun on my bare skin. That's why having access to a walled garden will be so good.'

'I see,' I say, and I do, I see her out there in my mind's eye perfectly. 'I've always been interested in taking up yoga myself,' I tell her, ignoring Chloe's groan. 'Being a successful lawyer is all well and good, but sometimes I do wonder if I'm neglecting my spiritual side.'

'Oh, please,' Chloe mutters. 'The nearest you've ever got to spirituality is communing with a bottle of whisky.'

'Maybe you're right, Chloe,' I say, frowning profoundly at Sky. 'Maybe I'm not capable of reaching out for a higher plane.'

'Oh, no,' Sky says, concerned. 'You're perfectly entitled to your belief, Chloe, but I think that everyone has it within them to set out upon the road to spiritual enlightenment.'

'Perhaps . . .' I begin, before deliberately reining myself in. I shake my head dismissively. 'No, it would be too much to ask . . .'

'What?' Sky enquires, leaning forward.

'I was just wondering, if you did move in here, if you might be able to teach me the basics, you know, just to get me up and running . . .'

'Of course I would,' she says, beaming again. 'Nothing would give me more pleasure than to help you find yourself.'

'Right,' Chloe butts in, getting to her feet and making a show of checking her watch again, 'we're going to have to draw this one to a close now' – she fixes me with a glare – 'aren't we, Matt? We've got someone else coming in a few minutes.'

I pick up the list from the sofa beside me and run my eyes down it. 'No, no,' I contradict her, 'I think Sky's the last.'

'No,' Chloe corrects me, 'she's not.' She smooths down her trousers and shoots Sky a quick, razor-edged smile. 'I'll show you to the door,' she says.

'Oh, OK.' Sky picks up her Indian tapestry bag and stands.

I stand, too, and walk over and shake Sky warmly by the hand. 'I'll give you a call,' I say.

'Great.' She wavers, self-conscious under Chloe's glare. She smiles awkwardly. 'I'd better get going, then. Nice meeting you both.'

Chloe walks Sky out to the front door and I wave at her as she sets off across the road.

'Reaching out for a higher plane,' Chloe sneers, coming back in to the living-room and giving me a withering look. 'Reaching out and making a grab for her tits, more like.'

'You're too cynical,' I tell her, doing my best to appear offended.

She drops down on to the sofa next to me. 'She was an airhead.'

'Just because she's got a different outlook on life from you, doesn't necessarily make her an airhead.'

'She was thick as a brick,' Chloe continues to rail, goggling at me. 'She's called Sky, for Christ's sake. What else do you need to know?'

'May I remind you that it's customary for parents to name their offspring, so you can hardly blame Sky for that, can you?'

Chloe hisses through her teeth. 'You astound me sometimes, you really do. Anyway,' she adds, 'I thought you were meant to be all cut up about H?'

'I am.'

'But you're still considering letting Sky move in on the grounds that she might indulge in a bit of nude yoga with you in the back garden?'

'I can think of worse qualities in a lodger.'

Chloe chooses to indulge me on this issue. 'Like . . .'

'Well, look at the others we've seen,' I protest. 'They've hardly been ideal, have they?'

'Keith was all right . . .'

'No, Chloe. Keith was not *all right*. I think we can safely assume that Keith was probably on day release from a nearby mental institution. Apart from his disturbing interest in the view of the cemetery from the attic, his overriding concern was' – I consult the notes I've been keeping – 'and I quote: "Have you got a cellar? Only I've got some stuff – *private* stuff – that I'd like to keep down there if you have." ' I look up at Chloe. 'Like the polished skulls of his previous landlords, no doubt . . .'

'OK,' she concedes, 'Keith was a little weird.' She checks her own notes. 'How about Alice, then?'

I just stare at her. I don't even bother raising my eyebrows. Alice's first question on seeing the living-room was which nights would she be able to use it for her Church of the Possessed Apostles seminars.

Chloe examines her notes again. 'William, then. He was nice enough. Good sense of humour, I thought.'

'You'd have to have with a face like that.'

'Ian?'

'He smelled.'

'Of what?'

'I dread to think.'

She examines her notes yet again. 'Dick?'

'I never trust anyone named after the male sexual organ.'

'Maddy?'

'Mad.'

'Julia?'

'Peculiar.'

'Jonah?'

'Unlucky.'

Chloe chucks her notes across the floor in frustration. 'Fine,' she says. 'Sky it is. But don't come bleating to me in a month's time when it doesn't work out.'

'Why shouldn't it?' I ask.

'For the simple reason that your motives for getting her to move in aren't exactly honourable, Matt. You want her in so you can shag her.'

'And learn yoga,' I add.

'Right. And when you've shagged her – assuming she's even remotely interested – and learnt yoga, what then?'

'Shag her again?' I suggest.

'And then?'

'Just what's your point?' I ask.

'My point, Matt,' she slowly spells out for me, 'is that

you can't sit there like you were this afternoon, whining like a wounded puppy about being on your own, and then go saddling yourself with a deeply dippy hippy who you couldn't develop a meaningful relationship with in a million years. She'll drive you nuts and you know it. Not to mention holding you back from meeting someone else . . .'

'Fine,' I say, depression swamping me, 'so if not Sky, then who? We've interviewed eight people today. And that was the A-list. The other people who rang up either couldn't string a sentence together, or tried to Scrooge me on the rent.'

Chloe leans forward and picks up her notes. 'All right,' she says, taking out a pen, and switching in to marketing mode. 'Let's do this scientifically. If the calibre of interviewees is poor, then what we need is a differently phrased advert. Let's make it as specific as possible, and hopefully that way we'll get you the kind of lodger you want.' She pats me on the hand. 'Come on,' she says, 'this will work. Describe your ideal lodger to me and I'll draft the ad.'

'OK,' I tell her, 'I want someone who's funky, not boring, and who'll become a great mate.' I think on this more. 'He – it should definitely be a he for the reasons you've already outlined with Sky – should be the kind of guy who'll chat with me in to the small hours and make me howl with laughter. Preferably, he wouldn't be in a profession or in the City, because I get enough of that at work. He should be creative, but not pretentious. Maybe a musician, or an artist, or—'

'Or Jack,' Chloe says.

'What?'

'Jack. I mean, that is who you've just described, isn't it?'

'No,' I say, then thinking, 'Well, yeah, but not really . . .

though, generally, yeah ... someone like Jack would be perfect.'

'You can't just try and conjure up another Jack, Matt. It won't work. He's gone.'

'I don't mean an exact clone of Jack,' I point out. 'I just mean someone who'll be as much fun to live with as he was.'

She shakes her head. 'You can't plan life like that, Matt. It doesn't work. It's like with H and Sky and anyone else you might be planning to slot in to your life. People have minds of their own. You've got to respect that and realize that they're not going to fall in to line just because it suits you.'

'I hardly think the two are comparable.'

'Who?' Chloe demands. 'H and Sky? They're more similar than you think.' She takes the bottle of Diet Coke from the table and, swigging, looks me over for a moment. She puts the bottle down. 'It's a matter of how you see them, Matt.'

'Oh, right,' I say, stiffening, 'and how exactly *do* I see them, Chloe?'

'Home truth?' she checks, cocking her head at me.

'Home truth.'

'As pawns.'

'Pawns?' I ask, gobsmacked.

She lights a cigarette and blows smoke across the room. When she speaks, she's emphatic. 'Yes. Look at the facts. You want to manipulate Sky in to a situation whereby you can get your Tantric rocks off, and, of course,' she adds with a smile, 'learn the finer points of yoga, whilst simultaneously relieving your mortgage payments. And with H, you went about setting her up in exactly the same fashion, double-booking the stag and hen so that you could make your move. Just because your motives with H were emotional doesn't make them any less cynical. You were interfering with other people's lives to make your own better.'

I sit here stunned. 'You're ... you're meant to be my friend,' I stutter. 'I told you that stuff about the double-booking because I wanted to show you how much H meant to me. Not so ... not so you could turn it round and use it against me.'

Unimpressed, Chloe picks up the Diet Coke bottle and takes another swig.

'And I'm not a control freak, either,' I snap, snatching the bottle from her and filling my glass.

'From what you've told me about H, you don't know the first thing about her. Or care ...'

'Care?' I splutter, spilling Coke down my shirt. 'How can you say that? I'm in love with her. Or I was. Or I was heading that way, anyway ...'

'No, Matt,' Chloe asserts. 'You thought being in love was the next life stage you should be going through. It was like buying a flat to you, or getting a promotion at work. I'm not saying you're not heavily into H; you obviously are. But love? Come on, you can't be serious. You'd only just started getting to know her.'

'Good God,' I gasp, swivelling round to face her and sitting back against the arm of the sofa. 'This is rich coming from you. Who was it who got me to go over to their flat to make their new boyfriend jealous?' I demand. 'If that's not being manipulative, I don't know what is. Manipulation,' I carry on, warming to my theme, 'is a practice indulged in by every person on this planet every day of their lives. It's an essential component of the human condition.'

'Granted,' she responds. 'But giving Andy some food for thought and potentially screwing up the weekend for a dozen people are two very different things. I'm simply suggesting that you should be a little bit less ambitious, and perhaps give a little bit more thought to why exactly you're manipulating someone to begin with. Take Andy. He had potential. Right from the word go.'

'As did H,' I protest.

'Yes, but I already knew Andy quite well. It's not like we'd only just met. All you had to work on with H was a drunk hump. I mean, correct me if I'm wrong, Matt, but it might have been more shrewd to get to know her a little better before throwing yourself in up to your neck.'

I stare at her agog. My mouth is open, but for once I can't think of a single thing to say.

H

I hope Amy has more of a sense of reality than I do.

'Ready?' she asks, turning round to look at Susie and me. I have to say that despite my allergy to all things wedding, she looks stunning. I don't know how she manages to look so different considering her wedding dress is just that: a wedding dress. But she does. She has a radiance about her, and a sense of excitement which is so unlike the Amy I know, I want to pinch her just to check that she's real and she's not an impostor from one of her bride magazines.

She shakes out the train of her dress.

'Don't tread on it, you two,' she warns Susie and me, raising her eyebrows before turning back to face the vicar.

And then we're off. The church doors are open and we're walking up the aisle. I suppose I haven't wanted to think about it too much, the actual service, but now that it's happening, I feel very odd. As if I'm on TV.

There's a blur of faces and hats on both sides of me, until Chloe leans out of the aisle in slow motion and points a camera in my face. The flash blinds me for a second and I pull up my arm, my bouquet in front of my face. I haven't seen her since she ceremoniously dumped my brother's best friend. And although she's bosom buddies with Jack and Matt, I wouldn't give her house space and she knows it. Which probably explains why she's trying to trip me up. I scowl at her.

And I look ahead and I can see Jack turning round. He looks grey and clammy, as if he's about to puke. He sort

372

of half-grimaces and then turns back to face the altar, his shoulders tense as a plank.

But I'm not interested in Jack. I'm interested in the immobile figure beside him.

Turn, I plead in my head.

Turn round and see me.

Because I need to see his face.

I hadn't even noticed the organ playing, but I do notice the silence as we all stop at the end of the aisle and the vicar starts to speak. I can see Amy's eyes shining as she looks at Jack and he reaches out for her hand, his fingers catching hers, but still I'm staring at Matt.

He's stepped back and he's at a slight angle and he straightens up, staring towards the ceiling and taking deep breaths.

Maybe he's nervous too.

It's an odd thing, sex. Because as soon as you've had sex with someone, they never look the same to you again. I suppose it's because you've seen what their bug-eyed face looks like right up against yours, or how they look when they orgasm, or how they look when they sleep.

But looking at Matt, I'm reminded of the very first time I saw him in Zanzibar with Amy and how gorgeous I thought he was.

It seems such a long time ago.

As the introduction to the first hymn starts, I watch as he reaches for his order of service and even though he's close enough to touch, it feels as if I'm looking at him through the wrong end of binoculars.

I look down at the words, feeling horribly self-conscious as Amy's voice echoes in my head.

It was last night and Amy was sitting on her bed at her mother's house, one knee tucked under her chin as she finished painting the last of her toe-nails.

'So how are you feeling about seeing Matt?' she asked.

'Fine,' I lied. Because I didn't feel fine. About anything.

'Shit!' she said, suddenly.

'What?' I asked, looking at her in the round mirror, the tweezers I'd been using hovering above my eyebrow.

'Matt,' she said, looking up at me. 'I forgot to tell you. He knows about Laurent.'

I turned round to face her, my stomach lurching. 'How?'

'Stringer was in the steam room with us.'

I think back to Leisure Heaven and the guy with the towel over his head and I feel something inside me shift in horror.

'That was Stringer?'

Amy obviously clocked my face, because she leaned back, opened the drawer by her bed and pulled out two cigarettes. She lit them both, handed one to me and beckoned me over to the window.

'Yes, the heavy breather. He heard you raving about Laurent and told Matt . . .'

I could see our reflections in the open window, Amy's wedding dress hanging on the wardrobe behind us, like a ghost.

'I guess that's why he was so horrible to you,' said Amy, blowing smoke out in to the garden, before adding, 'I can't believe I'm getting married tomorrow and my mother still doesn't know I smoke.'

I inhaled on my cigarette, barely hearing her.

'Are you OK?' she asked, peering at me.

'Yes,' I said, vaguely.

'Sorry to tell you like this, but I thought it might be better if you knew.'

But now, as Susie and I sit down in the front pew, I just feel embarrassed and slightly sick.

Matt knows that I slept with Laurent. Right after sleeping with him. No wonder he was cross. If he'd done the same to me, I'd have gone nuts.

But maybe he meant it when he said that the sex didn't

mean anything to him. Maybe he genuinely didn't enjoy it.

So why do I feel so vain? Why is my ego shouting out: look at me, fancy me in my girlie dress, with flowers in my hair.

But it's all a load of bull.

I've ruined everything because I negated Matt and me with Laurent.

And what was that all about? I feel hideous thinking about it. Because the sex wasn't as good as it was with Matt, if I'm really honest. Matt was more fun and Laurent more romantic maybe, but I made a huge mistake thinking that Laurent was exotic. He wasn't exotic at all. The only thing that was different about him was that he wasn't one of Amy's mates and he wasn't another standard London bloke, like Gav.

I look at Jack and Amy. They look like little kids, staring wide-eyed at the vicar, nervous in front of the congregation, but even though everyone is watching them, they seem totally wrapped up in each other.

And I can feel tears pricking my eyes. Because despite my cynicism, looking at them both now, with Jack almost strangled by his cravat, it's obvious to everyone that they love each other. And all this time, I've been secretly terrified of this happening, that Amy getting married would mean that I'd lose her and that I'll be alone without an ally in the world. But this doesn't change a thing. She's Jack's soulmate. They're in this together and all this time, me bellyaching hasn't even touched it.

I look up at the stained glass as they make their vows, my eyes filling with tears. Because I'm happy for them, but so sad for me.

It was supposed to be me up there with Gav, not Amy and Jack. But now he's about to make this same commitment to someone else. And looking back at the petals of the carnations in my bouquet, I realize it's never going to be me and Gav. He's gone. Finally gone.

Maybe Gav's what all this has been about. Sleeping with Matt and Laurent, being angry and cross with every man unfortunate enough to stumble into my path. And then there was Ben, who was completely spot on: I have made my job the be all and end all of everything. And whilst I want to be successful and make the most of all my hard work, surely it can't be at the expense of my life.

I've been so busy and so angry and it's all because I haven't wanted to let Gav go. And as I sit in the pew, with the sunlight streaming through the stained glass windows in dusty, coloured streaks, I watch Jack and Amy kiss as man and wife and I finally say goodbye.

Susie

Amy bunches up her dress, shuffles backwards and with a giggle lands on the toilet seat.

'Strumpet,' I tease.

'That's *Mrs* Strumpet to you.'

'Amy?' It's H outside.

'We're in here,' she calls, flushing the loo. I follow her out and stand looking at her in the mirror. Her tiara is wonky, she's got lipstick marks on her cheeks and there's mascara smudged under her eyes from where she cried at Jack's speech, but it doesn't matter a bit. She still looks beautiful.

She grabs H and me in a hug and she looks at us all, reflected in the mirror.

'You were fabulous today,' she says.

'Don't!' I say. 'You'll set me off.'

'And me,' says H.

Amy pulls us both in tight. 'You are my special girls,' she says, kissing us both on the cheek, but the moment is interrupted by Jack.

'My wife,' he shouts, bursting through the door and throwing a fist into the air. 'Where is my wife?'

He stops as he sees us all.

'Well, ha-ll-oooo, ladies,' he says, raising his eyebrows up and down.

He looks absurd and absurdly happy at the same time and I can't help but laugh as he holds out his hand to Amy.

'Excuse me, girls,' she laughs, her eyes locked with Jack's. 'It looks like I've just been asked to dance.'

Jack whisks her off her feet and she squeals as he pulls open the door and carries her through it. I'm about to follow them when H stops me.

'Susie?' she says.

I turn around to face her.

'Um,' she hesitates. 'I just wanted to say, if I don't get another chance, good luck in the States.'

'Thanks,' I say, genuinely surprised by her sincerity.

'When you're back, I thought maybe we could hook up for a drink or something?'

And I smile at her, because I doubt that it will ever happen, but I hear what she's saying.

'OK,' I nod. 'That'd be great.'

And we look at each other for a moment as the water passes under the bridge between us.

'Let's go boogie,' I say.

'I'll be out in a moment,' she says and I nod.

The disco is about to start in the main hall and the microphone squeaks as the DJ announces himself.

I walk over to the present table to check on Torvill and Dean. I've wrapped their bowl in a big pink bow and there's a plastic bride-and-groom decoration embedded in their gravel. I'm sure they'll be safe with Jack and Amy.

'There you are.'

I turn round and see Stringer grinning at me.

'Hello,' I say, reaching up to kiss him. 'How are you?'

'Knackered,' he says, taking both my hands and holding them out. 'Susie, look at you,' he says. 'You look fabulous.'

I curtsey, delighted by his compliment, because although I say it myself, I do feel more like a princess than I've ever felt.

'You don't look so bad yourself,' I say, fiddling with his

tie. He's changed in to a suit, having been racing round with the caterers. 'You did so well with the meal.'

'I can relax a bit,' he says. 'Just a few more things to sort out.'

'No way,' I say, hearing 'Tainted Love' starting up on the disco. 'Come on, this is one of my favourites. You're dancing with me.'

'You can't dance to this,' he protests, as I drag him along by his tie, but Stringer has obviously been to ballroom lessons and can dance to anything. I've never known anyone with so many swanky moves.

'So?' I ask, as he rocks me back and forth. 'How did it go with Karen?'

He grins widely as I twirl under his arm.

'It goes,' he says.

I tease him with a discreet pelvic thrust and he laughs and looks up at the ceiling.

'Yes, even *that* goes,' he says, 'thanks to you.'

'The pleasure is all mine,' I giggle. 'And Karen?'

'She's wonderful,' he says, happily. 'I hope you get to meet her one day.'

'Maybe I will. You can write to me in California and tell me all about her,' I say. 'You can write can't you?' I check.

And with that he picks me up and twirls me round so hard, my head spins.

Matt

I watch Jack and Amy tripping the light fantastic with a bunch of other couples on the dance floor. It's the last dance and the scene is suitably serene. Jack and Amy are looking wonderful, Amy's parents are looking on in admiration, and Jack's divorced parents are even looking one another in the face. The lights are low and, for the first time this evening, the local DJ has managed to restrain himself from bellowing encouragement over the music.

That said, sitting here at the edge of the dance floor, fumbling with the bottle of champagne that Stringer was kind enough to get one of his members of staff to fetch for me a couple of minutes ago, I find I'm bizarrely detached from the whole situation. Like one of the goldfish Susie gave Jack and Amy as a wedding present, I feel there's an invisible barrier preventing me from doing anything other than looking on. I can't quite put my finger on why. I mean, I should be on a high. I didn't let Jack get too trashed at the pub last night. I got him to the church on time. I remembered the ring and I didn't drop it. Even my speech went down well – remarkable, considering the fact that I only got around to writing it after Chloe left on Thursday night. Maybe it's what she said to me and what I've thought about it since that's left me feeling so odd.

She was right. About everything: my attitudes towards Sky and H and my addiction to mapping out my life without knowing what the terrain really looks like. I did call Sky yesterday, but it was a courtesy call, letting her know that I wasn't going to ask her to move in. The reason I gave her was that I'd changed my mind about getting a lodger at all. And it was the truth. And it still is. I'm not going to get a lodger. I checked out my finances yesterday after the favourable result we obtained in Tia Maria Tel's case. With the raise I'm pretty much guaranteed to get as a result at my upcoming pay review, I'll be able to cover the mortgage comfortably on my own. Money wasn't the reason I decided against a lodger, though. It was down to what Chloe said. About my being too dependent on other people for my happiness. I came to the conclusion that the best way to get on with my own life was by living on my own terms: alone. Just me and whatever the future holds in store.

I look up and see Jack waving at me, before putting his arm back around Amy. I smile back. A shell of hope bursts inside me. One day, that'll be me. One day, like Jack, I'll meet someone and get to know them and fall in love. But in that order. I'm done with trying to grab it all at once. It doesn't work. And until that time arrives, I'll keep my eyes open. I meet new people every day. Who knows who they'll turn out to be if I give them time?

I notice Chloe disentangling herself from Ug's primitive advances on the dance floor. She comes over and sits down. 'Not dancing?' she asks.

I pop the champagne cork and fill my glass. 'No.'

She puts her arm around my shoulder and gives me a squeeze. 'Thinking about H?' she asks.

I nod my head, scanning the dance floor for her: she's nowhere to be seen. 'Sort of.' I turn to Chloe. 'But don't worry, it's not in the way you think. I was just thinking I should maybe speak to her, apologize for acting so ungraciously when I was wasted, that's all. Wipe the slate clean, you know?'

Before Chloe has a chance to reply, the room bursts into a round of applause and cheers. I watch Jack and

Amy following Stringer across the dance floor towards the exit.

'Come on,' Chloe says, pulling me to my feet. 'They're off.'

I put my glass down and follow her through to the main doors and out in to the bustle of bodies, as everyone gathers outside to say their goodbyes.

'Matt!' Jack shouts, pushing past several people to reach me. 'There you are.' He checks out the smiling faces around him. 'Awesome, or what?' he comments, grinning. The space clears for a second and I catch a glimpse of Amy. She looks incredible. He shakes his head, as if he can't quite believe his luck. 'Fantastic,' he says, 'Fan-bloody-tastic.'

'You've really gone and done it now,' I tell him, as he hugs me.

'Haven't I just?' He pulls back, his hands resting on the shoulders of my morning coat. 'And haven't *you* just? You've been brilliant,' he tells me. 'Top stag. Top speech. Top all-round bloke.'

'You two take care on your honeymoon,' I tell him.

'Damn right.' He stares me in the eyes for a couple of seconds. 'You gonna let me return the favour some time?' he asks.

'Yeah,' I tell him without hesitating, 'as soon as the time's right.'

'Matt,' Amy says, appearing suddenly, slipping in between us and giving me a kiss. 'Thanks for everything. You've been a star. And thanks for everything you said in your speech about us being made for each other. It means the world to me.'

'I meant every word,' I say, but then they're gone, swept back away from me into the circle that Stringer's created for Amy to throw her bouquet.

'On the count of three,' Amy shouts, turning her back on the assembled girls. 'One . . .'

'Two,' the crowd joins in.

'Three!'

And the bouquet's spiralling upwards, falling to earth only seconds later into the waiting hands of . . . Stringer.

'Oh, shit,' I hear him saying. His face is beetroot. He turns to Susie, who's standing next to him, and hands her the bouquet. 'For America,' he tells her. 'Who knows who you'll meet?'

Then I'm looking at Jack and Amy as they climb in to the back of the cab and wave goodbye. The cab pulls off seconds later and, gradually, the shouting dies down, leaving only the sound of the tin cans tied to the back of the cab as they clatter along the gravel drive. It's only then that I realize I'm still holding the open champagne bottle. I raise it in the direction of the disappearing cab and then lift it to my lips and drink.

'Any chance of a refill?' someone to my left asks.

'Sure,' I say, turning round and seeing H standing by my side. She holds out her glass and, after only the slightest hesitation, I touch the neck of the bottle against its rim and begin to pour.

H

Sunday, 00.05

I look at him, my hand trembling as he fills up my glass.

'Do you want to go back inside?' he asks.

There's so much to say and I've been so nervous about this moment all day that now it's finally come, my mind has gone blank.

'Let's go for a walk,' I manage.

I watch our feet stepping in time along the gravel path and I shiver. Without saying anything, Matt takes off his jacket and puts it round my shoulders.

'Thanks,' I whisper, clutching my glass.

'Shall we?' he asks, nodding to a bench between two yew trees.

I kick off my shoes and hug my knees up as we sit down and we're both silent, looking at the trees in the moonlight. A few yellow lights streak along the motorway at the bottom of the valley, but otherwise it's silent. Just the wind in the trees.

'Good wedding,' I say, turning to face Matt. 'Your speech was excellent.'

'Thanks,' he says.

And there's another unbearable silence.

'Matt?'

'So?' he says at the same time and we laugh.

I shake my head. 'This is crazy. I've been avoiding you all day.'

'I know,' he says. 'Which is a shame, because I wanted to tell you earlier that you look wonderful.'

I look over my shoulder at him.

'Thanks. You don't look so bad yourself,' I say, swallowing hard as my eyes meet his. 'I'm really sorry, Matt.'

'I was about to say the same to you.'

'I mean about Laurent,' I say. 'I know you know. Amy told me last night all about Stringer overhearing us in the steam room.'

'Yes, well I wasn't exactly very gracious about it. All that stuff I said to you . . .'

'I guess that makes us even.'

'I guess it does,' he says.

I take a sip of champagne and sigh, looking up at the dark sky. I can hear the crunch of gravel on the drive as the guests start to depart.

'I feel so empty,' I confess.

'You can't be after all Stringer's food.'

I hang my head and smile.

'I sat in the church today and all I could think was that everything I've done has been because I was feeling heartbroken about Gav. It's taken me all this time to realize it.'

'How do you feel about it now?'

'OK, I think,' I shrug.

Matt takes a swig of champagne.

'I'm sorry, though. About us, I mean,' I say, looking back over my shoulder. 'I didn't mean to, but I used you.'

Matt doesn't respond. He holds the champagne bottle and looks at his feet.

'D'you know what? I seem to spend my whole time apologizing to people. Why do I always get things so wrong?'

Matt leans forward and puts his elbows on his knees. 'You're not the only one. I've got a confession, too.'

'Oh?'

'I think you should know that I booked Leisure Heaven

deliberately. I looked through that envelope in your bag, the night you stayed.'

'You didn't!'

'I wanted to surprise you,' he says.

'You managed that.'

I shake my head, ashamed and sad all at once. Because it could have been a good plan. In a parallel universe things could have worked out between us, but now it's all gone to waste. We managed to go from being acquaintances, to lovers, to enemies in such a short space of time. And now we're left with this emotional fall-out. Matt clears his throat.

'So? What about you? How's your French bloke?'

I put my legs down on the ground and turn to face him, shocked that he doesn't know. 'Oh Matt. It's not what you think. It was a total disaster.'

'So you're not still seeing him?'

'No. But his wife is. And his kids.'

And suddenly I feel lost and I can't name the emotion, but it feels something like grief. For Gav, for Laurent, for Amy, for my youth, for Matt, but most of all, for me. I take a deep breath.

'Fucking men,' Matt jokes as if sensing it.

'Yes, fucking men,' I repeat. 'Never a good idea.'

And then instead of crying, I laugh.

Matt tips some more champagne into my glass. 'To new beginnings,' he toasts.

'To new beginnings,' I repeat.

Matt shakes his head and looks out over the view and we seem to be silent for ages.

'I wonder how Jack and Amy are getting on,' he says, eventually, which is odd because that's exactly what I was thinking, too.

'Consummating probably,' I say.

Matt laughs. 'Or sleeping. Aren't you exhausted?'

And all of a sudden, I realize that I am. I shiver and yawn at the same time.

'Come on,' says Matt, helping me to my feet.

Everyone has gone when we get back to The Manor and the duty manager is locking up. There's one cab left on the gravel drive and Matt goes to talk to the driver.

'We might as well share it,' he says, opening the door.

I look behind me out of the back window, glad to be in the warm as the cab pulls away. The duty manager turns the lantern out above the grand entrance. I watch as the drive turns blue in the moonlight and the grass lawns fade into black.

And I don't know where we're going, but I do know, as I turn back and settle my head into the crook of Matt's arm, that everything is going to be all right.